THE
STONE KEEP

The Stone Keep

S. K. MARLAY

HEROIC

Heroic Books

First published in Great Britain in 2021 by Heroic Books.

Paperback ISBN: 9781914342042
Ebook ISBN: 9781914342134
Audiobook ISBN: 9781914342226

Printed and bound in Great Britain by Clays Ltd, Elcograf S.p.A.

www.heroicbooks.com

This book is printed on paper from responsible sources

FSC
www.fsc.org
MIX
Paper from
responsible sources
FSC® C018072

For Conor, Maya-Rose, Éanna & Aodhán.

Most of the names in this book are Irish and some are based on an ancient Irish tree alphabet.

A guide to meaning and pronunciation is set out at the end of this MS.

PART I

THE KEEP

CHAPTER 1
BOND

Warm light spilled through the kitchen doorway, a golden path for the small boy who came running, trailing laughter into the summer's evening. Above him the Keep stood black against the red sky. He trotted to the light's edge and paused.

'Eadha!' he called, imperious. 'Eadha! Eadha!'

From the darkness came soft arms, circling his tummy and heaving him awkwardly into the air.

'Eadha,' he said again, happy now, resting a head of shining hair against a shoulder not much higher than his own and kicking his legs in glee. Eadha staggered under his weight but still held on, pressing her face briefly into his hair. For Ionain was her heart's ease, and holding him the closest she ever came to feeling she was home.

A moment later and Ionain had wriggled free and was running again, on out into the twilight, his bare feet pattering on paving stones still warm from the day's heat. He shrieked with delight as Eadha chased after him, until the two tumbled in a laughing heap on the grassy mound where the kitchen yard opened out into gardens beyond. As they fell, the first stars appeared above them, silvering the still waters of the lake. Behind them, in a half-circle curving out from the West Tower, lights flickered into life in the servants' houses. This was Ailm's Keep, drawn from the earth by Channeller Huris almost four centuries before.

Ever afterwards, Eadha held on to the memory of that moment like a talisman, the way she might keep a piece of dragonglass deep down in her pocket. Proof that before there was power, there was love. The last clear moment before it all began.

The two children were curled in a sleepy huddle under the rising moon, Ionain's arm flung across Eadha's neck, his soft hair tickling her nose, when a hand caught her shoulder and shook her back to wakefulness. It was Beithe, Ionain's nurse, stooping over her. She looked stricken, the angular lines of her face all collapsed into fear.

'Quick, child, up, up.'

Eadha sat up, rubbing her eyes. Beside her, Beithe was shaking Ionain, but he was fast asleep and wouldn't wake.

With a grunt, Beithe bent down and caught him up in her arms. In the same moment Eadha realised the pounding she could hear in the distance was the sound of fists battering the oak doors of the Keep, as hard as if to shatter them into pieces. And she knew something was very wrong.

'What's...' she began, climbing to her feet, but Beithe cut across her.

'For once, young one, no questions. There's no time. A man is coming. A bad man, and if he catches Master Ionain out here, alone and undefended, he will likely kill him.'

As she spoke, Beithe shifted her grip on Ionain to hold him more tightly with one hand, turning back towards the Keep. Eadha could see Ionain's head over her shoulder, still asleep though he was beginning to stir. His face was hot and sticky, with strands of hair stuck to his cheek.

She gawped at Beithe, unable to make sense of what she'd just said. It was as if she'd pointed to a clear blue sky and said the dragons had come to burn the Keep to rubble.

'But why...'

'Will you whisht I said? You need to run, get yourself to your uncle's cottage quick as ever you can. It's not safe for you to be outside either. He'd channel anyone on a whim, that one—even a child.'

But as she spoke Ionain had come fully awake and was instantly furious at finding himself being held like a baby. He started kicking Beithe's shins, pushing his arms out rigid against her shoulders, trying to get free.

'Let me down!' he shouted.

But Beithe only gripped him harder.

'Hush, young master, there's no time. I've to bring you to your room, your father said,' and even as she spoke, she was moving, turning away from Eadha. But catching sight of her over Beithe's shoulder Ionain cried out,

'Eadha. Eadha comes, too.'

Beithe sagged then, her head dropping. For this was a thing decided long ago, when Ionain was even smaller than he was now, Lord Ailm's only surviving child, and Eadha one of the pack of Fodder orphans that tumbled through the Keep, half-clad and half-fed. Still barely able to walk, Ionain had followed her even then, stumbling after her on unsteady legs, the wild-haired girl not two years older than him, but who led the rest of them a dance through the Keep's crumbling halls. And Eadha had stopped and she'd seen him, the lonely boy, barely more than a baby but already forgotten, as his mother birthed and lost two more sons after him, leaving him to roam the Keep's halls with only the echoes of his voice for company. And for all the world it had been a recognition; a finding; two small, lost souls finding home in each other. Ionain would not be separated from her since.

With her free hand Beithe seized Eadha's wrist.

'Come on then, you as well, but hurry or we'll be too late,' and she shambled into an awkward half-run, Ionain still clutched to her chest, dragging Eadha after her.

Now they'd reached the kitchen, a stab of too-bright light after the night's soft dark. It was thronged with people and with panic. Stumbling along behind Beithe, Eadha stared up in bewilderment at the huddles of kitchen maids and stable-hands, some in tears, others white-faced with fear. Who was this man coming, that terrified everyone so?

Head down, Beithe threaded her way through the crush, making straight for the tunnel of dragonglass that linked the kitchen to the main Keep. As she did, Ionain's father, Lord Ailm, came hurrying in from the stables. Catching sight of Beithe and her charges he crossed the flagstones in two quick strides and said, so quietly Eadha had to strain to hear, 'Get them to his room quick as ever you can, before you're seen.'

Eadha stared up at him. Ionain's father always looked stricken, his face marked early and deep by failure, the first Lord Ailm in ten generations born without the Channeller's gift—the power needed to grow the Keep's crops and hold the Keep itself whole. But this was different. Now he looked petrified, with the same staring fear Eadha had seen in Beithe's eyes when she'd shaken her awake in the garden.

Beithe said nothing in reply, only nodding grimly and hurrying on. Behind them they heard Lord Ailm raise his voice,

'Quick, all of you. The great Lord Huath is to honour us with a visit. Set the lamps in the Great Hall, stoke the fires, fetch out the sweetmeats we set by for the winter feast. It should be just enough to feed Lord Huath and his men.'

At his words Eadha stopped dead. She and Ionain had hunted

together all summer long to find the wild raspberries and blackberries to make those sweetmeats. In return, Beithe had promised them a plate piled high with sweet things on feast night. It was one of the only days of the year Eadha ever felt full, that lovely tight feeling in her belly of not wanting more. She had to go back, save their precious hoard. But Beithe was too strong, ignoring her squirming, her bony fingers crushing Eadha's hand as she dragged her on out of the kitchen and into the dragonglass tunnel.

They were halfway down the tunnel when a voice cried out behind them.

'Beithe. He's here.'

It was Sepp the quartermaster, calling after them in a voice so full of fear it reached all the way down the tunnel and pulled Beithe up so she stopped stock-still and Eadha ran right into the back of her. Setting Ionain down, she caught Eadha by the shoulders.

'We're too late. I have to go back. Listen to me, child. Get himself up to his room, fast as you can. Don't stop for anything and whatever happens don't either of ye come out until I say. D'ye hear me?'

Beithe's eyes darted between the two children and the look in them was so absolute neither child dared say anything, only nodding together, mutely, their eyes wide.

'On with ye now, go!' she said then, giving them each a hard push-off between the shoulder blades before turning back to the kitchen.

On they ran, Eadha ahead, holding Ionain by the hand so he wouldn't fall behind. Down the long dragonglass tunnel with its flickering candles set in the marble floor. Out into the Great Hall, slipping between the V-shaped columns holding up the walkways that criss-crossed its vast space. Along by the slate fireplaces where a solitary fire cast its shadows, on towards the spiral stairs up to the east wing and Ionain's room. And it would have been almost like one of their games except that as they ran, from beyond the Great Hall doors there came an almighty commotion of horses' hooves and men's shouts, as if a great company had come riding down from the Blackstairs to storm Ailm's Keep.

Now they'd reached the foot of the spiral stairs, its curves twisting up and around the trunk of one of the yew trees that held up the hall's ceiling. Crouching down so they were hidden by the bannister, the two of them began scrambling up the steps. As they did, through the iron leaves that twined along the bannisters Eadha glimpsed Sepp hurrying towards the doors. In the same moment they slammed open as if forced apart by an invisible hand, rebounding off the walls with the sharp crack of something breaking.

A deep voice drawled, silkily powerful.

'Is no one come to greet me?' and a man with white-blond hair, dressed all in black, came strolling into the centre of the Great Hall.

At the sight of him the two children froze mid-step.

'Lord Huath, my humblest apologies, we had no word of your arrival...'

It was Lord Ailm, hurrying across the hall, his hands outstretched in greeting.

'Don't cluck, Ailm, it makes you sound like a woman.'

As his father spoke Ionain had huddled down, pulling his arms and legs in like some small wild animal trying to make itself invisible. Panic seized Eadha. This was all wrong. They couldn't stay out on the stairs like this, they'd be seen. She started tugging Ionain as hard as she could, trying to get him moving again. But his whole body had gone rigid and he wouldn't budge. As she pulled, she squinted out through the gaps in the bannister, trying to keep track of Lord Huath.

Directly underneath them she could see Sepp, Beithe and the other Keep servants, lined up now in two rows. They were all standing stony still, their fists balled and their bodies rigid like statues, as if some vicious beast had come prowling among them and even the tiniest movement could mean death. Their terror caught at Eadha then, too, the gut-twisting terror that had come rushing in with the man with the white-blond hair and sent its tendrils winding about every soul in Ailm's Keep.

As Eadha watched, Lord Huath turned away from Ionain's father, and called up to a cross-walk opposite where she was crouching.

'Sister, stop lurking up there and come greet your brother.'

Lady Ura, Ionain's mother, was standing on the cross-walk, silently watching her husband and her brother meet. As Huath spoke, from her perch halfway up the stairs Eadha was close enough to see how Ura's hands shook as she straightened her skirt, where it had caught on her softly rounded belly. She was only just beginning to show; her baby was not due until winter. But her voice was steady as she moved on down the steps to greet her brother.

'Brother, what a surprise. To what do we owe this honour?'

'How could I travel west of the Blackstairs and not call upon my sister? In truth, I was sent by the Masters to chase down a will o' the wisp of a tale of marauding dragons that signally failed to maraud in my presence. There I was with a wagonload of Fodder and no sport, grown weary of travel rations and sleeping on hard ground. I thought, where would I find a bed for the night? And it came to me, why here, in dear old decaying Ailm's Keep.'

Huath glanced at his brother-in-law and away again, up to where the dome of the Great Hall was hidden far above them in darkness, as it had been for almost a quarter-century now, ever since Lord Ailm's father, Ionain's grandfather, had died and with him the channelling gift in the Ailm Family. Without the gift Ionain's father had no means to light it.

'But where are my manners? You must be weary of huddling

7

here in darkness with no Channeller to light the place. Such a Great Hall deserves a great light.'

Stepping away from his sister, Huath twisted his wrist, like one grasping a rope and pulling.

As he did, Eadha saw a silver thread spring to life in the firelight, unspooling from Huath's hand and shooting the length of the hall, then disappearing beneath the staircase where she and Ionain hid. As the thread snaked underneath them she heard a thump. Peering down she saw Sepp had collapsed unconscious, his head twisted at an awkward angle, his eyes closed and his arms outflung. Eadha's throat tightened. She had to stop herself from crying out in panic. Sepp was a bull of a man, he'd spent years on dragon patrol with Ionain's grandfather. What could have made him fall like that? And why was no one moving to help him, the stable lads on either side of him staring straight ahead as if they'd been turned to stone?

The next moment Lord Huath went flying up into the air. Still linked by the silver thread to Sepp's unconscious body, he spiralled towards the dome. As he flew, he sent flames of were-light from his fingertips, dozens of tiny golden flames, each one dancing as if it was separately alive, their light illuminating the carvings that curved across the dome.

Wonder blanketed Eadha then, snuffing out even her fear as she gaped up at the man flying far above her, his hair shining white in the swirling lights, diving and rising like a swimmer through the air. Her mouth rounded in an "o" of amazement, a tiny indrawn gasp at the impossibility of it. Between her arms she felt Ionain half-rise to his feet, transfixed, too.

'Come, sister, you really must see these carvings; they are quite remarkable,' and before Ionain's mother could say anything, with another flick Huath swept Ura off her feet.

As Huath's power whipped her up into the air, Ura let out a cry

8

of fear, her hands going to her rounded belly. And between Eadha's arms her cry was echoed by a terrified whimper from Ionain as he saw his mother being yanked up into the air like a toy puppet on the end of a string. She'd never heard Ionain make a sound like that before, at once horror-struck and stifled, too frightened to cry out. This was not to be borne.

'You mustn't do that. You might hurt the baby in her tummy and Beithe will be cross.'

Without realising she was doing it, Eadha had risen to her feet, her small dark head appearing over the top of the bannister, her high voice calling out, clear in the silence.

Hearing her, Huath's head whipped about like a snake. With heart-stopping speed he swooped down towards her.

'What have we here? Ailm, Ura, have your people been so long without a Channeller they've lost all proper deference? Are they so keen to be Fodder?'

The next moment Eadha was enveloped in the iron grip of Huath's power as he snatched her, too, lifting her up and out into the empty air of the Great Hall and leaving her hanging there, her arms and legs dangling uselessly. Right up to her he flew, his were-lights shooting down to swarm about her head. With a flick he yanked up her head and arms for a clearer view.

'So, Ailm, are you breeding tiny rebels out here in the mountains far from the heart of things? Have you forgotten who grows your crops and keeps the roof over your head?' he called. 'Perhaps your Fodder need a little reminder of what happens to those who defy their Lords' Channeller.'

Eadha could feel every eye in the room staring at her as she hung there outlined in were-lights: her arms forced out cruciform, her chin pointing up to the dome, her dark hair hanging down. Unable to cry out, the tears of terror in her eyes unable even to fall as Huath's power encased her from head to foot and held her rigid, dangling helplessly in the air high above them all. If Huath let her go now, the fall would kill her.

For a long, long moment there was silence, and in that silence Eadha understood they were all powerless. Lord Ailm, Lady Ura, Beithe, Sepp, everyone. There was nothing any of them could do to protect her against this man. And in that same silence she knew she hated him for it. Would hate Huath all her days for the power he had and how he wielded it, to tell everyone else they were powerless and that he would hurt them. Hurt them all just so they would know how powerful he was.

So the silence in the Great Hall stretched and stretched until at last it was broken by the sound of a child sobbing with terror. It was Ionain.

'Another stray?' called Huath. 'Shall I bring this one out, too?'

Now at last his sister Ura spoke, calling down from the cushioned perch high in the dome where Huath had deposited her. A Channeller eyrie, accessible only through a Channeller's art.

'It's your nephew Ionain, brother. He is just frightened. That girl is a servant. She looks after Ionain while his nurse sees to me and the baby. She meant no harm, she is merely ignorant; of Channellers, of your might. I pray you let them be and come dine. You must be hungry if you have come from dragon patrol.'

Huath stared at Eadha one long moment more as she dangled there in the open air, then gave a short laugh.

'A miniature protector for your tiny saviour, how quaint.'

With a wave of his hand he lowered Eadha back down onto the staircase beside Ionain. Landing on the step he bent down to stare at them.

'How is the great hope of Ailm's Keep? Run along then, tiny mouse, and be sure to defend young master Ionain. He is his Family's

10

only hope of salvation.'

Wordlessly Eadha caught Ionain's hand. Together they scrambled up the remaining stairs and fled through the archway, away from the man with the eyes that did not care if they lived or died.

Inside Ionain's room all was peaceful, the only sound the fire's embers as they gently cooled and settled, throwing off the last of the heat of long-ago summers. Utterly spent, Ionain crept beneath his bedcovers and was asleep within moments. Eadha curled up on a sheepskin rug in front of the fire and, after a little while, fell into a half-sleep broken by visions of whirling were-lights and shadowy faces looming at her out of the darkness. Sometime in the night she was woken by Ionain whimpering. He soothed at once when she climbed in beside him and curled into his back. Breathing in his downy softness, Eadha finally found peace and dreamless sleep.

CHAPTER 2
BACKWARD SHADOWS

It was early the next morning. Not a soul in the Keep was stirring. The air was chilly with the first hint of autumn and the two children were hiding together under the blankets, poking out their noses to watch their breaths frost on the cold air, passing the time until they could go down for breakfast.

'Tell me the new one, the one about the battle between the First Channeller Erisen and the dragon Kaanesien,' whispered Eadha, pulling the cover back up over her head.

Ionain's tutor had just begun teaching him the Channeller histories, the war of the Four Brothers, the founding of the Great Families, the great dragon battles.

'Alright, but you mustn't interrupt or I'll lose my place,' said Ionain, wriggling down beside her, his tawny hair dark in the half-light, so they seemed to be in a cave of their own making. As he began, his voice took on the slightly sing-song tone of someone reciting a story learned by heart.

'Not much is known of the dragons save only they are a nightmare brought screaming to life. These days they rarely venture far from their colonies off Westport, but centuries ago, when channelling was still young in the world, the dragons were far bolder, flying as far east as Lambay. For they hated the Channellers, seeking out their great works only to destroy them; burning the alabaster towers they raised from the ground, razing the golden fields of wheat they channelled from the soil. Most ferocious of all was the dragon Kaanesien...'

There was a rush of cold air and bright light. It was Beithe, snapping back the covers.

'I'll give you ferocious. Those are not your stories, young one. They're Great Family tales, not for the likes of you and me.' As the two children climbed reluctantly out of bed she went on, 'Now, young sir, I've to get you presentable, though how I'm supposed to do that is anyone's guess. Your uncle has decided to grace us with a house raising this morning before he leaves and afterwards, you're to be presented to him.'

All the terror and the wonder of last night came rushing back at Beithe's words.

'He's a Channeller, isn't he, that man who came last night?' said Eadha.

The shadow of last night's fear crossed Beithe's face as she looked down at Eadha, before it hardened into something closer to anger.

'That man is Lord Huath, the most powerful Channeller in all of Domhain. He's to raise a pavilion for his sister before he goes. A crop of wheat would be more useful but he's far too grand for that. Only raising castles and tormenting frightened children will do the likes of him.'

She flapped a sheet at Eadha.

'Away with you now down to the kitchen, see if you can make yourself useful. Your aunt is in with Lady Ura since first light, patching something half-decent together for her ladyship to wear.'

'But...' said Eadha, not moving.

She was looking at Ionain's face, which had gone pale and

frightened as he stood, frail in his night vest by the side of the bed. She knew he was remembering last night's terror. A mutinous expression settled across her face as she stared at Beithe, folding her skinny arms across her chest. She would not leave him like this, not while that man was still in the Keep. Glancing across at Ionain and back at her, Beithe's face softened.

'Himself'll be alright. His uncle won't harm him now, in front of everyone. Not even he's that brazen; the fear was only if a chance had presented itself, all innocent-like, for some class of an accident. It's yourself you should be worrying about. You could've gotten yourself killed last night shouting out like that. Sepp's still not right after what that man did to him; it'll be days before he's back to himself, though we're not allowed say anything about that, o' course. Now go before I have to run you out. I can't be standing here talking to children with the whole Keep in an uproar.'

It was some hours later. All of the Keep was gathered down by the lake, staring at a wide circle newly scored into the soil at the water's edge beneath the yews.

Squeezing through the crowd until she came out beside Beithe, Eadha saw a strange woman in a grey cloak standing in sunlight at the circle's centre. Her face had a faraway look, as if she was focusing on something past them all. A little distance away, half-hidden beneath the trees, stood a large covered wagon made of wood bound in iron, its heavy doors held shut with loops of chains.

'Who's that?' Eadha whispered to Beithe.

'That's Lord Huath's Keeper, Terebitha,' Beithe whispered back. 'She holds his power for him or some such. Don't be asking me what their kind do, only that it spells pain for the rest of us. Now whisht before you get yourself in trouble again.'

Around them the crowd's mood was sullen, as if, like Beithe, their terror from last night had hardened into something deeper, more mutinous. From the Keep came a small procession headed by Lord Huath, resplendent in a white cloak lined in gold, followed by Ailm, Ura and Ionain. Ionain had been dressed in a fine embroidered tunic and dark-red breeches. He had his mother's golden skin, and tawny tangled hair all his own, that he tugged at when he was anxious. Eadha could see a hand already wandering upwards as he stood a little behind his mother, watching as his uncle strode into the centre of the circle.

'Ready, Terebitha?' he called. The grey-cloaked Keeper nodded and straightened, bringing her attention back from wherever it had been. Turning to face the silent crowd Huath called, 'Deprived as you are of the Channeller's might here in Ailm's Keep, today is a timely reminder of its power and its glory. May all who hear this give of their strength to the greater glory of channelling, now and forever.'

As he spoke, Terebitha had taken up a position just outside the circle. Just like the night before, Eadha saw a thread spring into life, unspooling from Huath's wrist and snaking over towards Terebitha. Unlike with Sepp, however, this time Huath's thread seemed to pass straight through Terebitha, arrowing onwards across the garden and towards the iron-bound wagon. For a long moment it pulsed through the wagon wall. Eadha stared at it, open-mouthed. Then it shuddered and broke apart. Now, instead of one single thread there were multiple strands, all shooting back out of the wagon and converging on Terebitha. She staggered a little as the shining strands hit her, then steadied herself. Like a weaver working a loom, her fingers flashed between the different threads as if testing them, then with a flick of the wrist she sent them all on in one single, thick strand of power into Huath.

'Look,' said Eadha, tugging at Beithe's hand, transfixed by the beautiful shining threads, gleaming yet transparent in the shade beneath the yews.

'Shhhh,' said Beithe. Looking up Eadha saw that Beithe, and everyone else, was looking only at Huath, as if waiting for something to happen. Could she not see what was already happening, the sheer power that was pouring out of the wagon, through Terebitha and on into Lord Huath as he stood there by the lakeside, until he seemed to shine with it?

Radiant with power, Huath walked to the point that marked where the cornerstone of the new building would rise. With a single gesture he drove his yew staff deep into the earth. Gripping it with both hands the power poured out of him, down the staff and into the ground. Then, with a steady tread, he began walking the outline of the building, energy pulsing down his staff and into the earth with each step. From deep underground there came the grinding, groaning sound of shuddering rocks. The ground around began to vibrate, so hard that Eadha had to grip at Beithe's hand or fall. Now Huath was moving to the very centre of the circle where, bowing his head, he stretched his arms out wide, then slowly raised them. As he did, with a great juddering the walls of the new pavilion shouldered up through the earth, the rock shaped underground before being summoned by Huath to face the sun and sky once more. Up through the air it rose, its roof and walls of marble, the doors and windows already formed, the walls shaped and carved.

Within moments the building was complete, only a small central circle left bare above Huath's head, just as it was in all Channeller buildings, marking the spot where its Channeller had stood as he drew his creation up around him. With creaks and cracks the new walls settled into place, and Huath appeared through the doorway looking pleased with himself.

'Well, sister, how do you like your new pavilion?'

Lady Ura's face, Eadha saw, looked as strained as it had last

17

night, while the crowd remained stubbornly silent.

'Truly, brother, I am so grateful.' Behind her Ionain was peeping awestruck at the new building standing where moments before there had been only grass and soil.

'Come, nephew. Stop hiding behind your mother's skirts,' said Huàth. 'I have a gift for you.'

From inside his robe he produced a yew staff similar to his own. It was a beautiful thing, shod in silver and engraved with the emblem of House Debruin, Huath and Ura's Family.

'Carved from the yew trees that grow at the heart of the Masters' House on the Islands of Lambay; the very wood used by the First Channeller Erisen when he defeated the dragon Kaanesien.'

The staff dwarfed Ionain; he looked very small holding it in both hands as he stood beside his uncle in the shadow of the new-channelled pavilion.

'But you must put it away now, until the day you turn sixteen,' said Huath.

'Why must I?' said Ionain, crestfallen.

'Because it is a Channeller's staff. Only a Channeller may wield it to do all the things his art entails. Your sixteenth birthday is your Reckoning Day, the day you will be tested by the Masters of Lambay to see if you have the Channeller's gift. Only if you pass your Reckoning will you be permitted to wield that staff.'

Beside Eadha, Beithe let out a tight sound, between a hiss and a gasp as Huath finished speaking.

'The beast. He couldn't resist it. Praying for him to fail, no doubt,' she muttered.

Eadha tugged at her arm.

'Is it true?' she whispered. 'What he's saying, about Ionain doing a test?'

'Aye, child,' Beithe whispered back. 'In truth, ye all have to be

Reckoned once you turn sixteen, but these days the only ones with any real chance of being gifted are children of Great Families like young Ionain. That's what centuries of only marrying each other gets you; a shrinking pool of gifted ones and every one of them afraid to stick a toe outside it.'

Up on the dais Ionain was staring up at his uncle, still clutching the silver-tipped staff.

'But what if I don't pass? Like Father?'

His voice was so quiet it was almost inaudible, but still everyone in that place heard him.

'What happens if I fail?'

Eadha saw the gleam in Huath's eye as he bent down so his face was level with his nephew's.

'We must just hope it does not come to that. I would, of course, do my best to protect you but the Masters' rules on the matter are clear. If the gift is lost to two generations in a Family, then the Keep—and the lands and the title—are forfeit. One dry generation is tolerable, but two? No.'

Ionain's eyes had grown huge as he took in what his uncle was saying, the fate he was laying on him, the whole future of his Family resting on his small shoulders. His face had gone paper-white and Eadha could see it beginning to crumple. He was going to cry and then Huath would say something cruel, something humiliating; he wouldn't be able to resist it. Feeling Eadha tense beside her, Beithe laid a warning hand on her shoulder. She was not to shout out this time, not again. But even as Beithe's fingers tightened, a thrill ran through the watching crowd and a voice cried out,

'Look! By the West Tower!'

Every eye looked skywards then and all saw it, a blink of sunlight in the empty sky above the West Tower.

'Dragon!'

Huath was the first to react, spinning away from them all back towards the Keep, shouting as he did, 'Terebitha! The Fodder wagon!'

'My lord, the Fodder are drained. Several threads expired during the house raising...'

'Curse you, Ailm,' snarled Huath. 'This is exactly why Ailm's Keep cannot be without a Channeller of its own. I've had to waste half a wagonload of Fodder doing your work. If this dragon escapes me now I will hold you personally responsible. Terebitha!' he shouted once more. 'I have some power left, enough for the chase. I will ride ahead, you follow after with the wagon.'

Even as Huath spoke, one of his men came running from the stables with a horse already saddled. Swinging himself up, Huath urged it into a gallop across the Keep lawns, over the lake-bridge and east, into the forest leading up into the foothills of the Blackstairs. Within moments he'd vanished beneath the trees.

In the hubbub Ionain was left standing alone in the newly raised doorway, still clutching the Channeller's staff Huath had given him. Eadha climbed up beside him. Together they squinted up at the bright speck of the dragon, still just visible as it danced across the sky, like a spark blown on the wind.

'Will he kill it, do you think?'

Eadha looked sideways at the small, worried face staring up at the sky.

'No. It'll be long gone before they even reach the Blackstairs,' she said, trying to sound certain, to fill her words with all the lofty assurance of being a whole year and a half older than him. Ionain flushed, embarrassed and relieved.

'I just... you know.' He opened his hands wide in wordless, helpless knowing.

And she did know, would have asked him the same question if he hadn't asked her first. Because, she thought, asking the question was like saying a prayer. An incantation breathed out and up into the sky to make the thing said not happen. To hold that flying, dancing spark away up there shining in the sun, safe.

'Come on,' she said then. 'Before anyone remembers to look for you,' and she nodded towards the forest. Ionain's face lit up. Laying down the staff he took off towards the tree line, running as if his life depended on it, head down, fists and legs pumping. Eadha ran after him, sure-footed as she hurdled the grassy mounds, quickly catching him up so their escape became a race, ducking under the trees and down mossy ways until they reached their favourite hollow. It was what she loved most, that flowing sense of being at full stretch. Watching though, as she always did, Eadha slowed just enough as they burst down the dip so Ionain could pull ahead at the last moment, whooping in his delight at beating her.

A little later the two of them lay opposite each other across the hollow. Each of them was sprawled on a thick oak branch. Eadha was winding two ropes together to make a ropewalk to string between the branches. As she did, she thought about the silver threads she'd seen stretching from Huath twice now, by the lakeshore and in the Great Hall, how they seemed to fill him with power. She looked across at Ionain. He was lying with his face pressed against a bough in a slant of late afternoon sunshine, picking away at bark that had come loose underneath. Would he be a powerful Channeller like his uncle some day? Would those silver threads fill him, setting him free of the bonds that held everyone else earthbound, so he could fly up into the air and send fire dancing from his fingertips?

But even as she thought that, Ionain burst out, his voice muffled against the branch, 'Everyone's going to be waiting for me to pass that Reckoning, aren't they? To see if I'm a Channeller.'

Eadha remembered then the wrenching pity she'd felt watching him up there on the dais.

'We all have to be tested, Beithe said so,' she replied, gently. 'It's not only you.'

'But if I fail, my Family loses the Keep, Uncle Huath said.'

'Well, it's years and years away. Not 'til you're sixteen. And you will pass, I'm sure of it. You have your uncle's blood and look how powerful he is.'

'But what if I fail?' said Ionain stubbornly. 'Father did.'

'If you do we'll run away, you and me together. Be like Naoise and Narun in the Tale of Brothers, hide out here in the forest,' said Eadha, waggling her rope end at him with a comical expression. 'Remember Beithe told us how Naoise was mistaken for a bear.'

'Eadha, stop,' cried Ionain, his voice high and harsh with tears held back. 'It's not funny.'

She fell silent then, looking across at Ionain where he lay desolate, the whole fate of his Family and the Keep resting on his small shoulders.

All around her was still, the deep quiet of ancient forest, broken only by the distant echo of voices from the Keep. It all seemed as it had only yesterday, when she and Ionain ran wild together through their domain, and hid from Beithe and her chores, and told each other stories of dragons and battles in the high mountain passes, and it had seemed as if it would all go on forever the same. Yet everything was changed, for now she knew it could all be taken away, pulled down in an instant.

And all of it came down to power. The having of it, the not having of it; the beauty and the terror of those silver threads. It had always been that way but she hadn't known it, until now. And now she knew, she could never unknow it. Nothing would ever be the same again.

For a few moments Eadha lay still as her world shifted itself around her. Then with a deep breath, she pulled herself upright and tossed one end of the rope so that it landed across Ionain's back, startling him so he was forced to scramble up and catch it before it fell to the ground. There was no point in talking, no words she could say to lift the fate his uncle had laid on him. But they could build their ropewalk together and hang side-by-side from the branches until their clothes were dangling over faces bright red from the blood rush, and rub their hands along the bark to make better calluses for climbing, and generally lose themselves in being seven and eight years old, and free on a sunny afternoon deep in ancient woods.

CHAPTER 3
A FALCON'S FLIGHT

The winter that followed Lord Huath's visit was one of the coldest in living memory, the snow lying high up the Keep's walls. Deep in the mid-winter Lady's Ura's baby was born, the longed-for second son. But Orran was a sickly child, struggling to catch his breath from the moment he came into the world. All the life of the Keep was diverted towards keeping his frail flame going. Ionain was left to run wild and Eadha ran with him, the two of them slipping out of the Keep each morning and into the forest where they could run and tumble like wolf cubs through the dips and hollows. Food was short, as it always was in winter. Both children were nimble foragers, Eadha especially deft at hunting out animals' winter stores hidden under the snow. They knew as long as they returned with something to show for their wanderings, Beithe wouldn't scold them. So, each morning they'd snatch bread from the kitchen and stay out for the day, returning only as darkness fell and the wolfhounds paced out to meet them.

They heard no more of Lord Huath and no other Channeller came to Ailm's Keep for many years. All that remained was a blurred memory of lights and fear. After that day in the forest, Ionain hardly ever mentioned what Huath had said to him, when he gave him the

Channeller's staff. But Eadha knew not a day passed without him imagining a glorious Reckoning where his Inquisitor proclaimed him gifted, his parents cried tears of joy and pride, and all the people of the Keep cheered his name to the rafters. And not a night went by when he didn't wake soaked in sweat and tears from some new version of the nightmare where an awful silence fell in the Great Hall as the Inquisitor turned away from him shaking his head, the servants removed all the wonderful food, and there was a loud banging at the door as the Masters came to take his home away.

Without ever speaking of it, Eadha didn't return to her uncle's cottage at the edge of the Keep, where she'd lived since her parents had died when she was a baby. Instead, each night she slept curled by the fire in Ionain's room, mute witness to his night terrors. And when Ionain's nightmares woke him, her silent presence by the fire eased him, as he listened in the dark for her soft breathing and, reassured, drifted off again until morning. All through that winter, and the years that followed, each remained all to the other, and together the two of them formed a perfect sufficiency. He gentle, she fierce, a closed loop that needed no other.

So the years passed in Ailm's Keep, first slow then fast, until the winter Eadha turned seventeen. The winter before Ionain's Reckoning.

* * *

It was the dead time of early winter, weeks before the fires of the midwinter festival would bring their hope and warmth. The heat of summer had faded to memory, commemorated only by the fierce orange of the few remaining leaves that hung like tattered flags from the beech trees by the Keep yard.

Wrapped and hooded in her aunt's old cloak, Eadha crossed

the lake-bridge, heading on out of the Keep. At just seventeen she was tall for her age, so people often thought her older than she was. Old enough that she was expected to be of use, she chose to be out herding with her uncle rather than closed away with her aunt and the other seamstresses at the Keep. Out in the fields she could breathe, with only the sky above her and the sheep and goats for company. In truth, she knew she was no help to her aunt, her long frame hunching awkwardly over the fine cloth, inevitably pricking her fingers and staining some precious remnant of lace or silk being made over for Lady Ura's wardrobe for Ionain's Reckoning. It was to take place the coming spring, on the day he turned sixteen.

To the left of the lake-bridge was the willow maze, where she and Ionain used to hide when Beithe was on the rampage. Those days of the two of them running wild together were over now though. She no longer slept in the Keep. Since summer's end, instead of sleeping by Ionain's fire she'd returned to sleep on her old cot bed built into the side of the chimney stack in the loft of her uncle's cottage. It was cosy and warm and smelled of the chestnut wood her uncle burned on winter nights. But still she found it hard to sleep sometimes. She missed Ionain's quiet presence always just an arm's length away, and the airy dreams she'd only ever had in the high rooms of the Keep.

Where she was out in the fields, Ionain was mostly closed away indoors being prepared for his Reckoning and to one day become Lord of Ailm's Keep. His younger brother Orran had died two years ago aged just seven, his weak chest failing when a bout of influenza swept through the Keep. It had left Ionain as the only child once more, his Family's one hope of being restored as a Great Family with a Channeller lord.

Heading on out of the Keep, Eadha turned down the long avenue towards the village. At this time of year, it was sodden, with a thick rut of mud down the centre and pools of water that wouldn't dry out until spring. She'd been sent by her uncle to bring a flock of hardy fell sheep to pasture in the hills above the disused quarry for the day. In the bag slung across her body beneath her cloak was a bannock, a soft yellow apple, and a leather bottle of water. As she walked, she slipped her numb hands into the bag, seeking the heat of the bread, still warm from the Keep ovens.

The sheep were skittish in the fog, inclined to scatter at the least noise, but she was a canny herder and soon enough had cajoled and connived them up onto the fell where the mist had already cleared and there was still good enough eating in the grass for them to settle.

Once they were set, she clambered up onto a rocky outcrop that would give her a good view over them all. Her scrambling disturbed a falcon, and it broke with a screech from its hidden perch on the overhang, swooping low across the fell. During lambing season, they were a menace but now it flew on, out across the valley and on towards the snow-covered Blackstairs. Its flight reminded her of the dragons she still saw from time to time, flying high above her. They were mostly headed on into the high peaks, where the females sometimes bred in the spring. Those peaks were the boundary of her world. It was the one thing she envied Ionain: how he'd crossed the Blackstairs several times already, on trips south with Ura to visit her Debruin relations and allies in the city of Erisen, the great marble city raised by and named for the First Channeller.

As the sun climbed to its highest point and the mists below finally cleared, her heart gave a leap to see a familiar tawny-haired figure scrambling up the steep brae that led directly from the Keep. Even from a distance she could see Ionain was grinning widely. It meant someone, somewhere, was annoyed, most likely his latest tutor. He must have skipped his lessons to be out and about at this hour.

It meant there would be another row, tonight or tomorrow.

Not with his father; Eadha suspected he secretly sympathised with Ionain's escapes. But Ura would be quietly disappointed, and Beithe or Sepp would call on Eadha's uncle to complain she'd no sense.

Ionain wouldn't care, of course; he never did. He'd always had that way of sailing across the top of things. It wasn't that he didn't know people were upset with him, more that he wouldn't let them change his course in any way. As though the great challenge Huath had laid across his life when he was seven years old had simplified everything else for him, down to the bare bones of what mattered to him, and no one could touch him there.

Eadha knew, of course, how his parents and everyone else in the Keep felt. Ionain might ignore it, but she felt it for him. Every sigh, every pointed silence when he skipped lessons to join her out herding, or the two of them disappeared off hunting for the day. But for all that, she still met him where he was. She owed him that, not to let it touch them either.

As Ionain reached the fell-top she delved into her bag. The bannock's crust was stiff with cold now but still soft inside as she tore it, offering half to him as he clambered up to her perch. He took it but shook his head when she offered him her apple, wrinkly but sweet and tasting of summer. She ate it in five quick bites.

'Logicales?' she asked, after a bit.

Shaking his head Ionain lay back on the rock.

'History of the dragon wars. The Battle of Westport.' Eadha snorted. Ionain had been telling those stories since he was a young boy and could tell them far better than any dry tutor.

When they were smaller, Ionain had insisted she come to those lessons with him. Ura had tolerated it for a while, and it meant she'd a basic grasp of reading, writing and map-making. Maps had been her favourite lesson; her nose almost on the page as she painstakingly traced the delicate blue of the Anala sea, stippled with

29

the black of the dragon archipelago off Westport. But Ionain's tutor (a pompous, ungifted Debruin cousin) had shaken his head when he saw she'd sketched in a tiny dragon, all claws and wings, to mark their island domain.

'Art is the preserve of the Masters, and the Great Families, and rightly so, for nothing we ungifted could ever draw can match the wonders of a Channeller's illusions.'

She'd stopped going to the lessons at the same time as she'd moved out of the Keep, after Orran died. She hadn't drawn since then either, but still she dreamt of dragons. Each time she saw one flying overhead, it would follow her into her dreams for days afterwards. Dreams where she flew up alongside it, up into the bright air of morning, to arrow across the icy peaks. Dreams so real that when she awoke, they ached like memories.

After a short silence between them, Ionain poked her hip and when she turned towards him, waggled his closed fist at her.

'Put out your hand and close your eyes.'

As she did, he dropped something hard and smooth into her palm. As soon as she held it, before she even saw it, she knew it for what it was. In the sunlight it glowed with veins of red and gold, too-bright colours for a winter-bleached hillside. It was an amber shard, no bigger than her cupped palm, a model of the White Tower of Erisen. It was perfection miniaturised, tiny windows and arches all picked out on the smooth amber, as perfect as it had been the moment it was channelled by Ionain's great-grandfather a century ago. He'd been a Master Architect, one of the greatest of his age, and had channelled this model as a toy for his grandchildren. She looked down at Ionain.

'Won't your parents mind?'

He shrugged.

'You know Father; he won't care—and Mother is consumed by

the Reckoning preparations. I doubt she'd notice if I took an actual building as long as it wasn't needed for the ceremony.'

'I don't need a birthday present, you know.'

'We've been over this. I know you don't need a present. I want to give you a present. Your proud independence remains intact and is in no way compromised by this spontaneous giving of a gift that will not incur a debt of any kind towards me. So go on, like we practised. Just say thank you.'

'But you'll get into trouble.'

'Try it, go on, just for fun. Thank you, Ionain. Thaaaaank you.'

She looked across at him, his tawny tangled hair full of burrs, his blue eyes laughing up at her from under his hand, a lion cub still. Accepted the clench of happiness that propelled her up onto her feet, where she executed an exaggerated bow from the waist.

'Thaaaank you, kind sir.'

Ionain scrambled to his feet then, too. Now he was standing in front of her on the rock. He swirled his hand regally as Eadha straightened up to face him, then intoned in his most pompous voice, 'You are most welcome, my lady. And happy birthday,' before leaning in and kissing her on the cheek. And on that frozen rocky outcrop high above the Keep, everything stopped as the two friends pulled back and stared at each other.

He hadn't planned to do it, Eadha could tell by the shock on his face. He'd just been caught up in the joke. But when his lips touched her cheek it hadn't felt like a joke. It had felt as though he'd just swung open a door inside her heart and now the space inside her was five times greater than it had been before. And he felt it, too; she could see it in his eyes as the shock in them faded to be replaced by a question. A question her heart already knew the answer to. For it was truth, that kiss. It made no sense, and she knew there was no room for it in his world. But it was truth, and her heart would not let her deny it,

31

not now he'd set it alight. So, she looked him in the eye and kissed him back, a soft brush across his lips. And they were so warm and alive that she wanted only to be kissing him still. But Ionain flushed up bright red and stepped back a little from her.

'Happy birthday,' he said then again, for there not to be a silence.

'Yes,' she said, and it was her turn for her cheeks to burn red.

They both sat down again, closer now though, their hips touching, facing outwards as the heat on their faces slowly cooled.

From where they sat, they could see the lane leading up to the Keep. As they stared down at it, not looking at each other, a solitary rider appeared, picking his way around the puddles. Behind him a cart was just turning onto the lane. Glancing sideways Eadha saw Ionain was staring at them intently. Quietly she said, 'Red doublet, packages tied on the back. Spices for the feast?'

'Silk. More of the finest Erisen silk. Can't have enough silk for a Reckoning,' said Ionain, hunching his shoulders.

'That cart with two big rolled-up bundles, getting stuck halfway up the lane?'

'Ah, the featherbeds for the Debruin cousins. Mother is convinced she will be shamed for all eternity if Lady Mana sleeps on a lumpy mattress.'

'Blue with a yellow stripe, single rider on a fast horse?' Ionain sat forward as Eadha said that, staring down at the new rider already turning in towards the Keep.

'Those are the Manon Family colours. His twins Coll and Linn passed their Reckonings when they turned sixteen last month. Linn's the first girl to pass in five years, so Lord Manon is thrilled. They'll be off to First House on Lambay in the spring to start training. That must be his acceptance of Father's invitation. As if any of them would miss the show of the year. Come all, see the young lord bring glory or ruin to the once noble Ailms. If he fails, you can say you were there for the fall of a

Great Family.'

Turning towards him, Eadha held out the amber tower he'd given her on the flat of her palm.

'But if you pass, you'll be able to do this. And go there,' she said, gesturing towards the Blackstairs and all that lay beyond; the white city of Erisen with its marble towers, the twin islands of Lambay where the Masters had trained generations of young Channellers for near on four hundred years.

Ionain said nothing. It was the one thing he wouldn't talk about, even with her. What would happen if he passed. Eadha understood. All around him for years now his Family had been working up to his Reckoning ceremony with a kind of fanatical optimism, as if by building it into the shape of a victory they could somehow force the power to be there, inside him. But Ionain couldn't even let himself think it, the possibility he might pass. It meant too much.

As the Manon rider disappeared into the Keep the silence between them grew heavy, and in that silence Eadha felt Ionain slipping away from her, back into his old familiar world of worry and waiting.

'I'd better go down,' he said at last, not looking at her as he climbed to his feet. 'Mother will be looking for me to tell me about the Manon letter. She'll be upset if she finds I'm gone.'

Eadha said nothing, only nodding as Ionain jumped lightly to the ground. Raising his hand behind him in farewell he disappeared down the brae.

She sat on, staring at the spot where he'd disappeared, as the sun faded behind the hills and the mist reclaimed its old ground. It felt colder with Ionain gone, the chill needling through her layers, but still she didn't move, drawing her legs into her, her hand cupping her chin so her fingertips were touching the spot where Ionain had kissed her.

33

It was almost dark when she finally roused herself to begin rounding up the flock for the long trudge back down the fell. But as she counted, she realised with a jolt that two sheep were missing.

The first was easily found, a silly ewe tangled and bleating in a blackberry bush. Eadha was untangling the heedless creature, trying to avoid pulling too much wool, when she heard a panicked cry from the far side of the hill. There was a steep drop down to the quarry on that side, the grass over there quickly giving way to treacherous shale. Breaking into a run, she raced towards the sound.

As she ran, there was a rushing sound of stones giving way, followed by the flat thump of body hitting rock. The yearling must've wandered too close to the edge and slid right off the shale, over the drop. It'd been saved only by a narrow outcrop that jutted out about five feet down. The creature lay on the ledge, unmoving but still breathing, winded by its fall. Directly beneath it were the steep pits of the quarry. As soon as it tried to move, it would surely topple over the edge and fall to its death.

Throwing herself down flat on her stomach, Eadha strained towards the trapped animal, stretching her staff out as far as it went, trying to hook the creature's neck and pull it towards her. But it was just out of reach. She needed to get closer. Cautiously she inched out over the loose shale, but as soon as she did the stones began to gather speed beneath her. She only just managed to push herself out of the rush as a hail of pebbles clattered down and off the ledge below.

Panting, her heart thudding with the terror of almost going over the edge herself, she dropped her head.

'Stupid, stupid, how could I be so stupid?' was all she could think. Sitting there mooning over one impossible kiss while the sheep she was supposed to be minding went wandering off. How could she lose an animal so cheaply, so early in the winter, with food already short? They would all be so disappointed in her—her uncle,

Lord Ailm, who'd never said a cross word to her in her life. Even Ionain. She could see it, the look in Ionain's eyes when he heard what she'd done. No. She couldn't bear it, not after that moment of heart-starting joy on the fell. She wouldn't bear it.

It was almost completely dark now, winter's night coming on quickly as she lay there panting, the first lights shining out in the village below. Jamming one hand under a tiny outcrop for grip, her arm trembling with the effort of clinging on, Eadha reached out again, swinging out over empty air, trying once more to reach the yearling. As she swung out over the drop the rush of the air beneath her brought her back to the silent swoop of the morning's falcon. Hanging there, half-suspended in darkness, the world about her seemed to narrow to a falcon's flight. Now she was the hunter, arrowing into the darkness, seeking out her prey. And there, from one heartbeat to the next, there it was, glimmering in the quarry far beneath her: a living, silver force, shining out in the darkness.

Even as she saw it, beyond thought she knew the way of it: a thread that spooled out from the heart of her, arrowing towards that shining force. Without needing to think, in her mind she reached out along that living thread and pulled it hard into her. As she did the world went white about her, then snapped back to black as inside her head a star exploded. Life filled her, shining, pulsating life pouring into every cell of her until she must surely burst with the effort of holding it in.

She let go of her handhold then, dropping fast and hard through the winter night down the stony drop, to land lightly on the narrow ledge where the sheep lay. It was just starting to come round. She caught it up with one hand. Panic-stricken, it began kicking every part of her, fighting to get free. But she held it easily as she climbed back up the near vertical cliff, strong and sure in the darkness. Not until she'd reached the fell-top once more did her knees buckle, the energy that had poured into her from the silver thread she'd caught suddenly spent. She collapsed onto the ground, the sheep writhing out of her arms and scrambling bleating back to the herd.

For a moment Eadha lay there, panting, staring up at the dark sky where the constellation of the Sidhe, the Old Ones, had appeared low on the horizon. But the sheep were milling about anxiously, infected by the yearling's panic. There was nothing for it but to haul herself carefully back up onto the grass and shepherd the flock on down the fell-side, the dark path between the starlight and the firelight.

CHAPTER 4
THE WILLOW MAZE

As soon as the sheep were safely penned for the night Eadha was away, back down the tree-shadowed avenue towards the Keep. The moon had risen enough to light her way, reflecting on puddles already freezing over and mud churned up by the day's traffic. The whole way down the fell she'd shivered uncontrollably, her body aching as if she was running a fever. All she could think now was to crawl into her cot bed and draw the covers over her head until the pain left her. But even as she forced her shaking legs on down the lane, she heard feet coming up behind her, moving more surely and swiftly than her own. Turning, half-fearful of what else this strange night might have in store, she made out the features of the singer Magret.

Beithe's cousin, Magret was a short, vigorous woman with a narrow face framed by cropped white hair. A singer of renown, she had a voice of that still purity that cuts to the listener's heart and is the answer to every question that lies there while the song is sung. She could easily have found a berth at any of the Great Family houses but chose instead a nomadic existence, travelling from House to House throughout Domhain, there to mark Reckonings, betrothals and homings. Eadha knew her from when she'd come to visit Beithe over the years, when her travels took her near enough to Ailm's Keep, and she'd sung at Orran's homing when he'd died two years ago. Now she had come to Ailm's Keep to take charge of the music for Ionain's Reckoning ceremony.

As she drew closer Eadha saw she was bleeding from a deep cut on her temple and her face looked drawn. Peering at Eadha, she asked, 'Child, what has you out at this hour?'

'I was out herding on the High Fell. I had a bit of trouble with a yearling, and it took a while to get them back down in the dark,' Eadha replied. All she wanted was to get away to her room until she could make her own sense of what'd happened in those moments suspended above the quarry. Magret gave her a sideways glance.

'What trouble?'

'It slid down the shale side and almost fell into the quarry. I had to scramble a bit to get it out.'

As she spoke the two of them had reached the Keep courtyard. It was lit up with torches in expectation of Magret's arrival. She pulled up her cowl over her forehead, as if to conceal her temple, where the blood from her cut showed black in the moonlight.

'Do you want to come to the cottage, see to it before you go in to meet the Family?' asked Eadha.

'Do I look a sight?' said Magret. She spat on the corner of her cloak and rubbed at the dried blood until all that was left was the cut itself, just under the hairline. 'Now?'

Eadha nodded. 'You'd hardly see it.'

'Such a stupid thing. I passed the quarry on my way here and took a notion I might find some quartz stones. But I spent too long picking around and ended up having to make my way out in the dark. I must've tripped, for one moment I was climbing over some rocks and the next I was face down, every bone aching and this cut on my temple where I banged my head.'

Magret paused and looked directly at Eadha as she stood poised to escape into the moonlit gardens and home.

'You must've been right up above me when I fell. Strange, how these things happen.'

She turned and rapped her staff on the high doors. They opened to engulf her in a rush and hubbub of greetings and light and heat, while Eadha slipped away unseen.

The next morning, she woke early, her head finally clear of the throbbing pain that had pursued her the whole way from the fell and into exhausted sleep the night before. She could hear the soft sounds of her aunt and uncle stirring below, gently coaxing the fire back to life, murmuring back and forth in the short codes of lives long since so intertwined as to be indistinguishable. Light shone up into the loft from below through gaps in the wooden boards. Eadha curled into herself under her blankets, savouring the perfectly even warmth between her body and the air in her dimly lit cocoon, stretching gently and pulling back when her feet touched the cold sheets beyond her little nest.

Something was happening. She could feel it in her chest, some new life stirring, born of yesterday, of those fleeting kisses on the fell and the silver thread she'd caught in the darkness, both wound together into some newborn thing. It was too small to see, a silver fish that darted out of sight as soon as she tried to look at it, but she could feel it inside her. She hugged her arms around her legs, trying to hold it in, but the excitement pushed her legs scissoring down between the sheets, so she climbed from the bed, down the twisting stairs to her aunt and uncle below.

All the Keep cottages were the same, channelled a generation before by Lord Ailm's father from a golden-red cedar wood. A curving roof flowed in a wave across the houses, creating the nooks and lofts such as the one Eadha slept in. Outside the wood had weathered to a silvery grey, while inside the warmth of the cedar-red remained. The cottage was furnished with chairs and a table Eadha's uncle had carved from stone taken from the disused quarry. Over the years he'd taught himself how to carve stone by hand rather than a Channeller's art; skills that had fallen into disuse generations ago along with so many others, ever since the gift of channelling first appeared on Domhain four hundred years before. Such work was forbidden by the Masters. Only Channellers could grow crops or raise stone but, unable to provide for his people, Lord Ailm turned a blind eye to her uncle's carving and Beithe's vegetable plot hidden along the tree line at the forest's edge, never asking where the carrots that turned up in her stews came from.

Eadha filled a bowl with porridge from the pan hung warming over the fire and made for her usual spot on the stone seat that ran along the inside of the firewell, while her aunt cleared the breakfast things and her uncle made ready to set out for a day's herding in the far pasture. Theirs was a quiet house, with little asked and little answered, as though the two adults had been silenced long ago by some great trauma, one that had left them locked in silence, the only gift they had to give Eadha that of withholding. She thought it must have something to do with her parents and how they died, if only because they never, ever, spoke about them. As she grew older and the urge to know grew stronger, she sometimes even, almost, nerved herself to ask her aunt, but then she'd meet the wordless grief in her aunt's eyes and her questions would stay, unasked and unanswered.

It was a whole world of not asking she lived in, she thought sometimes—not just with her aunt and uncle, but with the other Keep servants. There was a weight to them all, as if they carried a heavy, unspoken burden. Only Beithe seemed made of hard enough stuff to take the asking of questions, but she had her own ways of shutting down nosey children, most often with the flat of her hand.

As Eadha sat by the fire, hugging her own new secrets to herself, they all heard footsteps on the landing outside. It was Magret come calling.

'Come in, come in,' said Eadha's uncle as her aunt urged Eadha to show manners and give up the good seat. But Magret wouldn't come in.

'It's Eadha I'm after,' she said. 'I've always wanted to visit the Keep's willow maze and Lady Ura tells me she knows it best.'

Soon the two were out in the Keep gardens, Eadha leading her around fire-berried bushes and under black-limbed trees until they reached the willow maze. It was bare now for winter, but still dense with intertwined branches. In the clearing at the heart of the maze some tree stumps were set in a rough circle, still scattered about with piles of favourite pebbles, oddly shaped twigs and once colourful flowers she and Ionain had collected, now faded down to heaps of stems and limp leaves.

'Eadha,' said Magret. 'There is something I need to tell you.'

Eadha felt oddly unsurprised. There'd been something in Magret's manner ever since she'd met her the night before on the lane, some suppressed eagerness.

'When you rescued that yearling last night, what do you think happened?'

Eadha shrugged. Yesterday's fog seemed to have crept into her memory; all she could remember now was a sense of tremendous effort and the overwhelming exhaustion that followed.

'I don't know. The sheep was in trouble. I felt bad, and I didn't want to let everybody down. I reached out to hook it and then suddenly it came up and free.'

'Eadha, can you sit here, please?'

She came and perched uneasily on a stump opposite Magret. Moving with incredible swiftness Magret caught Eadha's head on either side, holding it in an unbreakable grip.

'This may hurt a little, but it will only last a moment.'

The next second Eadha felt icy hands reach inside her skull. She screamed in shock. A presence had entered her mind as if it were just another room to be walked into. She squirmed and pulled, trying to break free, but Magret's arms were like bands of iron clamped on either side of her head, immovable.

Desperate then she turned inwards, instinctively trying to push out the invader inside her mind, but nothing happened. She could still feel the calm presence moving about in her head. It wasn't painful after the initial shock, but it was utterly alien, the fundamental wall between her mind and the world outside ripped down. Her every thought was naked and exposed. This was not to be tolerated. More surely now, for she'd walked this path once before, she reached out to Magret and pulled along the silver thread she could sense linking them together. As she did, she felt strength pour into her once more, as it had done the night before, powering up from the depths of her until it shot through into the surface of her mind; a giant wave exploding out from the silvery heart of her, driving all before it. Magret was helpless before this tsunami of Eadha's violated rage, swept out of her mind on the thump of a heartbeat. She collapsed onto the leafy ground at Eadha's feet.

Eadha's only thought was to get away. But as she staggered into the maze, she heard Magret's voice calling after her.

'Eadha, Eadha, don't go. I'm sorry, I had to do that. Eadha, that was a Reckoning, that's all, please just let me explain.'

At these words Eadha stopped. She was due her Reckoning after Ionain's Reckoning day, along with all the others who'd passed sixteen since the last time a Channeller had visited Ailm's Keep. Was Magret an Inquisitor then, sent early from Lambay? It made no sense. Peering through the branches she saw Magret pull herself back up onto the tree stump and hunch over, forearms resting on her thighs and head bowed.

'Eadha, I know you're there. I need you to listen very carefully. You have the Channeller's gift. From what I can tell, a rare gift, strong and sure. I guessed as much last night when you channelled me in the quarry, drawing the power to rescue that yearling. How else do you think you were able to climb up a vertical cliff carrying such a weight?'

Eadha reeled in her hiding place, sitting down heavily on the damp leaf carpet between the bare hedges. Not since she'd been a very young girl playing games of make-believe with Ionain had she ever even imagined she might be a Channeller. Even in those games Ionain would always argue she couldn't play the Channeller, because girls hardly ever were. No more than one or two in a generation and always the daughters of Great Families, not girls like Eadha from a family with no name, no history of the gift.

The realisations began to multiply, bursting silently one by one in her mind like a shower of stars shooting across a winter sky. All was changed by this. She could make everything right again, the way it'd been in Ailm's father's time. She could be the Keep's Channeller. Grow the crops, guard the animals, heal the buildings, even protect against dragon raids. She could live in the Keep again. And Ionain, he was finally free of the shadow that'd darkened every day of his childhood. He didn't need to be a Channeller to save the Keep. She could do it for him. His Reckoning didn't matter anymore.

Magret, making her way along the maze, came upon the hidden girl, arms around her knees, head buried. She put her arms across her shoulders, wincing in sympathy.

'There now, it's a lot to hear, I know.'

But Eadha's eyes, when she lifted her head, were blazing.

'How can you know? Are you an Inquisitor? Were you sent by

43

the Masters? How can you be sure?'

'I have some skill of Reckoning, yes, but no, this wasn't your official Reckoning. That is still to come. I would wager my life you are a Channeller born. The way you channelled my energy just now for the power to throw me out of your mind is the purest proof there is.'

Unable to contain herself Eadha jumped to her feet, ready to run the entire way to the Keep to find Ionain, to say the words to break the curse that'd held him for so long. In her mind she was already there. He was already hugging her so hard she could hardly breathe and—her throat tightened in sudden longing—then he would lean in and kiss her, only this time he wouldn't be pulled away from her by the old worry and waiting. This time they wouldn't have to stop.

'But Eadha, I need you to listen to me now.'

Magret's sober tone jolted Eadha back, to the frosty morning and the damp leaves and the bareness of the willow branches that surrounded them.

'This power, it is not something to be taken lightly, a toy. There is so much you don't know. Your life, the life of everyone in Ailm's Keep, is so different to that of most people on Domhain. Without the gift there's been no channelling here for many years apart from the occasional rampage by Lord Huath. Growing up in the Keep, almost part of Lord Ailm's family, channelling has doubtless been a thing of legend for you, this great power that will bring prosperity back. It's what they do so well, the Families and the Masters, telling their children only of the beauty and nothing of the darkness of it.

'But all you've been hearing is one part of a brutal story. Yes, channelling can draw life from the soil, slay dragons and all the other wonders Ionain has doubtless talked of to you. But power cannot come from nothing. It has to come from another; one man's power is another man's pain.'

She paused and stared at the listening girl.

44

'Eadha, I will not speak of this here, now, in this place. You need time to heal from your efforts and I need time to recover. Even with all my skill in shielding, I am weak from what you've done to me these last two days. But heed this. You must swear you will speak of this to no one and you must not use this power again before your Reckoning day. Ionain will have told you channelling unschooled by the Masters at Lambay is utterly forbidden. Lord Huath arrives soon for his nephew's Reckoning ceremony and he is not someone you want to cross.'

Eadha's natural composure had returned. Already taller than the slight singer, she stared at her, unblinking, until finally she nodded a brief assent. And while she still wanted to race to find Ionain, race until her legs ached and her breath gave out, a part of her rejoiced at holding this new, strange feeling to herself for a little longer.

Magret left her then, needing to return to the Keep before she was missed. Left alone, Eadha struck out for the forest. She would live with her aunt's anger when she returned late, chores undone. For now, the cottage, even Ailm's Keep itself, felt too small to be borne. Only the forest, stretching up into the foothills of Mount Lein, its roots reaching fathoms below into the earth, felt deep and wide enough to hold her.

As she ducked in under the bare canopy, the low winter sun shone almost horizontally across her way, lighting the branches from below, throwing out shadows of tree trunks. Moving from shade to light she saw a family of roe deer, picking delicately beneath the spread of a chestnut tree for the nuts shining from their spiky casings. As she watched they startled to the crack of a branch, and as they raced off, she raced after them, lean and swift, a young wolf. On silent feet she leapt across ivy-covered trunks fallen across her way, bent low to pass beneath hanging branches, easily keeping pace with the deer as they flowed on. Her breath came smoothly, and her legs ran surely and effortlessly through sunny clearings and down dark tunnels overhung with dead and matted leaf fall. A fierce joy rose in her. It was not until the deer stopped to graze in an open clearing that she understood. This, this surging power, this was channelling.

She wasn't far from the hollow where she and Ionain had built ropewalks as children. They criss-crossed the air in a layered web, a record of their childhood like the rings of a tree, the older, lower-down ropes green and slippy with moss, the newer ropes stretching far above them, strung by herself and Ionain between the topmost branches as they grew taller, climbed higher with each summer. As she stood there a memory of Huath in the Great Hall all those years ago came back to her. Closing her eyes she concentrated, imagining herself floating up into the chilly air. For some time, nothing happened, and then, slowly, unsteadily, she began to rise towards the trees. She was almost level with the first ropes when, as suddenly as snuffing out a candle, the power went out of her, spent, and she began to fall back down.

At the last moment her outflung arm caught rope. She hung there a moment then pulled herself up onto the ropewalk and across to Ionain's favourite branch. She could still feel flickers of the flame that had driven her as swift as the deer deep into the forest. She wished Ionain was with her. He would know what was happening to her. Closing her eyes she imagined his face, not trapped in its habitual scowl of worry but smiling with relief and happiness. With the last embers of power within her she reached out across the ropewalk, across the forest and into the Keep.

'I will make everything right,' she whispered.

For one tiny moment she thought she felt him respond, a tremor running back down a long thread stretching between them, before tiredness overcame her. As she'd done every night since she moved out of the Keep, she curled into the memory of his warmth and fell asleep, cradled in the branches of the tree.

CHAPTER 5
WAITING

The days after Eadha learned she had the Channeller's gift passed in a daze. Each morning she took the sheep up to the fell then sat for the day staring out across the valley towards the Blackstairs, dreaming of all that lay beyond them for her now. Her world had exploded outwards and filled with possibilities she hadn't dreamt of since she was old enough to know better. She was gifted. She was going to be a Channeller.

She ransacked her memories for every scrap of every story about Channellers Ionain had told her when they were small, back in the years before Orran died and the weight of expectation had grown too heavy for him to talk about it anymore. How those found gifted at their Reckoning were summoned to the Masters' House on the islands of Lambay, where Channeller apprentices had been trained for the last four hundred years.

She pictured how she'd ride out from the Keep across the Blackstairs, on past the white towers of Erisen to be welcomed by the Masters on Lambay. How she'd learn the ways of power; the growing of crops so plentiful the people of the Keep would grow fat and lazy, the shaping of stone to make the Keep whole once more. She would become a dragon warrior with a staff as fine as the yew staff Huath gave Ionain all those years ago, her power flowing through it and out into great bolts of power as she battled dragons in the skies above Westport, just like in the stories. And for as long as she lived, Lord Huath would never threaten the Keep or Ionain again.

Ionain. Each time she thought of him, her whole body flushed with the memory of their kiss. In her mind Ionain and her newborn power were mixed together, all part of a single explosion as her life became something so much greater than she'd ever thought it could be.

Those first few days she was so preoccupied, she barely registered that Ionain didn't come again to find her on the fell. When she did, a part of her was relieved. She remembered how easily Magret had stepped into her mind and shuddered at the thought of how brutally someone like Lord Huath might use that power if he thought someone was keeping a secret from him. She knew she couldn't risk telling Ionain anything, but she'd never kept a secret from him before. A part of her didn't trust herself not to blurt it out the minute she saw him, just to see the look on his face. But as the days stretched into a week and still Ionain didn't come to find her, a chill crept into her thoughts. Why did he still not come?

The first Reckoning guests were due to start arriving soon, and Beithe had everyone in the Keep terrorised, clearing and cleaning. One morning, a week after her encounter with Magret in the willow maze, Beithe caught Eadha by the shoulder as she headed out herding and swivelled her instead towards the Lady's Well.

'Lord Huath's wife Mana arrives tomorrow. Lady Ura says we've to clear out the Well in case her ladyship takes a whim to sit there. Though why anyone would ever sit in that awful, draughty spot is beyond me. On with you now and mind you clear it properly.'

The Lady's Well was a marble cloister on the very edge of the

Keep. In times past it was where the ladies of the Keep had sat while the old Lord Ailm wove illusions from the great dragon battles high above them in the evening sky. Its tiled floor was covered with mosaics and a stream sang down its centre before beginning its quick fall towards the lake.

Without a Channeller for more than quarter of a century, these outer parts of the Keep were beginning to crumble, dissolving gently into the gardens that bided their time beyond. In the Lady's Well the mosaic tiling had begun to crack and heave, pieces of broken tiles scattered about the floor. Crouching down, Eadha held her hand out over the jewel-coloured shards. Inside, her newborn gift kicked in sudden longing. She tried to picture power flowing out of her into the stone, commanding it to flow back together and become whole once more.

'Hey, Beithe said I'd find you here.'

It was Ionain, come up silently behind her. She started, snatching her hand back and almost toppling over, just catching the stream's edge to steady herself.

'Do you remember what we did with those, the last time we were here?' Ionain said then, looking down at the small pile of tiles.

The familiar memory steadied her, and she smiled.

'They were our drums,' she said. 'That's how we got caught by Sepp that day. I was battering them with a stick when you decided to sing along at the very top of your voice. Stealth was never your strong point.'

Ionain laughed.

'That's how the Dragon Song is meant to be sung: at the top of your voice as you ride west across the stony barrens to Westport to fight dragons, because you're terrified you're going to be burned to death by some enraged dragon mother and singing is the only thing you've got to keep you going.'

Turning on his heel Ionain threw his head back,

'Westward the dragon flies and so must I

Naught but a yew staff by my side

My one heart's wish that you are there to keep for me

When I ride to Westport's shore, but it cannot be

When I'm gone, when I'm gone

Say that you'll miss me when I'm gone.'

As he sang, Eadha saw the two of them riding west together to join the Channellers' never-ending battle against the dragons, fighting to hold them back to their island colonies off the west coast. And the longing to tell Ionain her secret was so strong that before she could even think she'd started turning towards him, her mouth open to tell him everything.

The look on his face as he finished singing stopped her.

'I'm glad I found you here. I've been wanting to talk to you about the other day.'

Eadha stared. He looked down at the ground, not meeting her eyes, one hand on his head, twisted into his tangled mop of hair, the old familiar tell of worry.

'I shouldn't have done that. Kiss you.'

A chasm seemed to open up inside her then, splitting her down the middle. Glancing up and seeing the expression in her eyes Ionain hurried on, 'I mean, not that I didn't want to, only... I've no right to do anything like that. Not until after my Reckoning.'

Eadha frowned and said, 'But it doesn't make any difference to me what happens at your Reckoning. It never has, not ever.'

Ionain half-smiled then, the look of strain on his face fading a little as he said, 'You know you're the only person on all of Domhain I'd believe when they said that?'

'Well then?' said Eadha.

'But it matters to me, whether I pass or not. I need to know who

I am before... before I start anything else. Even that.'

'Why though? You'll still be you, I'll still be me. We'll still be us regardless. Power won't change who you are.'

Ionain looked at her directly then and, just for that moment, of the two of them he seemed for the first time ever to be the older one.

'You know that's not true, Eadha. Not on Domhain.'

Eadha remembered then the power coursing through her that night on the fell. How it had changed her whole sense of the world, made it seem limitless and without boundaries. And she knew that though she'd spoken the truth, Ionain was right, too.

As she thought it, Ionain leaned in, so close his forehead was touching hers, his warm breath mingled with hers.

'Will you wait, Eadha? Until then?'

She looked into his blue eyes so full of worried earnestness. In truth there was no choice in this. She would always wait for him. She nodded wordlessly and with a quick, relieved grin he nudged her in the shoulder.

'Now push up if you want my help to get this done, before Beithe comes to tell us how we've gotten it all wrong.'

They eventually got the Lady's Well cleared to Beithe's grudging satisfaction, but in the days that followed it began to seem as if there would never be any end to the Reckoning preparations. The food, the clothes, the invitations endlessly talked over and worked on as winter began to loosen its grip and the months shortened to weeks.

To Eadha's annoyance, in those final weeks her aunt commandeered her to help to prepare the formal robes for Ionain's ceremony. Last worn by Lord Ailm for his own failed inquisition decades ago, they'd been handed down through generations of Ailm lords, heavy ornate things embroidered in gold and silver thread and embellished with jewels. The colours had begun to fade with age, the cloth decaying in spots or tearing with the weight of the precious

53

stones. It was delicate work, searching through the many folds and with the gentlest of touches repairing and renewing.

For Eadha it meant sitting day after day with her aunt and the other seamstresses in the sewing room in the East Tower with its corbelled windows on all sides, filling the room with the light needed for the fine, precise work. She hated it, the smallness of their world, and she hated those robes, the thought of their dead weight swallowing up Ionain's slight frame, imprisoning him. She was put to hemming the plainer undergarments, a task where her clumsy fingers were less likely to do harm.

Halfway through one morning's work the quiet of the sewing room was broken as Lady Ura and a small convoy of noblewomen swept in, pulling Ionain along in their wake. Relatives and allies from the Great Families had been arriving in the Keep for the Reckoning for days, chief among them Lady Mana, Lord Huath's wife, there with her two small daughters. Now they wanted to see Ionain dressed in his ceremonial robes.

Sitting in the corner of the sewing room Eadha didn't look up at Ionain. She knew he hated all of it: the fuss, the women cooing and laughing above his head, the way his mother steered the conversation all the time back to her powerful brother's wife, because she knew if Ionain failed his Reckoning, Huath's favour might be the only thing that saved them from destitution. All his life he'd been stared at and talked over, as people wondered if he'd be the salvation or the ruin of his Family. More than anything he wanted to be able to just walk through the world and look out at it, rather than always be looked upon, and these final weeks before his Reckoning were the worst of it. Knowing this, the only solidarity Eadha could show was to keep her head bowed in awkward silence.

After much discussion Eadha's aunt stepped forward with one of the ceremonial robes, and the room fell quiet. Ionain was made to strip, standing pale and skinny in the centre of the room. As soon as the robe was draped across his thin frame it was obvious it was far too long. He was swamped in it, like a very young child dressing up in their father's clothes.

'Well, if even the robe doesn't fit...'

It was Lady Mana, her voice loud in the silence. Around her, her attendants turned their faces away, giggling.

'Remove it, please,' said Lady Ura, nodding meaningfully to the seamstresses.

But the gold ties used to hold the robe in place had become knotted. For long stretched moments Ionain was surrounded by a huddle of seamstresses nervously unpicking the knots, trying to hurry but not tear the precious fabric while Ionain stared at the ceiling, blinking his eyes furiously.

Finally, mercifully, he was released. Eadha tried to catch his eye, but they were fixed only on the door and escape, and in a moment he was gone. All afternoon she looked for him, clambering up onto the Keep roof, even hiking out to the ropewalk dell, but no one could hide like Ionain when he did not want to be found.

The next morning, she woke before dawn. Her sleep had been broken by a dream in which she'd taken Ionain's place in the sewing room, immobilised beneath the jewelled carapace of heavy robes and undergarments. She stood surrounded by noblewomen who looked on in the same scornful silence as she tried again and again to find and hold the thread of power and channel it through a needle held by Lady Mana.

Every morning since the willow maze, when she passed through that dreaming state between sleep and wakefulness, in her mind's eye she saw a shining thread leading towards her sleeping aunt and uncle; the same silver path she'd seen leading to Magret. This morning, troubled by her dream, with eyes still closed she reached towards her aunt, catching her shining thread and unspooling it very gently towards her. As she did a shock ran through her. Where before she'd taken power from Magret only to fling it out immediately once more, this time she just lay there for a moment, sensing it pour softly into her, building in the very centre of her until her aunt moaned in her sleep and Eadha quickly dropped the thread.

Wide awake now, she concentrated on the energy fizzing gently within her. Holding one hand out in front of her, she imagined a tiny were-light and sent the energy inside her flowing into her hand. Immediately, a scalding flame burst into life above her hand, burning her palm. With a start she flung the light away from her. It flew about the room, whizzing in a circle above her head while she sucked at her burnt hand. Terrified something would catch fire or that the little light would go shooting off downstairs, she closed her eyes and concentrated on the feeling she'd had in the woods, of power being snuffed out. After a moment the were-light wavered, came to a halt, then vanished. Heart pounding, Eadha lay back.

That morning her aunt found it difficult to get up, sleeping on well past her normal hour for rising. It was not her way to complain but Eadha could see a stiffness in her as she left for the Keep. After she and her uncle had left, Eadha stayed sitting with one of the Keep cats for company and stared a long time into the fire.

In the days that followed, Eadha took to waking every morning before her aunt and uncle. She would stealthily draw power as they slept and sit there in her loft practising. She learned to control the tiny were-lights so they floated safely above her hand, sending them dancing about the room, first one, then many in interweaving patterns flashing round her head. And every day her aunt and uncle were weary, unrefreshed by their nights' sleep, bodies aching and minds dulled. They put it down to a winter chill, and her aunt brewed up warming potions and scolded her uncle for not wrapping up as he headed out across the frozen ground to tend to the Keep animals. As if from a distance Eadha sensed their weakness bore relation to her power. But so absorbed was she in the cocoon of her newborn gift that the lines of pain being slowly drawn down their faces were blurred to her, as if seen through a pane of frosted dragonglass. She held any thought of it away from her, as something to be faced, but not now.

On a day when snow blanked the world, her uncle sent her to the granary to go through their scant store of seeds. Huath had promised them a crop raising when he came for Ionain's Reckoning. She was to see if any seeds had sprouted or shrivelled. Remembering Ionain's stories of Channellers drawing whole fields of golden corn from the soil she stood there in the musty darkness, the tiny casings in her hand, called up her power and felt them start into life. One seed split apart as she watched, a tendril nosing out onto her palm where it curled about itself, drinking in the life that pulsed through her skin. A perfect leaf, then another and another formed along the tiny stalk. Heart pounding, she hid the budded seeds behind the granary in a pot packed with soil and a prayer, then stepped out into the early end of winter's day.

The moon's crescent was stamped silver in a corner of the sky. Above her, crows gathered, calling harshly to roost. All around evening's tide was rolling in and into it Eadha dived, lifting herself up into the air, grinning as the crows startled when she flew in among them, before plunging into the pines of the forest beyond the Keep, feeling their branches brush soft against her face. Hidden just inside the tree line she flew, swift and solitary, a lone wild thing, until across a field of snow she saw a yellow light, brightening as evening's dimness faded to night's black. It was Ionain, trudging back to the Keep from an afternoon's hunt, a candle lantern swinging in his hand. She dropped down to earth then. As he neared, she called to him from beneath the canopy.

'Catch anything?'

'Eadha, is that you? What are you doing out? You must be freezing,' he said, holding his light up to see her.

Just for a moment she fingered the truth, held it palm out in her hand towards him, until, remembering her promise to Magret, she moved on to a half-lie of firewood and chores.

'Beithe wanted me to get some wood in, start it drying out.'

'It's far too dark for that now, you goose,' he said. 'Come on, I'll walk you back to the cottage.'

They walked along in silence a while, their arms linked tightly against the cold, and Eadha was as warm as she'd been wrapped in her power flying among the pines.

'I'm sorry for the drama in the sewing room the other day,' said Ionain.

She hugged his arm.

'You're better than me, I would've torn that stupid robe right off. They're horrible people. They'll regret their sniggering when there's a Channeller back in Ailm's Keep.'

Ionain looked at her, startled by her fierceness, then squeezed her arm in return.

'Maybe. That would be fun.' He puffed out his breath. 'Just imagine their faces, Lady Mana and all the whole superior lot of them.'

Too full of her secret to trust herself to answer him without shouting it out to the snow and the stars Eadha slipped out of his arm then, stepping from the circle of candlelight so Ionain could no longer see her.

'Anyway,' she called to him with a grin, as she rose invisibly into the air. 'Like I've always said, if you don't pass we can just disappear...'

'Eadha, don't be an idiot, where are you?' he called.

She'd flown up above his head, looking down at his pin-prick of light in the darkness around them. In the next moment her snowball caught him square on the back of his head, exploding with a soft floof. He hadn't a chance. She was a will o' the wisp, now in front, now behind, peppering him with snowballs and disappearing, flying up into the air safely hidden by the darkness. Pinned down by having to keep his candle burning Ionain was defenceless, first cursing and then laughing at the white balls raining down on him until at last he gave up and pelted off towards the Keep and shelter.

By the time they reached the gardens they were both red-faced and sweating, full of the electric calm that comes from laughing your heart out. As she turned to go into the cottage Ionain caught her arm and pulled her hard into a tight, wordless hug before releasing her again and swinging away across the frozen lake.

As she stepped inside, her breath still coming in white puffs, Eadha felt as though the cottage had shrunk around her or she had grown giant-sized, the life and the love inside her too much for this small space. But the slow dance of fire-shadows on the back wall, the quiet gestures of her aunt and uncle in the dim light cast their spell, shrank her down to girl-size once more, and the waiting went on.

CHAPTER 6
THE HIGHEST NOTE

Since arriving at the Keep, Magret had been assembling her choir for the Reckoning from a mix of house servants and crofters. Eadha had been included—more, she thought, so Magret could keep an eye on her, rather than because of any great singing ability. More than once, she'd sensed that Magret was looking to talk to her, but each time Eadha managed to slip away just as choir ended, before Magret could get her on her own. She'd broken her promise to Magret not to start using her gift and she didn't want to be faced with that fact, not yet.

Each morning the choir rehearsed in the Great Hall, where they would ultimately welcome Ionain to his inquisition. As Eadha's channelling skill grew she often arrived in rehearsal with a surfeit of the energy drawn from her aunt and uncle, roiling gently within her. Slowly at first and then more surely, she learned to channel that unused power into her singing, so it grew in power and purity, and her voice soared above the others', dancing through the age-old melodies and up into the silent space above.

Only Ionain knew her well enough to know she couldn't normally sing like this, but he was shut away with visitors day after day and never heard her. The older singers around her, kitchen servants and farm hands, remembered only that her mother had sung with an aching clarity at Lord Ailm's Reckoning twenty years before and they rejoiced in her, at this proof of a mother living on in a child. For the first time Eadha felt shame at her deception, and all the while Magret watched her from her stand on the podium.

She'd been awake from before dawn, practising her flying as her aunt and uncle lay unconscious below. The effort had for once used up most of the energy she'd drawn from them. Now she stood in the centre of the choir in the Great Hall with almost all her power already spent. As the singers hummed and coughed around her, in those last few instants before their voices would dissolve together into a single song, Eadha saw Ionain's familiar tawny head appear through the stone archway above. It was the first time she'd seen him in days, not since their walk in the snow. He leaned over the cross-walk and gave her a wave. She grinned back at him and mimed throwing a snowball.

With a sweep of her arm Magret gestured to the choir to begin. Their voices rose in the canto to welcome Ionain at the start of his Reckoning ceremony. It began with a single deep voice, a subterranean thrumming that seemed to rise through the floor, beating inexorably forwards. Gradually each layer of voices added its own melody, sonorous and sweet intertwined, filling the great space with a multitude of harmonies until every voice stopped together on a heartbeat and the sound collapsed into silence. This would be the moment when Ionain reached the stage and turned to face his Inquisitor.

Eadha and the other sopranos were to lead off the second canto, starting high and cascading down before lifting again to the highest note of all. As the first song neared its end, she felt the last traces of the power she'd drawn that morning ebbing away from her.

Glancing up she could see Ionain's head, watching from the cross-walk above, his chin resting on his forearms. He looked preoccupied, as if his mind was far away. In that moment Eadha was gripped by the need to be seen by him, for him to hear her voice soaring above all the others.

Closing her eyes she focused, finding the now-familiar threads leading to the singers around her. With the gentlest of touches she reached to first one, then another and another, pulling tiny sips towards her, feeling power build within her. Below she watched Magret mouth the count, raising both hands above her head as if reaching for the notes with the singers. With a sweep of her own she shot the power from the centre of her, sent it pouring into her voice so that it flew up and up, and as they reached the highest note, she sang it out with such purity and power, a thing of such outrageous freedom that it forced the breath out of every listener in the room, as if to hold up the beautiful sound a moment more before it fell to earth. She saw Magret's eyes widen and Ionain's head lift to stare at her, but in that instant she didn't care, utterly absorbed now in the flow of her power.

In the same instant there was a commotion at the oak doors, a ferocious hammering as if someone was trying to smash them apart. The singing stuttered to a halt, voices falling silent. House servants peeled away from the choir, running to open the doors before they were broken down. Lord Huath pushed past them without a word, flanked by guardsmen who swiftly took up positions at every doorway and stairwell.

He stalked to the podium, his eyes scanning the choir. As he did, every head in the room bowed down, every breath coming shallow with fear. In the centre of the choir Eadha was close to collapsing in sudden terror. Magret's warnings came screaming back to her as she felt something stir in front of her, as if a much larger creature were unfolding itself where Huath stood, his power radiating out from him. The heat of that power began building against her skin, a prickling, crawling sensation. She remembered how easily Magret had entered her mind, knew it would only be seconds before her every pathetic attempt at channelling, the tiny lights, the forest flights, the budded seeds, would be laid bare to Huath's pitiless gaze.

Within her, she felt her own power still pulsing gently with the energy she'd drawn moments before. Now in her mind's eye she grew a sheet of ice above it, dull thick ice, a blank surface that would reflect the glare of the winter sun and blind the eye. She sent her silver fish diving, deep beneath the ice into the depths of her, to hold, perfectly still. But the heat of Huath's power was relentless; in only a few heartbeats more her ice sheet would shatter, and she would be exposed.

But even as she clenched her fists, waiting for his strength to overwhelm her, Magret spoke. Her voice was quiet, deferential, but it rang clear in the silvery acoustics of the Great Hall.

'Lord Huath, pray forgiveness for my intrusion, but I felt you would wish to be informed of the presence of your nephew Ionain above you. While I would not presume to know your purpose in this moment, it would be a tiding of such joy to your sister and Lord Ailm, if you have sensed the first flickerings of power even before the young master's Reckoning in a few weeks.'

The hot breath on Eadha's skin snapped out as Lord Huath's head shot up to see Ionain's scared face peering down from the crosswalk above. It was enough to end his inquisition. Released, Eadha saw how Lord Huath visibly damped down the power flowing through him. Then he straightened and turned with a wide smile.

'Why, nephew, how remiss of me, I did not see you there. Come, let us go and speak to your father. If what I sensed as I rode in is any guide, then you have a powerful gift indeed and your Reckoning day will be one spoken of for years to come.'

From where she stood watching in the choir Eadha saw disbelief then hope chase a dawning joy across Ionain's face as he took in what his uncle was saying.

'Oh, Uncle. Truly? You sensed something? Some power? I never...'

Visibly overcome, Ionain stopped then, looking down for a moment and drawing a deep, shaking breath before looking up again, his eyes blazing with happiness.

'We have to go tell Father and Mother,' and he raced down the steps, jumping the last few to embrace his uncle before pulling him away with him.

Left to itself the choir broke apart, scared and bewildered, no heart left in them to sing again that day.

CHAPTER 7
THE FODDER WING

As the choir dispersed Magret began gathering up her music sheets. Head down, Eadha started shuffling out with the rest. She was still shaking from the fright of almost being caught by Huath and had to fight down the urge to push past them all and run on out of the Keep and into the forest, get as far away as she could from his searing, scouring power.

'Eadha, can you come here, please? I need another pair of hands to carry these manuscripts.'

For a moment Eadha thought of pretending she hadn't heard Magret. But the people around her were already looking at her; there was nothing for it but to turn back.

Magret handed her the bundle of manuscript sheets and nodded for her to follow. She crossed the Great Hall, making for a dark hole in the wall underneath the spiral staircase, half-hidden behind a bust of Ionain's grandfather. Eadha's steps faltered. Magret was headed for the entrance to the Fodder tunnel, that connected the Great Hall to the Fodder Wing.

Its black mouth had always frightened Eadha, like something lying in wait beneath the stairs, a pit waiting to swallow any who came too close. She tried to force herself to follow Magret, but even as she did a long-buried memory stirred, like a shadow unfolding from a corner of her mind.

They'd only been about eleven and ten, she and Ionain, on the run from Beithe and her chores, when they'd hidden inside the tunnel entrance one sunny afternoon. She'd faltered then, too, when Ionain had tugged at her to come further in.

'We're not allowed,' she'd said. 'It's only for Channellers.'

'It's alright if you're with me,' Ionain had told her, already gone on ahead, pushing against a door stiff with age. Inside, a dim light filtered in through filthy, narrow windows set deep in the wall. 'We can play hide-and-seek.' It'd always been his favourite game. Eadha wanted to say no, but the darkness seemed to have swallowed her voice. Ionain had already disappeared, though she could still hear his light footsteps as he searched for a hiding place.

'...Twenty-seven, twenty-eight...' she'd intoned, almost whispering, as if afraid something might hear her.

'...Fifty-two, fifty-three...'

She could no longer hear Ionain moving. Stepping further into the room her voice faded into the silence, her feet soundless on a floor carpeted by the dust of years. In the dimness the far wall seemed strange, misshapen. Peering closer her foot clanked against metal, and she started back. An iron chain stretched into darkness. In front of her the stone of the wall swelled out at intervals to make a row of narrow seats. They were of a part with the wall; they must have been made at the same time as the Fodder Wing was first raised, part of its reason for being. Below the seats a stone rivulet ran the length of the room, discoloured by dark stains still visible through the dust. As she strained to see an old pain seemed to open out before her, yawning in front of her like a black pit so that she scrabbled backwards, petrified. Groping blindly, she felt her way back to the door, scraping her thigh against a jutting table leg.

The darkness was multiplying, out of the corners, down the tunnel, flowing around and over her until she was choking on it. She could find no trace of Ionain, no tell-tale breathing, no creak of floor. She felt her way by touch, running her hand along the wall, across the air of empty doorways, listening for any sound that might show her where he'd hidden. She froze, holding her breath, listening, listening, but there was nothing, nothing but the dark and at its heart those seats of pain and the dead river beneath. It came over her then with iron certainty that she would never leave here. That the darkness had swallowed Ionain and now it was coming for her, to chain her to those stone seats and drain her dry, until there was nothing left of her but a stain on the stone.

So loud her voice tore in her throat she'd screamed his name then, 'Ionain! Ionain!'

'I'm here,' he sang out cheerfully, uncurling from beneath a broken chair by her feet. 'Silly, you always do that. Just when you've almost found me, you always give in and call out.' Furious with fear and relief Eadha hauled him with her back out into the brightness of the Great Hall.

Now, six years later, she stared at that lightless mouth, and the nameless horror of those stone cells gripped her once more. She couldn't go back in. But Magret was unyielding, her face grim as she stepped out, caught her by the arm and dragged her the last few steps into the tunnel.

Though there'd been no Channeller to use it since the death of old Lord Ailm, as they ducked through the opening Eadha saw signs of recent passage, the dust stirred up in places, torches casting an uncertain light.

As soon as they were out of sight of the Great Hall Magret turned to Eadha with a furious whisper.

'You stupid child, have you any idea of the danger you were in just now? I warned you not to channel before your Reckoning and not only do you ignore that, but you stand there in the Great Hall brazen as you like, drawing power from all around you and roaring it to the heavens with the most brutal Channeller in the entire Domhain outside the door. Did you think your power would not be felt? Oh, you little idiot, you are playing with something you have no conception of. Being surrounded by the blind does not make you invisible. To those that have eyes for power, everything you do with your gift might as well be written in lines of fire across the sky.'

Eadha's eyes filled with tears, but there was no hint of compassion in Magret's face.

'Come. There is something you must see,' and taking a torch from its brazier Magret pulled her deeper into the Fodder Wing.

As they reached the room where she'd counted all those years ago, Eadha realised there were signs of occupation. A lighted candle on a righted table, a water jug and some husks of stale bread. And along the far wall, in the stone seats, were people. Four of them, sat in a row, in tattered clothes and bare feet. Two men, two women, all of them slumped as if too exhausted to hold themselves up. Peering in from the doorway, as her eyes adjusted to the dim light, she realised with horror that what was keeping them in their seats were the iron chains that bound them there.

'So, child, and what do you make of this?' asked Magret, moving to hold her torch over one of the men. His face had caved in, worn to the bone, and he lay like one utterly spent. As the light cast its feeble shadow across him, he stirred weakly, too tired to rouse himself to look back at the woman and the girl staring at him. The other three paid them no heed at all. One of the women was resting her head on the shoulder of the other woman, their eyes closed as if they were asleep, or unconscious, but Eadha saw they were still holding hands, tightly, as if they'd braced themselves together against some impact.

'I don't understand,' she replied. 'Who are they?'

'These, my dear, are Fodder. The inevitable end of a path that leads from you sipping power from your fellow singers and whoever else you have been thieving life from, all the way to this foul place, to these poor husks of what once were men and women. Huath drained them for the power to do his inquisition, after your little stunt in the choir.'

Eadha was crying now in earnest. She didn't need Magret to explain any more, she understood. She'd always known but had been so entranced by her power she'd held that knowledge away. But Magret continued, in a harsh, angry voice.

'This is your gift, child, look upon it. To drain the life from the people around you and play lords and ladies. To take their life-force to make dancing lights and fine singing. Is the journey from Erisen to Ailm's Keep too long, too tedious? Well then, drain a crofter or two, so much more civilised, don't you think, to arrive in time for dinner? Perhaps you grow bored of your castle; why, summon the Fodder and a Master Architect will draw from them the towers of your dreams in no time at all.'

Eadha tried to turn and run, but Magret held her in an unyielding grip, fingertips tightening down her arm as she tugged uselessly.

'No, you will see this. You will not just run away to join those pampered idiots on Lambay, all trace of the reality of their power carefully hidden away from them so they drain and play away with no idea, no thought of the consequences of what they do until they are too far gone to ever care.'

'You're hurting me, please, let me go,' begged the distraught girl.

'Oh, and did you think of the hurt you were causing your aunt and your uncle these last weeks, as you drained them for your sport?'

This brought her up short. She sagged then and would have

fallen but for Magret's hold on her, as the full force of what she'd been doing to her aunt, her uncle, hit her.

'But I didn't mean...'

'Oh ho, you learn fast. The perfect Channeller answer. They never mean to hurt people, all they want is to build a beautiful house or draw out the crops. The harm they do is merely an unpleasant by-product, not to be talked of in polite society.'

Magret spoke with a controlled rage, eyes blazing as she gestured towards the pathetic heaps before them.

'We have to help these people. I'll bring food and clothes from the storerooms,' stammered Eadha, desperate to somehow make things right.

'You will do no such thing. We will do nothing. We will leave this room and it will be as if we were never here.'

'What do you mean? We can't leave them here in this cold, they might die.'

'Child, you would be condemning yourself and everyone working in the Keep to suffering far worse than theirs, if you were to lift a finger to interfere with Lord Huath's Fodder. There is nothing you can do here that will not make things far worse for many more people, people you love. Fear not, they will not die, though they may wish for it. Lord Huath needs them to draw power for the Reckoning. They will be fed and kept alive until then at least and quite possibly afterwards. Huath is well aware of his sister's squeamishness about the realities of channelling.'

Magret drew her out of the room and, stepping carefully, led them both out through the rear of the Fodder Wing. The first frost had thawed, uncovering a clear day. Eadha's face was ashen and tear-stained, and she was shivering uncontrollably. They walked unspeaking back to Eadha's cottage, empty at this time of day. The embers of the fire were still warm. Magret stoked it up with logs from the woodpile outside, while Eadha walked over to the rainwater barrel at the side of the house, plunging her head into the icy water. The cold helped restore her to some sense of herself. She folded her aunt's cloak about her and sat on the stone fireseat.

Magret's normal calm demeanour had returned, the livid rage revealed in the Fodder Wing hidden once more. Speaking more gently than before, she addressed the silent girl.

'This knowledge is painful, I know. And it is not your fault you did not know before this. You grew up with Ionain, so all you heard was the fairy tale the Great Families tell their children about channelling. Only about the power, its might and its beauty. Not its source.'

'But Beithe, and Sepp, they must've known. Why didn't they tell me the truth of it?' said Eadha.

'Why bring in the darkness?' said Magret simply. 'Old Lord Ailm was a cruel man and every person in the Keep suffered terribly under him. These last years, while Ionain's father had no gift, have been a blessed respite. Can you blame them for choosing to forget for a little while and letting you have a childhood unshadowed by dread?'

Eadha tilted her head back against the chimney wall and looked across at the woman opposite.

'And now it's too late. It's only a matter of days until my Reckoning. You know this. When I am Reckoned, my Inquisitor will see my gift just as you did, and then I will be sent to the Masters' House on Lambay. There I will be taught in the ways of channelling. I will become a Channeller. This is the way of it, I have no choice in this. Why show me those poor people now, when it's too late, when there's nothing I can do?'

'Because you can refuse. Because you have the chance to be something extraordinary, something almost unheard of: a gifted child who escapes the poisonous grasp of the Masters, and the seductive enchantment of Lambay. A powerful one who chooses not to use her power to inflict pain and suffering in the name of her own self-glorification.'

Magret had risen, unable to sit still, eagerness in every line of her stance, holding herself back as if fearful of scaring the girl away, but willing her to heed her words.

'I don't understand. My Reckoning is set. I can't refuse to appear.'

'Yes, but knowing you have the gift, there is a way for you to conceal it from your Inquisitor. You got part of the way there this morning yourself. I saw how you damped down your power just as Huath reached out to search the choir. It would be a deeper, stronger concealment than that, but you have enough time to prepare for it. I can teach you.'

Eadha stared into the fire, at the flames leaping hungrily up along the line of the wood where it had been split by her uncle and herself in the autumn. She wished she could set a fire inside herself, burn away this revulsion. All the joy she'd felt in her gift these last weeks, the excitement and pride that she would be Ionain's saviour, the Keep's protector, ripped down to reveal the dull horror of those dark rooms, echoed in the lines of pain etched on her aunt and her uncle's faces.

How could something so beautiful, so joyous be the cause of such pain? In the days since Magret had revealed her gift, Eadha had come to love her power, her silver fish flashing through the depths of her, always ready, always eager. The threads linking her to the souls around her, was she to cut them all, for always?

Magret had subsided back into her seat, knowing that to push now was to drive her away. There was a long silence, filled only by the quiet crackle of the flames. Eadha looked up at Magret across the firelight.

'All I've thought since that day in the willow maze was that I could be the one to save the Keep. If Ionain fails his Reckoning, I'd step in, be the Keep Channeller, stop Lord Huath from taking it over.'

But Magret was already shaking her head.

'It doesn't work like that. If Ionain fails his Reckoning, then the Keep is lost to the Ailms. You passing your Reckoning wouldn't change that. You don't come from a Great Family, you have no Name. It would take you years to become a full Channeller, years more before you could earn yourself a Family title and land. Ailm's Keep would be long gone by then, taken over by an established Lord like Huath.'

Magret subsided again, as Eadha stared at her hands and fought back tears. She would not cry again in front of Magret. After another long pause she lifted her head again and said, 'Even if I can't save the Keep, you still have no idea what you're asking of me. Sitting there with no power and saying I should give it up. Go back to being a helpless nothing. You've no idea what you're asking.'

'You are right, I don't. It doesn't make me wrong. Stop thinking for a minute about what you want and think for a moment about what you know in your heart to be right. You have a chance to get out now, before you are twisted and corrupted by the Masters on Lambay to the point where it will be impossible for you to see what is right anymore,' said Magret quietly.

'You said almost. That I would be something almost unheard of. So there have been others? Others like me?'

'Child, you must understand I cannot speak of this to you. Not now, while you might still choose the Masters' path or be taken for it. After your Reckoning I can speak to you more freely. But I can say you are not the first to have triggered their gift before the Masters reckon them, and so earned themselves this chance to choose the path they take. You would not be alone.'

Eadha stood up then, arms wrapped about her, eyes still staring into the fire. Her voice was very small, almost inaudible, but steady as she said, 'I will refuse.'

Magret bowed her head then, in thanks, in pity for the straight figure before her, rigid with misery.

'Tomorrow we will begin your lessons in concealment.'

Eadha stayed standing until Magret left. Then with unsteady feet she climbed the stairs to her nest, crept beneath the covers, and cried and cried.

CHAPTER 8
THOUGHT-WALLS

Eadha slept badly that night, her head filled with nightmares about the people in the Fodder Wing. Dreams where she knelt pouring energy into the first man to try to revive him, only for a woman lying beside him to begin screaming in pain. She would turn then to pour power into her until the bearded man began to scream. On and on it went, endlessly round and around as she kept draining one to try to save the other, her ears filled with the sound of their screams.

Waking in the thin pre-dawn light her throat closed at the thought of her aunt and uncle sleeping so trustfully beneath her. For the first time her silver fish began to feel like a disfiguring growth inside her. Her head was heavy, thick with loss and the effort of not reaching for her power for comfort. The morning stretched colourless before her, and the morning after that and on and on, one long featureless path of self-denial.

Pushed out to choir by her aunt, all anyone was talking about was the news Huath had sensed power in Ionain. Eadha stood silent in the middle of the chatter, her arms wrapped tightly around her, earning a rebuke from Beithe.

'Have you nothing to say? I thought better of you. To be gifted is all that boy's wanted since the day he was born. Put out he'll be leaving you behind once he passes his Reckoning, are you? But that was always the way of it.'

Eadha said nothing, but a warning twinge of worry cut through her own sadness. It had been her power that Huath had sensed yesterday, not anything from Ionain. Magret had only said it was Ionain to deflect Huath before he caught her. But now that lie seemed to be taking on a life of its own.

At the end of rehearsal, Magret gestured to Eadha to follow her once more. Together they made their way deep into the forest beyond the Keep, far from any prying eyes. It was a long, chilly walk, each closed away from the other in their thoughts, up to where the trees began to thin on the shallower soil of the foothills of Mount Lein, stopping at an open space at the very edge of the tree line. They eyed each other warily, Eadha half-expecting more anger from Magret. Instead, to her surprise, Magret took her hand.

'I am sorry for yesterday. I should have spoken to you sooner about your gift and how it lets you draw on others. It is a hard thing to hear, and I delayed longer than I should have, thinking I had more time, before any Channellers began arriving for Master Ionain's Reckoning.'

Eadha thought of the last weeks, of the beauty of the little were-lights darting about her room, of flying through the snowy forest and watching the seeds stir into life in her hand, and knew in her heart she wasn't sorry she'd had that chance to know magic, even if she would never draw on people again.

She said nothing and after a short pause Magret said, 'Tell me how you created your barrier yesterday.'

Eadha explained about the ice sheet. Magret was impressed.

'You did well. A Channeller as strong as Huath would expect to identify anyone using the gift in a heartbeat. You must have shut yourself down very fast.'

'The ice was about to crack when you spoke up and pulled the heat away. I couldn't have held out much longer.'

'In the olden days during the Channeller wars, it was a prized skill to be able to slip close to an enemy Channeller without being detected. It is less important now, with all the Channellers united through Lambay. Indeed, such skills are not taught on Lambay, on the basis that concealment of the gift goes against the whole idea of cooperation. Although, of course, some Channellers will always be more distrustful than others and so the knowledge has been preserved in a few places.'

Magret produced a yellowed book from beneath her cloak.

'This is a text that has survived from the time of the Channeller wars. It has some skills in it that I daresay even Lord Huath is not familiar with. My family has a long history of power, mostly as Watchers, but we have never been supporters of Lambay, so it has never come into the hands of the Masters.'

'A Watcher?' interrupted Eadha. 'Is that a type of Keeper?'

Magret grimaced as she shot back, 'Ach, where to start with that? The Masters would have us all believe that power is this rigid thing. You are a Channeller or a Keeper or nothing, because it suits the world they have built for themselves. But just think, girl. Power is life; life is power. You know this, you have felt it yourself.'

Eadha flushed at the reminder of how she'd drawn power from her aunt and uncle.

'Just as life comes in many forms, so, too, must power. I am one who can perceive power. I see the threads that link us all and can even follow along those threads to look into an unguarded mind, as I did with you. But I do not have the ability to manipulate those threads, like a Keeper, or draw life along them, like a Channeller. We call ourselves Watchers, and we have always been there, even if the

Masters choose to ignore us. No more than other forms of seeing or using power have always existed or been coming into existence, for as long as there is life. But enough chat about gifts and their uses. Today is about learning to hide the gift you have,' and she handed Eadha the book.

Eadha opened pages stiff with age and dried ink. Images glowed up from the paper, pictures of tiny figures swimming across the page, of wolves poised to spring and on one page a fish leaping from the water as it swam upstream.

'These notes were written by Channellers over generations. Power is a difficult thing to convey, because every Channeller experiences it differently; some will talk of colours or lights, of swimming through water, while others talk of animals, birds, fish. Truth be told, I cannot comprehend your gift, but perhaps some of this might speak to you.'

Looking closer Eadha saw how even the words contained pictures, lovingly drawn in fantastical detail, an eagle whose wings formed the shape of an m, a fox peeping between the legs of an n. And everywhere the silver threads, radiating out from figure to figure, hands raised towards each other. There was so much joy, so much love and pride in the gift that even in her sadness it made her smile.

'In hiding your gift, the trick is to create an illusion of transparency. If you simply build a wall in your mind, the Inquisitor will see you are hiding something and will use his strength to break it down. You must give the impression he is seeing all of you, while hiding your power as deep inside yourself as there are depths.'

Magret pointed her towards an illustration in the book of a man standing above another man, gripping his head between his hands as Magret had done to her in the willow maze. Inside the seated man was drawn a mat, itself woven from even smaller images: hands, faces, trees. From behind the weave a light glowed.

'See how he does it, creating a wall made of thoughts. I want you to think of all the things that fill your mind on a normal day. Family, or chores or choir practice, say. From these you weave a thought-wall, a set of images woven tightly together that you place across the space where your power resides. It needs to be smooth so the Inquisitor will not see the join between your actual thoughts and those you are using to conceal your power. You use your power to fire the thought-wall into life, so they move and change the way true thoughts flit through our minds.'

'Alright,' said Eadha, taking one last look at the image before closing her eyes. In her mind's eye she wove together images of herself out herding, Beithe catching her swiping apples from the pantry, her aunt sat by the fire on a winter's evening. But each time she felt she'd created a reasonable imitation of her mind's normal flow, Magret would step into her head and shatter her flimsy illusion with a flicker.

As Eadha groaned out loud after yet another failed attempt Magret said calmly, 'This is a deeply demanding art. Your difficulty is you cannot do what you have grown accustomed to; reach out and draw power from another. Instead, you must learn to draw from your own life source. The Masters teach us that power can only be taken from another, because it suits their purposes. For them the gift has always been as much a means of dominion over others as it is a way of creating wonders. They say this is how it must be, using people as Fodder to drain for their power. But go back a few hundred years when channelling was new in the world, and it was well-understood a Channeller could draw small amounts of power from their own life source. Only a spark, for sure, with little strength, but enough for minor acts like firing a thought-wall. Then again, it is always easier to reach out and snatch fruit growing in abundance in another's orchard than it is to patiently cultivate it in your own.'

She pointed again at the illustration.

'Study the image. See where the concealer has drawn a silver thread running from his mind's eye to his centre. This is where you must find the power. In your heart, in your belly. Nothing in these images is without meaning. See how the thoughts in his wall reflect the images that surround him. He has taken the thoughts that mean the most to him. This opens his heart so the power can flow from it. This is what you must do. Think of what matters most to you, and with that open your heart.'

Bowing her head, Eadha tried again, and this time into her wall she built memories that were closer to her heart; of drawing the map of Domhain when she was younger, of racing through the forest, and of Ionain climbing up the fell to find her on her birthday.

Now it was stronger. Magret was right. These thoughts sparked something deep inside her, a pulse of electricity that shot up into her mind, to fire her wall. But still Magret was able to break it. It took her a few moments longer, but each time Eadha felt her needle into the wall she'd built so carefully and twist until it shattered.

'That's better,' she said, stepping back after breaking Eadha's latest attempt. Eadha, though, wanted to scream in frustration.

'How are you able to break it then?' This time the look in Magret's eyes was sympathetic.

'The thoughts you've chosen, they're precious to you but some are also stained with worry, and that creates a weakness. All I have to do is press it. If you are going to use them, you need to find a way to keep that fear out. But it grows late. We will take this up again in the morning.'

The sun was setting when Eadha returned to the cottage. To her surprise, Ionain was sitting at the table with her uncle. Beaming, he sprang to his feet as she came in, coming over to take her coat before hustling her on upstairs to her loft. There he flung himself into his old spot on her bed, his back against the chimney wall, and drummed his

82

feet on the floor, bursting to talk.

She sat beside him gingerly, her head aching from the long afternoon of shattered thought-walls. Ionain shifted around so he was looking at her.

'I feel like I haven't stopped talking since Uncle Huath arrived yesterday. Mother and Father and everyone are so excited. Uncle Huath told Mother if the flare of power he felt yesterday was anything to go by, I might be a really gifted Channeller, powerful like him. He said in all the Reckonings he's done, he's never felt a flash like that, and my Reckoning should just be a formality now. Mother almost cried when she heard.'

He sprang up again then, unable to hold himself still, his eyes shining in the dim light that came up into the loft from below.

'All this time I've been so worried about failing, I wouldn't let myself think what it would be like to actually pass...'

'How does your uncle think it happened yesterday, the flare he sensed?' asked Eadha, and though her voice was steady, inside she was fighting down a growing sense of panic.

'I don't know. Nobody knows really. I was watching the choir and feeling scared about the Reckoning and wishing I could be down there with you instead of having to march in on my own in those stupid robes. Father thinks that's where the power was awakened; seemingly it can happen sometimes, in moments of stress. I don't care where it came from, I'm just happy it came, and Uncle was there to sense it.'

Listening to Ionain talk, his voice so full of excitement, Eadha felt sick. It seemed as if everything she'd touched since discovering her gift had turned out ill. She'd almost killed Magret in the quarry, drained her uncle and her aunt's life-force, and now, unwittingly, she'd raised the stakes even further for her dearest friend for the defining event of his life.

If after all this Ionain had no gift, his devastation would be even worse now his hopes and the hopes of his whole Family had been raised to such a pitch. And if he failed, he was on his own. For with her promise to Magret not to use her power, she'd abandoned him.

Ionain was still talking, oblivious.

'Mother and Mana both say I mustn't do anything else with the gift now. We have to respect the sanctity of the Reckoning ceremony. But Father is sending for Master Dathin to be my Inquisitor now instead of Uncle Huath. He's the senior Master on Lambay. Now they think it will go well, they want to make a bigger show of the whole thing.'

Eadha pulled her legs up and wrapped her arms around them. She couldn't trust herself to say anything, lest she began to sob and beg him for forgiveness. But even as she curled in on herself, Ionain flung himself back down on the bed beside her. He was silent for a moment then reached out and took her hand, working his fingers in between hers.

'I know I said I needed to wait until after my Reckoning before we...' He paused and took a deep breath. 'But it's different now. Now I know I have worth and that I will be able to protect you.'

Eadha's heart froze. He was going to kiss her, and she couldn't, she couldn't let him. Not when it was all based on Magret's lie, not when she'd abandoned him.

'Hey, what is it? What's wrong?'

Ionain slid off the bed and crouched in front of her, trying to make her look at him. She couldn't though, avoiding his eyes even when he gently pushed her hair back from her face.

'What did I say? Is it your own Reckoning you're worrying about? I'm sorry, I've been so focused on mine I keep forgetting you must be worried about yours, too.'

He rubbed her arm consolingly.

'It will be over quickly, don't worry. For you and the others it's just a formality. No one's expecting any of you to be gifted. All we need is for my Reckoning to go as we all hope now. Don't you see? Then I'll be the Lord of the Keep, and I'll be so much freer to choose who...' and he flushed up bright red.

A sob rose in Eadha's throat then. She couldn't let him make promises to her like this. Leaning forward she threw her arms around his neck, hugging him so hard he rocked back on his heels and had to grab the bedframe to stop them both toppling backwards in a heap on the floor. As he steadied himself, she burrowed her head into his shoulder so she wouldn't have to see his face, see those trusting eyes, while all the time the words she couldn't say to him pounded through her mind.

'I picked them. I picked them over you. I picked those starving, ragged people over you. I picked Magret and her secrets over you; and if you fail your Reckoning now I can't use my powers to protect you because I've sworn not to channel anymore.'

With tears in her eyes, she pushed Ionain away then, hustling him bewildered back down the stairs to her uncle, where she filled the room with empty, half-hysterical small talk. All just to stop Ionain saying something else fine, something kind, something only he would ever think to say to her. Because if he did, her fragile promise to Magret would shatter into a million pieces like her failed thought-walls in the woods, and she knew she would not be able to make another one.

CHAPTER 9
RECKONING

Spring rain fell softly, warming the frozen earth, filling the Keep gardens with the newborn laughter of winter's thaw.

Eadha's aunt slipped out in the earliest light to help Lady Ura with dressing for the ceremonies. It was Ionain's sixteenth birthday, his Reckoning Day.

Both her aunt and her uncle had regained their strength, now Eadha no longer drew power from them. She by turn woke each morning to a memory of loss, a hollow place.

After a few more chilly afternoons in the woods with Magret she'd finally come by the trick of the thought-walls. How to fire a small spark from within herself, drawn from belly to heart and on up into her mind, using it to power a mental barrier woven of thoughts and memories. Now each morning after she awoke, she bricked in her power behind a thought-wall fired by her heart's will, practising for her own Reckoning day when Lord Huath would examine her mind and she would hide her power from him. He would never know what he had in front of him, and she would not be called to Lambay. She would never draw power from Fodder. She would keep her promise to Magret.

But she could still feel it, her silver fish flickering in the depths of her and the effort of denying that part of her was wearing her down. Day by day she withdrew from everyone around her as the effort of concealment took its toll. It was easier to step away from those she loved than to constantly patrol her boundaries, watching she didn't make a slip in word or deed. This was what it was, to deny a part of herself. She had to become someone else. Someone harder, someone silent. And all were so preoccupied by Ionain's Reckoning that no one seemed to notice.

She'd moved the pot with the seeds she'd sprouted to a hidden spot by the chimney stack in her room, as the air outside was still too cold for them. They were growing strongly, and each morning before she left to go herding, she'd crouch down to stare at the bright green leaves as they spindled upwards, their bright beauty forcing her each time to remake the promise she'd made.

Ionain's inquisition was to take place at midday. By midmorning the Keep was overflowing with people. The whole village had been invited and they milled about in the courtyard, stiff in their best clothes, ineffectually shushing their children as they dashed about. Inside the Great Hall, Eadha and the rest of the choir were assembled on the dais specially built for the ceremony, the adults standing, the younger singers, including Eadha, sitting cross-legged on the floor at the front. Eadha had made sure she was sitting in the middle of the front row, so she'd be directly behind Ionain when he reached the dais.

In front of the choir, the hall was thronged with Great Family representatives all resplendent in their court wear, the Channellers among them marked out by the silver brooches on their tunics or cloaks, the Keepers by a wide silver wristband. In truth, Eadha didn't need those markers to know them. She could feel the power radiating from them even as they stood there. All the Channellers she saw were men, forbidding in the absolute security of their power. Some, like Lord Huath, were heads of Great Families in rich cloaks and furs, while others were dressed in the grey of a Lambay Master. These men spent their lives on the islands of Lambay training the next generations of gifted youngsters, securing the Channellers' rule over Domhain as they'd done for four centuries now. If Ionain passed his Reckoning they would be his tutors for the next two years. Each was a master of his art, one of the most powerful Architects, Growers, Tellers or dragon slayers on all of Domhain. Eadha's power twisted behind her thought-wall as she stared at them from the dais, trying to imagine what that must be like. To spend your life devoted to mastering your gift; the power they could contain, the wonders they could create.

Lord Ailm was walking among the guests, quietly greeting each one, nodding deferentially to the Masters and the Channellers. Eadha saw how they barely seemed to register him, glancing at him and then away, as if his presence embarrassed them. That had been his life, she thought, ever since the day he'd failed his own Reckoning almost twenty-five years ago. Feeling her eyes on him, Lord Ailm glanced over at Eadha. She saw him take in where she sat and understand why—so she'd be beside Ionain, no matter what happened. With a nod he tipped his head towards her in wordless gratitude, before turning back to his guests.

The Great Hall itself was lit all the way to the ceiling with were-lights circling slowly, placed there by Lord Huath with his Keeper, Terebitha. She was standing by the entrance to the Fodder Wing. Magret had explained to Eadha that as Keeper, Terebitha was not being drained by Huath. Rather she guided the flow of power from the people hidden in the Fodder Wing on to Huath. She would amplify or reduce the stream, switching from one person to the next as each one weakened, to ensure a steady flow of power onward to Huath.

Closing her eyes Eadha concentrated, and as she did, in her mind's eye the silver threads of power running from the Fodder Wing into Terebitha sprang into view. The Keeper glowed with energy, the silver threads from the tunnel merging as they reached her into a single, thicker thread stretching between herself and Huath. Like someone working a loom Terebitha's hands moved swiftly, shuttling between the threads. As one faded it was dropped and replaced by another, then picked up again once the thread had regained some strength.

Bonfires had been lit for the crowds outside for the air was chill. Their flickering light shone through the windows of the Great Hall, bringing to life the stained-glass images; scenes of long-ago battles between dragons and Channellers, golden sunflowers being coaxed from the soil, porcelain white buildings towering above the tiny figures of the Channellers raising them. Within the Great Hall the bare yews had been garlanded with fresh pine and candles set the length of the spiral staircases.

In the sewing room, Eadha knew, Ionain would be submitting to the last moments of fussing by Lady Ura and her seamstresses. He would dress in the plain undershift, then the ceremonial robes would be draped across his slender frame, each layer carefully wrapped and tied, before the outer tunic embroidered in gold and red was lowered over his head and fastened about him.

Even as she thought that, silence fell in the Great Hall. Ionain and his mother had appeared on the cross-walk above the Great Hall. Lady Ura came on down the spiral staircase and went to stand beside her husband, while Master Dathin took his place on the dais, waiting to receive Ionain. With a sweep of her arm, Magret gestured to the choir to begin.

As their voices rose Ionain began his slow descent of the

staircase, his steps matching the beat of the first canto. His head was erect, tawny hair catching the candlelight as he made his way through the centre of the assembled crowd and up onto the dais. With perfect timing, long rehearsed, he turned to face the Master in the moment the choir fell silent.

Master Dathin was a bear of a man, his cloak pinned by a silver dragon, marking him as a dragon slayer. Ionain looked heartbreakingly slight stood before him, his face paper-white. He placed his hands on either side of Ionain's head as Magret had done with Eadha weeks before. All the congregation bent their heads, the one concession for the boy on the dais before them. Everyone except Eadha, who kept her eyes fixed on Ionain. As she watched she saw his eyes widen and knew he was feeling the shock of the Master entering his mind. Involuntarily he stepped back a little towards her before steadying himself, closing his eyes and holding himself still as he'd been trained to do. Now Ionain was so close to her the tip of his robe brushed her left knee.

Still watching, Eadha saw a small frown begin to appear on Dathin's face. His brow furrowed, as if searching further for something he'd expected to find quickly. The silence in the Great Hall began to stretch thin. Eadha's heart started to hammer in her chest. If she couldn't use her gift, she so badly wanted Ionain to have his wish. In her heart she knew he must have power, but in times of stress his instinct would be to retreat, and no one could hide like Ionain. His gift could be hidden deep within him in simple fear.

If he had the true Inquisitor's skill Master Dathin would surely eventually find it, but what if he mistook it? What if he took it for a weak gift, not worth cultivating, or for the lesser Keeper's power? Anything less than a resounding hallelujah in this moment would surely break Ionain's heart, make him feel he'd failed his Family. Still Master Dathin frowned. He was not finding it, the gift he'd come expecting to find.

She couldn't leave Ionain there, alone before the world. She could see the thread leading to her dear one, this most familiar of all paths. Quietly she dropped her palm, so it touched Ionain's robe where it rested against her knee. From belly to heart her power surged but this time, instead of earthing it in a thought-wall as Magret had taught her, she threw open the doors of her heart, urging it on out of her. Released after all those weeks confined, her gift flew, rocketing out of her along the link from her palm into Ionain. She felt it steady him, fill him. She poured all of her love, all of their shared life into him and saw Master Dathin's head shoot up in astonishment.

He dropped his hands to his sides and turned beaming to the assembled crowd to sound the formal words of finding.

'Rejoice, for the Gift is with this child. May all his days be filled with power and may all who hear this give of their strength freely that his power might be great, to the glory of his days and of Domhain.'

An enormous cheer rose through the Great Hall then, resounding to the domed ceiling above. Magret swept the choir into the song of rejoicing. Eadha had dropped her link to Ionain as soon as the Master's head went up. And if anyone had been watching her, they would have seen her eyes widen in shock as she stared down at her empty palm. They would have seen her mouth crumple and her voice fail her so she could only mouth along the words as it hit her what she'd just done, what she could never now undo. But no one was watching, and no one saw, every eye in the place on the golden-haired boy radiant with relief as Ionain turned to receive his acclaim.

As Eadha watched, Ionain's father and mother stepped forward, kissing him on each cheek, followed by members of the wider Family each in turn carefully embracing him. Then Master Dathin stood once more to formally summon Ionain to the House on Lambay.

'Ionain, son of Lord Ailm. You have been Reckoned and found

to be truly gifted. In the name of the Masters of Lambay, upon whose authority I speak, I hereby requisition you as one gifted in the ways of channelling, to report to Lambay soonest, there to be trained in its arts.'

Watching, horror-struck, as Master Dathin declared Ionain gifted, all Eadha could think was that it'd been such a small thing, what she'd done, a reaching out to her dearest one. But now even as she watched it was growing huge, bigger than her, bigger than Ionain, her little lie becoming fact, the foundation stone for a new reality where everyone believed Ionain was the gifted one and the Keep was saved. It was all going too fast, and she wanted to scream to them all, 'Stop!' She did, but in the same moment she couldn't. Her throat closed over and the words wouldn't come. She couldn't do it, not in front of them all like this, exposing Ionain, exposing herself. It was all going too fast, she needed to think, she couldn't think, there in the heart of it all as the choir sang and the crowd cheered.

The formal words spoken, the festivities could at last begin. In front of her she saw Ionain turn to his mother to beg leave to remove the stiff robes; with a smiling gesture she shook her head, pointing towards the long line of guests pressing forward to congratulate him, each one to be greeted and thanked.

Meanwhile Eadha stood invisible in the choir as it sang on, songs of praise and thanksgiving. Nothing about ending or regret, she thought, no gesture towards the innocence soon to be lost in the brutality at the heart of the Channeller's art. It was only and all about the power, the getting and the glory of it. From her place facing the choir Eadha saw Magret glance at her, but she was certain in herself she hadn't seen the gift she'd given Ionain. She'd been too close to him for anyone to see where she ended and he began, her power flowing seamlessly, invisibly between them.

At the entrance to the Fodder Wing Master Dathin's Keeper took up position beside Terebitha. The two women nodded coolly to each other before each concentrated on their Channeller's calls. So began a display of the Channeller's art such as hadn't been seen in the Keep in a generation, as each of the two adepts sought, genially and with impeccable manners, to outdo the other. Children were lifted and swept up to the ceiling, shrieking in terrified delight. Rainbows arced from one end of the Great Hall to the other, only to dissolve into multi-coloured raindrops that melted before they could touch the elegant outfits of the guests below. Images of dragons were chased by hunters across the ceiling, fragile snowdrops opened their petals at the guests' feet.

At last, the songs were done and Eadha released. Seeing her standing alone Ionain came rushing over to her, catching her up in an enormous bear hug that lifted her off the ground and twirled her around. In all their life together she'd never seen Ionain as he was in that moment; blazing with such relief and happiness he seemed to shine. Setting her down, his arms still around her, he whispered into her ear,

'You'll wait for me? When I'm away to Lambay? Everyone says the time goes quickly; two years and a few dragons then I'll be home again and everything will all go on just like now, only so much better, I promise...'

This was the moment when it all pivoted, there in the still centre of the Great Hall. She could see it almost as if it was happening, as if she'd split in two, and one part of her had taken him by the arm and led him out into the courtyard. Out there it would be chilly and quiet, just the two of them alone together as it had always been. She would look into his eyes and tell him what had really happened in those flashing moments up there on the dais. How her life had flowed into him so that just for that moment, her gift became his gift and Master Dathin acclaimed him a Channeller. But there the vision stopped, and her heart failed her. Even in her mind's eye she couldn't do it, could not make herself picture the joy on his face dying at her words, could not imagine the look that would come into his eyes as she told him that in the very crisis of his life she'd made a lie of him, of who he was.

So, after all, she didn't speak, there in the still centre of the crowd, only hugging him back wordlessly instead. The next instant Ionain was gone, swept away on a wave of well-wishers, cheering his gift and his name.

CHAPTER 10
CHOICES

Down the tunnel of dragonglass Eadha fled, out into the kitchen, her mind focused only on escape. The mood there was sombre and resigned.

'Hush now, we always knew this time would come to an end. We were blessed to have such a long run of it; there's not many on Domhain can say the same,' Beithe was saying to one of the maidservants as Eadha hurried past, head down. The girl's eyes were red, as if she'd been weeping.

'Better Master Ionain be found gifted than have one such as Lord Huath come to rule over us as Channeller. That's what we faced had he failed. Master Ionain's a gentle soul. He will not be cruel, or not more cruel than he can help. And we will endure as we always have, Sister save us.'

'Sister save us,' came the quiet reply, like a prayer.

Unheeded, on out into the night air Eadha went. It was as cold and quiet as she'd imagined when she'd stood in Ionain's arms, the shock of the night's chill enveloping her like one burning, but she was alone beneath the silent sky. There was a wave reared up behind her, higher than the North Tower, higher than the Blackstairs, come roaring up to fall on her. A wave of all she'd done, and what she'd failed to do that night, and if it hit her, she would drown. Stumbling a little she forced herself into a run, past the silvered yews and the moon-shadowed lake, on towards her uncle's cottage. Inside it was silent and dark. Everyone was still up at the Keep. Reaching her loft she sat cross-legged on the bed, the same spot where Ionain had sat only a few days ago and tried to kiss her.

In the distance she could hear the sound of the party, spilled over into the Keep courtyard where the bonfires still burned, and the wine still flowed beneath the night sky. Already she could picture the scene in a few hours' time as night swung on towards morning and the revellers departed. Her aunt crossing the yard and heading up to Ionain's room at first light, helping Beithe pack his clothes, laying out his travel cloak for the journey across the Blackstairs to Lambay in two days' time. Her uncle out in the stables with Sepp, provisioning the horses for Ionain and Lord Huath's party, checking they were properly shod. Going over the weapons, sharpening swords and spears, for the Steps across the Blackstairs were still treacherous this early in the spring. Every one of them, Ionain most of all, convinced he was gifted. And she the only soul in all the world who knew he was not.

What had she done, oh, what had she done?

She curled into herself, clenching her fists so hard her nails broke the skin, as her treacherous mind ran on, imagining Ionain arriving on Lambay to be greeted by the Masters. How they would step back, with their wise, grave faces and call on him to produce a were-light or lift himself up into the air, just like she'd done in those first days after she'd triggered her gift. He would stand there, his face bright and full of pride, so determined to restore his Family's honour. And he would fail.

A moan escaped her then as she pictured her friend standing

bewildered and alone in front of Master Dathin, his huge, hulking frame looming over him as he tried over and over to find the gift he did not have. How could she have been so stupid? What did she think she could achieve by stepping in and giving him her power for those few seconds, when it was a lifetime he needed it for?

She stared down at her hands, remembering the flashing moment on the dais when she'd unleashed all that pent-up power from inside herself and sent it pouring into Ionain. And even in the heart of her shame she still felt the subterranean joy of it, the sense of release when she'd reached inside herself as Magret had taught her. But what she'd gifted to Ionain hadn't been the fragile spark Magret had spoken of. It had been something far greater, as though in reaching for that spark she'd uncovered instead a great well of power fathoms deep inside her and in one pulse sent it pouring into Ionain.

Closing her eyes as she sat on her bed, she reached inside herself once more, trying to find again the handholds that had led her down into the depths to that hidden well of power. But there in the silent loft her power made a liar of her, staying stubbornly earthed as she failed and failed again to come by the trick of it, to find again the door she'd opened in her heart.

As she hunched there on her bed trying to replicate what she'd done earlier, she heard the cottage door open and close softly. It was her aunt and uncle back from the celebrations. She could just make out their quiet murmurs as they prepared for bed, their voices sober and resigned, like Beithe in the Keep earlier. Sitting above them on her cot-bed Eadha closed her eyes, trying once more to reach for the power inside herself. But now all she could think of was their life-force, shining just beneath her; how easy it would be to simply reach out and draw energy from them as they slept so trustingly below. Panic twisted her stomach. She had to get out.

Standing on her bed, she pushed open the loft's skylight, pulling herself out and onto the roof, away from temptation. Along the wave of timber roofs she ran, before dropping to the ground where they sloped lowest, landing on a grass mound, the outermost of the circles that ringed the lake.

Under the night sky her panic did not seem so large, the stars able to prick it. She sat herself under an oak tree by the forest's edge, out of sight of any stray reveller from the Keep. Through the still-bare branches she caught sight of the Sidhe burning bright. She and Ionain would always start their adventures when they were little by solemnly plotting their way by the Sidhe, the Dancer's Staff pointing them to the Steps across the Blackstairs. She remembered Ionain's face, how it had shone as he embraced her in the Great Hall earlier and his whispered words, 'Will you wait for me?'

Was that who she was? It was what Magret demanded of her, what even Ionain expected now. That she was one who waited, who denied the power inside her. One who endured, repressing who she was, eternally standing by instead of doing. And as the emptiness of that life clutched at her she forced it down inside her. Down with the shame at what she'd done to Ionain, and the unspeakable fear she would lose him the moment he found out the truth, and underneath it all the bone-deep yearning to be loved, all of it, compressing them deep inside her as she sat on the damp grass under the night sky, so that together they hardened into a stone of pain lodged inside her chest. Coal hard, diamond hard, that stone was and with all her strength she struck against it; and there at last, it was. A tiny spark flaring in the darkness, struck from the flint of pain lodged in her chest.

In front of her, on her outstretched palm a were-light flared into life, bobbing and dancing, bowing to its sister stars above. She had found it. The way back down, a way to draw on her own heart's strength for power and send it out of herself into the tiny were-light, into Ionain. And as she stared at the were-light she knew this little thing had been born not just of her need to protect Ionain, but of her fear. Of being rejected, of living out her days suppressed, battening down the love and the power within.

Beneath the paling stars she stared at her palm, at the single empty point at the heart of the flame, the point of blackness where air and life met and became fire. And as she stared at it, she saw the hidden path out of what she'd done to Ionain. She would not wait, she would not endure. She would fight. With her power she would fight; for her love, for herself. Closing her eyes then she let the wave of fear and shame that reared up behind her come crashing down. For now she had hope, a rope she twisted around her hand until it pulled her up and out into the wave's curling heart, a tunnel of shimmering green, racing along it until she shot out and back once more into the night's sky, wiping away her tears, while, still dancing in her palm, the tiny flame held away the darkness until morning.

CHAPTER 11
SEE THAT YOU DO

'Let all those who have passed the age of sixteen come forward for their Reckoning.'

It was almost noon of the following day. Lord Huath sat resplendent in a red velvet cloak in the centre of the muddy village square, its gold lining gleaming in watery sunshine just breaking through after early morning rain.

In front of him all those from the village or the Keep who, like Eadha, had passed the age of sixteen were being herded together, ready for their Reckonings. There were ten in total, mostly from the village, with a couple like her, grown children of Keep servants. She was the youngest of them. She knew them all to see, though she was close to none of them. Ionain and her own company had been all she'd ever looked for.

All were subdued and anxious, their parents ringing the edges of the group protectively. Eadha stood at the back while her uncle talked quietly with some Keep servants.

She had not slept all night and was glassy-eyed with exhaustion, but as she stood there waiting for her turn she felt no fear, only calm certainty. It was like preparing a house before visitors arrive, hiding away all private things, arranging it carefully to give the right impression. Inside her mind, just as Magret had taught her, she'd packed away all thoughts of her channelling gift into presses, onto shelves out of sight, then woven images of careful tedium into a thought-wall that now lay draped across her power, fired by her own heart's will.

Glancing across the square she saw Magret standing with Lord Huath's party. No doubt she was come to see if she'd manage to keep her promise, to hide her channelling gift so she wouldn't be summoned to Lambay. Though she tried to hide it, Eadha could see the strain on her face. She'd taken a great risk, trusting Eadha with her hatred of the Masters. She needed Eadha's thought-wall to hold against Huath's inquisition as much for herself as for Eadha. Terebitha, Huath's Keeper, stood beside her. But there was no sign of Ionain. A chill wormed its way into Eadha's thoughts. This wasn't like him, not to come and support her on her Reckoning day. Surely he'd come riding up at the last moment. But he didn't come, and now it was too late, as Huath began the inquisitions.

Many of them flinched with shock when he stepped into their minds, some starting to cry and others trying to squirm away. Each time after a moment's focus he waved them away. The square was so still the nervous coughing and shuffling of those still waiting to be tested could be clearly heard. From outside the square, birdsong flowed into the silence, the clatter of still bare branches tossed on the spring wind. Eadha's turn was almost upon her. She saw Magret push her way to the front of the group to have a clear line of sight.

Now it was her turn. She stepped forward and saw recognition in Huath's eyes.

'You are the niece of my sister's seamstress, are you not? Ionain's little playmate?'

'Yes, Lord Huath, may it please you,' came her dutiful reply, keeping her eyes low and her voice monotonous. Even so she sensed a flicker of something; some straightening as if Huath was bringing his energies into full focus. Eadha braced herself and there he was, stepping fast and hard into her head. This was no cursory examination. Huath was far, far stronger than Magret, the scale of his power almost enough to overbalance her. But she steadied herself and there it was, so carefully arrayed right in the centre of her mind for Huath to find. Just enough of her gift and not too much. She could feel Huath examining what she'd laid out for him, expertly weighing it. For just a moment she felt him pull back and sweep all through her mind, but she'd prepared for this and held steady. He flickered across the studied domesticity of her thought-wall with its images of milking goats and (nice touch, she thought) her humble awe at his display of power on Reckoning Day. As quickly then he was gone, out of her mind, dropping his hands. She allowed herself the tiniest release of breath as he called across to his party.

'Terebitha, it seems we have not entirely wasted our morning here. We have one of your kind here, a Keeper, strong and true if I am any judge.'

Huath glanced down at Eadha.

'Well, girl, it seems you will keep your vigil at my nephew's side a while longer. Congratulations. In the name of the Masters of Lambay, upon whose authority I speak, I hereby requisition you as one gifted in the ways of Keeping, to report to Lambay soonest, there to be trained in the ways of keeping and assigned to a Channeller fate willing. Report to Lord Ailm's quartermaster at the Keep, he will provide you with a mount. We depart for Erisen and thence to Lambay in the morning.'

She turned to face the crowd. She'd been the last to be tested and people had already begun to disperse. She saw them standing in knots on the edge of the square and looking back from up the lanes as word spread outwards that Lord Huath had declared her a Keeper. She didn't know what reaction she'd expected, but it hadn't been this. Muted, serious, men and women she'd known all her life looking at her and then looking away, glancing towards her uncle. Her uncle. He stood as though turned to stone, staring expressionlessly at Eadha, still standing in Lord Huath's grasp. Sepp hurried over and took him by the shoulders, murmuring in his ear and shaking his head before turning him back towards the Keep, staggering slightly like a drunken man.

As Huath re-joined his party, Eadha was left standing alone in the centre of the square until at last Magret came over and embraced her carefully, like some fragile thing that might break if she was roughly handled.

'You did your best, child. It was a brave effort; don't blame yourself. Huath was just too powerful. At least he did not find your full gift,' Magret whispered quickly in her ear before turning to Lord Huath.

'My lord, if I might, I know the family well. I will bring her home and ensure she is readied for the journey.'

Huath nodded in Magret's direction, already clearly bored.

'See that you do.'

PART II

LAMBAY, FIRST ISLAND

CHAPTER 12
THE STEPS

Shortly after dawn the next morning, Eadha made her way across the lake-bridge to the Keep courtyard where Ionain, Lord Huath and the rest of their party were gathering for the journey across the Blackstairs. Across her chest was a small bag with Magret's book, the amber tower Ionain had given her, and a change of clothes her aunt had packed for her, after she and Magret arrived back from her Reckoning with the news of her summoning to Lambay.

Her uncle hadn't returned to the cottage at all, while her aunt had been like a sleepwalker woken from a dream, staring stupefied as Magret gently explained what Eadha would need for the journey. After Magret left, her aunt had busied herself in familiar work, deftly pulling apart some old clothes and piecing them together to make warm layers for Eadha's trek across the Blackstairs. As she sat by the fire that night, her aunt, who never held her, laid one hand on Eadha's head with awkward tenderness before slipping away to bed in the alcove in the far corner. She lay there, unnaturally still, facing the wall until Eadha climbed the stairs to her nest above.

When Eadha came down from her loft the next morning, her bag already slung across her chest, her aunt and uncle had been standing by the cottage door, their faces full of wordless grief. Eadha's heart caught at her then.

She thought of Ionain's whispered words when he embraced her in the Great Hall and catching her aunt's hand she said, 'It's only two years and when I return it will all be as before, I promise, only better, as Ionain will be Lord and I will be his Keeper.'

For this was her plan, conceived as she sat beneath the spreading oak by the lake and called up a were-light with her own heart's power. To make a kind of truth of her accidental lie, by following Ionain to Lambay and supplying him with her heart's strength, so he and all the world would go on believing he was gifted.

As she came into the courtyard, it was already full of horses and people. Their party were fifteen in all—Ionain, Huath, his guardsmen, Terebitha as well as Sepp and several other Keep men. Magret was to ride with them as far as Erisen. The Keep men would stay with them through the Blackstairs then turn back. Although the winter snows had melted, the way was still difficult this early in the spring. Packs of wolves and solitary bears roamed the foothills, hungry after the long winter, while she-dragons were known to fly out from their colonies off Westport to birth in solitude in the high passes in late spring, hiding their brood until they were strong enough to fly.

In the centre of it all was Ionain. His parents were embracing him, his father stern-faced, his mother in tears. He was in high spirits, laughing and joking, coaxing a smile out of his mother, reassuring his father before swinging up onto his horse and urging it into a canter. Slipping into the crowd unnoticed, a sudden terror gripped Eadha. It was one thing to make tiny were-lights that sat in her palm; another thing entirely to send her power into Ionain under the eyes of the Masters. What if she failed and Ionain was exposed, or she was caught? But even as her head filled with panicked imaginings, Ionain's horse came around and he saw her standing there.

112

His face lit up.

'Hey, sleepy-head. Good of you to join us,' he called, grinning.

And it was his old grin, the one that threw open every door in her heart. It was as if he'd heard her question and sent his answer flashing back to her across the courtyard. She would not fail. Their bond was too strong. It was, after all, why she'd been able to send her power into him on the dais at his Reckoning. That hadn't changed. It would never change.

With a whoop, Ionain urged his horse into a gallop, on out of the yard. With an indulgent smile, Huath gestured to the rest of the party to follow him, calling back over his shoulder, 'Fear not, sister, I will make sure he arrives safely at First House.'

That first day they made good time, climbing steadily. Luck was with them as the Steps were little damaged by the winter storms. They paused at the crest of the first peak for one last look back at Ailm's Keep. Only the North Tower could be seen, spearing above the surrounding forests. To the east the sea glittered in fleet sunlight, choppy with white tops racing wave after wave to the shore before the hard spring winds. They turned and descended into the stony valley below.

Ionain rode with his uncle at the head of the party, while Eadha and Magret were near the back. Bringing up the rear was a windowless, iron-bound wagon, its wooden wheels juddering along the steep paths.

'Huath's Fodder wagon,' said Magret quietly, seeing Eadha glance back at it. 'Bringing those people you saw back to Erisen. They won't take those wretches out while young Ionain is here. Too much of a shock for him. You'll see when you get to First House. For the Masters it's all about the stages. Corrupt them first, before they ever see the people they drain.'

Magret had been gentle with her, since that dazed walk back to the Keep after her Reckoning, when she'd said, 'You did your best, girl, Huath was just too strong for you to fully hide it from him. You did well to have him think you only a Keeper. Take comfort in that. Hand on heart a Keeper does less harm, and if you work at your craft, you may even be able to shield the Fodder a little from the really savage Channellers.'

Apart from that, though, Magret spoke little to her now she was marked for the Masters. As they rode through the mountains side-by-side Eadha yearned to question her. Magret, after all, was the one who'd first taught her how to draw a spark from within herself to fire a thought-wall, and explained that the ability to draw and use life as power came in different forms. Maybe she might understand the nature of this newborn strength inside her, how she'd been able to send it pouring into Ionain at his Reckoning. But that would mean telling her Ionain was powerless, and that secret couldn't be spoken aloud to any living soul, not if she was to keep him safe. So, she held silent.

That night they camped under a rocky out-hang deep in the mountains. It was bitterly cold. Eadha was put sleeping alongside Magret, and under the cover of her blanket she tried to return the little book of drawings Magret had given her in the forest. But she wouldn't take it.

Propping herself up on her forearms, her face just visible in the dim firelight, she whispered, 'Your need of it is greater than mine, child. Do not underestimate the danger you face, bringing your gift to that place, the very heart of their power. Even if they do not uncover you for what you truly are, a Channeller born, it will take all your strength to resist the lure of their seduction. Keep the book with you and when next we ride together, give it to me then.'

Long after the others had all fallen asleep, Eadha lay awake, Magret's warmth beside her and the familiar shape of Ionain curled beside Huath on the other side of the campfire. As she'd lain down she felt something dig into her side. It was a package her uncle had pressed into her hand as she left the cottage that morning. Unwrapping it carefully she saw it was a fish carved by him from silver ash, curved in a semi-circle, tiny scales in miraculous detail ridging along the delicate surface. All that night she held the little thing, warm in her hand, as she drifted in and out of a fitful sleep, each time rousing to see the stars had swung further in their long dance across the sky, until she pulled herself up, weary and unrested into grey morning.

Cloud blanketed the mountains as they set off, the only sounds the occasional clink of sword against sheath and the rumbling of wagon wheels over stony ground. They reached the highest point of the Steps at about mid-morning. Lord Huath called a brief halt and Sepp sent Eadha to refill the water bottles, pointing her towards a ridge.

The clouds had lifted off the Blackstairs during the morning and retreated to the sky, where they raced each other across the sun, their shadows tracking them through the mountains below. Up shale and over ridge Eadha scrambled to where, in the lee of a cliff face a lake lay utterly still, a shard of sky fallen into the mountain. She crouched down by the water's edge, unwilling to disturb its perfect smoothness.

After a quick glance to make sure no one was watching her, she put down the water bottles, closed her eyes and focused, pulling gently on the thread that ran steady now from belly to heart, calling up a miniature were-light in her hand. She felt a start of joy at seeing her power respond. It was quicker even than when she'd drawn strength from her aunt or uncle, because now she was drawing only on her own heart's strength. Staring at the dancing flame, she itched to try it out properly. Could she make a fireball, or lift off the ground and fly once more? But she knew it was far too risky with Huath so close by, and so instead, turning her hand palm-down, she held the little light out over the water to see its reflection, smiling as the mirrored flames bowed to each other.

The next moment her were-light flickered and was almost snuffed out by a downdraft of air.

A shadow passed above her head. Long and sinuous, the dragon spread its wings to their fullest extent as it glided low across the lake, bending its neck to drink from the icy waters as it flew, then raising its head again, drops glittering on its scales. Its wings beat the water once as it climbed from the surface, sending waves racing to Eadha's feet where she crouched still, at the water's edge, watching its flight in disbelief.

In all her life she'd never seen a dragon this close. When they crossed the sky above Ailm's Keep they always flew far above them all, so high they seemed no bigger than eagles. But the dragon gliding away from her above the surface of the lake was fifty feet or more in length, more again from wing-tip to wing-tip, and as it flew the reflected sunlight seemed to ripple across its scales like a silver flame.

She rose to her feet the better to watch its flight, the tiny were-light dancing forgotten on the palm of her hand, and all she could think, with a savage joy, was she'd never seen anything more glorious.

Even as she stood, the dragon reached the far end of the lake. But instead of flying on out across the mountains, with a single tilt of its wings it curved about and came flying swift as thought to where she stood. With impossible grace it reared up to its full length to stare down at the tiny figure below it, the were-light still cupped in her hand.

For a long, stretched moment there was silence, as the dragon stared down at the girl, and the girl stared up at the dragon.

'Mahera,' the dragon hissed then, as its wings beat down, once, twice, flashing, almost transparent in the sunlight, and from inside

Eadha there came a galvanic kick, as her power lit up inside her in recognition.

But already behind her there were voices shouting at her to get down, to come away. With another sweep of its wings the dragon immediately shot upwards, wheeling about as it rose. Clenching her fist, Eadha killed her were-light with a thought.

As it flew up into the air, Lord Huath's guards came racing over the top of the ridge and scrambled down to the water's edge, readying their bows. Lord Huath appeared behind them, laying his hands upon their arrows, power flowing from him until they glowed red and shot high into the blue sky, after the disappearing shape of the dragon. But though they flew fast and hard, the dragon was already away, shooting up and over the next peak and lost from sight. Lord Huath cursed, grabbing a bow and shooting one last arrow straight up into the sky so it plummeted into the lake, the waters bubbling and hissing with the heat of its passage.

'Did you see, the bitch was heavy, she must be due soon. We'll have to send a hunting party,' he shouted as he turned back towards his mount.

There was a new urgency now as they began their descent. Huath had to keep the party together while they were still in the mountains but as soon as they reached the relative safety of the foothills, he and Terebitha galloped on ahead. As he left, Eadha sensed the massive draw of power he took from the Fodder sitting invisibly in their wagon. She wondered at the toll it must have taken on them as the two horses raced away, their speed limited now only by what bone and heart and sinew could take, power coursing through them from Huath, impelling them ever faster. Lord Huath was in his element, a fierce joy in him now the hunt was on for the she-dragon.

All Channellers spent at least a year on the western borders after they'd won their staff on Lambay, patrolling for dragons, raiding out onto the islands to keep their numbers down. It was difficult, dangerous work, for the dragons were cunning and ferocious, savage fighters when defending their colonies. Huath had stayed on in Westport for years and tales of his ferocity in battle were legion. He and Terebitha had gone ahead to Erisen to assemble a full hunting party and return to the mountains, to try to kill the she-dragon before she could hatch her brood.

With Lord Huath gone, the mood relaxed. Ionain dropped back to ride alongside Eadha. It was the first time they'd talked since the party in the Great Hall after his Reckoning.

Glancing across at her he said with a grin, 'You look very calm for someone who was only just saved from being incinerated by a dragon.'

Eadha gave a small snort of laughter, Ionain's words releasing her from the slightly stunned daze she'd been in since the dragon had flown over her. Then, more soberly, she said with a shake of her head, 'I don't think she was going to hurt me.'

'What was it like?' Ionain said then, and quietly, 'Truly?'

She looked across at him, and in the same quiet voice, so Huath's guardsmen wouldn't hear her and think her crazed, said, 'It was beautiful. They leave that part out of all the stories. How beautiful they are.'

The two rode on for a little while and in Eadha's mind she saw once more the sunlight glittering on the dragon's scales as it dipped its head into the lake and heard the single word it had called her by, as it reared up before her. Mahera.

'I'm sorry I missed your Reckoning yesterday,' said Ionain then. 'I was all set to go but Mother said now I'm to be a Lord Channeller I shouldn't be hanging about down in the village. I didn't want to fight with her when I was leaving so soon after.'

Eadha glanced across at him.

'It's fine, don't worry.'

'What was Huath like as an Inquisitor?'

'Very strong,' said Eadha, 'but after all it's only a keeping gift. It didn't take him long to see it, so it was over quickly.'

Ionain frowned.

'Don't say *only a Keeper*. I know it isn't as strong as a Channeller—as my—gift, but I think it's amazing you're even a Keeper when you're not from a Family and no one was expecting anything at all. And it means we might even be paired together with you as my Keeper. Like Erisen and Beithe.'

'If I remember rightly Beithe sacrificed her life for Erisen in the final battle with the dragon Kaanesien. I may be fond of you, but I wasn't planning on dying for you.'

Ionain laughed delightedly.

'Hmm. I shall have to make a note of that to the Head Keeper when we reach Lambay. Keeper has attitude problem, lacks willingness to die for me. Seriously, though, it's going to be so much fun. Huath's told me a little about it. He says they've halls just for building illusions, combat yards and handball alleys for training, these huge studios where we'll channel buildings out of stone, greenhouses where we'll learn to channel every kind of fruit and plant there's ever been. I'll be flying within the year, actually flying, can you imagine that? He told me Second Island is wilder than anything I can imagine, though Mother wouldn't let him tell me anything about that. She kept going on about how we have to respect the Stages. But he's told me all about the Masters on First Island, so I can tell you who's decent and who to watch out for.'

As they'd been talking, the pace of their horses had slowed so they'd fallen behind the main party. Now Ionain nudged his horse closer to Eadha, so close his leg bumped against hers and he said more quietly, 'I used to imagine this when I was little, you know. Us.

119

Riding across the Blackstairs to Lambay together. But I never, ever thought it would really happen. It's as if all those years of waiting and worrying were a price I had to pay, and in return I'm finally allowed to be happy. I'm going to be a Channeller. I have worth, I can save my Family. And you're coming with me; we get to be together through it all,' and pushing himself out of his saddle he leaned across and kissed her hard on the mouth.

It was a rough and clumsy kiss, his nose bumping against hers, broken in an instant by the up-down of their horses' trotting. But to Eadha it was like a benediction; for the choices she'd made and the secrets she'd kept.

Ahead of them Sepp turned in his saddle and shouted to them to catch up. Ionain leaned forward and urged his mount into a canter, Eadha following behind more slowly. She was riding into the heart of the great lie that channelling was built on, a lie of power without price. And into that big lie she was bringing her own, smaller lie; that the beautiful boy she'd loved her whole life was powerful, too.

But in return for that lie, she was riding beside Ionain across the mountains they'd dreamed of since they were tiny, and a dragon had spoken to her beside a shining lake. That was enough and more than enough for now.

CHAPTER 13
LAMBAY

The east wind whipped the waves into white tops that curled and collapsed at their feet where Eadha and Ionain stood, staring out to Lambay First Island. The island's shoreline was densely wooded, the only sign of human habitation a narrow stone dock directly opposite.

As they watched a grey figure appeared through the trees. Walking up to the water's edge, he held a yew staff straight out in front of him. Light began pulsing the length of the staff in a steady beat. In answer a massive, grinding refrain came rumbling over the sound of the waves, as tonnes of rock lifted themselves from the seabed to form a slender walkway running from shore to dock, water pouring off the stones as they settled inches above the waves.

From behind them a deep voice spoke, 'Come along. The way won't stay raised all day.'

It was a man wrapped in Master's grey, already mounted on a silver cob. As he spoke, he rode out onto the narrow stone with practised ease. Ionain and Eadha swung up onto their horses and followed him, picking their way more gingerly across the stones. Eadha's mount had caught her nerves, whinnying when waves splashed across the path and hit her legs, the stone slick and slippery. Ionain trotted closer so his horse nuzzled hers, calming it enough to continue. Slowly they picked their way the length of the land-bridge and came together onto First Island.

At the dock, Ionain leaned in to Eadha and said in an awed whisper, 'That's Master Fionan. Uncle Huath told me he always comes to meet the new apprentices; he's our senior Master for the first year. Uncle says he's really strict about training. He was in charge of the Westport posting for new Channellers for years, but then he got badly burned saving a Keeper from a dragon. That's when he came back to First Island. Huath says it's why he's so strict; because it might save our lives someday.'

With a brief glance at Ionain that was enough to silence him, Master Fionan led them onto a curving path that climbed steeply away from the jetty, up under the trees. Eadha thought she glimpsed a wagon similar to Lord Huath's Fodder wagon hidden behind a clump of bushes, but if she did, it didn't follow them on the path to First House. As they rode deeper in, the roar of wind and waves fell away. It was so quiet that they could hear birdsong and the muffled clop of hooves on the matted forest floor. Here and there they saw the remains of fantastical buildings half-fallen in, branches threaded through what once were windows, roots snaking down crumbling stairs.

After a short climb they reached the end of the tree line. The ground fell away beneath them into a deep half-valley that flowed out into a sandy bay. On either side forest stretched down to the sea, while before them a carpet of grass unrolled down the hillside to fetch up against the walls of First House, cupped in the valley and facing away from them out to sea.

Channelled originally by Erisen the First Channeller, it was made over to the Masters as a training school in the shattered years after the Channeller wars. A hulking grey building built to withstand winter storms, it formed a long rectangle with narrow outstretched wings at either end that created a sheltered space between the House and the valley side. Nestled there were the south-facing greenhouses, home of the Master Grower. At the northern end, still deep in shadow, stood the stone handball alleys and battle-yards where they would be trained in the art of combat.

Perched high on the hill staring down at the great grey walls of First House, Eadha's stomach clenched in fear. This was not a place to be bargained with or withheld from. In its terrible strength it demanded her soul. She wanted to turn and run, back through the forest, across the land-bridge and not stop running until she was back in her aunt and uncle's cottage, sitting by the fire, listening to them weaving a day from small deeds and unwavering love.

Then Ionain's voice broke into her thoughts and with it her reason for being there, on a windy hillside out by the sea, with the might of Domhain's Channellers assembled below her.

'Come on,' he called back to her over his shoulder as he kicked his horse into a canter down the hillside. 'Time enough for daydreaming of epic victories when we've settled in.'

With a nudge Eadha sent her horse after him and moments later they arrived in through a stone archway into a stableyard.

Groomsmen took their mounts and Master Fionan led them on into First House. Inside it was unexpectedly bright and warm. Circular light wells pierced the ceilings to make alternating pools of light and dark, candles flickering in bell jars set in recesses along the walls. A long corridor opened out into a round central hall, panelled in oak and topped by a dragonglass dome. It was already almost full of people, a mix of grey-robed Masters and new apprentices.

Food was set out along the sides, piles of freshly channelled strawberries and soft purple plums, warm bread with mounds of butter, hot chocolate drinks steaming in silver cups. Eadha had to resist the urge to gawp; she'd never in her life seen so much fresh fruit, with winter only just past. Log fires burned in enormous slate fireplaces set at intervals along the walls, while above them were-lights circled just below the dome.

'Excellent, I'm starving. Come on,' said Ionain, leading her into the round room and making straight for the food. Following him more slowly, Eadha cupped her hands around a goblet of fragrant hot chocolate. As she did someone called Ionain's name. It was a tall, dark-haired boy dressed in navy leggings and sheepskin cloak. Alongside stood a girl, strikingly similar in looks but dressed in hunting gear; dark-green tunic, leggings and soft brown boots, lean and strong.

'Hey there, we heard all about your Reckoning, it's all anyone is talking about. Is it true you almost knocked over Master Dathin your power flare was so strong?' said the boy.

'Eadha, this is Coll and Linn of the Manon Family. Our grandparents were apprentices here together,' said Ionain, who'd gone bright red. 'And they should know better than to listen to gossip. Of course I didn't knock Master Dathin over. I was just glad to pass.'

Another voice broke in.

'Well now, if it isn't the most exotic and wonderful twins. I bow before your mighty power, my lord and lady.'

The speaker was a large, florid, fair-haired boy. Even at sixteen the large man he would become was evident in his thick neck and broad shoulders. He was dressed warmly in furs, sweating already in the well-heated room.

'Ailm, good to see you,' he nodded to Ionain. 'Family back from the brink, eh?'

His eyes flickered restlessly about the room to the other new arrivals, already beginning to coalesce into small groups of twos and threes, before coming back to rest on Eadha.

'Well, well, have we another Channeller, Ionain?'

'Don't be daft, Senan, of course not. You know as well as I do there's never been a girl Channeller from outside the Great Families. This is Eadha. She's a Keeper and we're all very proud of her,' said Ionain. Eadha said nothing.

'Strange,' said Senan. 'I thought I sensed something.'

Eadha tensed then, afraid she'd let her thought-wall slip and he'd seen her true power. But Senan had already lost interest.

'Never mind. It must've been someone else, there's so much power sloshing around this place, it's hard to read it.'

'...Thirty-seven, thirty-eight,' Coll was counting quietly under his breath. 'I'd say forty all in as there are bound to be stragglers,' he said, before turning to Ionain and smiling. 'The Masters must have been mightily relieved when House Ailm came good at the last moment with a Channeller and a Keeper. Makes the numbers a little less dire this year.'

Ionain grinned back.

'As if it was ever in doubt. Good hearty stock, us northerners.'

'My, and don't you bounce back quickly, too,' drawled Senan. 'It's as if House Ailm was never away. But my cousin's class ten years ago had twenty-five Channellers. What do we have—fifteen, and the rest just Keepers? We might need to start thinking about allocating more than one Keeper girl to a Channeller to get the birth rate up, eh, little Miss Not-Channeller?'

Senan raised an eyebrow at Eadha before drifting off across the room, helping himself to fruit and nonchalantly greeting other students. Eadha was left standing unnoticed while Ionain chatted and laughed with Coll and Linn. Watching him so relaxed and happy, all Eadha could think was how this place *fitted* him, like he'd pulled on a coat made specially for him. But at the same time there was something different about him, too, since they'd walked into the Round Hall. He was standing straighter, his words that bit more clipped and precise as he talked to Coll and Senan. For the first time in her life, he seemed almost lordly.

Seeing her standing alone, Linn turned to talk to her.

'Don't mind Senan,' she said, her voice kind. 'He can be a little direct. I think you're lucky to be a Keeper. I doubt I'll be so much as allowed outside on a wet day, you'll have much more freedom.'

'Why wouldn't you be allowed outside?' asked Eadha.

'Linn's a Channeller,' said Coll. 'The first girl Channeller for five years. She's worried she's going to be wrapped up in cotton wool until the Masters have married her off to some nice Channeller boy to make lovely Channeller babies. Isn't that right?'

Linn rolled her eyes at her brother.

'Once I can use my power, I'd like to see them try.'

'Watch out, Ionain. Looks like Ailbhe's on her way over. Seems we're not the only ones to hear about your oh-so-strong Reckoning,' Coll muttered to Ionain.

Eadha glanced in the direction Coll was looking and saw a tall, exceptionally pretty girl heading for their little group from the other end of the Round Hall, a bright smile on her face. She was richly dressed in a travelling habit, her hair caught up in a filigree net that reflected the were-lights above them.

'But I thought she and Gry...' said Ionain, looking suddenly disconcerted.

'Didn't you hear? Mr First Family failed his test, only managed to pass as a Keeper. I'd almost prefer to have failed completely. There's something humiliating about being quite so mediocre.'

Senan had wandered back to their group, and his tone was gleeful as he watched Ailbhe push her way through the crowd towards them, nodding hellos to other apprentices as she passed them.

126

'Of course, that means any match between Gry and Ailbhe is off now. There's no way her father would let her marry a Keeper. Serves her right. Remember how she wouldn't even look at any of the rest of us when we were younger, she was so sure of her First Family match. About time she learned a little humility. I'm going to enjoy this,' he chuckled, waving cheerfully towards Ailbhe as he spoke out of the side of his mouth. 'I'd make her work for it, Ailm. Doesn't do to make it too easy for those Keeper girls. Let the mating season begin.'

Beside Eadha, Ionain had gone red again at Senan's words. Ailbhe reached them just as Senan finished speaking, but before she could say anything, a gong sounded, summoning them all into the next room.

Eadha fell in behind Ionain as they all filed in. As they walked, he began talking confidentially to Coll, their heads bent together, already completely at home with all these people whose names she only knew from his tutor's stories of old. Manons, De Paors, De Lanes. To her these were the names of ancient dragon slayers, Master Architects, Growers and Tellers. But to him they were his friends, the sons and daughters of people who'd trained on Lambay with his uncle or grandfather, who'd come to stay at Ailm's Keep for his Reckoning. And though she'd known this, not until this moment had she understood it; that Ionain was already a part of this whole other world she neither knew nor understood.

But as they stepped through into the next room those thoughts were driven out of her mind by the heady smell of a room filled with books old and new, bound in calfskin on shelf after shelf of varnished oak stretching away as far as she could see, towering above the group of new apprentices as they filed in. This was the Library, a long, high room, its dark wooden floor burnished by the passage of generations of Channeller apprentices. Here, Ionain had told her, stood all the records of Channeller lore and history. The annals of the Four Brothers, the first Channellers; the witness accounts of the Channeller Wars, collected by Lady Huris when peace finally returned to Domhain; the vast body of dragon lore added to each year by Channellers returning from the western borders.

The shelves stretched far beyond the reach of human hands, yet there were no ladders. Eadha saw instead that dotted about the shelves were cushioned nests where Channellers could fly up to sit and study, like the nooks in the dome of Ailm's Keep. Breathing in the dry air, watching dust motes spin slowly in the slanting sunlight, just for a moment she let herself imagine using her power to fly up to sit in one of them and read about the dragon wars. But Master Dathin was standing there waiting for them, immense in his black cloak, while from behind them Master Fionan called, 'Channellers to the centre, Keepers to the side.'

Rows of chairs cushioned in red velvet had been set directly in front of Master Dathin. Plain benches stood sideways on. As Ionain took his seat on one of the red velvet chairs, Eadha, who'd been quietly shadowing him, had no choice but to go and sit on a Keeper bench.

She suddenly felt very exposed. She was joined by a dark curly-haired boy dressed in beautiful soft leathers who grimaced companionably and whispered, 'Doesn't take them long to separate the wheat from the chaff.'

It was Eadha's first chance to take a proper look at the group. Apart from the boy sat beside her, all the Keeper novices on the benches were girls. All were elegantly turned out for the journey to First House in riding habits with soft leather boots. As they sat down, they quickly broke into small groups, whispering to each other beneath their hands as their eyes darted about the Channeller apprentices in front of them. At the centre of one of those groups was Ailbhe, the girl Senan had talked about. Up close she was just as pretty, but now Eadha could see the tension in her gaze and in that of the other Keeper novices, as they studied the Channeller apprentices intently. To Eadha, it felt as though she'd walked unawares into a game that was already under way, one being played with deadly seriousness by the people around her, but whose rules she didn't know.

Directly in front of her sat Ionain on a plush wide-armed chair, eyes shining as he waved at this and that person. Beside him sat Coll and Linn. In front lounged Senan, one leg crossed above the other knee and an arm draped over the chair as he leaned back and candidly assessed the group about him. Linn was the only girl on a red velvet chair. All the rest, she counted fifteen, were boys, richly dressed sons of Great Families nodding familiarly to each other and staring about confidently.

Following Eadha's gaze the boy beside her said quietly, 'Better get used to it. All the rooms are the same; red velvet in the centre for the Channellers, wooden benches sideways on for us Keepers. After all, how are you to know you're special, unless someone else is being treated as less than you?'

There was no time for Eadha to answer though, as Master Dathin had begun to speak.

CHAPTER 14
FEALTY

'Welcome, newly Awakened Channellers, to this, the four hundred and fifteenth year of the House at Lambay. Only the most gifted in all Domhain are invited to our islands, where generations of Channellers have walked before you. Each of you is here because you have a rare and priceless gift. A gift upon which Domhain depends to survive and to prosper.'

From where Eadha sat, she could see Ionain's profile. The relaxed expression he'd had chatting with Coll and Senan had disappeared. Now he was completely focused, sitting bolt upright, his jaw set as he listened to Master Dathin.

'Look about you, to the left, to the right. You are the elite. You are the future of Domhain, its salvation and its glory. Here on Lambay you will find the training, the knowledge, and the wisdom to unlock the power that lies within you. I will not deceive you. The way of the Channeller is hard. We expect the very best from you. Complete dedication to the realisation of your power, fealty to the Masters, and devotion to the way of the Channeller. Those who win through to bear the yew staff are the leaders of our land, heads of our Great Families. Defenders of our realm, Master Architects, Growers, and

Tellers. Succeed here and you will be set upon a life of power, honour, prestige and wealth beyond measure, first among men and women. May the power newly Awakened within you flow all your days in channels true, to the glory of your days and of Domhain.'

As he paused a young man dressed all in white handed Master Dathin a large, beautifully bound book.

'These are the Annals of the Four Brothers, the first record of the birth of the Channeller gift. Every Awakened Channeller must swear their fealty on this, the wellspring of our history.'

At a gesture Master Dathin rose into the air to where the spring sunshine shone aslant through the dragonglass dome. Four young men came to stand by them, one at each corner of the group. One by one they lifted the newly Awakened Channellers up into the air to face Master Dathin in the bright silence above where they could be heard, some faltering, some steady, but all repeating the same oath.

'I swear fealty to the Masters in my thoughts, words and deeds. For channelling is the power and the glory of Domhain and I its vessel now and always.'

Ionain was the last to be raised up, his voice ringing clear and vibrant in the hushed room, his face shining with determination.

'Channellers, please follow Master Fionan now. He will guide you to your apartments in the Channellers' quad. Keepers remain.'

Master Dathin left then, and the Annals were replaced in a glass case just beneath the dome. The Channeller apprentices filed out behind Master Fionan. With them gone the room felt empty.

A severe-looking woman in black, who'd bowed deeply as Master Dathin passed her, now took his place. Her voice flat and toneless, she addressed Eadha and the other Keeper novices, still perched awkwardly on their narrow benches.

'I am Fiachna, Head Keeper. Here on First Island you will learn that as Keepers, our vocation is one of service to our Lords'

Channeller. For our gift only gains meaning in submission to theirs, in carrying their powers upon which all of Domhain depends.'

As she spoke, Eadha saw how Fiachna's pale face had become flushed.

'Only in submission are we truly blessed. You will have the privilege of studying alongside the Channeller apprentices for the first few months, as the skills taught are common to both Channellers and Keepers. Never forget, however, that this privilege is subject to strict compliance with the Keeper's Code, which was created to ensure we never lose sight of our place. A copy is nailed above each bed in your dormitories. Read it, memorise it, for it will guide your steps throughout your time here on Lambay and afterwards in service to your Lords' Channeller. We begin with Matins in the temple at daybreak tomorrow.'

Eadha, though, didn't hear a word of this. She was too busy watching Ionain disappear from the Library with the other Channellers. Unease gripped her. She hadn't thought she'd be separated from Ionain like this. Her whole plan rested on being able to get close enough to him to send her powers into him without it being seen by anyone.

As she watched, Ionain stepped out through the doorway at the far end of the Library without a backward glance. Eadha bowed her head, trying to hold in her mind a sense of the thread linking the two of them, but as he moved on deeper into the House it winked out and she couldn't find it again. Losing it unbalanced her, like being asked to stand steady on one foot.

She was being gently nudged by the curly-haired boy to stand up. As they shuffled out of the Library, he whispered, 'I'm Gry, from House Flemin. You?'

'Eadha, of Lord Ailm's household.'

'You came with Ionain then?'

She nodded distractedly, still trying to pick up Ionain's thread. Gry's face was sympathetic as he looked at her.

'You won't see him again today. He'll be off to the Channellers' quad where they all have their own apartments. No bare dorms for our Lords' Channeller.'

As Gry spoke, the Head Keeper Fiachna began shepherding them out through an oak door set in the immensely thick walls and on into a shadowed cloister. Along one wall figures were carved into the stone in bas-relief: familiar scenes from the wars and their aftermath. On the right, a colonnade overlooked a smooth lawn. It glowed in the late afternoon sunshine like a jewel set within the walls, water singing as it flowed up and out from a marble basin in its centre.

Fiachna pointed them to it.

'The Fountain of Beginning, where the First Channeller drew fresh water from the earth. The earliest known use of channelling, and the reason why Erisen chose to build First House on this spot.'

Now they were passing through a narrow tunnel braced with thick beams, then out into the sunshine, into the Keepers' quad, their home on Lambay.

At its centre stood a thicket of oak trees, still bare of leaves. Above their heads, high cross-walks linking each side of the quad intersected in the middle of the thicket. The buildings were of plain sandstone, each one divided into dorms with five beds each, although as the sole boy Gry had a room to himself. The dorms themselves had dark wooden floors with white walls, white beds and marble busts of past Keepers and Channellers set into recesses.

Eadha had been allocated to a dorm at the eastern end of the quad with four other girls, including Ailbhe, the girl Senan had teased Ionain about. Eadha's bed was in the far corner of the room, opposite a bright window.

As Head Keeper Fiachna had said, a copy of the Keeper's Code was nailed above each bed.

The Code of Keeping

A Keeper's role is to serve their Channeller with all of their gift and
their strength, to the greater glory of their Channeller.
Channellers must at all times be treated with the deference owed their
gift and their name.
Keepers must give way to Channellers. Doors are to be held,
heads bowed.
Keepers may not sit in the presence of a Channeller unbidden.
No Keeper may speak to a Channeller until so bidden.
No Keeper may visit a Channeller uninvited.

As soon as Fiachna left a babble of talk broke out, as the other four girls all embraced each other, asking after each other's families and gossiping about Reckonings.

Left to herself, Eadha quickly unpacked her one change of clothes, putting it in the locker beside her bed and hiding Magret's book and the amber tower underneath.

After a few minutes Ailbhe stepped forward from her little group, her hand outstretched.

'I'm Ailbhe, of House De Paor.'

'Eadha.'

'I saw you talking to my dear friend Ionain when we arrived. How do you know him?'

'My family are of his household,' said Eadha, flushing awkwardly.

'Ah. Isn't that good of him, looking out for the staff?' said Ailbhe. Behind her the other girls tittered.

'That explains why I haven't seen you before. Though perhaps you waited on me, when I visited dear old Ailm's Keep?'

Eadha stared at her. Ionain may well have visited the De Paor Family's home on trips with his mother, but this girl had never been to Ailm's Keep. If she had, she'd have seen her. Looking into Ailbhe's eyes, she realised it was a deliberate test. She was waiting to see if Eadha would dare to challenge her. There was a brief silence as Eadha took this in and realised, too, that she couldn't; she had too many secrets to keep to be able to afford to make enemies. After a moment Ailbhe turned away, satisfied she had the measure of her.

Addressing the other girls she continued, her voice lowering confidentially, 'Of course, Ionain was always terribly sweet on me. He used to follow me around everywhere like a little puppy when he and his mother came to stay with us. It will be lovely to see more of him now we're together on Lambay. Now, ladies. Hauls out, let's see what you've got!'

The four girls upended their cases. Heaps of clothes, silks and fine brocades, embroidered dresses and hunting gear cascaded onto the beds, the girls shrieking as they caught sight of each other's stash. Watching them, just for a second Eadha pictured the look on their faces if she were to use her power to call up a small fireball on each of those piles of costly clothes. She pushed the thought away, though, and after a few moments slipped out of the dorm unremarked.

Outside all was quiet. Through an archway opposite she glimpsed an open space encircled by trees sloping down to the sea. Out on the water, lights twinkled as sailboats made slow, steady progress towards Second Island, where the second-year apprentices lived and trained. But even in the quiet twilight she could find no trace of Ionain's thread.

Trying not to panic she hurried back into the main building. She peeped into empty classrooms with their rows of cushioned Channeller seats and plain Keeper pews sideways on, slipped past high-ceilinged studios filled with blocks of marble ready to be channelled into fantastical shapes. On and on she walked the polished, silent halls of First House until at the very furthest end away from the Keepers' quad, she reached another archway.

Stepping through, the towers of the Channellers' quad soared above her, carved and turreted with stained-glass windows and balconies bound in metal spirals. Chains of were-lights dangled from the walkways that criss-crossed the upper levels above the lawn. Voices called from house to house through open windows, white curtains dipping in the sea-breeze, bursts of laughter echoing around the green.

With a surge of relief Eadha realised she could sense Ionain's thread in a building on the other side of the lawn. Slipping across the grass she peeped in through the window, hoping to catch sight of him. She was looking into a fire-lit sitting room, the dancing flames reflected in the polished wooden floorboards covered with thick rugs. Along the walls stood rich rosewood sideboards bearing silver trays and delicate crystal decanters, while jewel-coloured cushions were scattered in front of the fire. To Eadha, used to the shabby austerity of Ailm's Keep, the room's opulence was overwhelming: a barrage of colour, texture and light.

As she stared, Ionain walked in laughing and chatting with Coll and Senan, his face bright with excitement. Instead of the relief she'd expected to feel, though, she felt a flash of anger. He clearly wasn't missing her in the slightest; she wondered if he'd even thought of her since that moment he'd taken his seat on a red velvet chair. She'd taken this enormous gamble so he could have his dream, everything she'd done had been for him, yet he seemed to have forgotten her the minute he'd arrived here, like a young prince coming into his throne.

The next moment a heavy hand caught her by the shoulder with a thud that set her heart slamming.

'Keeper, what are you doing here?'

It was Head Keeper Fiachna, looming over her, her heavy frame belying the soundlessness with which she had come up behind Eadha.

'I... I was looking for Ionain,' she stammered.

With grim satisfaction Fiachna said, 'When you arrived on this island today, you entered the service of your Lords' Channeller. Access to the Channellers' quad is forbidden to you unless by their express invitation. Nor may you address a Channeller by anything other than their proper title. Be thankful this is your first day otherwise your punishment for breach of the Keeper Code would be severe. Return to your quarters at once.'

As they spoke, heads began appearing at windows, peering out to see where the noise was coming from. As quickly as she could Eadha escaped, away back through the stone tunnel. Her heart was still racing; with humiliation, with hurt, but more than any of that, with fear.

She hadn't planned for this, had crossed the mountains and the sea to Lambay with a naïve certainty that she and Ionain would be together, if not in the same room, at least nearby. From Ionain's talk of a Master's House, she'd pictured it as another Ailm's Keep. But First House was something far greater, far heavier than that. Not just the scale of it, huge though it was, many times the size of the Keep, or the thickness of the walls. It was the power she could sense all around her, coursing invisibly along the corridors as Masters drew on Fodder, weighing her down, confusing her mind as she tried to find the link to her friend. And if Ionain was to be hidden so far away from her here in the Channellers' quad, if she had no way of getting close to him when the time came and she needed to give him her powers, then her great gamble, in coming here to this place that was so far beyond her, was lost before a single dice was thrown.

She needed to think, try to work out what to do. She couldn't face the girls in her dormitory. Instead, she sought sanctuary in the Library. It was dimly lit as she entered, lights burning here and there.

Checking first to make sure no one else was there, she reached inside herself, finding and pulling gently at the slender thread from belly to heart. It comforted her, to feel her power respond. This, at least, she was sure of. Willing it out of her, she lifted herself up in the moonlight under the dome, in unconscious echo of Ionain's bright flight that sunny afternoon. Wavering slightly, she came to rest in a cushioned eyrie and watched the stars rise for a while over the quiet sea, searching them for a way to reach her friend.

CHAPTER 15
MATINS

The next morning, she was hauled awake an hour before dawn by the tolling of the temple bells, summoning all to Matins. Groggily she pulled on the red Keeper robe laid out at the end of her bed. About her the other girls did the same.

As her head cleared, the dead thud of yesterday's panic kicked in her stomach, but the night's sleep had calmed her a little. Fiachna had said yesterday the Awakened Keeper and Channeller apprentices would study together. This surely meant she could get close to Ionain during lessons even if his quarters were at the other end of First House. She just had to be patient.

The other girls were filing out of the room. As she followed them, she bowed her head beneath her cowl and built her thought-wall, swiftly creating a new display, her silver fish flickering restlessly in the depths as the last blocks slid into place. She could not stop her worry colouring her thought-wall, though, staining it with her anxiety. With a final tug she pulled power up the thread. It lit up, thoughts set moving to circle in random patterns through the day.

As she lined up behind Fiachna, the other Keeper girls pushed in front of her, until she ended up at the end of the line. From her place at the front, Ailbhe glanced back at her, her face expressionless and said, 'Commoners go last.'

In silence then they followed the Head Keeper's swinging lantern through the cloisters, feet echoing on the bare stone, on into the temple. In the pre-dawn darkness, it was lit by torches set in braziers along the walls. Bundles of fragrant pinewood burned in fire-wells set at intervals up the centre aisle, creating circles of heat in the frosty air. In front of them, the Channellers were filing into their plush red-cushioned seats in the centre. The Keepers slipped into high-fronted Keeper pews that stood sideways on. In front of her, Eadha could see Ionain's tawny head in the middle of the Channeller apprentices, flanked by Senan and Coll.

Fiachna and the other senior Keepers stood behind the pews, cowls raised so their faces could not be seen, hands crossed and tucked into their sleeves, like living statues lining the temple wall.

As the bells stilled, four Masters paced slowly up the centre aisle, swinging incense-filled thuribles on long silver chains until the smoke filled the temple, drifting over the Keeper pews. Eadha's head began to swim as a potent blend of incense and some other, unfamiliar smell surrounded them, filling lungs and dimming eyes. At the same time, a single drumbeat began thumping from the back of the temple in rhythm with her heart. Gradually, it was joined by other deeper, more complex rhythms that built and echoed with fierce intent.

The incense and the pounding of the drums were making her dizzy; she had to put out a hand and grip the pew in front of her to hold herself steady. As she did, the first rays of sunlight lanced through the east-facing windows and the Masters stood as one and began to sing. Their deep voices rang out over the drumming, a chant that built from the depths and climbed into the frozen air.

In their song Eadha heard the ferocity and joy of power,

coursing through the heart, the body, the mind. From nowhere a wildness gripped her. Urged her to rip down her thought-wall, to reach out and drain the life-force from everyone around her until they collapsed in a pyre at her feet, and she rose like an arrow, blazing out with all the power she was capable of, shattering through the dome above, soaring up and up into the flaming heart of the sun to burn in an unending, glorious immolation.

Her power surged up inside her unbidden, demanding to be unleashed. With all she had, she struggled to hold it down, but even as she did the drums kept up their relentless pounding. Faster and faster still, they beat until at last they merged, collapsing down to a single racing drumbeat that arrowed into her mind to strike, shuddering, into her worry-stained thought-wall. For one frozen instant it held against the impact and then it shattered into unbeing, her true thoughts fled all through her mind.

Out of the corner of her eye she saw a hooded Keeper's head shoot up, whipping this way and that, like a blind person trying to locate the source of a sound. And down the row from where she sat, Gry's head inched about, his eyes sliding sideways towards her.

Eadha knew from all Magret had told her that her full gift must have shone out in the moment the thought-wall had shattered. Even now the Keepers' grasping, spidery senses would be spooling out towards her, to hook her in. The part of her that could still think through the drug-haze and the drumbeats was screaming, scrabbling to rebuild her thought-wall from the scattered, bewildered images ricocheting through her mind.

But each time she managed to cobble her thoughts together the relentless drums pounded them to nothing once more. And mutely, sullenly, deep inside her something else was resisting, too, would not let the new wall take hold. A part of her that'd stayed standing in the Channellers' quad last night staring in at Ionain's rich apartment.

That whispered to her it was all too hard. That maybe it was better like this. Better to be caught now before it all went too far. Better, maybe, to be found out and recognised for who she was, a Channeller born, and take her place like Linn, in a turret with stained-glass windows, and sit on a red velvet seat, and be kept in out of the rain.

But as she struggled on, the drumming finally stopped and the congregation rose to their feet. All around her the apprentices began to sing. It was the refrain of thanks, the same song she'd sung with the Keep choir at Ionain's Reckoning, what felt like centuries ago. As they wove the melody about her, from note to well-loved note she climbed. Pulled herself away from the seductive drumbeat of despair and desire. Remembered the promises she'd made and built back a shining thought-wall of music and memory that glimmered and reflected back the searching Keeper's creeping threads so that they withdrew from her mind, thwarted.

A little later, as the Keeper apprentices shuffled out through the temple doors, a voice spoke behind her.

'Are you alright?' It was Gry. 'You seemed a bit wobbly back there.'

'The smoke and the singing, I don't know, it affected me,' she replied, her head clearing quickly in the morning air. He fell into step alongside her.

'I wouldn't worry, that's normal. They burn molash potions with the incense to heighten the rush from channelling. You'll soon get the hang of it. You should see how it affects the new Channeller apprentices; they're far more sensitive to it than us lowly Keepers. Some have even been known to lose control.'

She looked at him sharply but Gry's eyes were wide, full of nothing but an innocent concern.

'How do you know so much about this place?'

'My cousin is a Risen Channeller over on Second Island—he'll graduate and be away to Westport in the autumn. He's told me a good bit about what to expect and my Family goes back a long way. We're descended from Shem. So, plenty of nurse's tales for me since I could first sit on her knee. I used to long for a story that did not involve dragons or buildings or battles; possibly something involving cows.'

Eadha realised then that Gry was the Mr First Family Senan had sneered about yesterday, descended from the youngest of the Four Brothers, the first known Channellers on Domhain.

'So, what happens now?'

'Well, breakfast in the ref now. Then a tour of First House from some insufferably smug Risen, hopefully not my cousin. After that the real work begins.'

At his words Eadha's anxiety stirred inside her once more; her thought-wall was back in place, but she was still no closer to a sure means of reaching Ionain unseen.

The refectory was in the main House, its east-facing windows lit by the rising sun as the apprentices trickled in, some as dazed-looking as Eadha had felt, the molash having clearly affected them, too. The same buffet was laid out as the day before, mounds of fresh fruit, warm bread and steaming hot chocolate. Raised on the thin rations at Ailm's Keep, all this plenty was intoxicating, and she piled her plate high. In front of her, two Keeper girls were chatting as they inspected a glistening pile of strawberries in a porcelain bowl, carefully selecting the ripest, roundest berries.

'They're very good; much better than our crops this winter,' said one.

'Mother always says Master Con could channel pomegranates from a teaspoon of soil in a snowstorm,' the other replied.

'But look out for the tomatoes; they're the hardest to get right. It's best to avoid them for the first term until the new Channellers get the hang of them.'

Standing behind them Eadha wondered if she was the only person on Lambay who didn't already know everything there was to know about the Masters' House, from the hazards of tomatoes and drugged incense to the Masters and their talents. She felt like someone playing a high-stakes game of Blind Man's Bluff, flailing clumsily as she tried to feel out the obstacles and pitfalls ahead while all around her the smugly sighted looked on, sniggering. How could she have thought she'd be able to outwit the Masters when she didn't know the first thing about this place she'd come to?

A group of red-robed Channeller students burst in, talking loudly, pushing and shoving each other in high spirits. Ionain was in the middle, laughing and ducking to avoid a cuff from Senan. They were followed more slowly by a clutch of Keeper girls, Ailbhe and the other girls from Eadha's dorm among them. All sat down at a long table, though not before Ailbhe and the other Keepers had bowed carefully to the Channeller apprentices.

Seeing Eadha, Ionain jumped to his feet, waving to her to come over, his face flushed with heat and excitement. Awkwardly she did so, Gry following.

'Eadha, there you are, I looked for you last night. You know Coll and Linn and Senan from yesterday. Everyone, this is Eadha, my friend from home. She's the one I told you about, who faced the dragon in the Blackstairs on the way here.'

Eadha smiled self-consciously.

'Yes,' snorted Senan. 'I've no doubt you played a major part in routing the creature. I heard Huath chased away the bitch a few days ago but not before it hatched, so they're hunting for its spawn now.'

'It was so fortunate your Uncle Huath was with you in the mountains, a dragon slayer of such power,' said Ailbhe, leaning in to the conversation, gazing wide-eyed at Ionain. 'Though no doubt some of you will be equally powerful once you have your yew staffs.'

The talk turned to the different Lords' Channeller, with Ionain loyally backing his uncle against younger Channellers recently returned from the western front with tales of new techniques, new slayings. But when Gry ventured an opinion Senan's head whipped about like a snake.

'Ah, the boy Keeper. How are you doing in your Keeper dorm? I heard your mother cancelled all the winter festivities at House Flemin after your Reckoning rather than face the pitying looks from her sisters. I think I'd prefer no power at all than to be a Keeper. So very mediocre, don't you think? At least being powerless has that whiff of notoriety, eh, Ailm? What girl in their right mind would have you? Far too much of a risk, I would've thought. Unless, of course, Linn takes pity on you.'

Gry had flushed at Senan's onslaught but his voice was calm as he replied, 'At least my parents didn't have to endow a whole wing of First House to ensure I passed the Reckoning, because we already have a Channeller in the Family.'

'How dare you.' Senan sprang from his chair and had to be held back by Ionain. 'You're lucky we're not permitted to use our power yet or I would show you what a real Channeller looks like.'

'What did he mean, not permitted to use power?' Eadha asked Coll beside her as Senan subsided, still muttering.

In between mouthfuls of food he explained, 'Well, as Master Fionan will doubtless tell us at great and pompous length later this morning, it's all about the stages. Our bodies and minds must first be purified into worthy vessels for our power. So, no flying or raising buildings or anything else fun for us until Master Dathin deems us worthy.'

It was a reprieve, an unexpected gift of time. Time for her to find the way to reach Ionain with her power unseen, to keep her promise, after all. And the sweetness of it, that flood of relief that rushed all through her was so strong and sudden that Eadha swayed slightly in her seat.

She straightened up, looking about the sunlit refectory with a new sense of possibility. Ionain glanced her way and she grinned impulsively across at him. He smiled widely in response, blue eyes shining with their old shared laughter, before turning towards a knowing kick from Coll.

From the darting looks of Ailbhe and the other Keeper girls around her she knew that in that one moment, with that one shared smile, she'd made an enemy of Ailbhe after all, but just then, just there, she didn't care.

CHAPTER 16
THE HANDBALL ALLEY

Later that morning, Eadha and the other novices stood shivering in the stone handball alley at the northern end of First House. Though the high walls sheltered them from the sea winds it was still bitterly cold there in the thin spring sunshine. Master Fionan stood before them holding a net of handballs, small balls made from twine and covered in leather. He was a tall, slim man, well-muscled with keen eyes and an amused expression. His long hair was tied back, and his cloak had been put to one side. He was younger than either Dathin or Fiachna, though Eadha could see no trace of the dragon-burns that had ended his posting in Westport. She tried to picture it, being caught in the path of a dragon's fiery breath, but Fionan had started speaking.

'Awakened, today begins your first Stage: preparing yourselves in mind and body to be worthy vessels of power. You will need immense physical strength, agility and flexibility to contain and use your power effectively, whether in the peaceful arts of building and growing, in dragon combat or in the weaving of lays and illusions.'

'We begin with handball. It is a sport that requires speed, agility and coordination of the hand and eye, all essential when wielding the yew staff. May I have a volunteer?'

Ionain's hand went up to cheers and back slaps from Senan and Coll. He was standing in the middle of the group of Channeller apprentices directly in front of Master Fionan, while the Keeper novices stood in a separate group a little to one side, watched over by Head Keeper Fiachna. Throwing the ball in the air, Fionan whipped his hand forward, smashing the ball against the far wall, where it rebounded and came shooting back towards Ionain, hitting him hard in the chest. He doubled over, all the breath knocked out of him.

'As I said, speed and agility. Also, quick reflexes.'

Laughing good-naturedly Ionain picked up the ball and Master Fionan began by walking him through the serve, showing him how to place his feet to react swiftly to the flying return, how to twist his body to avoid being hit, how to throw himself across the court in a diving catch and hit the ground in a roll rather than smashing shoulder to the ground. Soon all of them were playing with varying degrees of success, the air filled with the sounds of balls hitting walls and various tender body parts as they ricocheted back.

Standing there in the spring sunshine, watching Ionain throw himself around the alley, Eadha was still fizzing; with the relief of knowing she didn't have to find a way to supply power to Ionain for weeks yet, and with another, deeper feeling she wouldn't admit to herself but that filled her until she almost had to rise up onto the balls of her feet to hold it in. The feeling of being, just for a little while, free. She'd come to this place to protect her friend, but for now he didn't need her. She was free to just be; in this place of power and wonders, she had nothing to do but train like all the Great Family apprentices who stood around her, with their ancient names that spoke of dragon slayers and Master builders.

When her turn came to step into the alley, she threw herself into the game. Her hands were callused from working in the fields, making it easier for her to strike the hard ball. She adapted quickly to the game's rhythm, anticipating the flight of the ball and positioning herself instinctively to send it flying back against the wall and beyond reach.

As the morning wore on Master Fionan set up a tournament. It quickly became competitive, with all the new apprentices keen to give a good account of themselves in this first test. Ionain was knocked out early on, sprawling red-faced on the ground as Linn defeated him with a final smash that bounced off three walls before whizzing past his outstretched hand.

Eadha came through the first three rounds, Ionain loudly cheering, 'Victory to House Ailm!' when she defeated yet another Keeper novice in a closely fought game.

Next up was Ailbhe. She came stepping daintily, her shining hair tied into a neat bun. They were well matched, Ailbhe with the superior skill and experience, Eadha relying on her longer reach and natural agility to stay in points. Almost all the other novices had been knocked out at this stage, the Keeper novices returning to stand by Fiachna, who made them stand in strict rows, while the Channeller apprentices sat high above them on the alley walls, feet dangling as they looked down at the two girls racing about the alley, diving and twisting. Ionain continued to noisily cheer Eadha on from the side, while Ailbhe's dorm-mates cheered for her. Ailbhe was perfectly composed, not a hair out of place, skin only lightly flushed as she served the ball hard, fast and low. Eadha had the impression that it was almost as important to Ailbhe that she made it look easy, as it was to win. But Eadha could see she was beginning to tire. Saw, too, the quick, irritated glance upwards when Ionain gave a particularly loud cheer.

'Come on, Eadha! Show them what us northerners are made of!'

'Here it comes,' she thought, and there indeed it was, a

deceptively quick serve, sent deliberately high against the wall so it would shoot back directly into Eadha's face. Ailbhe, it seemed, was sending her a warning. She would not be beaten, in anything.

In response Eadha felt her power start to uncoil, surging up inside her. In her mind's eye she saw her silver strength so easily channelling power to her legs to somersault back and out of the flight of Ailbhe's serve, saw herself coming around to whip the ball back and into the calm, composed, utterly entitled face of the girl beside her. But in the same moment she knew that was not a choice she had; not if she was to keep her promise to protect Ionain. With an effort she pushed her power back down and braced instead to take the blow. As the ball slammed into her temple her neck snapped back and she went flying backwards onto the ground.

Master Fionan hurried over to where Eadha lay dazed, blood trickling down the side of her forehead and into her hair. Above her Ailbhe launched into the expected apologies, her pretty face twisted into an appropriate, if blatantly insincere expression of concern. Ionain jumped down from the wall, but the Master waved him back before placing his hand across the cut and calmly asking her, 'How is your head?'

'It's fine, just a cut.'

'Still, we can't have our apprentices wounded on their first day, and we wouldn't want to leave a scar now, would we?' And there was enough of a smile in his eyes to show he knew that Eadha, and doubtless all the other apprentices, had been wondering what dragon-scars he still bore.

He closed his eyes and Eadha sensed him draw power. Instinctively she tried to follow it, a thread running across the alley and out into the quad behind, but there she lost its path, unable to trace where the Fodder were hidden. Even as she did, she realised with a start she'd seen no trace of Fodder at all since they'd arrived on First Island the day before—no Fodder wagon, no Fodder Hold like that in Ailm's Keep. Wherever they were keeping the people they were using as Fodder, they were well-hidden. Fionan stretched his hand out just above her cut, there was a tingling and the pain disappeared, snuffed out.

Reaching up she felt the skin on her forehead. It was whole, the cut healed. Master Fionan handed her a cloth to clean away the dried blood and turned away to look up at the rest of the class gathered on the walls above.

'For those of you from the Great Families this may come as a surprise, but you are not loved, out there, in the world beyond your Houses, beyond Lambay. There are many people—the ungifted, the poor, your own servants and bondsmen—who chafe under the Channellers' yoke. They depend upon us and yet they hate us for it, for our power and for the price it exacts. All this you will understand better as you progress. But know this. It is natural for you to see each other as challengers, as these two young ladies just did. But never for a moment lose sight of the fact that when you leave this House you are all on the same side, facing a common enemy. You are the elite, you are not loved and all you have is each other if we are to maintain the rule of the Great Families into future generations.'

He paused a moment, then smiled.

'Now. I appear to have some power left over from that healing. Who would like to see how this game can be played?' and sending the ball against the end wall above he raced to the side wall, running vertically up it. With a flick he pushed off to reach the ball in mid-air as it came flying back, before somersaulting down to land lightly on the ground. Taking off again he whipped the ball improbably high into the sky, then went shooting up into the air to meet it as it came down, volleying it with his foot against the end wall in mid-air then diving headfirst down onto the ground where he rolled at the last second to come up and catch the ball calmly in one hand as it flew back once more.

When at last he floated down to the ground, calm and unruffled, excited apprentices clustered about him, teeming with questions. Sitting on the ground dabbing at her forehead Eadha saw reflected in them the hunger she'd had, the hunger she still had churning inside her. The beguiling, seductive appeal of the power, the excitement of being able to pass beyond normal human boundaries, to become something more, effortlessly soaring above the rest. But Fionan was well used to managing eager new apprentices and shepherded them to line up into their separate Channeller and Keeper groups for the trek back to First House.

As they walked Gry caught up with Eadha.

'Unintentional, my foot. Ailbhe De Paor was the junior Erisen champion in handball when we were younger. She knew exactly what she was doing when she smashed that ball at your face. What did you do to annoy her so?'

'Smiled at the wrong person, I think,' said Eadha.

'Well, try not to make a habit of it then. With those Great Family girls, it's a hazardous undertaking.'

'Why?' said Eadha then, turning to look at Gry.

'One word,' he replied with a wry grin. 'Power.'

His grin widened as he took in her look of incomprehension.

'You really have wandered into the dragon's den without a staff, haven't you?' He gestured towards the high walls of First House ahead of them. 'This place, it's all about power. Having it, keeping it.'

Stung, Eadha replied, 'I know that.'

'But not just in the way you think. How do you become powerful?'

'By being gifted.'

'True. But how do you stay powerful? By marrying someone

gifted. This place, it's not just a school. It's a Great Family mating zoo, where all of us Great Family offspring try to pair up with each other in such a way we can be sure our children will be gifted, so our Families can stay powerful. We're all terrified of ending up like Ionain's Family—having the Channeller gift die out and trying to survive on scraps while you spend years praying the next generation will be born gifted.'

He shrugged then.

'Ailbhe's from one of the most powerful Families on Domhain and only the top Channeller apprentice will do for her. She thought I was a good bet because of my bloodline, before I went and let everyone down by only being a Keeper. I suppose I shall just have to cope with the devastation.'

Eadha glanced at him. He was grinning widely, and anyone less devastated looking it was hard to imagine. His grin faded a little then as he went on more soberly, 'I do feel bad that it's turned out like this for her, under pressure to find a Channeller to pair up with. She's the kind of person who should really be running a small country, or at the very least head of a Family. Instead, she's stuck as a Keeper novice where the only measure of success is finding a powerful husband. With the added bonus that if you marry early, you'll probably duck out of a Westport posting because there are always more Keepers than Channellers. Us Keepers are a bit more likely to get fried by a dragon than a Channeller.'

'But no one's even used their power yet. Why set for Ionain now?'

'He's her best bet. He's from two ancient families and everyone's heard about the huge flare of power at his Reckoning. Master Dathin said the last time he felt a flare that strong was Huath's own Reckoning thirty years ago, and he's easily the strongest Channeller on all Domhain. It's a match both Families would support; they've been allies forever.'

They'd reached the Keepers' quad, where she followed Gry up the stairs towards their dorms. Glancing at her as he turned towards his own room, his expression suddenly serious he went on, 'This isn't a game to these girls. I know Ionain's your friend, but he's away in the Channellers' quad and he can't protect you here. So be careful. Now we'd better get changed; we've history of channelling next. Want to wager we'll get the Four Brothers for our first lesson?' and as he walked down the white-washed hallway towards his room, he began reciting the opening words of the Annals of the Four Brothers in a sing-song voice.

'*There was once a primitive land whose people dwelt in ignorance, huddled in hovels, their fields barren and their buildings ramshackle, scourged by the dragon menace.*

Unto this land four brothers were born, the first of their kind, Channellers born,

and their gift was to be the salvation and the glory of the land...'

CHAPTER 17
PURIFICATION

So began Purification, physically the toughest of all the stages Eadha, Ionain, and the other apprentices would face on First Island.

From the first their routine was relentless, with every moment of every day scheduled, from the clanging instant the temple bells hauled them out of bed before daybreak for Matins until they collapsed exhausted after Vespers at evenfall.

Each morning after Matins they stood for an hour in silent meditation. Fiachna and her Keepers patrolled the ranks of sleepy novices with bamboo switches, swishing them smartly across the back of anyone found dozing. From there they marched to the shore below First House and straight out into the freezing waters of the bay, swimming a half-mile out and back. Soaked and shivering, they then staggered back up the beach and on to a ten-mile circuit of the island. Up into the hills and through the forests behind First House they ran, along narrow animal tracks and over fallen trunks.

They trained in handball and staff combat, the stone yards at the House's northern end filled with the thump and clack of yew staffs as they learned to whirl, feint and strike, in readiness for the power that one day soon would pulse through the long staves.

The training came more easily to Eadha than most, hardened as she was from years of herding. Even so, her back was often raw from the swoosh of Fiachna's switch, quick as a snake to catch her nodding off during Matins or Vespers. She knew it had to be harder for Ionain but he gave no sign of it, throwing himself into the training with a determination she'd never seen in him before. But though they all quickly became fitter and faster, their bodies responding to the demands made of them, the Masters were relentless, upping the intensity every few days so no matter how much stronger they became, the exhaustion never lessened. Yet they all persevered, through the stiffness and the pain, drawn on by the siren song of power for those who made it through.

Despite the exhaustion, though, Eadha never lost sight of her real reason for being there on Lambay. From the first day's training she was studying the routine, trying to work out when she could get closest to Ionain, to give him her powers when the time came.

She realised immediately Matins was no use. He was too far away from her on his red velvet seat in the central aisle, with Masters all around him. Meditation was too heavily supervised, the Keepers and the Channellers standing in their separate groups watched over by Fiachna and her black-cloaked helpers. The daily run, she thought, was her best chance. Fiachna ran with them, but the apprentices always ended up strung out along the course, the faster ones running on ahead, the slower ones falling back. The Keeper novices started behind the Channellers, but she was faster than most of them. It wouldn't be difficult to pull ahead mid-run, she thought, when they were deep in the forest, and come alongside Ionain for a few moments. That was all she'd need.

But it was hopeless. Every time she tried to drift ahead unobtrusively, she only ever managed to pass one or two Channeller stragglers before Fiachna would spot her and snap, 'Keeper Eadha. You must stay behind the Channellers. Fall back at once,' and as she slowed, Ailbhe and her friends would overtake her on either side, ramming her with their shoulders so she stumbled and went sprawling on the muddy track, while they ran on.

Still, she didn't panic. Afternoons were given over to lessons in four of the main arts of channelling—Building, Growth, Combat and Illusion. As the apprentices weren't allowed to use their power yet, these first lessons were just demonstrations from the different Masters. In the days that followed they saw towers of ivory and gold raised up around them by the Master Architect, only to be sent flowing back into the earth at the end of the demonstration as if they'd never existed. They watched as Irial, a Master Combat, did battle in the air above them with a group of older Rising Channeller apprentices come visiting from Second Island. Using their yew staffs they sent balls of white-hot fire shooting at each other, weaving golden nets of power as traps for the unwary. It was the first time Eadha or Ionain had seen the full wonders of what channelling could do. Eadha was entranced, watching them like one starving, sending out tendrils of her awareness to sense the threads, how the power flowed along them, how the Masters shaped that power into their creations. But the demonstration that brought Eadha the greatest longing of all came at the end of their first week, when Master Ruadh, one of the Master Tellers, wove for them the story of the final battle between the first Channeller, Erisen, and the dragon Kaanesien, said to be the mightiest dragon ever to have lived. It was the last great battle between Channellers and dragons before they retreated west to their colonies on the islands off Westport. As the apprentices sat in front of him, using only his hands Ruadh shaped a great golden dragon in the air above their heads.

'The dragons are our greatest menace, a nightmare come

screaming to life. Yet for as long as there have been dragons there have been Channellers, the only ones capable of standing between the people of Domhain and fiery destruction.'

But as Eadha craned her neck to stare up at Ruadh's creation, all she could think of was the dragon rearing up before her by the lake in the mountains. How beautiful it had been, and how her newborn power had leapt inside her in joyous recognition.

Even in the midst of all the wonders on display, Eadha still kept a hold of her true purpose. Here, she thought, at the start of each Master's demonstration. As they all crowded around the Master, she'd surely be able to slip behind Ionain, even just for a minute. But once again, Fiachna was watching.

'Keeper Eadha. Step back,' she would hiss each time she tried to sidle alongside Ionain, her hard hand landing on Eadha's shoulder and yanking her back.

The third time it happened was during a demonstration from Master Con, the most gifted of all the Master Growers, in a sun-dappled greenhouse at the southern end of First House. He was an older man, white-haired and slightly stooped, yet Eadha could feel how readily power still flowed into him. As the apprentices clustered around him, he spread his fingers wide over a pot packed with earth. Closing her eyes Eadha sensed the soft pulse as Con sent power snaking into the soil, the tickle of the seeds' answering start as they heeded the call to live, sending out their tiny shoots, drinking in the life Con was pouring into them so they shot upwards, pushing aside the soil, their tendrils wavering in the air, blindly seeking Con's fingers, following them, up, up, twisting around his fingertips, as leaf after leaf fell open like a skirt falling to reveal the tiniest, roundest tomatoes shining on the stems.

'So, life begets life,' murmured Master Con as he lifted the tomatoes away from the stem and passed them round the class to taste. As the tomato burst on Eadha's tongue it tasted of summer, of colour, of magic. She remembered the afternoon last winter when she'd made the grain sprout with the power nestled in the palm of her hand, and inside her buried gift twisted in longing, sharp like a needle pressed into her side. But then with a mental shake she reminded herself of why she was there. With the other apprentices distracted and murmuring to each other, this was her chance. She began to sidle unobtrusively closer to where Ionain was standing with Senan and Coll. She'd almost reached him, too, when Fiachna hissed at her once more, forcing her to drop back. This time, as she did, Ionain glanced around at her, and in his eyes for the first time she saw a mix of irritation and embarrassment.

Eadha flushed hotly as Ailbhe and her friends sniggered, and in front of her Coll and Senan nudged Ionain knowingly. Though he was facing away from her, she could see the back of his neck, which had gone bright red. Of course he didn't understand why she needed so badly to be beside him. All he could see was her embarrassing him in front of his new friends.

Standing there Eadha wanted to scream with frustration, and underneath that was a growing fear. Because she was beginning to realise that what she'd thought would be the simplest thing of all, to stand for a moment beside her best friend in all the world, had become something almost impossible. But if she couldn't find a way to do it, then the moment channelling began, Ionain would be exposed.

After Master Con's demonstration had ended, the Keepers stood in a line, heads bowed, to allow the Channellers to leave the greenhouse first. Peering up at him as he passed, Eadha saw how Ionain didn't even glance her way, his jaw still set in annoyance.

'I wouldn't blame him, you know. He's under a lot of pressure, trying to restore his Family after a dry generation. He needs everything to go perfectly. And this place changes people.'

It was Gry. He'd dropped back to the end of the line of Keeper novices to walk out with her, commiseration in his voice.

Stung, Eadha answered, 'Not Ionain.'

Gry snorted.

'Even Ionain. That's what this place is for; to change people, make them into good little Lord Channellers. If they don't change, then Lambay is failing. And it never fails.'

Eadha said nothing, only hurrying on ahead to her dorm room to get changed for Vespers. As she pulled on her robe, she pushed down the gnawing fear. So the Code meant she couldn't get close to Ionain during the day. There was still the evening time, the short window after Vespers, before lights out, when they were free. And Ionain was a Channeller apprentice, not bound by the Code the way she was. She wasn't allowed to go visit him, but he could come and go as he pleased, and from the very first, many of the Channeller boys had used that privilege to come visiting the Keeper girls before lights out.

Some, like Senan, were only interested in using their visits to flex their new status as Channellers, turning up unannounced at bedtime for what he called 'inspections', so that Eadha, Ailbhe and the other girls in their dorm, Siofra, Muir and Cara, had to drag themselves back out of bed and stand at attention, their heads bowed, as Senan sauntered up and down the line, peering at each in turn while they stood there, legs shaking with tiredness. Standing at the end of the line, Eadha's power, blocked away behind her thought-wall and unused since the day she'd arrived on Lambay, would begin to churn inside her. She had to fight to keep it down as Senan's flushed, excited face loomed over her.

'Common,' he called her, because she was a commoner, the only one in her dorm not from a Great Family.

162

'Common,' he would say to her as she stared straight ahead, not meeting his eyes.

'You look tired this evening, Common. Training not going well? Breeding will tell, you know. The lower orders just don't have the stamina, my father always says. What do you think?'

'I don't know,' she would reply.

'I don't know what?' he'd say then, satisfaction creeping into his voice at catching her out.

'I don't know, my lord,' she would correct herself then, her voice carefully toneless, though inside her power was raging, longing to strike out at him. 'I am sorry, my lord.'

Other Channeller apprentices were more low-key, calling to ask out particular girls and going walking with them in the dusk. Gry hadn't been joking when he'd called First Island a Family mating zoo. Couples were quickly forming. It was all the girls in Eadha's dorm ever seemed to talk about. Who was seeing who, which were the most likely pairings.

Ionain, though, was one of the few Channeller apprentices who didn't come at all. Not once during Purification did he come to visit her. For the first few weeks, as she watched other apprentices appear night after night, she told herself he was exhausted. Or it was as Gry had said. He was focused on his training, determined to wipe out his Family's shame. But he didn't look exhausted, in lessons, or as he tumbled past her each day in the pack of Channeller boys brimful of excitement and entitlement, while she and the other Keepers stood aside for them, their heads dutifully bowed. He didn't look exhausted at all.

CHAPTER 18
IMMOLATION

By the sea the transition from spring to summer was almost imperceptible. On Lambay, as the days stretched towards midsummer, the view from the windows of First House was unchanged, the sea just a little calmer, the grass a little greener.

Within First House Eadha's days had settled into a seemingly endless rhythm of training, demonstrations and study; of Ionain hidden beyond her reach in his quarters or striding past her, his blond head just visible in the crowd of Channeller boys.

And every day they were marinated in power, stewed in it. Their days spent training for it, watching the Masters use it, and all the while prevented from touching it themselves. Eadha could feel the pressure building; not just inside herself but in all of them as day by day they watched yet another Master's display of wonders and still they were forbidden from using their own gifts. Pent-up, unused, it churned and churned inside her until she felt it had begun to curdle, that soon it would burn its way out of her whether she willed it or not.

It bled into her dreams, so that night after night she dreamt of power; of repairing the Keep to the cheers of Lord and Lady Ailm, of growing whole fields of golden corn, of weaving beautiful illusions just as Ruadh, the Master Teller did. She knew she shouldn't dream such dreams. That long ago and far away, someone had told her channelling Fodder was wrong and she'd made them a promise. But in her dreams, just as on First Island, there were no Fodder, only the wonders channelled by the Masters, and every morning the ache deepened as she dragged herself away from the sweetness of her dreams, back into the chilly reality of being nothing but a Keeper novice on a hard bench bowing to Channeller apprentices and every day it grew harder and harder to remember why.

'Apprentices. These last months you have purified yourselves, rendering your bodies vessels worthy of holding power. I am pleased to say your Purification is now almost complete. Seven days from now, at the full of the moon, you will begin your training in the uses of power.'

A thrill ran through the assembled apprentices at Master Dathin's announcement, just as they rose for the final Matins chant on a sunny morning in late summer.

Eadha, standing there anonymous beneath her hood, knew this was the moment she should panic. But standing there she felt only a kind of numb acceptance. It was as if the tendrils of molash smoke she breathed in every morning at Matins had built and built up inside her mind until they'd clouded it to everything but power. Ionain, soft Ionain with his tawny hair and his gentle smile had faded away into the gloom, lost to her like a prince in a story hidden high above and far away in a glass tower guarded by spells and enchantments. And her own strange new gift, where she'd sent her powers out of herself into Ionain at his Reckoning, had been nothing but a mirage. That was not power, the Masters told them, over and over, with every superhuman display. For power was something taken, something used, to make the user powerful beyond imagining.

So, she'd failed then. In seven days the Masters would ask Ionain to use his gift and he would have nothing. Maybe it was for the best. After all, he was powerless. An empty vessel. Wasn't that what she'd been taught? That all that mattered was power; the shining hard certainty of it, the churning longing to finally release all that pent-up strength in one fiery blaze of immolation.

'Playtime's over,' muttered someone behind Eadha as she walked through the cloisters after Master Dathin's announcement. The next moment she stumbled forward as Ailbhe and her friends pushed past her, an elbow catching her squarely between the shoulder blades.

'It is not known when dragons first came into being, but Channellers have been fighting to hold them back to the islands off Westport since the days of the Four Brothers.'

It was later the same day, and the Master Librarian was teaching them Dragon Lore in the Library.

Next spring, on Second Island, they'd be trained in dragon combat. Here the Librarian was teaching them the dragon's anatomy. On a wide table he unrolled sheets with drawings of dragons in flight, in battle, their mailed bodies lying on the desolate sandy shores of western Domhain, the leathery wings pierced by Channeller fire, scales torn from their bodies.

'The dragon remains the single greatest enigma of life on Domhain,' began the Master Librarian. Of all the Masters, he was the one who used his gift the least, unless you counted flying up to fetch books from high shelves. Yet on First Island everyone knew the Librarian ranked only after Dathin and Fionan in seniority. At first Eadha had wondered at this, in a place that rated power above all else. But then she thought of the years Ionain had spent being taught the historic might of ancient Channellers and she realised it was because the Masters had always understood that owning the story of their power was as important as the power itself.

That afternoon, as they gathered around the table, Channellers in front and Keepers behind, Ionain ended up standing directly in front of her.

Eadha stared at his back, so close in front of her. She knew she should take her chance, the chance she'd been looking for since their very first day. But what, after all, she thought then, dully, was the point? This was only one class. It wouldn't prove anything. She needed to be able to get close to Ionain every single day, and she knew by now that was impossible. So she stood there, staring blankly, and didn't move.

The Librarian was still talking.

'The dragon's body may grow anywhere from fifty to a hundred feet in length, covered in scales hard as the finest chainmail, the wingspan stretching the length of the Library roof above your heads. Razor claws the size of a man's arm, teeth of unbreakable ivory set in jaws in which two people could easily stand. In truth, there is no way a creature of such enormous weight and size should be able to take to the air.'

And yet they do, thought Eadha, picturing dragons like the one she'd seen above the mountain lake, swooping on the sea winds, folding their wings to plummet straight as arrows shot from the blue sky towards the Channeller ships that put out from Westport towards their colonies. In all the battles, no Channeller had ever come close to understanding the source of a dragon's power. They were fiercely loyal even in death, preferring to immolate their fallen, gathering above a battlefield to create a flaming pyre of the body and the sands around it. From such funeral pyres came dragonglass, the enormous heat fusing the sand into a smooth, thick glass so prized by Channellers for their Keeps.

Afterwards, as they filed out of the Library, Eadha felt the fog inside her lift a little. To be reminded there was a world beyond this closed universe of Channellers, that the dragons were flying far above them all on the world's winds, with a power beyond the Masters' understanding. Her mind going to her own gift hidden away unused behind her thought-wall, she thought to herself, that was a thing worth knowing.

The Librarian had dismissed them early, leaving them with a rare free hour before Vespers. As she turned towards her dorm a familiar voice spoke behind her.

'Hey there, you haven't been over to my rooms yet.'

It was Ionain, standing there, just himself, grinning at her. It was, she realised, the first time she'd been on her own with him since their first day on the island. Since then, she'd only ever seen him in the ref or in class, or else going about with Coll, Senan or the other Channeller apprentices. Automatically she began to straighten to attention, bowing her head as the Code demanded. He waved her to stop, a pained look in his eyes.

'Don't, Eadha, not to me, not when we're alone. Will you come?'

With a suddenly singing heart she nodded, following him to his rooms at the western end of the Channellers' quad. She hadn't been there since the day they arrived and Fiachna had caught her peering in. It was as luxurious and richly furnished as she remembered. As they came in, a cheery fire was burning. They sat down on thick velvet cushions scattered in front of it.

Seeing him up close for the first time in months Eadha realised Ionain had changed, his face leaner and harder, tanned by the long days outdoors. There was less of the cub about him now. He'd grown as tall as Eadha finally, their eyes level as they sat. For the first time in her life, Eadha realised, she was not looking down at him, he not looking up at her. A kind of grief shot through her, as the loneliness of the last few months hit her.

Something must have shown in her eyes then, because Ionain reached across and touched her hand.

'Eadha, I'm sorry. I know it's harder for you here. I wanted to come see you in your dorm, I did. I just thought after that first day in handball with Ailbhe it would...' He stopped himself and glanced around the room, with its silver decanters and cut glass, the thick rugs scattered across the polished floor.

'You know, I still can't believe I'm really here. I feel like a fraud most of the time,' he said then. She looked at him.

'You don't seem like a fraud. Whenever I see you, you look like you were born to be here.' Ionain frowned then, pulling his hand back and turning to face her more directly.

'You know what's at stake here, don't you? My Family was so close to losing everything.'

'I know...'

'No, you don't know. Everything depends on me succeeding here.'

He took a deep breath then and looked across at her.

'Look, don't take this the wrong way, Eadha, but you need to try harder.'

That hurt. She stared, stunned and fighting the urge to scream at him, 'Don't you know how hard I am trying? Every single day since we got here, I've been trying to find a way to get close enough to share my gift with you, so you won't be found out as a fraud. But you're so caught up with trying to be the perfect Channeller apprentice, you're making it impossible for the one person you actually, truly need, to get anywhere near you.'

She said nothing, however, biting it all back, though she couldn't stop her eyes from filling with unbidden tears.

Seeing them, Ionain scrambled up so he was crouching beside her, reaching out his hand to push her hair out of her face.

'Hey there, no, I'm sorry, I didn't mean...' He closed his eyes for a minute and then opened them again.

'All of this. The Code and the bowing, people pairing off together, it's all just a game. None of it is real for us. But it's a game we have to play. That's all I meant. You need to try harder, to play the game. Fit in, don't draw attention to yourself. Maybe don't glare quite so hard at Senan when he does those daft inspections.

The way Mother always explained it to me is you have to become a mirror. You mirror back to people like Ailbhe and Senan what they expect to see. Someone like them, so they don't see what's really there and then they leave us alone. So I have to be the loyal son, be friends with the right people, make the right... alliances. But Eadha, that's all it is: a game. A treasure hunt, where we've come to steal the treasure and bring it home safely, so no one can ever threaten the Keep again.

Another year of this, a few dragons and we'll be home again. It doesn't touch us, you and me. We're what's real. All this silliness, the robes and the bowing, it'll all be forgotten, nothing but funny stories to tell Sepp and Beithe and everyone.'

And just like that everything made sense once more. The choices she'd made, the reason she was here with her true powers hidden deep inside, ready to be gifted to the boy sitting in front of her. She let out a great, shuddering breath, that turned into a laugh, her first real laugh since the day they'd crossed the land-bridge together onto Lambay.

'When did you get so wise?' she said then, poking his knee so he almost unbalanced from his crouch.

'Oh, I've always been wise. You were just too busy bossing me around to notice,' he said, embarrassed, and as she grinned back at him his words about mirroring clicked softly into place in her mind, and she saw at last how she'd be able to share her gift with him.

She scrambled to her feet, her heart pounding.

'I have to go. There's something I need to do before Vespers,' she said, her grin broadening as he stared up at her, bewildered at the sudden change in her.

'It's going to make everything alright. You've made everything alright,' she added, crouching back down and hugging him with all her strength, before hurrying out the door.

Down the halls she ran, back to the Keepers' quad, taking the stairs two at a time.

All this time she'd been focused on how to get close enough to Ionain to send power to him unseen. But his gentle words about mirroring had changed everything. They'd spent weeks watching the Master Teller weave the most fantastical illusions: dragons, castles, battles in the air above their heads. But what if she used that power to create something far simpler? Something that couldn't be seen, but that would hide her power behind it?

A mirror. If she could hide the thread of her power behind a mirror illusion, then she wouldn't need to be beside Ionain at all. She could send it to him over any distance without anyone ever seeing it.

An unfamiliar quiet hung over her dormitory, broken only by the hiss of a dying hearth-fire. The other girls must have already left for Vespers. She pulled Magret's book out from beneath her clothes where she'd hidden it the very first day she'd arrived on Lambay. The pages glowed up like a shout in the silent room with its dark wooden floorboards, its white walls and even whiter busts of bygone Keepers in alcoves between the beds. She began turning the pages, searching for a half-remembered drawing of a Channeller weaving a mirror illusion to reflect the beautiful face of his lover.

She was concentrating so hard she didn't hear the door behind her open, didn't feel the quiet footsteps across the floorboards, didn't sense the eyes over her shoulder. The first she knew was a hand, too quick for her to catch, snatching Magret's book from her grasp and swinging it above her head out of reach, a child's game played with deadly intent. She whipped around to Ailbhe's face, inches away from her own.

'Now, now. Think carefully, Keeper Eadha, before you do anything rash.'

Ailbhe's face was calm yet powerfully pleased.

'Please, give it back.'

Stepping back and out of reach Ailbhe glanced down at the page.

'It looks quite like instructions for the use of power. How would someone like you come by something like this? Stolen perhaps, on your special little visit to Ionain's rooms?'

She smiled at Eadha, but her mouth was stretched, like a snarl.

'This needs to be reported to Head Keeper Fiachna.'

She turned on her heel, sauntering towards the door, tapping the book against her thigh.

'I drew them,' Eadha blurted out. 'The images. I dreamt them and painted them. I was thinking of bringing them to the Head Keeper myself. My gift, it's strong, I think, my lady.'

Ailbhe paused at the door, stayed standing with her back to Eadha for a moment before turning and walking to the fireplace. She propped the book on the mantel then picked up a poker and stoked the fire, tossing on a log as the flames stirred back to life. As she crouched there, her shining hair a halo of reflected firelight, she turned to look up at Eadha.

'What would you know of gifts? Or strength? What are you, after all? Some wild child raised hundreds of miles from the nearest Channeller. What could you possibly know of our power, our legacy?'

She stood and pointed to a marble bust behind Eadha's head.

'Do you know who that is?'

Half-bewildered by the abrupt change of direction, Eadha shook her head mutely, her eyes locked onto Ailbhe's. Even in her terror she could feel the pent-up power radiating from Ailbhe as she stood there. A question half-formed in her mind—how could this girl only be a Keeper, with that much power inside her? But there was no time for such thoughts. Ailbhe was still speaking.

'My great-grandmother. First-ranked Keeper of her year, one hundred years ago. And over there, by your bed, my great-aunt. Head Keeper on Second Island for twenty years. But you? What are you? A freak, a gamble no one is willing to take. A Fodder wagon Keeper riding west to an early death in a dragon's breath.'

As the elegant girl with her elegant words like knives sliced away at her, in the deep heart's core Eadha's own power, so long buried, uncoiled now, stung to angry life. Filling her so she had to rise up on the balls of her feet, flexing her fingers to hold it in. Ailbhe turned back to the mantel.

'So, little freak. It's not enough for you to be allowed here on this sacred island. You think you can win through to be the next Lady Ailm, is that it? You know, I almost envy you your mediocrity. The freedom of it. Do you know how long I've been perfect? Since I knew there was a perfect to be, I've been perfect. The perfect hair, the perfect manners, the perfect smile,' and just for a second Ailbhe's voice wavered, before she checked herself and went on, her voice hardening again. 'Can you even begin to understand what it means? To set the bar so high that now for all my life anything less than perfection will be accounted failure?'

Staring at Eadha she tossed Magret's little bound book onto the flames.

'No!' screamed Eadha. Ailbhe looked at her, unmoved.

'Consider it a warning. You do not get to take what is mine. Understand? Now do hurry or you'll be late for Vespers.'

In a moment she was gone. Eadha skidded over to the fire where the book's pages were melting and twisting as the flames climbed around them. From inside her, her power flowed down into her hands, so she could reach in and lift out the charred remains. With a flick she killed the flames and the room filled with the acrid stink of smoke, melted ink and burnt paper. The front and back of the book had burned away, the pages inside eaten by the fire, so the once glowing colours were run and charred to brown and black, the pages buckled and jagged.

Cradled in her hands she huddled over the small burnt thing, grief and rage fighting within her. Grief for the desecration of that perfect, joyous thing, for the loss of her one link to a world beyond this place that had no place for her. Rage at the girl who thought she could order her away from the person she loved most in all the world. It was no contest. Her anger, after all, had been building for months, since the day she'd arrived on Lambay and they'd sent her to sit on a wooden bench, stoked by all the petty humiliations, the nicknames, the bowing, the denial of her; her power, her gift, her dignity. Rage won, a blackness rising all through her until it blinded her to everything but the pretty, dark-haired girl hurrying across the lawn to Vespers.

Rising to her feet she ran to the open window, her power surging inside her as she did, so that without breaking her stride she leapt out through it and landed lightly on the ground two storeys below. Ailbhe was just disappearing through the entrance to the cloisters at the far end of the Keepers' quad. Her own power wasn't enough to reach Ailbhe from here; she needed more. Without even needing to think she reached out as she'd seen the Masters reach out, day after day, the silver thread of her power snaking out instinctively to find and draw into her the life-force of the Fodder hidden far beneath her feet. She would show Ailbhe who was mediocre, who was nothing. Around her the world whited out as a tsunami of Fodder life-force poured into her. This was more like it. She would show them all.

She took a deep breath, concentrating her power around her hands, feeling them begin to glow as she called up a fiery bolt the way she'd watched the Master Combat do. She only had seconds before Ailbhe disappeared into the temple, but that was all she needed.

She drew her arm back, ready to send her power bulleting through the air after the disappearing girl. But the next second she went crashing to the ground, as someone caught her around the waist and knocked her over. She went sprawling, the bolt scorching through the grass and spending itself uselessly in the ground. Twisting her head around she found herself staring up at Gry. He'd half-fallen across her, using his weight to pin her down. With a grimace he stood, then reached out a hand to pull her up. Glancing round she saw Ailbhe was gone. Gry was already stepping away. As he did, he looked back over his shoulder towards her.

'Come on. There's something I think you need to see.'

Eadha's rage was already subsiding. She felt hollow, as if a chasm had opened up inside her and she was standing on its edge, staring down at what she'd almost unleashed. She began shaking uncontrollably, her body shuddering with the power she'd drawn and not used. She didn't resist when Gry took her by the hand, leading her out of the quadrangle through the archway that faced out to sea.

The evening had the still brightness of late summer, only the faintest hint of dusk around the edges. There was no one else around, all were in the temple. They passed the stone jetty on the shore directly in front of the House, where visitors from Second Island docked, climbing the hill to the right of the handball alley and ducking in under the treeline. Here the trees grew right up to the water's edge, a dense undergrowth crowded around their trunks. Eadha had never come this way before. Gry pushed ahead, bending the branches so they could pass. After a little while the land ended, the ground dropping away beneath them into a narrow ledge of shingle, the stones clacking as the sea rolled over them, like a gambler rolling dice in his hands.

They were looking across a narrow inlet at a shallow cove beneath a headland. A ship was moored just offshore, its rowboat beached on the shore. Armed guardsmen were helping those on board to climb out. They moved awkwardly, half-falling out. After a moment Eadha realised it was because their hands and feet were chained; as she watched, one woman stumbled and fell on her knees in the water—in climbing over the gunwale, she'd tried to stretch her chained leg too far and toppled over. A guard jerked her back to her feet. There were about ten or twelve of these chained people, all dressed in worn, shabby clothes, their hair lank around their faces. They moved slowly, as if exhausted. A woman dressed in a Keeper's robe appeared from inside the cove and gestured them towards her. A guard handed over a rolled-up sheet of paper. Moments later the people had disappeared into the back of the cove, the guards were rowing back out to the ship and the beach was empty.

Gry whispered to Eadha, 'My aunt Hera was a Keeper novice here thirty years ago. She told me about this cove. There's a whole network of underground passageways, caves and shafts beneath the island so that Fodder can be brought in by boat here and held underneath the House to be used for power without ever being seen. The Masters have been doing this a long time; they've engineered the system to make it nigh on impossible to see what's really happening.'

Eadha said nothing, but her eyes filled with tears of shame. She'd done it again, what she'd sworn to Magret she would never do. She felt sick, the stolen power heavy like a stone inside her.

'We should get back,' Gry was whispering. 'It isn't a good idea to be caught near here.' They made for a small beech coppice in front of First House. Heads ducking under the branches they slipped beneath its cover and sat down on a fallen tree trunk. Through the leaves they could see the lights twinkling out on Second Island as night began to roll in.

'I made a promise,' said Eadha after a little while. 'Not to channel people again. But all it took was one Great Family girl sneering at me and I broke it, just like that. Drawing power without even thinking about what I was doing to those people beneath me.'

Gry was silent for a few moments before replying, 'These first few months here, all the training, the pampering for the Channeller apprentices, the speeches about them being an elite. It's all a bit of a conjuring trick. You know that bit where the conjuror keeps you busy, looking at his right hand waving, while the left hand is busy popping the flowers into the hat? The apprentices don't need all this preparation to be able to use power. They just use it, channel the Fodder.'

Eadha bowed her head at the truth of that, remembering how easily she'd done it at home in the Keep.

'But do you think if, on our first day here on Lambay, they lined up people in front of the Channeller apprentices and said off you go, channel the life-force out of them, they would do it? Some would, like Senan. There will always be the ones who enjoy hurting other people. But the rest, no. They have to be seduced, brought along step by careful step from the moment they pass their Reckoning. You're unique. You're gifted, part of an elite, with everyone from Keeper down bowing to you at every turn.

And oh look, see the wonders of channelling, what it can do; the golden crops, the majestic buildings. And oh yes, this is how it must be, because before channelling men lived in hovels and starved, because otherwise the dragons will come and burn us all in our beds. Surrounding them in a web of imperatives, while all the while the one irrefutable truth about channelling, the people being drained for all this wealth and power, are hidden away out of sight, underground, never seen or heard.'

Gry paused, then went on, 'What they're doing here, they call it purification, but it isn't. It's seduction. Seducing decent people into believing they're so special it's their right to drain Fodder. They deserve to drain other people's life-force because they spent a few weeks going on early morning runs and learning how to grow tomatoes. It's why I'm grateful every day I'm only a Keeper.

And us Keepers with our bare dorms and our plain wooden benches, our desperation to marry the strongest Channeller? Half our purpose here is to make them feel just how very special they are, a handy onsite reminder of their status as the elite. And as they get more and more used to being fought over by pretty girls, to their special apartments and their servants, their cushioned seats and being first in line for everything, they will cling for dear life to the one thing that buys them entry to that world, the only thing that separates them from us, their ability to channel.'

He looked directly at Eadha then and shrugged.

'So, don't be too hard on yourself. This place has been seducing gifted kids for four hundred years. Did you think you'd be immune?'

'How did you know?'

'I sensed it, that first day at Matins. Nothing since then, though, you've hidden it well. You'd know, anyway; the Masters would be down on you in a heartbeat if they knew you were hiding a Channeller gift.'

She hesitated then. Should she tell him? That she was hiding more than a Channeller's gift, that she could draw power not just from others but from herself, too? But, she realised, she couldn't do it. Even as Gry sat there with his kind, open face, breaking the Masters' spell, making sense of it all. The habit of secrecy was too strong in her. She'd been hiding too long and too well and it was, after all, not her secret to tell, not if she was to protect Ionain. So she said nothing, just listened silently as Gry went on.

'But you need to understand, this is only the beginning. When channelling proper starts next week the stakes are going to get higher. The choices we make, they get starker. And the walls you build, they need to be higher.'

He let his words hang for a moment then smiled ruefully.

'I sound more like my old nana every day. Soon I'll be walking the halls ringing a bell shouting, "here be dragons." But, Eadha, you've been lucky twice now. Today was your second escape. I doubt you'll get another.'

CHAPTER 19
HARVEST

That night, her back still smarting from Fiachna's lashes for missing Vespers, Eadha waited until Ailbhe and the other girls had fallen asleep then slipped out of her dorm, through the Keepers' quad and up into the forest behind First House. Tucked inside her tunic were the remains of Magret's book. Though the outer pages were badly burned, she could still make out the drawing she'd been looking for when Ailbhe caught her.

In it, the Channeller had used their power to create a mirror that hung in the air, reflecting their lover's face back to them. Her plan was to use the same mirror illusion to hide the silver thread of her power. Swiftly climbing the same forest track they ran every morning in training, she made her way to the ruins of a summer pavilion at the western end of the island. The whole forest was dotted with ruins like it, fantastical buildings summoned from the earth by long-ago apprentices practising their art, then left to crumble back into the forest. After setting a couple of were-lights on the ground, she stepped into the centre of the cracked and broken floor, bowed her head and summoned up a silver thread of power. Reaching out her hand she sent the thread into a marble pillar that lay covered in ivy on the ground. Long and slender the thread stretched, no wider than her little finger, but clearly visible to anyone with eyes for power.

Then, with her other hand she began to weave a mirror around the thread, copying the gestures in Magret's book. As the mirror covered the thread like an invisible sheath, it gradually disappeared from view. If a watcher came into the pavilion now, all they would see was the light from the were-lights, reflecting on the narrow mirror sheath that completely covered the line of her power. There was no trace of her silver thread; it was completely hidden from the sight of any Channeller or Keeper.

She had seven nights to be ready to share her gift invisibly with Ionain, sending it down the silver thread. Each one of those nights she slipped out into the forest, staying out 'til dawn practising, until she was sure she could do it perfectly, the sheath hiding her power from the moment it sprang from her hand and arrowed towards its target. As she sent power out of herself, night after night, into it she poured all the repressed loneliness and frustration of the last few months, so that night by night it grew. No longer a tiny, newborn thing but grown tremendous, fierce and sure.

And in returning to her powers, she remembered herself. Took back from Ailbhe, Senan and the Masters the right to have the last word in who she was. Found, as she pulled her power from belly to heart and out, that the months of training and meditation had made her stronger, faster. That the tiny were-light she'd first made the night of Ionain's Reckoning had been growing all the while inside her, into a steady fire that would warm her if she let it.

Once more she could fly. Drawing only on her own heart's strength she'd never be able to fly as fast or as high as someone channelling strength out of many Fodder, but it was enough, to be able to rise unseen among the trees, weave between the branches, feel the whisper of pine needles against her face as she dove through the canopy reborn.

Up all night practising, exhausted by the time Matins came around, she would pull her cowl about her head and half-doze through meditation, but she struggled to find her normal fluency in training, her arms and legs trembling with tiredness. Ailbhe and her cronies were quick to spot her new shakiness. She took so many 'accidental' blows to the head from them in handball she ended up being suspended from handball training for several weeks and sent to the Library to catalogue accounts of dragon patrols. Yet despite that she was happier than she'd been since she'd arrived on First Island. In going back to her power, she'd recovered a part of herself that'd been shut down. She felt stronger, more able to endure the daily humiliations, Ailbhe and Senan's bullying, now she knew no matter what they did, the steady flame of her power burned on inside her, invisible to them all.

With channelling proper about to start, the Masters eased back on lessons and the apprentices had a little more freedom in the afternoons. In those quiet hours she would slip away to the beech coppice in front of First House where she and Gry had talked, to practice, or sleep or just sit staring out to sea. On the last evening before channelling began, as she sat with her back against a tree trunk at the copse edge, she heard feet moving softly behind her. It was Ionain. He sat down beside her, nudging her over to make room.

After a few moments' silence he said, 'I can't believe it's actually going to start tomorrow, finally. I don't feel any different. Senan and the twins talk about being able to see threads when they inhale the molash at Matins, but all I can see is a sort of shimmer in the air.'

'I wouldn't worry, half of what Senan says is bravado,' Eadha replied, her mind automatically going to her gift, reassuring herself it was there, ready to be given to him. Even as she did, she felt an

183

involuntary twinge of pity for Ionain; to not be able to see or sense the silver threads that joined them all, that for her now formed a part of the colour of the world.

The summer evening rolled out before them, hours to go before darkness fell. Wordlessly Ionain held out a hand to her and they locked their fingers together, Ionain's hand dry and warm in hers.

More quietly he went on, 'Linn told me Ailbhe's been bragging about putting manners on you. I wish you'd told me.'

Eadha's mouth turned down as she fought to keep her voice steady, trying not to picture Ailbhe's face as she threw Magret's book on the fire.

'It's fine. I'm fine. Ailbhe doesn't scare me.'

'What did she do?'

'She... she sent me a warning.' She glanced across at Ionain then, and though she tried, she couldn't keep the question out of her voice as she went on, 'She seems to think she has a claim on you.'

Ionain was shaking his head in frustration.

'I'm so sorry. It's just our Families—all the Great Families—they get a bit crazy about this stuff, and Ailbhe thinks...' he stopped himself then before going on, 'But Eadha, listen, it's only them. It's not me.'

'She seemed very sure, though. That she was going to get what she wanted. In the end.'

'Stop it, Eadha. That isn't fair. Not when we both know who we've always been for each other. How could I even see someone else that way...'

Ionain's face was twisted into a mix of hurt and frustration as he turned to face her directly. But the months of loneliness and isolation on Lambay had cut too deep; she needed more than this if she was to hold on, and so she said, 'No, Ionain, I don't know, not anymore.'

Ionain dropped his head then and was silent for a moment. When he looked up at her again the look in his eyes was almost angry, his voice rough with the words she was forcing out of him.

'You have to know. My whole life...' he paused before going on, 'the shape of love in my heart is you. So how could I ever?' And then they were kissing, soft at first and then fierce with all the pent-up longing strung out between them ever since they'd first kissed each other high on the fell above Ailm's Keep.

Behind them the temple bells began to peal, summoning them to Vespers, breaking them apart. They stared at each other, their faces flushed and for a moment they seemed almost like enemies, as the enormity of the promises they'd made to each other hit them both.

'I'd better go,' said Ionain then, climbing to his feet.

Eadha nodded, though she didn't move. But as he slipped out of the coppice she called after him, 'Good luck tomorrow. I know you'll show them all.'

That night after Vespers, Eadha stayed out practising the whole night, only returning to her dorm just before the bells for Matins sounded. Though she hadn't slept she was keyed up, her power surging inside her, barely hidden by her thought-wall, ready to flash across to Ionain the moment he needed it. But as she walked into the temple, when she looked across to Ionain's usual spot she saw he was pale and upset. Around him, the Channellers were whispering among themselves, having to be silenced by Master Dathin when he rose to address them all.

'In keeping with tradition, the first trial of the Channeller apprentices occurred before dawn this morning. I am pleased to say that all bar two of this year's students proved more than adequately receptive. I have posted the rankings outside the temple. These will be posted weekly until the spring trials. Keepers, your assessment will take place before Matins tomorrow morning.'

After Matins the apprentices crowded around the rankings, looking for their names. Senan's name was at the top, followed by

Coll and Linn.

Ionain's was one of the two listed at the foot of the page as unranked.

As Eadha stared at the ranking sheet she heard Senan mutter, 'So much for the great flare of power at his Reckoning. I always knew it was too good to be true. That Ailm bloodline is tapped out. It's embarrassing really, how they're trying to cling on to the Keep. I wonder if he'll be sent home.'

As Eadha turned around, she saw Ailbhe's normally composed face was stricken, while her friends hovered uncertainly. There was no sign of Ionain. He'd left straight after temple, pushing ahead of the other Channeller apprentices and disappearing in the direction of the main cloister.

The other apprentices soon dispersed to their quarters, and Eadha was left standing alone by the board, filled with a mix of fury with herself and a rising sense of panic. She'd been so focused on working out how to share her powers with Ionain, she'd forgotten to do the most basic thing: find out exactly when his test would take place. When Master Dathin announced the testing of the apprentices she'd assumed it would be in class, not in some pre-dawn visit to their rooms. How could she have been so stupid? Surely the very first lesson she'd learned on this benighted island was that she knew nothing about the place, to assume nothing. Now all her planning and training had come to nothing through simple carelessness. Ionain had failed his test.

She needed to find Ionain, find out what would happen to him next. Was he going to be sent home? Could he ask the Masters to retest him? Even as the thought gripped her, she was moving, her steps quickening as she hurried out of the temple in the direction she'd seen him take. He was probably going to his quarters to get away from the other apprentices gossiping about his shocking failure. But when she peered anxiously through the archway that led to the Channellers' quad, she saw Coll talking to a manservant at Ionain's door.

He was shaking his head as he answered Coll's query, 'No, sir. I am sorry. Master Ionain has not been here since before Matins.'

All that morning she scoured First House and its many outbuildings, even climbing up onto the roof, sure she'd sense his silver thread if she came close to him. Finding no trace she widened her search, down to the coppice where they'd met the night before, then on up into the forest behind the House. But no one could hide like Ionain when he didn't want to be found. It was almost dark when she finally returned to her dorm. Having found no trace of him all day, as she climbed the stairs she felt desolate, just about convinced the Masters must have already shipped him off the island.

As she came into the room, Ailbhe and two of the other girls were talking. Ailbhe looked as distraught as Eadha felt. She felt an unfamiliar twinge of fellow feeling, at each of them in their own way as tied up in Ionain's destiny as the other.

Siofra was sitting beside Ailbhe on the bed, her arm across her shoulder saying, 'It really is awfully bad luck, for you to have a second one fail their Channeller test. At least Gry has some power.'

'Go easy, Siofra,' interrupted Cara then. 'You know it isn't definite yet. He'll be retested before they make any final decision.'

'When?' Eadha blurted out. The three girls stared at her. Eadha never spoke directly to them, or they to her. Eadha reddened under their surprised gazes but repeated her question.

'When will they retest him?' For a moment, she saw how they thought about not answering but then Siofra relented, with a small roll of her eyes.

'Not tonight. They're testing us just before dawn, so there isn't time to do a ceremony for him, too. But tomorrow night or soon after.

187

They won't wait long to find out for sure.'

'Thank you,' said Eadha then, though the girls were already turning away from her. She made for her bed, trying not to let on that she was barely able to stand, on legs suddenly shaky with relief and remembered exhaustion.

That night she slept in her bed for the first time in weeks. When Fiachna shook her awake in the pre-dawn darkness, a candle lantern in her hand, she quickly and easily identified the silver Fodder threads running from behind a screen at the back of the dormitory. After Matins her name stood at the head of the Keeper rankings, followed by Gry and Ailbhe, as the novice with the fastest and most accurate thread identification.

'Let the Keeper girls try to twist that,' she thought with some satisfaction, before slipping away to sleep in a nook in the Library, knowing there were sleepless nights ahead.

In the end it was three nights before the Masters tested Ionain again, three nights Eadha spent hidden on the cross-walk closest to Ionain's bedroom window, watching for the lanterns to come swinging through the quad. She was so exhausted she kept slipping in and out of sleep, jolting herself awake, terrified she'd missed them. Her vigil was finally rewarded when she saw a line of lanterns emerge from the other end of the walkway, passing close by her hiding place and entering Ionain's quarters.

Eadha concentrated, seeing Ionain's thread colour change and deepen as he awoke. With the skill born of those long nights in the forest, she pulled her powers from within herself, from belly to heart and out, and sent it flying invisibly through the air to pulse imperceptibly into Ionain. As it did, she felt an answering start. With her gift flowing through him she knew he would be able to see the silver Fodder threads the Masters wanted him to see.

Not long after the swaying line of lanterns passed her once

more. She pulled away then, knowing as she did, she'd left enough power with him that he would feel its pull for the rest of the day. As she fell into exhausted sleep, she remembered that first exhilarating race with the deer through the Keep forest last winter, and wondered what he would do with his first heady dream of a day.

Later, at Matins, she watched blearily as his familiar tawny head sat, proud and erect, taking his place among the Channeller rows. The news had gotten around, and she saw the quick pats on the back from Coll and Linn, the nod from Master Fionan as they rose to chant. In the classroom a new ranking sheet had been posted, with Ionain's name now in fourth place. They headed away out to handball practice. Still suspended, Eadha had to report to the Library, where the Master Librarian set her cataloguing old dragon reports.

Eager to be out and hear what Ionain might do with her power, the day dragged. Finally released she hurried to the beech copse. She was sure he would come again to find her, talk over the day, tell her all that'd happened. She sat, she paced, she climbed into the trees and practised her flying hidden among the branches, but he didn't come. She stayed so long that in the end she was almost late for Vespers, forced to use her last dregs of power to quickly fix the familiar mess Ailbhe had made of her bed in the dorm, before racing across a walkway and discreetly hurdling down onto the lawn in front of the temple doors, slipping inside just as they closed.

That night Ionain was all Ailbhe and her friends could talk about. He'd been so full of energy he'd beaten all comers at handball. Master Fionan himself had challenged him to a game where he'd almost bested the Master before he ran out of steam. Lying on her bed, listening to the giggles of the excited girls, Eadha felt a flash of annoyance that her life-force, given so unstintingly, should be spent so cheaply on training ground games and impressing Keeper girls. But then she closed her eyes and thought of that well-loved thread

shining in the night with relieved joy and went to sleep well content
with her day's work.

CHAPTER 20
THE PRICE

'I still remember the day I first channelled almost thirty years ago. I know today will be one you, too, will remember for the rest of your lives as the day you truly came into your power. May you dedicate yourselves to its mastery, to your glory and the glory of channelling now and always. Let the channelling begin!'

All the assembled Channeller apprentices gave a great cheer as Master Fionan finished speaking, smiling broadly as he surveyed the eager faces in front of him.

Fiachna stepped forward then, as dry and as stern as ever.

'Keepers. Today a number of you will have the honour of being personally assigned to a Lord Channeller, to support them in the drawing of power. I will call out the pairings. As you hear the name of the Channeller to whom you have been assigned, please take up your position beside them. Those of you not paired today will be rotated in and out with the paired Keepers, so be assured you will also gain direct experience in keeping, to the greater glory of channelling, now and always.'

'Keeper Gry; Lord Coll of the Family Manon.'

'Keeper Eadha; Lord Senan of the Family De Lane.'

'Keeper Ailbhe; Lord Ionain of the Ailm Family.'

In front of her Eadha saw the quick pats from Ailbhe's friends. Ailbhe said nothing but her eyes shone as she walked over to stand beside Ionain.

'Paired Keepers, your first task is to identify a suitable Fodder thread for your Channeller from those available. When you feel the pull of your Channeller's call, you deflect it on through yourself to the Fodder, and then allow the Fodder's strength to flow back through you to supply your Channeller.'

Trying not to think about how happy Ailbhe looked, Eadha closed her eyes and did as Fiachna had instructed, easily finding a suitable thread and holding it loosely in her mind ready to accept the reach of Senan's power. Most of her, though, was focused tensely on Ionain.

She'd sent him her power earlier that morning as they stood in line outside Matins, feeling a quick rush of relief as her mirror-sheath held and her gift flowed invisibly into him. But now was the first real test of how well he'd actually be able to use the powers she'd given him. Would he understand how to use them? Not just see the silvery Fodder threads but be able to draw life along them, just as she could and as the Masters' demanded? Standing a little distance away from her, Ionain's own face was tense with focus as he listened to Master Fionan's instructions.

'We begin today with the summoning of were-lights. When you have taken the power into yourselves, you must bend your focus towards the palm of your right hand. There you picture the creation of a small light, about the size of an apple; the more clearly you can...'

He was interrupted by a small scream from Ailbhe and shouts of laughter from the Channeller apprentices standing around Ionain. A fireball the size of a large pumpkin had popped into existence in his arms. He looked half-terrified, half-exalted as the ball spun just above his hands; even from across the room Eadha could feel its scorching heat. Ailbhe, Coll and Senan, who'd all been standing beside him, backed away quickly, the two boys convulsed with laughter at the expression on Ionain's face as he looked at Fionan across the top of the rotating fireball, which had started sending out sparks in every direction.

'Lord Ailm. Might I commend you on your rapid progress but suggest that we leave the conjuring of larger fireballs until we are outdoors, where they are less likely to set First House alight?' said Master Fionan calmly before flicking open a window, lifting the fireball out of Ionain's grasp and sending it bulleting onto the training ground outside where it exploded harmlessly in a hail of fiery sparks, to the cheers of the entire class.

Standing behind Senan, Eadha ducked her head to hide her grin, and made a mental note to send Ionain a little less power tomorrow.

So, at last, channelling proper began.

Those first weeks Master Fionan concentrated on the lighter uses of power—summoning were-lights, powering up fiery arrows for battle. The young Channellers revelled in their newborn power, setting the tiny were-lights dancing in excited patterns about the classroom, sending them crashing into each other to create miniature explosions.

Soon they were learning to fly. Even the most disdainful apprentices, like Senan, couldn't help but whoop the first time they lifted themselves up off the ground and into the sky above Master Fionan's head, wobbling unsteadily before taking off in flying circuits of the training ground, the more daring shooting on out over the sea with Master Fionan shouting after them to come back for fear they would run out of power and go tumbling down into the water.

Games like handball took on a whole other dimension now they could fly up after the ball, somersaulting through the air and pushing off the alley walls. Out on the sea they powered tiny coracles in furious races around the bay, weaving in and out between the marker-buoys, doing their best to tip each other into the waves.

Watching from the sidelines as she kept for Senan, Eadha could see Ionain was in his element. Fuelled by Eadha's daily gift of power it was easier for him than any of the other Channellers, as he was using none of his own energy at all. Each day, she sent him both the power to be able to see and use the Fodder threads, and also some of her own life-force. In the Masters' lessons he needed to be seen to draw on Fodder, so that Ailbhe as his Keeper, and Master Fionan watching over them all, wouldn't see anything amiss. But Eadha couldn't bear the thought of him drawing heavily on Fodder and so she sent him some of her energy as well, so he'd need very little of their strength. It was her compromise, with herself and with the promise she'd made to Magret.

For Ionain, it was power without price, and he revelled in it. Master Fionan marvelled at his energy and ready strength. Fit and strong after the months of training, he gloried in his new abilities, throwing himself into the training and growing more adept each day.

From the first it was a straight three-way contest between Ionain, Linn and Senan to be the top-ranked Channeller in their year. While Senan might not have had Ionain's secret power source, he made up for it with his own enormous, bullish strength. It translated into a channelling power of unusual ferocity. Assigned as his Keeper, it took all of Eadha's skill in shielding to hold away his brutal power from draining her own life-force before she could deflect it on to his hapless Fodder. She quickly realised Fiachna had assigned her to Senan to protect the other Keeper girls from his clawing, vicious draws. Linn, meanwhile, had a dextrousness that meant she could do more than any of the other apprentices with even small amounts of power.

While the Channeller apprentices flew above their heads, Eadha and the other Keeper novices remained firmly earthbound, standing on the edges of playing fields or on windswept shores, learning to accept the reach of their assigned Channeller's power and send it on to the Fodder sources. They studied the strength of the different threads, learning to recognise their quality, when it was weakening, when to transfer away to a different Fodder thread and back again when the original Fodder source had recovered. They learned to measure how much strength their Channeller had drawn and how long it was likely to last, depending on what they were using it for, as well as how long a Channeller could retain unused the life-force they'd drawn, before it began to dissipate.

And every day, as they stood outside Matins, Eadha bent her head and sent her power into Ionain hidden in its mirrored sheath, giving him the strength to do all the Masters demanded of him. Learning, in a kind of shadow lesson to those she took each day with Fiachna, how much power she needed to give him each day and how long it would last.

In those first weeks, when she still had some reserves of energy and the Channeller training was relatively light, she thought her daily gift to Ionain was something she could absorb. But as the weeks turned into months and the demands grew greater and greater, she learned how wrong she'd been. It took everything from her, everything she had, to keep Ionain supplied with enough power.

She spent every spare moment either snatching sleep or eating, trying to find the energy to keep going from somewhere. She became heavier, rolls of fat appearing around her belly and her thighs until she felt she was trapped in a body not her own.

Her own performance as a Keeper suffered with everything else. Where she'd started out at the top of the rankings she quickly slipped down to the bottom, struggling at times to perform even the simplest manoeuvres.

Gry and Ailbhe, meanwhile, were easily the strongest of the Keepers, both adept at judging threads and maintaining their flow. Watching Gry calmly sustain the thread for Coll, one of the weaker Channeller apprentices, while he floundered in the air above him, a question started to form in Eadha's mind. But this and any other thoughts she had in those first months were quickly blotted out again by exhaustion. Bone-deep, heavy-headed, scratchy-eyed weariness that stalked her from the moment she woke until she collapsed onto her narrow bed each night. Soon she could no longer remember a time when she hadn't been tired. It fuddled her thoughts, sapped her energy so it was an act of will each day to force herself out of bed, channel her power into Ionain and with what little energy she'd left for herself, force herself to do all she had to do and could not escape, each and every long and weary day.

Through the haze of her exhaustion, she watched as Ionain shone, pouring everything she gave him into mastering the different Arts. Determined to restore the honour of his House, he spent hours after training each day practising combat stances, coaxing shoots from the soil in the greenhouses, raising frames from the earth as they'd been shown by the Master Architect. That small part of her that was not too numb with weariness to feel, was filled with pride in her love, in her own power, every time she saw his proud, lonely figure out in the darkness of the training fields, lit only by a were-light, pirouetting through some complex manoeuvre. From her hiding place in the trees, she would pull the last vestiges of power and gift it to him so he could stay that extra hour, often at the cost of a night outdoors when she collapsed, too exhausted to make it back to her dormitory before lights out.

And still, even though the Channeller apprentices were now flying and fighting, growing plants and raising rudimentary buildings from the soil, even though they were doing it all using the life-force of the people, the Fodder they shared First Island with—still they remained invisible, either behind screens for close work or directly underneath them in the Fodder Hold dotted about beneath First House and the training grounds. The apprentices studied the silver threads, but the people themselves remained an abstraction, a silent, invisible source.

Only once, after several weeks, did Master Fionan touch directly on the subject of Fodder late one afternoon as they sat, taking notes on the ways in which a thread might be identified through different types of building walls.

'You will be aware that channelling involves the drawing of life-force from others. This goes to the very heart of our power; it is the only means by which the wonders of channelling so essential to the functioning of Domhain society and the rule of the Great Families can be realised. Some of you may find what we have to do upsetting, distasteful even, and it is a testament to your kind hearts. But understand it is your absolute duty to press beyond simple sentimentality and act for the greater good, for the good of your Families and a stable Domhain society.'

Eadha had sat bolt upright as soon as Master Fionan had mentioned Fodder. She'd been wondering for months if the Masters were ever going to talk directly about the people they drained, and how the apprentices would react. But looking about the classroom, she saw nothing but bored disinterest. Apprentices variously lounged on their desks or leaned back in their chairs, weary from a heavy day's training and impatient for lesson's end. Ionain was sitting towards the back of the classroom beside Senan, and they were deep in whispered conversation, paying no heed to Master Fionan's words.

The next morning, sitting in the bright refectory after Matins, surrounded by the chatter of apprentices, Linn leaned in to Eadha and said quietly, 'I saw you yesterday in class, almost climbing out of your seat when Master Fionan mentioned Fodder. A friendly word of advice. It's not the done thing here, or anywhere else for that matter, to show too much interest in that subject.'

After Linn had left Gry looked up from where he'd been sitting opposite them.

'She's right, you know,' he commented. 'You had no channelling growing up in Ailm's Keep so you wouldn't know, but most of these will have taken that in with their mother's milk.'

In the morning light he looked pale, the shadows under his eyes clearly visible. From the first, Senan's mockery of his failure to make the Channeller grade had been relentless. As a First Family heir, Gry's name was the grandest of their year, and Senan took a vicious pleasure in pegging him down. For his part, Gry was not inclined to give his tormentor any satisfaction, batting back Senan's barbs with his own whip-smart wisecracks day after day. But now Senan had come into his full power, flying high above the Keepers, peppering the sand around Gry's feet with fireballs, it was getting harder all the time to look unconcerned in the face of the endless taunting.

He looked at Eadha's disbelieving face and shrugged tiredly.

'Look, all they know about Fodder are the scary bedtime stories nurses and big brothers tell them, about horrible, disfigured Fodder bogeymen who steal away children from their beds, or how naughty children can be turned into Fodder if they don't eat their greens. So, in their minds, what's behind those screens is probably a cross between the worst nightmares of their childhood and some pot of invisible golden power. They are equal parts uninterested and afraid to find out anymore.'

'So we don't see Fodder, ever?'

'Second Island. We can see them then if we want to—they think we're corrupted enough at that stage. What you'll find is that some avoid ever confronting the reality of what they're doing, while others,' he went on, glancing across at Senan, loudly holding court at the next table, 'enjoy it.'

So, the relentless grind of channelling and training wore on day by endless day, as the path Eadha had so impulsively set herself upon at Ionain's Reckoning narrowed and darkened about her until it began to seem that there was no end to it.

Standing beside her every day as they stood on the sidelines keeping for their Channellers, as autumn turned towards winter, Gry was clearly baffled by Eadha's growing exhaustion.

More than once he tried to talk to her, whispering over his shoulder, 'Eadha, what's going on? Is it your thought-wall? Is that what's wearing you out? Because I know some tips...'

But she would just stare back at him blearily, as if from a great distance, locked deep inside the misery of having to keep going when her entire body was ready to collapse.

It wasn't until almost two months in that Gry managed to catch Eadha on her own. The Channellers were beginning their training in aerial combat out over the sea north of Lambay, in preparation for their Westport postings. The Keeper novices had to row out in small rowboats, two to a boat, so as to be within reach of their assigned Channellers as they flew above their heads, then send their draw onto the Fodder, still hidden out of sight on Lambay island itself.

As Eadha climbed wearily into a rowboat there was a thump as Gry jumped in beside her, a determined look on his face. As soon as they'd rowed out far enough to sea to be out of earshot, he looked across at her.

'Alright. Spill it. What's going on? With your gift you should be able to keep for Senan in your sleep, even if he is a vicious brute. So why are you so worn out?'

A lump rose in Eadha's throat. It was, she realised, the first time she'd felt seen by anyone, since the day she'd kissed Ionain in the beech coppice. Ionain hadn't come to see her since then, too absorbed in his training, while the Keeper girls all ignored her.

Too worn out to think of a lie, but unable to tell him the truth, she stared at Gry wordlessly for a long moment before saying simply, 'I made a promise, a long time ago. One of those promises you can't break. Keeping it is taking more out of me than I thought.'

'Another promise? Besides promising not to channel Fodder? How very mysterious. You don't think you're maybe making too many promises?'

'You're one to talk,' said Eadha then, rousing herself. 'I've seen you keeping for Coll. You look like someone doing it in his sleep, too. So, have you been making promises as well?'

They'd reached the marker-buoy where they were to wait for the Channeller apprentices. Shipping his oar and staring back at the shore where Fionan and Fiachna stood watching them, Gry said, 'For your sake, I'm not sure that's a question I should answer. Once you know something it's hard to unknow it if you're ever asked by people of power. I will answer a different question, though. Over the last two years I've watched my Channeller cousin change from a decent boy into a swaggering, entitled, selfish thug. And I've walked the streets of Erisen at night when all the nice Family boys and girls are tucked up in bed and seen the dregs of channelling. And I've thought a lot about choice. That there is an element of choice, in how complicit we are in our destinies; in what we let the Masters see and what we let them make of us. If that answers your question.'

He glanced at Eadha then with a challenging look in his eye.

'So, back to you, Eadha of the many promises. Are you going to tell me what it is, this other promise you've made?'

Eadha was silent for a moment, leaning on her oar. In the distance she saw the Channeller apprentices lift off the beach and fly out towards them, Ionain's tawny head clearly visible out in front, jostling with Senan to be first to reach the Keeper boats. Ailbhe and the other Keeper girls in the boats around them were cheering him on noisily.

'In the spirit of not answering what we're asked, I've a question for you instead,' she said. 'Do you ever find it hard, giving it all up? Knowing you have something that'd make you the best and brightest of them all, and instead the Masters can barely remember your name?'

Gry leaned back in the boat and hooted at the sky.

'It's a bunch of old men in a house on an island, desperate to validate their own lives by indoctrinating another generation of youngsters to make the same choices they made. Why would anyone ever want their approval? It's a gateway to wealth and power, that's all, so be honest and say you want what they have and you're prepared to sell your soul to get it. But there are other options. Like just step out of their game altogether, say you're not playing.'

They were holding their boat steady just off the northwest headland of Lambay. From there, to the west Eadha could make out the mainland, the long silver beaches of Erisen where she and Ionain had crossed the land-bridge what seemed like a lifetime ago.

'We could just keep going, you know; row on to Erisen, go into hiding, try to find other people like us,' she said then, abruptly. 'We can't be the only ones who've stepped outside the Masters' game.'

Gry chuckled dryly.

'Not unless you happen to have some Fodder hidden beneath your seat. That wind is from the west and it'd take us most of the day to row against it. We'd be caught long before we ever got near the shore. And I'm not that kind of rebel. I'm a nice boy from a Great Family, who doesn't want to be poor, or cold, or on the run from the Masters, but just isn't prepared to fry people's brains and drain their life-force for a living. This is my compromise, my tiny fist-wave at the system and I've made my peace with it.'

Later that afternoon, as they tied up their boat at the dock below First House, Gry looked across at her and said, 'It's not forever, you know, all this. The Masters, First House. You've come so far. Now we just have to stay the course. Stay hidden and one day you'll be free of them, free to make your own choices, free not to make a horrible situation worse,' and draping a companionable arm across her shoulder, they climbed together back up the hill towards the Keepers' quad.

CHAPTER 21
ENTER THE DRAGON

In late winter the snow came, blanketing the training grounds of First House where the Channellers and Keepers practised. Every day it was cleared by Master Fionan's staff, driving heat into the soil to thaw it, and every night a fresh blanket fell.

In that frozen first hour before the snow melted, the Channellers practised their flying. They had leave to channel power to keep off the cold, surrounding themselves with their own personal pockets of warm air while the Keeper novices stood underneath them, often up to their knees in snowdrifts.

Already drained from supplying Ionain that morning, Eadha stood at the edge of the playing field, her face aching in the icy wind, her feet numb and swollen in her thin boots. A little distance away from her stood Ailbhe, warmly wrapped in furs and heavy leather boots, her face prettily flushed with the cold and shining hair peeping out from beneath her soft cap. As well as being paired with her as his Keeper, Ionain was spending more and more time with her outside of training, joining her in the ref each morning for warming drinks, or sitting beside her in the evenings when the Master Teller wove his tales above their heads.

Eadha told herself it didn't matter, to trust Ionain. That it was still all just a game, to hold to his words that day, months ago, in his apartment. But it was hard to remember as she watched the two of them laughing together, Ionain scraping snowballs from the tops of pine trees to land in soft puffs at Ailbhe's feet.

She sensed the change before she heard anything, a thrill running through the icy air. Master Fionan felt it, too, turning to gaze towards the hill above First House. A group of black-clad riders had appeared at the forest's edge. Pausing only to dispatch an apprentice to fetch Master Dathin, Fionan flew up to meet them as they emerged from the trees, pulling a large wagon behind them. It was similar to a Fodder wagon but larger and made all of metal, reinforced with inner and outer rows of bars. There was a dark shape lying on the floor of the wagon; too large to be a man. As the riders neared the bottom of the hill Masters began to appear from First House, pulling on their heavy winter robes, clutching their yew staffs. Eadha recognised the white-blond hair of Lord Huath at the head of the riders at the same moment that Ionain, still flying above them, cried out in a voice filled with fear and wonder, 'Dragon!'

Their training cancelled, the apprentices gathered in the refectory. Ionain, however, managed to wheedle his way into the main Receiving Room where Lord Huath was closeted with the Masters, pleading to greet his uncle on this rare visit to First House. He returned, eyes shining with excitement, climbing onto a table to report the news as everyone clustered round him.

'It's a young dragon. My uncle caught it four days ago. It's one of the spawn of the she-dragon we saw in the Blackstairs last spring. My uncle and his men have been hunting them on and off ever since. They killed two, one escaped west they think, but this one, the smallest, they managed to capture alive. Master Combat is beside himself with excitement. It's the first time Lambay has ever had a live dragon. It's too young to be a danger; it can't breathe fire yet and it's only the length of a man. My uncle says even one of us could put it down.'

Seven days later the apprentices crunched through the fresh snow on the training grounds shortly after Matins, on their way to see the captured dragon. It lay still in its iron cage a little distance away from the main House. Little was known about the stages of growth of young dragons. They were fiercely protected by the she-dragons, hidden away on the western isles or on the most impenetrable northern peaks until they were old enough to fly and breathe fire. The Masters were intensely wary of their captive. A full-grown dragon could best even the most seasoned Channeller unless he had massive Fodder resources at his disposal. The flame alone would kill anyone in its silent burning path and the Masters had no way of knowing how far the young dragon was from coming into its power.

Master Fionan and the Master Combat called them to a halt some way away from the cage. The dragon lay inert on the floor, curled like a cat, its haunches pulled into its belly and wings folded flat along its ridged back. Only the eyes gave any sign that it was anything other than a creature channelled from stone. They were great and golden, unblinkingly regarding the apprentices as they craned to see, straining against the barriers set in a wide circle around the cage. Eadha's heart began to thump unbidden in her chest, her silver fish flickering into joyous life. She closed her eyes, and there it was in front of her, shining, a piece of the sun fallen to earth, blinding in its purity. She gasped and stepped back, looking about her. Could they not see it, what they had lying there before them?

The Master Combat, apparently oblivious, was explaining the dragon scales; overlapping and interlocking, they covered the body in iridescent mail, hard as silver, flexible as skin, undulating sinuously when the dragon moved. They were impervious to normal weapons, shattering arrows and swords unless they were powered by a Channeller's art. Even then it took the power of twenty Fodder just to pierce the underbelly where the scales were thinner. In front of them the dragon had lifted its head as though it scented something. Eadha's power twisted in savage recognition. Behind her Ionain placed a hand on her shoulder.

'You're burning up.'

The touch of that familiar hand pulled her back into herself, breaking the dragon's spell. She leaned briefly, almost imperceptibly into the beloved touch then pulled away before it could be seen by Ailbhe or any of her spies.

That night she couldn't sleep. They'd had no further training that day, meaning for once she had power to spare, coursing restlessly through her. With a grin and no one to see her she spun a pocket of heat around her and flew down from the Keeper dorm through the quad tunnels and out into the winter night with its vertiginous carpet of stars flung from one horizon to the other, the sea below her pacing like a caged beast to the shore's edge and back. Lifting one hand above her she began to spin, faster and faster until she was nothing but a blur of energy, then shot up into the sky, up, up, whirling until the stars became streaks of light she was outrunning. Below her she saw the dragon, felt it quivering with longing in its iron cage. Down she dived to land in front of the golden eyes, hands cupping a single were-light. They regarded each other, the girl and the dragon.

'Mahera,' hissed the dragon, drawing its lips back, teeth already the size of Eadha's hand glinting in the light.

Wordlessly Eadha slipped her arm through the bars to touch the side of its face, the shining mail dry and warm to the touch. Closing her eyes, she pulsed her remaining power into the emptiness before her. She felt the dragon's hunger, felt a savage longing in that moment to let everything go, to disappear, when the dragon nudged her hand, breaking the link so that she returned to herself, almost falling to the ground in sudden weakness.

Training remained erratic for the next few days and Eadha was able to get away to the Library, sneaking down each night after lights out. She flew up to the shelves beneath the dome, to the books forbidden to apprentices. "Mahera", the she-dragon had said to her in the stony mountains and her child had repeated it underneath the eastern stars. If she could understand, if she could speak to it, then perhaps she could understand the intense connection she felt. At night she dreamed of the touch of the warm, dry dragon scales, of flying on dragon's wings through soft flakes of tumbling snow. She dreamt she stood on the training ground, keeping for Ionain when he flew back to earth and bowed before her. She looked down then to see she'd been covered in a dragon's iridescent skin; over her shoulders she felt the wingspan, light, tremendous as she spread them wide and sprang into the darkening sky.

Normal training resumed, but they were brought once more to study the dragon some weeks later. A late thaw had set in, so this time they trekked across muddy ground to its cage. It had grown rapidly, its head almost touching the roof of the cage. Below the open space where they stood, at the east dock, a full-masted ship had put in. It was a rare sight, the ship almost too large for the jetty normally only used for coracles travelling the short distance to Second Island. The white sails strained in winds blowing straight off the sea, drawing every eye. Seeing their gaze, the Master Combat explained.

'This will transport the beast to Second Island. It is growing rapidly and will need to be put down before it comes to pose a serious risk. The kill will form the basis of the final graduation trials for the Risen Channellers on Second Island later in spring.'

Eadha felt the words as a punch to her stomach. All the time the dragon had been on the island she'd been tethered to it, walking about First House on an invisible leash that ran from her to the impossible creature chained to an iron floor at the island's heart. In a daze she returned to the dormitory to change into her Vespers gown. The room was empty, a rare moment of solitude. From underneath her bed she pulled Magret's burned book, looking for something on the fire-eaten pages to make sense of what she felt. At its charred heart was the picture she was looking for, of a man and a dragon entwined. The man was holding his staff above his head, the dragon's wings raised about him; the colours of each had run into the other in the fire's heat. She'd always assumed it was a representation of a battle between man and beast, but now she had eyes to see she finally understood.

She slipped away in the early dark, back down to where the creature lay still. It watched her intently. She called up a were-light in her hand. The dragon looked at it pleadingly.

'I know,' she said. 'I understand. You want to do that, too. Let me show you. Mahera. Sister.' The dragon placed its head against the bars.

'Mahera,' it hissed in reply. And so quietly, patiently, Eadha set about teaching the chained dragon to channel power from within itself. Night after night she slipped out, pulling power up from inside her, showing the dragon how she created the were-light from the life-force within. And slowly, surely, the dragon began to respond. It was very young still, ramming its head in frustration against the bars when it could not produce flame. The cage was too confined for it to extend its wings fully, but it flexed them as far as it could, bending its long neck down to the girl like some creature caught and frozen in mid-wingbeat, holding perfectly still as it bent all its attention onto the hand cupped in front of it. At last it caught the trick, of pulling the thread of power from belly to heart to throat to produce a soft whoosh of flame, drawing its lips back in dragon laughter as she was forced to leap out of the way or be singed by a fiery bolt. But it didn't have the strength yet to burn its way out of the cage and escape, while Eadha, drained from supplying Ionain each day, hadn't enough power to be sure she could do it either.

On the day before the Masters were due to move the dragon off the island, Eadha reported to the infirmary, pleading illness. It was not difficult, for exhaustion had stalked her for months as she spent herself supplying power to Ionain. The sleepless nights with the young dragon had given her skin an even more waxy pallor, her eyes fever bright with effort. As darkness fell and the congregation gathered for Vespers once more, she lay in a narrow white bed in the infirmary. The room about her faded as she focused everything on the thread running to the cage, now on the dock.

The dragon crouched ready. And slowly, like someone unpicking a weave, she began to pour every atom of her being into the golden heart of the dragon. On and on it pulsed, each heartbeat sending more and more of herself until she felt she must disintegrate and reassemble once more in the belly of the beast until finally, ah, the silent dragon roared. Roared until the trees shook and the sleeping crows roused crying from their roosts. Threw back its head and roared its pain and loneliness and thanks in a great, fiery breath that melted the bars that had held it down so that at last it stretched its wings to greet the sea winds and sprang soaring into the stormy sky.

And oh, how she wanted to stay with it, within it there in the sky riding the night wind. Above the turret where she lay like one dead the dragon circled once before opening its wings to be carried home on the east winds of winter. And in her white bed Eadha lay, unravelled and alone.

In the clamour and the panic that followed the dragon's escape, Eadha's collapse went unnoticed. After several days, colour began to return to her cheeks and the Master Herbal, baffled but relieved, prescribed complete rest. Lying there Eadha floated on a soft cloud of exhaustion. Just to have it stop, even for a little while to step off the wheel she'd bound herself to that day so long ago when she stepped in to help her friend.

Ionain came to visit her, and Gry, both looking too big, too vital in the narrow white room with its narrow white beds. Ionain was preoccupied, angry, his normal good humour deserting him.

'They've gone too far this time,' he said, unable to sit still, shaking his head every time he looked at her. 'I can't let her keep treating you like this.' She tried to shush him, tell him it wasn't Ailbhe's bullying this time, but the effort it took her to say anything only made him angrier.

Though he didn't say it, she could see he was worried about himself, too. Without her secret supply his power had faded away. He couldn't understand what had happened, though Master Fionan was unconcerned, putting it down to nerves with the spring trials approaching.

Gry came each day, looking at her quizzically though he talked only of trivial things, matches, training, preparation for the trials. But on a morning when the air held enough promise of spring for the window to be cracked open for a while, he stood looking out at the training fields and said, 'Ours is an old Family. One of the oldest on Domhain and one of the furthest west. We sometimes still see dragons flying far above us like bright sparks blown on the wind. There is a lot we've forgotten, or chosen not to know, in making this world we live in now.' He turned to look at Eadha, lying there on the bed.

'Never be so arrogant as to think you are the first. Everything that ever happens has happened before.'

He turned and left the room, leaving the window open so the air about her became chilly with the hard challenge of the cold spring air.

CHAPTER 22
THE SPRING TRIALS

The guests had been arriving all morning, some on horseback across the land-bridge, others on sailing ships moored offshore, channelling in to alight on the dock. It was raining heavily but the Masters had raised a power dome above the combat field the night before. Parents and apprentices stood about inside the dome in small groups, and the air was filled with the hubbub of greeting.

Eadha sat a little way away from the combat field, on the edge of the handball alley, her back against the wall. Behind her the diverted rain spattered noisily into the stone alley. Only her face was visible, the rest of her wrapped and hooded against the chill in her Keeper's cloak as she watched the steadily growing throng. The elegantly ageless mothers, the proud, confident fathers, all impervious and certain to the core. And why not? This was their world, built by and for their breed, and it fitted them like a second skin. It was a power as insidious and implacable as any Master's inquisition, the power that radiated out from these Great Families. That with every large gesture, every loud laugh, every immaculate outfit said *we are better than you. You who are different, know that your worth is less than ours. Look at us and feel shame. Feel less than us and when you are on the floor, bow down to us.*

Eadha could feel it, the force field of dominance that flowed out from the crowd in front of her, as surely as she could see the power that shone from Master Fionan's staff to hold off the rain. It was the power she felt every day: in her dormitory, in class, in the refectory. Everywhere, like a pressure on the back of her head, pressing her down onto her knees.

But something had changed since she'd returned to her dormitory from the infirmary, thinner and paler. A dragon had called her sister, there, on that field under a dome of stars. She'd filled it with her heart's gift and it had burned the Masters' cage into a twisted heap of metal. As she sat there on the damp ground in her thin wool cloak it felt as strong as a dragon's mailed skin, impervious.

'Keeper, on your feet.'

Master Fionan's sharp tone broke through her thoughts.

'Lord Ailm's parents have asked to greet you; go at once. The trials start in a few moments, and you will need to be in position to keep for Lord De Lane.'

Fionan brought her over to the viewing platform, and her heart gave a lurch to see the familiar faces of Lord Ailm and Lady Ura, Ionain beside them, beaming. To her surprise Lord Ailm held out his arms towards her and enveloped her in a warm hug. As he did all the memories of her beloved Keep she'd so carefully hidden away came rushing back in a wave that raced all the way from the North Tower over the forests and mountains, across city and sea to crash against her heart.

'You are recovered, I hope? Master Healer told us you had been unwell.'

'Yes, my lord,' she replied.

'He fairly scolded Ionain earlier. Seemingly he insisted on staying by your side all those nights you were unconscious. The

Master is convinced that's why Ionain's power stuttered for a few days.'

Eadha looked across at Ionain, who'd flushed bright red as his father spoke. Before he could say anything, she turned back to Lord Ailm.

'Master Healer is as bad as Beithe when it comes to fussing, my lord,' she said. 'Your son will do you and all of Ailm's Keep proud today, I have no doubt.'

'Well said,' replied Lady Ura. 'Now come, Ionain, we're sitting with Ailbhe's mother and I want you to greet her before the trials begin.'

Dismissed, Eadha made her way over to the sidelines. As she did, she saw Ionain and his parents join an immaculately dressed, silver-haired version of Ailbhe. Moments later Ailbhe herself appeared beside them. She was as beautifully turned out as ever, in a tailored combat bodice and skirt showing her trim figure, though Eadha saw how her mother reached out to straighten her bodice and tuck her hair behind her ears. They all embraced each other, laughing and chatting together until Master Fionan called to the visitors to take their seats, and the contestants to take the field for the trials.

In combat, the apprentice Channellers were divided into two teams. An apprentice was knocked out if they were pushed outside the playing field boundaries or if they were knocked off their feet on the ground for a count of five. The winners were the team with the most members left standing at the end of the match. Ionain was the captain of one team with Linn. Senan was captain of the other team with Coll as vice-captain. In the overall table Ionain and Senan were equal on points coming into this final combat with Linn trailing them by a few points, her twin brother a distant fourth.

Linn was heavily padded with two Masters stationed on the sidelines to protect her. Gry had been assigned as her Keeper, as the

213

strongest of the Keeper novices.

As Eadha took up her position to keep for Senan, Ailbhe arrived at the sideline. Master Fionan stood in the centre of the playing fields and addressed the parents.

'Welcome to the annual spring trials. I am proud to say this is one of the strongest apprentice years I have ever had the privilege of training. Their skill, commitment and loyalty to the Channeller code is outstanding. I am confident that the future of the Great Families is in safe hands. My lords, lady, a clean fight please—you may begin.'

The teams quickly took up their positions. The possibilities were endless, and the captains would have spent days assessing the strengths and weaknesses of the different apprentices; who would take on who, who needed shielding, who could fight best in the air and who on the ground. Typically, both teams would go for a mix of players in the air and on the ground. The aim was to keep as many apprentices in play for as long as possible; if one side got a significant numerical advantage early on, it would all be over early. Even the strongest Channeller apprentice would not be able to withstand the combined strength of seven or more apprentices on the other team ganging up on him.

Eadha knew Ionain's instinct would always be to lose as few men as possible. That was his weakness when facing a ruthless fighter like Senan; he would spread himself too thin trying to save everyone while Senan would abandon the weakest players on his team or line them up as frontline fodder early on to protect the stronger players and save their strength.

True to form she saw Ionain and Linn take up positions at the far ends of the playing space; typical protector stances. On the other side, Senan and Coll withdrew three layers behind their players, forming a tight clump in the centre. Then the time for thinking was over as she felt the wave of Senan's onrushing channel hit her, harsh and demanding. For the spring trials the apprentice Channellers were permitted to use up to three threads, so the skill of their chosen Keeper came into play, ensuring they switched between threads at the right moments and maintained a steady flow. As each thread was slightly different there was always a moment of adjustment when a Channeller moved between them. A good Keeper would judge not only the strength of the thread but also the best moment to switch.

The teams had been carefully selected by the Masters to give the spectators an even contest, and so it proved. Ionain and Linn were everywhere, protecting their team, diving in with their staffs to head off bolts. Senan, meanwhile, sat back, husbanding his strength for occasional thunderbolts, watching as his team pulled the two opposing captains the length and breadth of the pitch. Slowly Ionain and Linn began to whittle away his buffer of apprentices, as first one, then several were knocked out of the field of play, blasted by bolts of pure power they could not deflect with their staffs. The playing field was ringed by Masters, ready to catch apprentices before they could sustain serious injury, though one student was hit so hard by Senan that he was catapulted out over the sea and it took the combined efforts of Masters Fionan and Dathin to create a safety net and prevent him crashing into the choppy waters.

They were entering the final quarter of the match when the last line in front of Senan and Coll was cleared away. They'd paid a high price in numbers for their strategy—only two apprentices apart from the captains were left on the field. But they were fresher; Eadha could feel Senan's ready power humming through her. By contrast Ionain and Linn were battered and weary. Ionain had only two lines of power left, one having dropped off, while Linn had just one. On Linn's signal their remaining five apprentices pulled in close as they advanced on Senan and Coll. Seven to four; though tired, the odds were in Ionain and Linn's favour. Now it was about running down the clock and holding on. Senan, who'd remained on the ground throughout, flew up into the air, holding his staff in combat stance.

'Hope you enjoyed the warmup. I suppose it's time we gave the visitors a real game, hmm?' Bowing his head he sent an almighty blast sweeping in a half-circle in front of him. It was so powerful it sent two apprentices tumbling at once; Ionain dove to try to catch one, and Senan immediately took his chance, sending a fiery blast hurtling straight at Ionain's exposed chest. The crowd, filled with experienced Channellers, gasped. Eadha's instincts took over. Closing her eyes, she sent her power rocketing into Ionain. Senan's blast still sent him flying backwards, hitting the ground with a sickening thud, but Eadha's power cushioned the worst of the impact. Linn was there in a heartbeat and in perfect unison his hand shot up as hers came down and she lifted him into the air before he could be counted out. The crowd whooped in relief and delight. Linn whirled about to face Senan, eyes blazing, while Ionain retreated dazed, shaking his head, two apprentices pulling in front of him protectively.

'See how far you get trying that on me.'

Senan knew as well as anyone there that a direct blow like that to Linn would get him sent off. He fell into a defensive stance as she flew at him. His line of power faded, the Fodder he'd drained now completely exhausted by his almighty draw moments before. As his Keeper Eadha needed to switch away to a fresh line. But she was drained herself from the surge she'd just sent to Ionain and instead of a smooth pickup she faltered, dropping the spent Fodder line but fumbling the switch to the fresher line. In that moment Linn swept in, crashing with her shoulder into Senan, knocking his staff out of his hands before shooting a ball of power from her palm into his chest. Unable to draw power from the Fodder Senan tried to channel power from Eadha instead but her thought-wall was too strong, blocking his draw so his channel came back empty. Left without any power to absorb the impact, Linn's blow sent him flying, sprawling in an ungainly heap just outside the playline. He was out of the match.

While Ionain and Linn's team turned to face Coll and the one other remaining apprentice, Senan scrambled to his feet, livid. He raced over to where Eadha stood and grabbed her by the shoulders, screaming into her face.

'You cheat! You dropped that Fodder line then shielded yourself on purpose. You sabotaged me to help Ionain, you'll be sent as Fodder for this.'

His eyes were blazing, his face bright red with effort and rage as he spat the words at her. Even as he did Master Fionan stepped in between them.

'Lord De Lane, you are correct. If Apprentice Keeper Eadha has deliberately failed in her sworn duty to her assigned Channeller she will be severely sanctioned. Might I remind you, however, of our esteemed audience.'

Senan's eyes darted up to where his father and the other Lords' Channeller sat in the gallery, then he clamped his jaws shut, turned on his heel and stalked over to where the rest of his team were watching the last few seconds of the match.

The Master Librarian, who'd been acting as a touchline umpire, gripped her shoulder. With a grim expression he gestured her towards First House. As she began the long trudge up the hill, she heard the gallery behind her cheering. Ionain and Linn's team had won.

Moments later came Master Dathin's voice, 'Lord Ailm, Lady Manon, as our victorious captains it is with great pleasure that I present you with these yew staffs, made from the wood of the temple trees. As worthy representatives of two of our oldest Families, I have no doubt that you will wield them well and to the greater glory of the Ailm and Manon Families.'

CHAPTER 23
THE SISTER

'Apprentice Keeper Eadha. You have been accused of a deliberate breach of your duty to your assigned Channeller, Lord De Lane, in knowingly withholding power to help Lord Ailm and Lady Manon's team. You will be aware of the seriousness of this allegation. The first rule of keeping is to provide unquestioning support to their Channeller, up to and including permitting them to draw on your own life-force in extremis. While we discourage Channellers from drawing on their Keepers other than in a true emergency, it is their choice to make, not the Keeper's to withhold. Master Fionan, what is your view of what occurred?'

Master Dathin was standing by the lectern in the Library, Master Fionan and the Librarian sitting behind him, their expressions stern as they stared at Eadha, who stood, head bowed, in front of them.

'Apprentice Keeper Eadha is one of our weakest Keeper students, with limited ability and little physical stamina, unsurprising given her lack of breeding. She was recently rested for several weeks in the infirmary due to exhaustion. Before that she was excused from handball training for several weeks following repeated head injuries sustained owing to poor reflexes and timing. We are all aware of her inappropriate previous closeness to Lord Ailm, in whose household she served before her Reckoning. This was already under review and the intention was to take appropriate measures in the move to Second Island. In the circumstances I am of the view that what occurred with Lord De Lane, while unfortunate, was not a deliberate withholding of power. I do not believe her capable of shielding herself from a Channeller of Lord De Lane's strength. I would hazard Lord De Lane's inability to draw power from her was due to a combination of fatigue owing to her inherent lack of stamina, together with excessive sentiment towards Lord Ailm; she was distracted by what to all of us appeared to be a serious injury.'

'Thank you, Master Fionan. Master Librarian, do you have anything to add?'

Barely glancing at Eadha, the Librarian's tone was dismissive.

'I concur with Master Fionan. She has proven a weak student and is too close to Lord Ailm given her lack of breeding and the availability of other more suitable partners. This morning's incident simply demonstrates the inadvisability of excessive closeness in a combat situation.'

Stood in front of the Masters, head bowed, Eadha was angry. Angry because she'd just saved their precious Lord Ailm. Angry because she'd moved faster than any of the Masters to shield Ionain and they couldn't even see it. Angry because these old men stood there and called her weak, she who'd just kept for the most brutal Channeller in the year and still had the strength to supply Ionain with all of his power.

She knew if she looked up now the anger would show in her eyes and some sense of self-preservation kept her staring at the floor. Moving soundlessly Master Dathin came to stand in front of her, placing his hands on either side of her head for an inquisition. His was an implacable force, filling her head, dominating every thought as he sifted through her mind. She was exhausted by the outpouring of strength to Ionain and shaken by Senan's screaming fit, but rage sustained her. In her rage she welcomed the intruder. He might be immensely strong from drawing the life-force of the poor wretches beneath them, but he would not break through her thought-wall if she did not will it. She would defeat him on his own ground and he wouldn't even know he'd been beaten.

'An interesting mind. Very clear, surprisingly so on such an eventful day but with little real strength. Masters Librarian and Fionan, I will concur with your assessments; there was no intentional breach, she was distracted by concern for Lord Ailm, and her poor stamina impacted her reserves, both of which while comprehensible are not acceptable. The apprentice must be sanctioned, and the issues identified tackled.'

Addressing Eadha directly Master Dathin continued, 'Apprentice Keeper Eadha, you are barred from attending the Trial Ball tonight. When you arrive at Second Island you will attend remedial Keeper training in the Fodder Hold. Perhaps this will instil an appropriate deference to your Lords' Channeller. Appropriate measures on the excessive closeness to Lord Ailm are already in train. Now, gentlemen, let us return to our guests.'

That night Eadha lay alone in her empty dormitory, listening to the distant music from the Trial Ball. In the early hours the other girls burst into the moonlit room, chattering excitedly. All the talk was of who had danced with whom, telling Ailbhe what a beautiful couple she and Ionain had made when they stepped out together on the dancefloor, he so fair and she so dark. They knew she had to be awake, but she lay stubbornly facing the wall, feigning sleep. She would not give them the satisfaction of seeing just how much they were hurting her.

They finally fell asleep just before dawn. Eadha uncurled from where she'd been laying, hunched and silent, for hours. Moving soundlessly past their sleeping forms she slipped on out of the Keepers' quad, making her way down to the dock. All traces of the melted and twisted metal of the dragon's cage had been cleared away. Sitting on the jetty, legs dangling over the edge as the seawater gulped and slapped at the struts beneath her, she stared up at the brightening sky and thought of the young dragon, finally able to stretch its wings wide on the winds and strike for home. She knew it most likely had flown far into the west, away from the Channeller strongholds of Lambay and Erisen, yet still she felt connected to it. At night she often dreamt of it, as she'd always dreamed of dragons. And on days when she could hardly climb from her bed with tiredness, when her power felt so puny, so constrained by the limits of her physical body compared to the immense well of Fodder lives the Masters drained at will, she remembered the power she'd given, that lay now in the dragon's fiery heart on the other side of the world and took comfort.

As she turned to climb back up the slope to First House, she could just make out a scorch line, almost overgrown now by fresh grass, as though the dragon had burned a line in the ground as it broke free. Following the line brought her to a copse of newly grown birch trees, still less dense than the mature trees on either side. The dragon must have destroyed a whole section of trees leading all the way back to the walls of First House. While the Master Grower had clearly been at work raising new trees, it was still possible to see where the new growth began, at a heavy oak door set in the wall.

Looking down Eadha realised the mound of soil she was standing on was a freshly dug grave. As she stumbled back in horror, she heard Gry's voice behind her. He was stepping out from beneath the trees, followed by a tall woman with a weathered face and kind eyes.

'Eadha, this is my aunt, Lady Hera.'

Reaching out a hand to help her down, Hera murmured, 'Yes, most unfortunate. Master Dathin told me last night at the Trial Ball they spared no effort in hunting the young dragon that escaped. When emotions run high the cost in lives mounts quickly. At a guess I'd say four Fodder at least are buried here.'

Tears started in Eadha's eyes. Gry put his hand on her shoulder.

'You weren't to know.'

'Is this where they bring them out?'

'Yes, normally the door and the burial ground are well-hidden by trees, but the dragon's fire burned away the cover for a few days. I wanted to show Aunt while she was here.'

Eadha stepped forward again, around the fresh graves this time, to where far older burial mounds shouldered out of the ground. These were not the graves of Masters; they were buried in marble in the crypt beneath the temple. The farthest grave was set on a rise against the wall of First House. Once it would have looked east to Second Island, before the trees grew up, before it was hidden from view. Unlike the others it was marked by a headstone.

'Sister' was the one word pressed deep into the granite.

'So much we must forget in order to make our choices bearable,' said Hera, who had come to stand beside Eadha. 'In my time here, there were rumours this grave existed, but I could never find it. I am glad to have seen it, this once.' Turning to Eadha she continued, 'Leah. Sister to the Four Brothers, eldest and most gifted of them all. She lived out her days there alone on the furthermost east island of Domhain, in a fortress raised just to hold her, too far from land to use her power to escape.'

She gestured across the sea towards Second House, black on the paling skyline. Eadha stared at her. All winter long she'd listened to the tales and watched the Masters weave illusions from the Annals of the Four Brothers, the founding tales of how channelling first came into the world.

'But the Annals—they don't say anything about a sister?'

Hera began walking back to the stableyard, the two apprentices walking with her. The land-bridge back to the mainland was being raised for departing guests and her horse was already saddled and waiting.

'No one outside of our Family speaks of Leah anymore,' said Hera, swinging up onto her mount. 'Our ancestor was the only one of the four brothers to leave First Island, horrified at what his brothers had done to his sister, moving out west to found our House. He passed on some memory of his older sister to his descendants, but you'll find no word of her here on Lambay.'

Gry turned towards Eadha.

'That was the part of the story that always frightened me the most when I was little. Not the battles, but how it's possible to make someone disappear so completely, as if they never existed, even a member of the Founding Family.'

'Her power didn't fit with the world her brothers were building; the world we live in now, of Fodder and Holds and Great Families,' said his aunt. 'As long as there have been Channellers, it has always been their way. To snuff out a challenge before it even knows itself to be a threat, Sister save us.' A memory stirred in Eadha, of Beithe comforting the maidservant in the kitchen of Ailm's Keep after Ionain's Reckoning with those same quiet words.

'She must have scared them very much,' said her nephew.

Lady Hera looked down at the two young people.

'But the dragons remember. Let us hold to that,' and urging her horse forward she began the long ride west and home.

224

PART III

SECOND ISLAND

CHAPTER 24
FORTRESS

Boat timbers creaked and sails snapped as Eadha and the other Keeper novices sat, capes drawn tightly about them. The sun burnt the skin in the thin sea air but there was no heat in it, whipped away before it could reach them. Head Keeper Fiachna tacked expertly into the wind, which dropped sharply as they sailed into the shadow of the granite cliffs of Second Island. Ahead of them, the last of the Channeller coracles bumped each other as they edged into the sea cave that was the only entrance to Second House. Salt-blasted and wind-chilled, they came at last into the still waters of the cave. A Master waited for them, holding a silver lantern. The Apprentice Master on Second Island, Master Joen, was as tall as Master Fionan, though of a far heavier build, barrel-chested with an impassive expression as he glanced over the twenty shivering Keeper novices sitting behind Fiachna, before nodding to her. She addressed him with the formal words of transition.

'Master Joen, I commend these Rising to your care, to be trained and held on this Island until they are deemed Risen.' Rising. This was their new title on Second Island. Where on First Island they'd been the Awakened, now they were the Rising; when they finally graduated next summer, they would be the Risen.

'My thanks to you, Head Keeper Fiachna, journey safe.'

A cylinder of light had been hollowed out of the cliff, steep stairs winding about it to the top. Where the Rising Channellers had flown straight up the light well to the surface, the Rising Keepers had to pick their way like ants up the rock face, holding hard to the thin railing that was the only barrier between them and the long fall to the cave floor. Eadha and the other novices emerged breathless into a courtyard deep within the walls of Second House.

The cliff where Second House had been raised was little more than a blasted rock at the end of things, the only green the hardy cordylines and saw-grass clinging to the stony ground. Faced with less space the Master Architects had raised their creation as high as they dared, a defiant fist raised to the winter storms that came roaring in from the icy tundra of the north. Channeller walkways crisscrossed the space above them, rising level after level. The buildings looked inwards, windows facing each other across the courtyards. Nestled within those mighty walls, yews flourished on smooth lawns and freshwater fountains drawn from deep within the rock played serenely.

Master Joen guided them about the cloisters and colonnades, just as Fiachna had done with them when they arrived on First Island. As they walked, he talked of the island's history, of the raising of the first building there by the First Brothers. He was a practised storyteller, turning what could have been a dry architectural tour into a stirring tale. He said nothing, though, of what Hera had told Eadha, of how the brothers had raised that building to incarcerate their sister Leah here, or of her lonely grave where they'd buried her on First Island. Of the raising of this place to contain whatever terrible wrongness in her that her brothers so feared.

As she listened to Master Joen tell his carefully edited tales,

Eadha realised she no longer knew what to believe from the tales of channelling and power she'd been hearing all her life. The stories woven by the Master Teller, the Annals of the Four Brothers, the rows of scrolls in the Library; none of it seemingly was about truth or the recording of facts. What it was about, what it was truly about was the creation of a story to make the now an inevitability. The Channellers' world of Fodder and Lords the only possible world. And a truth like Leah's truth, whatever it was, did not, could not, exist if it had no place within that one true story of now.

Just as on First Island, the Channeller apprentices were given opulent apartments. The winning captains Ionain and Linn had first pick, both opting for airy quarters high in the main towers. For the Keepers it was all change. On Second Island most of them were to be assigned to live with one Channeller, serving them as their personal Keeper alongside the ever-present, ever-wordless manservants. Those few not personally assigned to a Channeller would live in a Keeper dorm as they'd done on First Island.

The Keeper novices stood in a subdued group as Master Joen began to read the list of assigned pairings. So much turned on this one allocation for so many of the girls—their hopes of a life of status and ease as the wife of a Great Family Lord. Locked in her own misery, Eadha could spare some small sympathy for the pale, anxious faces around her. For the most part the list followed the expected lines; established couples were put together, though there were exceptions. Not being placed together was a clear signal the Masters did not approve of a pairing. There were tears; hands to the mouth and the turn away, the awkwardness of friends not knowing what to say as some couples were smoothly split and paired elsewhere.

In other cases, the pairings comprised an overt nudge. So Gry had been paired with Linn. The Master's logic was easy to see, thought Eadha, giving him a small wave as he went to stand beside Linn. Pair the one Channeller girl with the only boy Keeper. Linn was easily the most decent of the Channeller apprentices; Eadha saw how she and Gry greeted each other with a friendly eye-roll, and felt relieved for her friend. Mara, a strong Keeper girl from an impeccable Family was put with Coll, one of the weaker Channellers. And Ailbhe with Ionain. Eadha's heart twisted when she heard the two names called together. Like Leah, she was being cleared out of the way, written out of the story so the true story of a love-match between Houses Ailm and De Paor could be told.

As the lowest ranked Keeper, Eadha's was the last name read. There was only one Channeller apprentice left unpaired, and with sick inevitability she heard Master Joen announce his name: Lord De Lane. For the next year she would be keeping for Senan, the cruellest, most vicious Channeller of them all. This was no attempt at a love match. Master Joen had clearly been warned by Fionan about Senan's vicious temperament and, just as on First Island, she was being paired with him to protect the Keeper girls from good Families.

'Keepers, proceed at once to your assigned quarters and assist your Channellers in preparing for the Welcome Ball,' finished the Master.

Senan had chosen an apartment directly below Ionain's, in a tower looking out west towards First Island and Erisen. A long, richly carpeted hall led from the entrance to the main suite, a cluster of bright, beautifully appointed rooms leading off a central sitting room. Eadha was quartered in the Keeper's cubby, a plain, white-washed room just inside the main door with one narrow west-facing window set deep in the walls. As she set her bag down on the bed and began to unpack, she heard Senan's drawl, echoing down the hall.

'Of course you're staying the full night at the ball. It's the first night when they finally stop treating us like children and let us get our hands on the Fodder. You wouldn't want to miss that, would you? Your uncle told me to make sure you enjoyed all the benefits of Second Island. You're not going to be a prude now, are you?'

'No, of course not,' came Ionain's voice. 'I'm just not a big one for parties, that's all.'

'Leave it to me, I'll show you how to enjoy yourself in true Channeller style. Keeper, come here a moment.'

At this last Senan raised his voice. Reluctantly Eadha made her way down to the central chamber. Senan and Ionain stood outside on a stone balcony jutting over the sea. Waves could just be heard crashing at the base of the cliff far below. White curtains billowed as the two stepped back inside. Senan sat down at a desk inlaid with ivory and gold leaf, leaning back in his chair to stare at Eadha. Ionain moved away, pouring himself a drink from a beaten silver jug that stood on a sideboard.

'Pour me one, too. I'm gasping still from that race earlier—who would have thought Coll was such a neat sailor?'

Eadha stood unspeaking in the centre of the room.

'Keeper. About time. Lay out my clothes for the ball, would you? My manservant is ill, but I told Master Joen you can fill in until a replacement arrives from Erisen. That's right, isn't it? You were a servant or goatherd or some such in Ailm's Keep?'

Eadha flushed red but held her tongue. Ionain handed Senan a full cup.

It was the first time she'd been in the same room as Ionain since before the spring trials. Seeing him up close her heart gave the leap it always did. He did not look at her and went to stand again on the balcony.

'Now, Ionain, don't sulk,' Senan called after him. In a conspiratorial whisper he said to Eadha, 'Your little stunt quite took the gloss off Ionain and Linn's win at the spring trials. Everyone thinks you helped him by deliberately blocking my channel and I should have won.'

'But that's not true,' she blurted.

'Really? Well, in any event, I volunteered to help Master Joen ensure you never forget your place again and now here you stand, assigned to me. I hope you're looking forward to it as much as I am.'

Barely hearing what he said, Eadha was already hurrying over to the steps leading up to the balcony.

'Ionain, please, I'm so sorry if I spoiled your win. I didn't block Senan on purpose, if that's what you think—it was an accident.'

'Ah, ah, ah, naughty,' came Senan's voice as Ionain finally turned from looking out over the sea, no look upon his face that she could recognise.

Instead for the first time in her life she saw a resemblance to his uncle, Huath, some hardening about the eyes and the mouth. Staring into space, not meeting her eyes once, he spoke distantly, formally.

'Keeper Eadha. I appreciate I have in the past permitted familiarity of address because you are a member of my father's staff. I must, however, remind you that here on Second Island all Channellers should be addressed by their proper titles, both in public and in private.'

Eadha frowned, drawing her head back as she stared up at him, half-smiling as if to acknowledge the bad joke that this was, had to be. He'd never held a grudge in his life, couldn't bear to stay mad with anyone. She was the harsh one, the one who had to be coaxed out of a sulk.

'Ionain?' she said.

Ionain said nothing. He took a long drink and came down the steps past her to join Senan by the desk. She swivelled as he passed, staring at him in disbelief.

She knew his face so well—so much better than her own. All she needed was the slightest widening of his eyes, a sideways sliding glance as he passed her, and she would know this was not really happening. It was just some elaborate game and he'd forgotten to tell her the rules before they started.

But his features were frozen into a fine, tanned mask as he settled himself on a divan, flicking some imaginary dust off his trousers.

'Ionain?' she said again, still staring, mutely pleading until at last he raised his eyes towards her. Eyes that were just that, nothing more, shuttered and dark as he looked at her expressionlessly.

'I trust you will give good service to Lord De Lane during your time as his Keeper,' he said before taking another drink.

'Atta boy,' chuckled Senan delightedly. 'Now Keeper, run along, we have a Welcome Ball to prepare for. I will call you when I need you.'

Eadha swung about on her heel and left, willing the tears back, tipping her head up so they couldn't overflow down her face as she walked unsteadily back down the corridor that was suddenly a hundred miles long. In her room, her bag lay open and half-unpacked on the bed. Her eyes were caught by the soft gleam of amber, just visible beneath her spare tunic. She pulled it out. It was the little tower Ionain had given her for her birthday, over a year and more than a lifetime ago when he'd bowed to her, his face shining with laughter, and called her 'my lady'. Holding it loosely in her hand, she sat in the bare space of her room and stared at the wall as she heard the outer door open and close.

Ionain was gone, and Senan was already shouting for her to come and dress him.

His outfit for the Welcome Ball was elaborate; layers of fine cloth overlaid with an embellished tunic, heavy trews and calf-leather boots. With her aunt's eye she could see the hours of skilled craftsmanship in every panel of the tunic. He shrugged it on carelessly, tugging petulantly where it caught slightly around his waist. He'd become heavier in the quiet weeks since the spring trials ended; his powerful build needed to be active to hold off running to fat.

Eadha thought of Ionain. He'd always been light as a feather; she'd been able to lift him for years, until it became too much of an indignity for him to be given a boost up a tree or onto the cottage's curved roof. She loved the lightness, the spareness of him, the slender fingers, the elegant length. Her chest hurt her as she loosened the ties on Senan's tunic until he was satisfied. As he left, he turned at the door and called back to her.

'Make sure this place is immaculate before you come down; I expect I'll have people back later. Oh, and before I drink too much to remember, you are to report to the Fodder Hold tomorrow morning for your remedial training. Now, hold still.'

In the next instant Eadha sagged as though from a blow to the stomach. Swift as thought, Senan had channelled her, draining her energy so she sank to her knees in weakness.

'Just needed a little extra for the party, you'll be fine in a while,' and he was away, leaving Eadha sick and shaken.

CHAPTER 25
THE WELCOME BALL

Tendrils of music and laughter snaked down the corridor to wind themselves about Eadha, pulling her aching legs towards the Banqueting Hall. Enormous doors stood wide, revealing an antechamber that opened into the space beyond. Storey after storey it rose, the height of the tower. All the way up there were balconies and cross-walks and in between cushioned eyries, curtained nooks and spaces. The walls were hung with tapestries, while heavy red curtains framed the deep-set windows that led onto stone terraces built over the sea. As Eadha stepped into the antechamber, the setting sun shot its last golden flares through the western windows as it sank behind Erisen. Were-lights sprang into life all through the hall as the daylight faded, a relay of torchbearers catching and carrying the sun's light on into the darkening night.

Fires were lit at intervals all around the walls with alcoves in between, some filled with tables of laughing apprentices, others discreetly curtained. Just like on First Island, there were tables creaking with food: fresh-channelled nectarines, plums, strawberries from the greenhouses all piled high, luscious sweetmeats and cakes of every description. But this time there were also decanters of wine from the vineyards and barrels of beer brewed from force-grown hops standing all around the room, ladles and rows of goblets beside them.

On the balconies above, musicians played, fiddles and flutes swirling. Powerful bass drums, normally used to set the beat of a house raising, throbbed all the way down to the roots of Second House far below their feet. As Eadha arrived, Linn flew up in the air to where the fiddlers stood and taking a violin began playing a whirling frenzy of a tune, channelling her power into her fingertips until they blurred, moving across the strings with impossible speed, flying all the while higher and higher until she was playing from just underneath the tower dome. Beneath her the apprentices gathered, cheering and clapping, before others seized instruments, too, and the moment collapsed into shards of noise as fiddles and flutes, drums and tambourines began to sound from all round the hall in overlapping circles of noise and energy, while underneath the bass drums kept up their relentless beat.

In front of Eadha a red velvet rope barred her entrance to the main hall. A senior Keeper gestured her towards a bench set against the wall of the antechamber.

'Apprentice Keepers may only enter at the grace and favour of a Channeller.'

Behind her she saw Gry and a handful of other Keeper students sitting on plain benches. They were placed to face the hall so there was no choice but to watch the Channellers' party. She settled down beside Gry.

'Better get used to this,' was all he said before tipping his head back and closing his eyes.

As the evening wore on the volume increased, the laughter became more shrill, the whoops more hoarse. For these next two months, until midsummer when they rode away to Westport, Eadha's class would share Second Island with the just-graduated class of Risen. The Welcome Ball was the night when these two groups of Rising and Risen apprentices first came together.

Used to her smaller class on First Island, this doubled throng of sixty or so apprentices laughing and chattering in the Banqueting Hall seemed improbably large to Eadha. The skills of the Risen were also far beyond those of Ionain and his friends. For the last year on Second Island, they'd studied the crafts of illusion and dragon combat, and this was their chance to show off to the newly arrived class. All through the hall illusions swirled: star bursts of colour showering down from the dome, flowers that bloomed and faded beneath their feet in a heartbeat, tableaux from famous battles racing across the tapestries and out into the summer night to disappear in the snap of a finger.

At first their displays were greeted with sincere claps and cheers. But as the evening wore on and the newly arrived Keeper girls clustered in admiration about the older, more experienced Risen Channellers, Senan and some of the other Rising boys became disgruntled. They were not yet used to the free-flowing wine and beer; many had started drinking as soon as they arrived, skipping food altogether. As midnight came and went, it took its toll. Boys staggered across the floor, draping their arms possessively around their partners, slurring into their ears to come away. Couples began to disappear into the curtained alcoves set in the walls all the way up the hall, Keeper girls giggling as they were lifted up in the air by Channellers.

All through the evening Master Joen and other senior Masters came and went past Eadha in a steady rota. For the most part they sat in a curtained alcove just inside the hall. Never fewer than two of them, they watched unperturbed as the volume rose and the apprentices slurred and staggered about, though none were ever so far gone as to disturb the Masters' table. Though the Masters made no move to intervene, from the intent look on Master Joen's face as he watched the apprentices celebrate, Eadha had the sense he was noting everything they did; that this was as much part of their training as any lesson.

Remembering Senan's gleeful anticipation about finally getting his hands on Fodder, Eadha looked about for them, but she couldn't see them. If they were here in the Banqueting Hall, they were still discreetly hidden.

Ionain had arrived shortly after Eadha, sweeping past in a phalanx of Great Family offspring, Ailbhe at its head, regal in a red column of a dress. He didn't even glance her way as he passed the bench where she and Gry sat. He was dressed in an embroidered tunic Eadha's aunt had sewn for him not long before he left Ailm's Keep. She remembered how he'd grumbled about the fittings and the fussing. That all he needed was a warm coat and good boots, that he wasn't going to waste his time on parties when he could be learning illusions or flying.

The disconnect between then and now left her dizzy. When she closed her eyes and focused, she could run a thread between them, silvery and true in its mirrored sheath, snapping taut wherever Ionain went in the Banqueting Hall. Yet when she opened them again, there he was; drinking steadily, listening to Ailbhe and Senan, laughing loudly and not once acknowledging his oldest friend in all the world perched on a hard bench beyond a red rope.

Senan, meanwhile, had grown red-faced and irritated as the group he'd assembled around him in one of the alcoves began to disintegrate, people drifting over to watch the Risen Channellers weaving their beautiful tales. Eadha saw Ionain shuffle across the centre of the hall to join Ailbhe, followed closely by Coll. She'd never seen him drunk like this before, his face flushed and hectic, his hair in disarray. He clutched a wine goblet to his chest as if fearful of dropping it. Unable to hold it steady he called a servant over to refill it, swaying slightly on his feet until Coll dragged him to a seat where he slumped, propping his head up with his hand.

Shortly afterwards Linn passed by the velvet rope. Seeing Eadha and Gry seated there, backs and legs numb from their long vigil on the wooden seats, she waved them in with an expansive hand.

'Come in, come in, how silly, come in,' she cried, before wandering off unsteadily. Still weak from Senan's channel earlier Eadha filled a plate with food and she and Gry sat in a quiet corner out of the way. In the centre of the room Senan stood and called loudly to the Risen Channellers about him.

'It's all very well for you to play with pretty pictures, but is that really all you can do? Surely it's about time we used some real power?' He flew up and out onto the highest west-facing terrace, followed by some of the Risen.

'Very well then, cousin,' said a tall, blond-haired boy, laying his yew staff down. 'Ever heard of were-diving?'

'Excellent, that's more like it.'

'The rules are simple. One person sends a were-light diving to the sea as fast as they can, the other has to dive and catch it before it hits the water or take a dunking.'

'Alright. Ready? Go!' and using the power he'd taken from Eadha that evening Senan called up a shining were-light and sent it streaking down towards the waves far below.

His cousin raced to the balcony and in one fluid movement dived over the wall and powered down after the tiny light, arms straight out in front of him, legs kicking as he sent power pulsing through them, flashing past cliff walls slick with water. Although the light had a good head start from Senan's powerful throw he gained quickly on it and caught it well above the spray thrown up by the waves crashing below, swooping around gracefully and back up to land on the terrace without a drop on him. Half the crowd had arrived to watch the race by then, some of the Channellers flying out into the night sky for a better view. To the cheers of his Risen classmates Senan's cousin turned to him, laughing.

'Your turn!'

Lacking his cousin's experience, Senan's start was slower, but he accelerated hard and caught the little light just above the waves, wetting only the backs of his hands as he scooped it up and away. The game was on then, as Channeller after Channeller flew out into the night, plummeting towards the sea. The Risen showed them other games: obstacle races around the turrets, in and out of the windows, through tunnels. Others flew out with their Keeper partners, who shrieked and clutched them about the neck when they saw the sheer drop below. The mild night was filled with the sound of laughter and screams, lights winking in and out of existence.

But as the night lightened towards the east, one by one tired Channellers began to filter back into the hall. Eadha had put a shield in place after Senan's raid on her life-force earlier, well hidden behind her thought-wall so he would just think her still drained. She was glad of it then as from all around the room she sensed Channeller threads snaking out, seeking power to replace that drained by the antics of the night. Senan wandered over to where she stood. She felt his power brush against her wall and come away; after a moment's puzzlement he shrugged and thrust his goblet towards her.

'Keeper, fetch me a refill. I'll be over yonder,' gesturing towards an alcove where the curtains had remained drawn all evening. Gry smiled at her sympathetically as she got up, stiff from sitting all evening.

Pushing aside the alcove curtains to hand Senan his fresh cup, her eyes met a row of slumped forms; some fallen to the floor, others sitting, heads on the table. At first, she mistook them for drunk students. But as her silver fish gave a sudden leap of recognition, she realised that all about her were Fodder. Her eyes widened in shock as her senses registered the scale of the life-force sleeting past her from the alcove, out and up into the Banqueting Hall. Inside, her silver fish twisted as though it longed to join the streams of power as they flowed soundlessly by. So, this was how they did it. The Fodder were here in the Banqueting Hall, just as Senan had said, but still kept discreetly behind a curtain. That way the more squeamish Channellers wouldn't have to be faced with the reality of what they were doing, if they didn't want to, while the more brutal, like Senan, were free to come in and drain them directly if they wanted to.

In front of her Senan sat, holding the hand of a thin, dark-haired girl lying almost unconscious beside him. As Eadha watched she moaned and tried weakly to pull her hand away; it was almost entirely encased by his large hands as he gripped her tightly.

'Sit,' he commanded. 'This will be part of your remedial training anyway.' He held up the limp hand.

'Now this one is almost useless. If I take much more she will go past the point of recovery; she won't have enough energy left to eat and restore herself. A good Keeper would have switched me away a while ago. My father always says the trick is to keep them at the point where they are too exhausted to waste any energy talking or moving, but not so spent the thread is compromised and they tip over into an irreversible spiral.'

He dropped the girl's hand, losing interest, and she slid limply to the floor where she lay, breathing shallowly. At Senan's nod a manservant dragged the unconscious girl to the back of the alcove, where he opened a narrow hatch and loaded her body into it. Closing the hatch, he rapped once sharply on the side. The sound of distant machinery could be heard, echoing faintly up a shaft from far below.

To Eadha's questioning look Senan smiled.

'Fodder hatch. Sends the used ones back to the hold. We should get some fresh ones in a minute.' He sat back, staring at Eadha over his wine glass. 'Best cure for a hangover, a good drain. Young ones are the best; their energy is the most cleansing, I find. Second Island is known for the quality of its Fodder; only the best for us Rising boys. You'd make good Fodder, you know—all that fresh country air in Ailm's Keep, hearty walks with young Ionain. For your sake you'd better hope your remedial training goes well. There is only one way off this island—as a Risen. Fall at this hurdle and you'll spend the rest of your regrettably short life as a hangover cure for us Rising boys down in the hold.'

He pushed back the bench.

'Come and tell me when the new Fodder arrives, there's a good Keeper.' Senan had left the curtain ajar as he left, and through the gap Eadha could see the Banqueting Hall, grey now in the first light of morning. Half-emptied goblets stood testament to the night before on every surface, half-eaten food still piled on plates or ground into the carpets. Here and there students slept on velvet seats or slumped against walls, the occasional couple wandering past, holding each other up as their heads formed the apex of an unsteady triangle.

Senan wandered through the centre of the room, pausing to kick against an insensible form; Ionain passed out, still clutching his goblet, clothes stained and drenched from his failed were-dive earlier. Eadha drew the curtain and sat on in the alcove. The only sound was the shallow breathing of the people around her as they struggled to hold on to enough energy to keep breathing, while the Channellers in the hall beyond drained them again and again to stave off their hangovers. In. Out. In. Out. In.

CHAPTER 26
TWILIGHT

For the Rising Channellers, Eadha thought, the summer that followed on Second Island must have felt like a summer of perpetual twilight. Of mornings spent sleeping off the hangover from the night before, rising in bedrooms with the curtains closed against the bright glare of late afternoon sunshine, bathing and eating in a haze before dressing with care, channelling fresh energy and going in search of that night's party. Second House was hung with lanterns that came alive at dusk, drawing the apprentices on and out into the night. Every night after that first Welcome Ball there was another party hosted by the Risen somewhere on the island; in apartments, in courtyards, out on the battlements, down by the lake at the heart of the island.

It was a tradition as old as Second House itself and the Risen's first duty as fully fledged Channellers, this hazing of Ionain and the other Rising. It was also the Risen's last summer before they left on a year of dragon patrols, a life of sleeping on bare ground, living off rations and knowing not all of them would return. Taken together it made for a fierce intensity as the Risen determinedly lost themselves under the summer stars and dragged the Rising into the night with them.

Each Risen Channeller took it in turns as ringmaster for the night, competing to outdo each other in excess; the wine and beer, the exotic foods, the wildness of the music, the dancing. Smoking braziers burnt molash, the drug that had almost overwhelmed Eadha that first morning in the temple. Inhaling it heightened the rush of power, so the threads all about them were more visible, glowing in the smoke. The apprentices would lift glowing coals from the brazier with tongs and place them in a silver bowl, cover their heads with a hood and lean over, breathing in the smoke while the coal burned. Then lying back, they would drain power from the Fodder sat soundlessly by, hidden by curtains or screens, the drug heightening the senses so the life-force flowed into them with an almost ecstatic surge of pleasure.

And the power—the endless flow of those shining threads, that sent them racing out into the night, filled to the brim, bursting with possibility, rocketing up into the starry sky, burning it off as fast as it could be absorbed. There were flying races out over the sea, powered coracle races about the lake. They channelled power into horses and raced each other on a circuit around the lake and up into the foothills of the mountains at the eastern end of the island, hooves flying along paths lit by were-lights. There were drunken combat games, Risen versus Rising, Senan and the other Rising boys only half in jest as they strove to outdo the older boys and give a good account of themselves to the Keeper girls watching and cheering.

And slowly, night by night, the Fodder were more in evidence. Always discreetly hidden behind a curtain or a screen, but accessible now, to the curious. Some, Eadha saw, stayed away, avoided the curtained alcoves, changed the subject when it came up. Others, though, pressed eagerly in, gawking at these creatures finally revealed. They were almost always young—not much older than the Risen Channellers, young men and women, dressed in plain grey shifts. They were not chained like the people Eadha had seen in the Keep, but sat docile, heads bowed, never speaking, even when the Channeller students sat beside them, heads spinning on molash, seizing their hands to drain their life-force more directly.

As the summer wore on, some among the Rising Channellers became more interested in draining the Fodder boys and girls than in using the power itself. Groups of them would sit about a table, taking it in turns to drain the Fodder beside them, watching as they began to slump and eventually collapse, emptied. They would place bets on how quickly this or that person could be drained to the point of collapse, giggling when they fell, bragging about the ferocity of their draw, about how many people's life-force they could contain.

Of them all, Senan took the most sadistic pleasure in the effect of his channelling. Each evening as Eadha dressed him in his embellished tunics he would speculate about the quality of the Fodder that evening, wondering if particular girls or boys had survived the night before, chuckling when they disappeared, griping petulantly when the same faces appeared night after night, complaining about used goods. Eadha was his unwilling audience, bathing him, dressing him, and each night sitting for hours in the spectator section behind the red velvet rope.

'It can't be an exclusive party unless someone is excluded,' noted Gry dryly on yet another evening spent trying to get comfortable on the hard benches.

There was a pattern now to those evenings. Gry, Eadha and the other less popular Rising Keepers would spend the first hours as an unwilling audience to the Channellers' antics. The parties were increasingly uncomfortable viewing, as apprentices like Senan deliberately left open the curtains of the Fodder alcoves so they could be seen more openly. Slumped, drained and exhausted while groups of Channellers sat round the tables, drinking and eating heavily, pausing from time to time to inhale molash and top up their power from the nearest person. Eventually Senan would get drunk enough that he ordered Eadha in to act as his cupbearer, refilling his cup and following him about.

Senan, the twins and Ionain still formed the same core group as they had on First Island, but joined now by Ailbhe, Mara and their hangers-on. Ailbhe never left Ionain's side, keeping him supplied with wine, hanging on his words. He was often tipsy when he arrived for that evening's celebration, good-naturedly shrugging off Senan and Coll's teasing when he failed yet again at whatever contest the Channellers had dreamt up for that night: riding his horse into a ditch at the start of a race around the island, tumbling headfirst into the water during were-diving contests. Meanwhile the Keeper girls, fully armoured in their gowns, picked carefully at the food and drink. Never losing themselves in the revelries, but always there, cheering on their Channellers, eyes darting, watching the other girls for any hint of a threat, watching the Channeller boys for any hint of boredom, ceaselessly patrolling their little patch.

After that first encounter in Senan's apartment, Eadha had simply faded out of his world. Ionain didn't speak to her, didn't look at her, seemed to move in a reality where she didn't exist. Ailbhe and her friends, too, confident Eadha was no longer a threat, simply acted as though she wasn't there, as if they really had succeeded in driving her away. As she and Gry sat together on yet another night when Ionain, Ailbhe and their group had strolled past without so much as a nod in their direction, Gry nudged her.

'The Masters should really be making more of our powers.'

She was hunched on the bench, hands clasped around her knees in a half-trance of boredom, but this was enough to startle her into turning her head.

'Shh!' she muttered. 'Someone might hear you.'

'But these powers of invisibility we seem to have developed. Surely they could find some use for them?'

She sagged back, closing her eyes with a 'humpf' of a half-laugh. 'You had me worried for a minute there.'

'It doesn't excuse it, but I know you know he's under huge pressure. From his Family and the Masters to get things back on an even keel in House Ailm after a dry generation,' said Gry. He nodded across to where Ionain was running a hand through his hair, grown long and tangled, smiling at some whispered comment from Ailbhe. 'Secure the future.'

Eadha looked across at Gry's eyes; felt too raw for the sympathy there.

'I can say that. I can even think it, but I can't feel it,' she replied quietly. 'I can't feel anything. It's like the threads inside me—they've been severed and now I can't finish anything, a thought, or a feeling, because they just run into nothing.' She took a deep breath. 'I just can't shake the feeling that it's not him over there, that he isn't here. He's walked every step of my life beside me until now, but sometimes it feels like he didn't make it to Second Island at all.'

She subsided back into silence.

It made no difference, ultimately, for she still loved that shell more than any other thing in the world. But it comforted her a little to tell herself it was not her friend who stared past her as she poured Senan's wine, who spent every night so drunk he had to be helped back to his apartment by Ailbhe. That his soul had fled on the western winds as he sailed his tiny coracle across the open sea from First Island, leaving behind only the shell. That the real Ionain was waiting for her somewhere beyond Second Island, waiting until the day she could leave that place and never return.

CHAPTER 27
WORLDS ABOVE AND
WORLDS BELOW

It may have been a summer of twilight for the Channeller apprentices, but for Eadha it was a summer of two worlds. A world above and a world below, linked only by the slender shafts sunk into the cliffs beneath Second House. In accordance with Master Dathin's punishment for her failure at the spring trials, from her first morning on Second Island, Eadha rose just after dawn and slipped through the sunny morning halls to the heavy gate that barred the entrance to the Fodder Hold.

The first time she presented herself at the holds' entrance to begin her remedial training, she was ushered in by the Head Keeper on Second Island, Fiarone, the gate banging shut behind her. They climbed into a wooden box and with a jolt Eadha felt herself falling.

'Don't worry,' said Fiarone, the ghost of a smile on her pale face as she saw Eadha's knuckles whiten, gripping tight to the handholds cut into the box sides. 'It's Channeller operated, and we are not short of power down here.'

They passed several doorways cut into the rock as they

descended. Following Eadha's gaze Fiarone said briefly, 'Those upper levels are my office and the infirmary, below are the holds. I'm just about to start my rounds, so you'll come down with me.'

They landed with a soft thump on the sandy floor of the lowest level and stepped out into the main Fodder Hold. It was a cavernous space at sea level, a sequence of natural caves hollowed out further by the Channellers over generations. The walls were bare rock, fresh water running down them in places and collecting on the sand and stone floor into rivulets that led eventually to the sea outside. In front as far as she could see stretched row after row of bunkbeds, some four and five beds high where the cave roof permitted, others only one or two where the ceiling sloped down to the floor. The light was dim, torches set into the walls, hissing and flickering in the damp air.

Fiarone set off ahead of her, accompanied by a group of Keepers and guards. Eadha fell in behind. Many of the beds in the first section were occupied by sleeping forms and Fiarone stopped at each one. She would carefully examine the occupant, shaking them awake, taking their pulse, lifting their eyelids, measuring their waists and barking instructions back to the Keepers behind. Most were left to sleep on; some were lifted out onto trolleys and wheeled away back to the lift. In one case the person didn't respond at all, and shaking her head in irritation Fiarone gestured to one of the guards. He wrapped the body in its sheet and lifted it over his shoulder, carrying it away to the back of the cave.

In the next cave, people sat in long rows on stone seats hollowed out of the wall. Each seat had arms and a ledge in front. They were chained to the walls, the chains long enough to allow them to slump forward onto the ledge or sideways onto the arms but no further. Above them rose a shaft, hollowed out in the cliff, so their life-force could be more easily reached from the surface. Beneath the row of stone seats, a channel had been dug into the floor. As Eadha watched streams of urine trickled from some of the seated forms into the channel, which sloped down into the natural rivulets to be carried away. They were the Fodder currently in use, being channelled from far above by the Masters and apprentices going about their daily business on the sunny surface of the island. Once more the Head Keeper and her team examined each person, tipping up their chins to check the eyes, feeling some for signs of fever, measuring their weight, reaching briefly into their minds, assessing their strength. Some were pushed back upright if they were deemed strong enough to sit, their chains tightened, others unshackled and carried back to the bunks. Fiarone stopped at one fair-haired girl and turned to a young Keeper, clearly irritated.

'Why has this one not been kept for evening duty? We are short on presentables at the moment with the current attrition rate.'

'Yes, Head Keeper, I am sorry. Master Joen specifically required a full complement today as they are completing the library extension. I carefully assessed her and was planning to put her on a double shift, covering tonight as well.'

Fiarone thought for a moment.

'Very well, it's not ideal as she will be low by tonight and might expire depending on the games, but we are expecting a fresh shipment so we should have enough cover even if she does. Continue, but keep her watered and if the extension is done early put her down for a sleep—even a couple of hours and we might not lose her.'

Her rounds completed Fiarone returned to the lift, calling to Eadha to follow her while her team remained behind.

'Running repairs,' she commented as the doors closed. 'This is the largest Fodder Hold on Domhain and it's a logistical nightmare, trying to keep so many inexperienced Channellers supplied with power every night, as well as providing power to the Masters for the day-to-day running of the House. We have to run several shifts day and night and the attrition rate is high. Your classmates are a rough group, and when we lose Fodder it's a long journey from Erisen to bring out more. We're having to manage on a skeleton supply at the moment until the next shipment arrives. And then we'll have all the Masters claiming they need the fresh Fodder more; they all love that first draw.'

The lift stopped at a door cut from the rock.

'I'm going to assign you to Records. It's where we usually put Rising Keepers sent down here for disciplining. Good for motivation.'

They'd entered the Head Keeper's offices on the higher levels. Here the rooms were bright, with windows tunnelled from the rock looking out to sea, furnished with sturdy wooden tables and chairs. Eadha was directed to another group of Keepers, leafing through piles of paper.

These were the Records, details of the people sent to Second Island as Fodder. In each case they listed the age, gender, weight, as well as technical Keeper assessments of their reserves and the reason for being sent. Some were "swept"—unemployed, unskilled people who could be taken at any stage by a Master or Channeller for use. Others were deemed "volunteers"—skilled workers ordered by their Channeller to do a stint in order to make up numbers, or as a punishment for some minor transgression or simply because there was not enough regular work for them to do. Last were the renegades— those identified as opposed to or critical of the Channeller rule. Some were listed as having been captured on tracker patrol, others reported by Great Family members or Masters for holding problematic views.

After the first few confusing days the allocations began to make sense to Eadha. The renegades were the most dispensable and would be allocated where particularly heavy drains were likely, with a real risk of losing their lives or being permanently burned out over time. The swept were next, slightly less likely to be assigned to fatal work, and finally the volunteers, those with the best chance of surviving their time on Second Island and returning to Erisen; though whether they'd ever regain the strength to resume their former lives was a matter of luck.

They came in every shape, size and colour; young, old, men, women, soldiers, farmers, musicians, skilled and unskilled, ugly, beautiful. The Channellers didn't care; they were simply a resource, vessels for the energy that sustained the Channeller way of life. Eadha was put writing out fresh arm tags for each of the Fodder, with their basic details and most importantly their strength levels. A good Keeper would be able to maintain a steady draw of power across a Fodder pool of varying power, but here on the Island where the Keepers were less experienced, the Head Keeper took responsibility for delivering groups of Fodder with roughly even levels of strength, to minimise the chance of accidents. The main risk to a Channeller was if the power supply failed, if they or their Keeper misjudged how much was left and failed to switch away in time. This could prove fatal in battle or even if the Channeller was simply in mid-air, left without the power to land safely.

Eadha sat with a group of junior Keepers, listening to them chat, chuckling among themselves as they swapped tales of the different ruses tried by people to conceal their strength, trying vainly to hold something back. Some of the renegades, in particular, had rudimentary shielding skills, but an experienced Keeper could quickly break through them to find whatever pathetic stores of energy might have been hidden away; anyone found husbanding strength in this way was severely punished. Every time she heard the Keepers joke about breaking down Fodder defences, Eadha's senses went instinctively to her own thought-wall; the dense weave of thoughts Magret had taught her to use to hide her true powers, grateful there was at least one form of concealment Fiarone and her

Keepers weren't able to detect.

As Fiarone was fond of telling her team on her rounds, the best kind of Fodder was exhausted Fodder. Fiarone had none of the fanatical submissiveness of Head Keeper Fiachna. Her one over-riding interest in running the holds was efficiency, her goal to keep the Fodder permanently drained to the point of near-collapse, worked around the clock and given the minimum amount of time to rest and recover before being drained once more. That way they needed less supervision and had no strength to plot dissent or try to escape. She told of how, in generations past, Fodder had tried to escape from Second Island, killing guards and setting out in stolen boats. Her predecessors as Head Keeper had learned from that, honing their abilities to judge a person's reserves of strength almost to the last breath. Now they prided themselves on needing minimal guards down in the Fodder Hold, so skilled were they in ensuring their charges had nothing left in them to think or talk, let alone rebel.

Most of the Fodder spent all their time on Second Island below ground in the holds. Only a few were sent above ground in the service lifts that connected the holds to the school at various points. The Masters for the most part didn't need the Fodder especially close by to channel them. However, for the younger Channellers it was easier if they were nearby, and there was still a novelty, a seductive thrill in seeing the effect of their power as they drained someone. In the spirit of pandering to their every whim, some Fodder, drugged to ensure their docility, were sent each night to the parties above ground. These were the Fodder Eadha had seen that first night at the Welcome Ball, and every night after that. They were always the youngest and most presentable ones; as one Keeper observed while loading them into the service lift, the Rising Channellers didn't want to channel a woman who looked like their mother, it rather took the fun out of it.

'It's always the same,' remarked Head Keeper Fiarone on her

rounds one morning as midsummer approached. 'They arrive here from First Island hardly using their powers, but by the time the Midsummer Ball comes around we're flat out down here as they channel from first thing in the morning to clear the cobwebs until last thing at night to shake off the day; by the time they leave the island they won't be able to live without it.' And Eadha understood this was the whole point of the summer, with its endless parties and contests. It was as much part of the Masters' stages as the purification on First Island, the Masters' way of ensuring the Channellers were so hooked on power they couldn't contemplate an existence without it.

Each day Eadha was released in time to report to Senan's quarters and help him prepare for the evening's festivities. In his elegant suite filled with light and air, the sense of dislocation was absolute. The morning felt like a dream, a recurrent nightmare of slumped bodies and clipboard carrying Keepers. It was only when she saw her handwritten tags on the wrists of the Fodder sat in their alcoves at the end of the night that the day came about full circle.

In her weeks underground the Keepers were never so explicit as to say that Eadha might end up there herself. There was no need; a week in Records was all she needed to see how easily a person might fall foul of the Masters or the Families and end up in a Fodder Hold, watching their life-force trickle out of them, day by changeless day. Eadha understood. For those apprentices for whom the seduction of First Island did not work, the Masters did not hesitate to use fear, showing them the choice, after all, was binary; between being above or below, using or being used, living or dying.

All through the summer she hardly needed to send any power to Ionain as he was barely channelling. He drank so much at the nightly parties that Senan and the others had given up trying to persuade him to join their games. He'd wave them away with his goblet before handing it to the ever-present Ailbhe to fetch him a refill. It was as well, because as the weeks in the hold wore on Eadha's heart began to fail her. She would draw the line from belly to heart, but there it stopped, too full with what she'd seen in the hold to release the power on to Ionain. He had to know he had hardly any power now but he didn't seem to care, pleading a summer cold when the hangover excuse didn't work, or draping his arm about Ailbhe with a meaningful wink at Senan.

It meant she'd some spare strength in her for the first time since channelling had begun. And one afternoon, as she draped an embroidered tunic over his shoulder she deferentially, politely asked Senan that she be allowed to keep for him when he drew power during the parties.

'I've learned so much from my remedial training in the Fodder Hold and it would be of such help to me to practice with you, my lord.'

Senan was tickled by the idea he drew so much power at a party he needed a Keeper to marshal it. Soon he wouldn't drain power before any Channeller party game without calling Eadha over. And when she felt his channel reach through her, she would dutifully bow her head and relay it on to the young Fodder men and women beside her. Senan was an excellent Channeller, adept at judging the power available and with a cruel streak that took a vicious pleasure in pulling every last drop. But in Eadha he had a Keeper who knew each one of those Fodder victims' faces, ages and just how far they could be drained and still left with enough strength to lie awake a half-hour before sleep, whisper a word or two to the person on the bunk opposite, maybe even remember for a little while who they had once been.

Quietly, skilfully, she blocked his grasping threads when she judged they'd had enough and instead drew her own strength from belly to heart and out, back into Senan, shielding those morsels of life with her own.

CHAPTER 28
THE GIFT

Eadha's seat in the Records room was near one of the windows hewn into the cliff face. Outside cormorants wheeled and dived into the sea below, light winged terns arrowed past, dropping from their nests built far above on rocky outcrops. She missed flying. Second Island was less wooded than First, fewer places for her to hide and practice her own gift. As she worked writing out the endless tags, she watched the birds beyond the thick dragonglass, riding the updrafts, holding themselves perfectly still, not a scrap of energy wasted until, with a single wing flick, beautiful in its perfect economy, they dived on a tell-tale flash in the waters beneath them. That was how she dreamt of flying.

The Channellers were taught to glory in waste, in burning away the power as soon as it coursed into them, shooting up into the wind, pushing against it as a thing to be defeated. In her power she was more kin to the birds than to them, kin to the young dragon who'd flown with the world's winds in the darkness of winter's night all those months ago. Her power was limited by her heart, by her strength, and so she flew within the wind, let it take her where it would and was grateful for the impossible lightness of it, the brief absolution from the bonds that tied her to the earth.

As she sat staring out the window, Head Keeper Fiarone marched through the Record room, picking up followers as she moved towards the lift, Eadha falling in at the back. The rounds were particularly tense that morning as this was the day of the Midsummer Ball, the last and greatest of the summer parties. Fiarone was worried they might run low on power. Fodder were being pulled off day shifts and sedated so they'd be as rested as possible by evening. Eadha was standing near a tower of bunks, listening to Fiarone and her deputies mutter over attrition rates when there was a soft thump beside her. A girl hardly older than Eadha had slid from her bunk and lay unconscious on the floor beside her.

'What is it now?' snapped Fiarone. The Keeper nearest Eadha bent to examine the girl.

'A volunteer presentable, Head Keeper. Seems to be dehydrated and spent.'

'Oh, for goodness' sake, that's all we need. Apprentice Keeper. Bring her up to the infirmary, tell the nurses we need her in shape for tonight or I'll personally review their own files.'

Eadha bent and half-lifted, half-dragged the girl over to the lift. She was heartbreakingly slight, her thin, triangular face slack as Eadha tried to avoid bumping her against the stony floor. Once inside the lift Eadha laid her down gently onto a trolley and leaned against the wall of the lift to get her breath back. She knew the little face. She was one of the Fodder regularly sent up to the parties. Young and with a shadow of prettiness about her emaciated frame, she counted as a presentable. She was one of about ten girls of similar age who were most often sent up. They had no names down in the hold, but Eadha had given them names of her own—this one she called Donn, brown, after her hair, which even matted and lank was still beautiful. She lifted her hand, thinking to send a pulse of energy into her when

Donn's eyes snapped open.

'Don't.'

Eadha pulled her hand away in shock. The girl sat up, swinging her legs down, and swiftly loosening the trolley's wooden sidebar, jammed it into the gap between the wall and the lift, so that it juddered to a halt.

'That will give us a few minutes.'

'What are you doing?' asked Eadha, now thoroughly bewildered.

The girl lay back on the trolley, spent by her swift movements of a moment before.

'If you give me much energy now, then the infirmary will spot it and they might start asking questions.'

'You know?' asked Eadha.

'Of course I know.'

'Do you all know?'

'Not all of us, but some, we have eyes for power and can see the threads,' said Donn, drawing her knees up and clasping her hands about them.

She smiled grimly at Eadha's shocked face.

'Yes, it's almost funny. A whole island full of learned Masters, a hold crawling with Keepers measuring us down to the last breath and not one of you ever thinks to wonder what we can see. Don't worry, by the way, those of us who can see, we won't say anything about what you're doing. We'll take it to the grave.'

'I'm so sorry,' whispered Eadha.

'For what?' said the girl. 'You're one of the decent ones.'

'But how can you bear it, every day, being used up like that?'

Donn stared at her levelly.

'You have to break. That's what gets whispered to every person their first night in a Fodder wagon, or a hold, or some Great Family Fodder Wing. Accept that this is how it is and let go of any ideas you had about yourself, about what you might do, any hopes you might have had before. That way lies madness, trying to hold on to some rope made of dreams or love, hoping that you can climb up it and out, back onto the surface, back into your life. You have to let go, accept there's no way out, no way around, that this is all there is for you now. Once you're broken you can learn how to just exist, that the only way is to go through it. And then, if you do come out the other side, what you have is a husk that still walks, still breathes, that maybe one day you can fill up again with things that are worth something. You will never be the person you were, you had to give that person up to survive. But you might make a new person who is just as worthy.'

Eadha stood, frozen, staring at Donn.

'Here,' said Donn, scrabbling beneath her thin robe and pulling out a package. 'This is for you. As a thank you.'

'What do you mean?'

'There have always been those who hold back, quietly, gently, trying to spare us within the limits of their ways. It's like a whispered conversation that only we can hear, every night up there in the halls, the touch of those who refrain. But you, you shine. That's what we call you: Grianan, the shining one. You have something none of us have seen before. We see your light, the way you block the fair one's spidery threads before they can suck us dry. It gives us hope, that maybe it does not have to be like this, for always and forever.

'We know you've hidden yourself, that they cannot see what's inside you. But just for one night we can make you beautiful on the outside even if they cannot see what lies within.'

Eadha stared at the little package, the size of her hand.

'The power you leave us with, we have to use it up or the Keepers will detect it. So, we cast about for something we could do. Some of us were seamstresses in our old lives, and I could steal bits and pieces from the students' rooms when I am called there for private sessions.'

Seeing Eadha's distressed face, she lifted up a tired hand and patted Eadha's arm.

'Please, take this as it is given, with joy, not sadness. Being able to do something for another is, after all, the essence of living rather than merely existing. It brought us back to ourselves, for a little while, to do this thing.'

There was a sharp snap as the wood broke and the lift juddered back into motion. Donn lay back down as Eadha hid the package beneath her tunic.

'What is your name?' said Eadha, quietly, staring ahead as she waited for the door to open.

'Seoda,' she murmured, closing her eyes. 'Go, shine for us.'

CHAPTER 29
MIDSUMMER

Eadha did not touch the little package hidden under her tunic until after Senan had left for the Banqueting Hall, but the thought of it carried her through a trying afternoon. Senan was at his most viperish, keyed up about the Midsummer Ball and taking it out on anyone unfortunate enough to come near him. By early evening his bed was piled with outfits he'd tried and discarded, years of craftsmanship and toil tossed aside like so many scraps of paper.

'How am I supposed to appear in public if you can't even lay out a proper outfit?' he raged. 'This is the Midsummer Ball on Lambay, not some goatherd's campfire. Some of us have a Family name to uphold.'

The ball was the last big celebration, the end of transition on Second Island. The next morning the Risen would depart for their dragon postings and the Rising would finally begin their classes in illusion and combat.

It was also Senan's last real opportunity to pair off with someone before the humdrum of Matins and classes took over once more. For all his prowess and his impeccable Family name, his vicious temperament frightened even the Great Family girls, schooled as they'd been since childhood in soothing the egos of vain and pampered Channellers. He'd set his sights early on Linn, confident she couldn't resist the logic of a match with the strongest male Channeller. He hadn't reckoned with her complete disinterest and that, as a Channeller female, she outranked him and couldn't be bullied, impressed or ordered by him to do anything. Confused and thwarted by this unfamiliar impotence, as the days lengthened towards midsummer he turned to the Keeper girls from the Great Families, only to find he'd missed the boat. The best connected were already spoken for, or quickly paired off with Risen Channellers when they came to Second Island. Senan was one of the few left without a partner. Only girls from minor Families (and Eadha) remained, and Senan was never going to accept a consolation prize.

His best hope now was to detach a paired girl from another Channeller; something the Masters permitted but only if the Families and the girl herself agreed. So Senan, Lord De Lane, found himself in the utterly unfamiliar position of supplicant, on his best behaviour, trying to win over girls he'd mocked and teased unmercifully all year on First Island. It did nothing for his mood in private as all his suppressed rage and humiliation exploded in tantrums and punishments for Eadha, his luckless manservant, and any other servants who crossed his path. Having stormed his way through the afternoon he ordered Eadha to stay behind to tidy his discarded clothing before he swept out the door, resplendent in a white tunic embroidered in gold thread.

He couldn't prevent her from attending altogether; the Midsummer Ball was attended by all on Second Island bar the Fodder in the hold. The Masters and Keepers emerged from their studies, towers, and holds to say farewell to the Risen and mark the beginning of the new term. It was the only night all summer when Keeper students had the right to enter without waiting on the grace and favour of Channellers.

The room immaculate once more, Eadha stepped out onto the terrace looking west to where the sun was still high above Domhain's mainland, catching on the white towers of Erisen so that they glittered like sun on waves. Carefully she opened Seoda's package and unfolded what lay within. It was a tunic and skirt. The tunic had been skilfully pieced together from scraps of yellow and gold cloth of different hues, some embellished with sparkling stones, others plain and smooth. It was in the shape of a Channeller combat tunic—bare arms, crossed at the breasts to bind them steady, fitted at the waist. The skirt was a single piece of the softest cloth Eadha had ever felt, falling like water to the ground, so light it lifted at once in the sea breeze, ready to fly on the winds, white as a dove's wing, as a wave top, as a summer cloud shining in the sunlight. Eadha slipped them on, looking at her reflection in the window. She had no shoes apart from her sturdy Keeper boots, but this dress was light incarnate; she would fly to the ball, she thought, on bare feet that did not need to touch the ground, and who, after all, would even look at her?

And fly she did, dropping soundlessly from Senan's terrace, the air rushing about her, caressing her legs through the softness of her skirt. She landed soundlessly on the furthermost balcony of the Banqueting Hall and stared down at the crowded room below. Later they would disperse, into the alcoves, out onto the terraces and further on into the sky, but for now all were gathered in the central rotunda where Master Dathin stood to bid a formal farewell to the Risen. All these Risen Channellers were to depart for their Westport posting the next morning, along with the Risen Keepers assigned to them for combat.

After the solemn blessing glasses were raised and the music began, talk building from a subdued murmur to a steady roar as farewells were shouted and promises made. A few of the Keeper girls in Eadha's class had grown close to Risen Channellers, and as they said goodbye they were almost in tears, clinging to their soon-to-be departed Channellers' arms. The protocol was strict in these matters, though; no crying, just a proud farewell to the brave defenders, but the girls were still young and these Channellers were their futures and it was hard not to cry when your future is walking away from you and might never return.

Eadha stood detached, looking down on it all from her hiding place. But she owed it to Seoda and her friends to show them their dress, the thing of beauty it was. She descended the circular stairs, holding to the side to avoid attention and slipping into a Fodder alcove. Seoda was there with several of the usual presentables. Now she knew to look for it, she saw the quick dart of Seoda's eyes as she entered. She bowed wordlessly, holding the skirt out so they could see how it fell, smooth and shining to the floor.

'Thank you,' she mouthed, 'it's so very beautiful.' With the briefest turn of her head, Seoda flashed her a quick smile and Eadha was turning to go when she was knocked over by Senan as he pushed through the curtains.

'I beg your pardon, my lady,' he began. 'Here, let me help you up, I am so sorry. I did not expect anyone to be here so early in the evening.'

Taking her hand, Senan pulled her carefully to her feet. Only then did he meet her eyes, his own widening in surprise as he realised who it was, dropping her hand at once. He stepped back and looked her up and down.

'Keeper, where did you steal that dress? Have you grown so fond of the holds you want to spend more time down there?'

Eadha bowed her head.

'My mother is a seamstress at Ailm's Keep, she made it for me from leftover scraps Lady Ura gave her. I thought it right to wear it to mark the departure of the Risen, my lord.'

It was the right thing to say. Senan was counting on the Risen leaving to improve his chances of winkling a Keeper girl free from her soldier love. He smirked at being reminded and wagged a half-drunk finger.

'As long as it doesn't give you any notions. Silk purse from a sow's ear and all that. I'll be watching you. Anything out of line and I will confiscate it.' He sat on the bench beside Seoda, dismissing her.

'I won't need you for this one, but be around later.'

Heart thumping, Eadha took a goblet of wine from the nearest table and made her way swiftly out of the crowd, back up to the curtained balcony. Staring down at the revellers, she focused, trying to see how much power Senan was drawing from Seoda and the others; he couldn't need much this early in the evening, but it was a bad sign if he was channelling this soon.

As she concentrated, she saw Ionain enter the rotunda beneath her. He looked tired as he always did these days, his fair hair straggly and unkempt, his fine tunic marked by wine stains that wouldn't come out. Ailbhe was shadowing him, putting a hand on his arm when he reached for a drink. He ignored her, filling a beer tankard to the brim so it sloshed and spilled when he raised it to his mouth and drank deeply. He looked about the Banquet Hall as he did so. For a moment his eyes met Eadha's where she stood on the balcony, almost hidden in the curtains. She saw him take in her warrior's dress before he turned away. Leaning over to Ailbhe, he pointed her and the girls beside her towards the Master Teller, who was just beginning to weave an illusion. Then, as soon as they'd turned away he ran lightly up the stairs, two at a time until he reached Eadha.

Eadha's heart jumped as it always did, as it always would, to see him so close after weeks of passing him by each night in the party crowds, the familiar blue eyes for once staring straight at her with a look both intense and questioning.

'What are you doing?' he hissed.

'Nothing,' she replied, defensively. 'Just watching the party.'

'I mean that dress.' That hurt. She expected no less from Senan but she'd thought more of Ionain.

'Fine, I'll change,' she said, turning away.

'No,' he said, reaching for her arm as she twisted. 'I'm sorry. I didn't mean to be rude. There's nothing wrong with how you look.'

He reddened slightly, turning away to look out at the crowd.

'You look like you, the way you should look, the way I see you whenever I think of you. But wearing that dress, now people will notice you. I thought you understood. We've been doing so well and when I saw you standing here, looking like that, all I could think is now others will see you, too. And that could make things harder for you again.'

He turned back to her, smiling. And it was the old Ionain, her Ionain, with eyes that shone and a smile that swung open every door in her heart.

'But it's just one night, and it's the last night of these awful parties and everyone is distracted with farewells. Please don't take it off, it's beautiful on you.'

Now it was Eadha's turn to redden in confusion and turn away, looking down into the hall once more, her heart racing.

'It looks like your bodyguard will be a while yet. Master Teller is giving them the tale of Kaanesien and he hasn't finished the building of Erisen yet,' she said, after a short, charged silence.

Below them the Master was weaving an image of the dragon Kaanesien snaking around the towers of House Debruin.

Ionain chuckled suddenly.

'Do you remember how we used to drive Beithe cuckoo, saying we'd to finish our stories about Kaanesien before we could come down in the morning. Cook would lambast her when she burned the pot, trying to keep the porridge warm.'

'By the time we got down it would be this horrible, dried lump with black burnt bits on the bottom, but Beithe would be really hurt if we didn't eat it.'

The words tumbled out of her on a river of memory, as if she was back there in the Keep looking at her seven-year-old self.

'I used to slip mine to the wolfhounds when she wasn't looking.'

'Ahh, so that's how you did it; there I was like a fool forcing it down. I always thought you had this iron stomach, but you were faking it the whole time. That's so unfair.'

He smiled across at her again and she was home. The strangled numbness of the nights he'd blanked her; the mundane horror of the days in the holds with the tags, the chains and the worn-out husks of humanity—they all wavered suddenly, like the recollection of a nightmare fleeing as she woke.

So much so she almost blurted out, 'Ionain, I had the most awful dream. I dreamt that I lost you. I dreamed I was buried under your feet, down in the holds with all these people chained to the walls.'

But the touch of Seoda's silk dress against her legs silenced her in its stark, white truth. Instead, she stared mutely at his hand, so brown and slim and perfect on the balcony next to hers.

'Come on,' said Ionain after a pause, reaching across to take her hand and leading her out the window. 'I've wanted to do this with you all summer long. I haven't a lot of power, but I should have enough to keep you safe.'

He picked up her hands and placed them on his shoulders, then wrapped his arms around her waist and lifted them both up into the air, smiling a little self-consciously as they wobbled then floated gently in the air above the tower. His touch was warm in the cooling air, and he pulled her closer, wrapping his arms more tightly around her. She was still almost as tall as him and looking over his shoulder, she rested her head against his and closed her eyes. She sent more power flowing imperceptibly into him, smiling as she felt it flow on out of him then to cushion them both on the night air. Until that moment she hadn't known it was possible to be so simply, completely happy.

They stayed that way a little while, far above the Banquet Hall as the night darkened around them and the first of the Sidhe glittered faintly above Domhain's Eye. But when people began to appear on the balconies seeking the coolness of the night air, Ionain lowered them once more, touching lightly onto the balcony. They stepped apart to stare silently at one another.

Ailbhe appeared through the window almost as soon as they landed. The world turned and Eadha made an excuse, slipping away head bowed. Ionain caught her hand softly as she stepped behind him, holding it until she'd moved out of his reach, her fingers touching his until the last moment.

Down in the rotunda she was reluctant to leave altogether, her heart too full to do anything other than feel, the absoluteness of her relief filling her until she wanted to fly up to the domed ceiling above, burst through the dragonglass heart of it all and up and out into the night sky once more. She was whole again; she was still loved and she could bear anything. Gry came over, awkwardly resplendent in a deep red tunic that suited his dark hair.

'You look like you got a top up of your own,' he said, smiling as all around them the Channellers were disappearing into Fodder alcoves.

Eadha smiled back, unable to hide her happiness. As they talked, a bodyguard of silk and organdie swept past, Ionain's fair hair just visible in the centre. She raised her glass slightly in his direction and he grinned ruefully back over the heads of the Keeper girls surrounding him before turning back to Ailbhe. Not one girl looked at Eadha as they shepherded the couple on and out of the room.

'Ouch. That's what you get for looking presentable,' said Gry. 'No Winter Ball invitations for you this year.'

'Keeper, over here.' It was Senan, beckoning her impatiently from beside a Fodder alcove.

'No rest for the virtuous,' sighed Eadha, putting down her glass and padding on bare feet to where he stood, enjoying the soft swish of the skirt against her leg, shivering slightly as she remembered how Ionain's hands had pressed oh so warm into the small of her back as they spun above the highest tower. Inside the alcove Senan was already drunk and in need of a channel to clear his head and power up for a last were-dive with his cousin. Eadha bent her head as his thread sprang into life, barrelling through her and on to Seoda and her friends. With practised skill she funnelled the minimum from them, sending it back hard and fast so that it shot into Senan like a flaming arrow.

'That's more like it,' said Senan, grinning. 'You're good, I'll give you that, Keeper.'

It was a long night. Ionain and Ailbhe never returned, but both the Rising and the Risen were determined to make a night of it, running through all the old favourites one last time, diving, racing, illusions. Couples danced, flew, held each other with new intensity. Senan was in the middle of every race, every contest, drawing power almost continuously, running it down as fast. Eadha was shaking with the effort of managing the flows, substituting her power when she felt the Fodder could no longer take it, until she was so drained herself, she felt like slumping in beside them, crawling into a service hatch to be carried back down to the holds and oblivion for a little while.

Shortly before dawn the hall began to empty out, couples

slipping away onto balconies and up into eyries for a last embrace before Master Joen summoned the Risen to depart. Even the Masters' table was empty for once, all of the Masters having slipped away for a brief hour's rest before the formal departure later that morning. Senan at the last found himself standing alone in the centre of the rotunda, candles guttering around the walls, the fires almost out and the were-lights long since departed with their creators. He ambled over to the table, picking up and draining a half-full goblet of wine.

'Keeper,' he called to Eadha once more as she sat on a bench by one of the fireplaces, cold in her thin dress in the pre-dawn chill, trying to stir some last life from the embers. She stood obediently and came to where he stood, staring at her, his expression unreadable.

'A little bird tells me you were a naughty girl. What did I say about stepping out of line, hmm?'

'My lord, I am sorry, I thought I'd kept well for you?'

'You were seen with Lord Ailm at the start of the evening, sneaking out onto the balcony, no doubt giving him a twirl of your shiny dress.'

'My lord, I am sorry, I...'

'Did I give you permission to speak? Did I?'

'No, my lord.'

'It's simple. You have one thing to do, stay away from Lord Ailm. Lord Huath was very clear when he spoke to me. Ionain has to be saved from himself. He's too soft, he has this ridiculous notion of loyalty to you. He was doing so well, all summer. I blame you, running around half-naked in a stolen dress, making eyes at him, doing god knows what else to get your claws back into him. It makes a mockery of everything I've done for him this summer, if he goes crawling back to you.'

He seized Eadha's arm, half-dragging her across the empty floor.

'Lord De Lane, please, you're hurting me.'

He closed his hand even tighter around her arm.

'You think that's hurting you. You have no idea what I'm capable of. Here, let me show you what real Channeller flying is, not the prissy floating Ionain uses to seduce the ladies.'

Pulling her after him he lifted her into the air, hanging awkwardly by the arm. Out through the window he flew and up into the air, higher and higher. Up there in the night air it was freezing. Eadha's shoulder ached badly from being held, her arm twisted and raw where Senan's thick fingers dug into it.

'So, Keeper, how do you like it?' he shouted down at her. 'If I let go now just think how long those few moments would be before you hit the water. Just long enough for you to shit yourself before you die, I'd say.'

And he let go.

Eadha started to fall, faster and faster, her skirt tangling her arms and flapping around her face so she couldn't see, didn't know how far she was from the towers, from the cliffs underneath. Just as she started to gather her power to stop her fall, she felt herself caught by the arms once more, the jolt almost pulling them out of their sockets. It was Senan again, laughing hysterically. He flew them both back into the almost empty hall, landing them in one of the Channeller eyries just beneath the domed ceiling.

As soon as he let her go Eadha scrabbled backwards away from him in the enclosed space. The eyrie was a circular cushioned nook set in the wall of the Banquet Hall, accessible only by channelling. A velvet curtain could be drawn to give the Channeller within privacy. They were typically used as love seats, places for couples to hide away during parties. Still panting, Senan pulled the curtain across and turned to Eadha.

'So where did you really get that dress, hmm?' He reached across and fingered the soft material of the skirt. 'That's finest Erisen silk; even the Great Family heads would think twice before making a whole dress of that material, it takes so much Fodder to grow the crops in this climate. So don't tell me Lady Ura gave her servant scraps, you little liar.'

Taking the delicate white sheath in both hands he ripped it in two, so that it slit all the way up to her thigh. He put a hand on her knee, moving closer as she pressed as far back as she could into the cushions. He caught her chin in his other hand, tipping her head back, examining her face coldly.

'Just what is it that Ionain sees in you? You're no more than passably attractive, your power is pitiful, you have no name. It must be something else. What is it you used to do for the good little lord on those cold northern nights? Maybe I should find out for myself.'

He leaned in, twisting her chin towards him with his hand and lunging forward, elbow digging into her shoulder.

'One word, Keeper, one word and I will have you thrown in a Fodder Hold for the rest of your worthless life,' he grunted as she tried to squirm away from him.

A part of Eadha was terrified as she shook her head frantically, tried to push him away, tried to break his grip on her chin, the hard fingers squeezing her jaw, forcing her mouth open. But another part was detached, watching herself struggle as if from outside her body, wondering, instant by crawling instant could she do this, could she bear this, should she submit, dampen down the power she could feel rising within her, all to hide her secret, to protect Ionain, was it worth this?

And then the two parts of her collapsed into one and the answer was no. This was not to be borne. She was light, she was power, and she didn't have to bear this; she wouldn't bear this. As it had done all those months before in the face of Magret's inquisition, her strength powered up through her, in a boiling tsunami of rage, the force wave roaring up at Senan, hurling him back against the wall of the eyrie. In the same instant the curtain was rent aside and Gry appeared, blasting Senan with a white bolt of furious power as Eadha flung him away from her. The two blasts at once knocked him unconscious and he toppled, limp, from the eyrie towards the floor of the Banquet Hall far below. A fall from that height would kill him instantly. Gry dived after him, catching him just before his head hit a table and lowering him safely to the floor.

As Eadha looked on horror-struck, Channellers began to converge on Gry where he stood by Senan's unconscious body. Master Joen appeared, still pulling his robe about him, papers whirling up and empty glasses toppling over in the speed of his arrival. Gry looked up to where Eadha peered down from the eyrie and gave the tiniest shake of his head. His heavy frame dwarfing Gry, Master Joen spoke to him once, too softly for her to hear. He nodded briefly, closing his eyes and rubbing his neck tiredly. In the next moment Master Joen had marched Gry to the door of the Banquet Hall where he was taken away by a group of guards. It was a long time before anyone noticed Eadha stranded in the eyrie, where she sat, eyes wide and hands wrapped around her knees, holding her torn skirt about her.

CHAPTER 30
AFTERSHOCK

Eadha didn't see Gry again after he left the Banquet Hall with Master Joen but she heard Senan holding forth loudly on his fate later that day. He was none the worse apart from a headache caused as much by the wine as by the bolts of power that hit him. He gave no sign of having registered Eadha's blast, putting it all down to Gry. It was the story of the night, of the summer, the whole of Second Island convulsed by the news that a Keeper student had been revealed as a Channeller.

The Masters moved quickly to dampen speculation. They let it be known Gry himself hadn't been aware of his Channeller powers. Rather, in a moment of crisis when he believed Lord De Lane to be in imminent danger of toppling from the eyrie where he'd fallen asleep, his power had revealed itself as he leapt instinctively to his classmate's aid. Senan had agreed to support this version of events in return for escaping punishment for his assault on Eadha.

Eadha was interviewed by Master Joen and Head Keeper Fiarone in Master Joen's private study, a sunny book-lined room in the main quad. It looked out over the yews that shaded the central fountain, plashing quietly in miniature echo of the sea's ceaseless song beyond the thick walls. She nodded her head when asked to confirm what Gry had told them, that he'd intervened in the belief that Lord De Lane might be pressing her too strongly. She nodded once more when they directed her not to speak of this to anyone outside the room. Only at the end, as they murmured quietly to each other, expecting her to remove herself, did she speak.

'Master Joen, Head Keeper Fiarone, may I ask what will become of Lord Flemin?' Irritated at her presumption, Master Joen drew himself up to dismiss her, but Head Keeper Fiarone laid a hand on his arm and spoke more kindly.

'Eadha, this is a matter for the Masters and not your concern. Suffice it to say the ways of power have always had some fluidity and this is not the first time we have had to deal with a Keeper revealed as a Channeller. Lord Flemin will undergo a process of reconditioning with me in the holds. If we are satisfied, he will join next spring's intake on First Island as a Channeller student. Whatever happens he will not rejoin you in the Keeper class on Second Island. You may go now.'

Holding court in his suite with a group of Rising Channellers later that day, Senan was more brutal.

'The only reason he's not being sent for Fodder at once is because of his Family name. I heard his aunt is on her way here already. House Flemin is the main way-post on the route west to the dragon borders so the Masters can't afford to alienate them. But even if he's eventually released back into polite society his name is ruined. How could anyone ever trust that lying little Fodder lover again? Would you trust him to stand by you on a dragon patrol? He'll never be entrusted with any Family lands now, no chance. I'd say they'll assign him some role stacking scrolls in the Library where they can keep an eye on him for the rest of his days.'

'I wonder what they'll do to him down in the hold,' said one of the other apprentices.

'Channel him, no doubt, so he gets the message; you don't embarrass the Masters,' said Senan confidently. 'That would be fun, knowing I was channelling that snivelling Fodder hugger in the name of his re-education.'

When Eadha presented herself down at the Fodder Hold the next morning she was politely but implacably turned away by Head Keeper Fiarone.

'You have completed your remedial training to my satisfaction. I have recommended to the Masters that you be released from any further duties in the hold. Your class is one Keeper short now and they will need every one of you to give of your best to ensure the Rising Channellers are properly supported in their training.'

Ever since she'd learned that Gry was in the Fodder Hold Eadha had been holding fast to the hope she'd see him there. When Fiarone turned her away at the gate she sat up all the rest of that day and on into the night, ignoring the ache from the bruises on her jaw and arms, trying with everything she had to find a thread down through the rock to where Gry lay. But he was too far away, too well-shielded in the hold. She could find nothing to hold onto, no trace of him through the obdurate stone. Without knowing it she passed into a light sleep as the sun rose. She dreamt Senan was channelling through her and together they were draining Gry until he collapsed insensible onto the sandy floor of the hold and was dragged away.

Something broke in Eadha then. Classes had begun the day after the Midsummer Ball but they passed her by in a daze as she followed her classmates numbly from room to combat yard to building ground and back. She recoiled at the thought of keeping for Senan, terrified her dream was prophetic, that she would help drain her friend dry and not know it.

Fortunately, the early lessons in the new subjects of illusion and dragon combat focused on theory. There was little actual channelling or keeping. While braggish as ever in public, in private Senan was also uncharacteristically subdued, less given to flashy displays of channelling or bullying. He'd been sternly warned by the Masters over his assault on Eadha. She might be his inferior but as a Keeper she was still a valuable resource and outright assaults were frowned upon. He was therefore on his best behaviour. Eadha barely registered the change.

She was desperately lonely. Ionain was closeted away as ever, his brief emergence at the Midsummer Ball fading like some insubstantial vision under the harsh lights and noise of the nightmare that had followed it. She hadn't realised until he was taken how much she'd come to depend upon Gry's warm presence beside her all summer at the Channeller balls and parties, his wry humour in the face of the madness of the Channeller system.

On the nights she didn't dream of Gry she dreamt of Senan, of those frozen moments in the eyrie, the sound of his breathing, his fingers digging into her face. She pushed her bed against the door at night, lying there listening for any movement in the hall outside. When not in class she spent as much time as she dared outside Second House, pounding the running tracks along the cliffs, riding on horseback out around the lake and on up into the foothills of the mountains to the east of the island, getting fitter and stronger, her body returning to the lean hardness of her years in the Keep. But no matter how exhausted she was falling into bed, still she dreamt, and in her dreams she struck out as she'd done that last moment in the eyrie. When she woke, she found holes she'd burned into the immense thickness of the school walls. She knew real fear then, gut-wrenching, stomach-turning terror. That she would wake one night to the Masters pounding on her door, hauling her away to the nightmarish underworld of the hold where Senan, and Lord Huath, and Master Dathin and all the other Masters would come and drain her, night after night.

Ten days after Gry had been incarcerated in the holds, Eadha overheard Senan say Lady Hera was expected the next day.

'Come all the way from the wilds of House Flemin to plead for her nephew, no doubt. It's a wasted trip, he'll have to stay in the holds until next spring no matter what. There is no way he'll be allowed to rejoin us.'

'What about you, Senan?' asked one of the Channeller boys sprawled on the cushions in the centre of the main sitting room. 'Have you made your move?'

'You mean Linn and I? Well, she might deny it, but she knows full well her Family won't permit a match with that Fodder lover, even if he is allegedly some class of an almost Channeller now,' came Senan's reply. 'Linn's headstrong but I've written to my father. He's talking to her Family and to Master Joen. She'll be outflanked by Family and Masters and delivered to my tender care to make lovely Channeller babies before the year is out.'

Eadha slipped soundlessly from the room under cover of the snorts of laughter and snide comments on Linn that followed Senan's lordly prediction. Making her way unseen through the central quads she dropped down the light well that led to the sea cave entrance. There she settled herself for a damp night, wrapping her cloak about her as best she could, pushing herself into a cleft in the rocks where she'd be less visible. She woke at dawn to the echo of voices in the cave. A ship was heaving to at the stone jetty, an armed guard leaping ashore to make the ship fast. There was no sign of Master Joen or any other welcoming party.

Eadha watched until she saw Lady Hera appear on deck. She hurried forward then, conscious she made a bedraggled sight in her soggy cloak, hair damp and matted with sand.

'Lady Hera. I'm sorry to bother you, but could we talk?' The guards moved to shield the older lady, but she waved them away.

'Eadha, this is more than I could have hoped for. Of course, come here, child. What an awful time you and my nephew have had.' She embraced Eadha briefly, her thin arms holding her fast a moment before releasing her to move towards the steps.

'Come, we will climb and talk. I want to see if I can reach the surface before that thug Joen and his lackeys realise I have arrived early. It gives me some chance of speaking to Fiarone alone for a moment about how they are treating my nephew.'

They began the steep ascent up the rock face, Lady Hera setting the pace, Eadha behind her and two of her guards to the rear.

'Now, my dear, speak. I must save my breath for climbing.'

'Gry. Some of the Rising Channellers have said he may be used as Fodder as part of his punishment. That we might be channelling him during lessons.' She paused.

Lady Hera looked back at her briefly as they climbed.

'Spiteful gossip, nothing more. They are braggish ghouls, the lot of them, gloating over the misfortune of another whose boots they are not fit to clean. The Masters have to make an example of Gry, but he will not be drained as Fodder. They would not use a First Family heir so. They know it would alienate our Family for all time, even risk another Channeller war.'

For the first time in weeks Eadha felt that she could breathe all the way in, as the fear that had choked her throat since the moment Gry was marched away, eased slightly.

'Thank you,' she said. They climbed silently for a little then Eadha spoke once more.

'Could you give Gry a message for me?'

'Of course.'

'Could you thank him, for what he did? And tell him I'm sorry?'

Lady Hera paused a moment on the stairs to catch her breath, holding hard to the thin rail and gazing up briefly to the top, still far above them. She swung about then to stare down at Eadha, standing several steps below.

'The thanks I will relay. But why on earth would you be sorry?' Eadha looked away from that bright, direct gaze.

'It's my fault Gry is in the holds, that he'll never be able to go home.'

'How do you conclude that?'

'I wore a dress.'

'It must have been quite a dress.'

'We talked once, long ago, Gry and I, about how hard it is to refrain, not to show what you are capable of. That to be invisible, to endure the contempt and not rise to it, is the right thing to do. To play the long game.

But I was given a gift. A gift of the most beautiful dress. I wanted to wear it so I would be noticed, just once. Because I was missing someone and I wanted them to see me, just that once. But then it all went wrong. I was noticed, and Lord De Lane, he wanted to hurt me for having shown myself in a dress.

And when he attacked me, I hesitated. I tried to endure in the very moment when I should have said, enough. Gry, he knew. He knew better than I did there has to be a line. He stepped in to save me, even though he must've known I could save myself. Now he's locked away in there somewhere and I can't feel him anywhere, can't say I'm sorry, and thank you, for being so much better than me.'

'Eadha, my dear. Take it from an old woman who has worn many pretty dresses and turned many Channeller heads in her time. Never, never apologise for being young and lovely and wearing a dress so the boy you like sees you for the beauty you are.'

She continued on up the stairs then paused once more, out

of breath.

'Gry will be fine. Don't be misled by his doddery aunt who can hardly climb some stairs. He is the heir of one of the four Founding Families. The Masters would not cross us lightly and we look after our own. I understand you feel upset at what has happened to him and fear, no doubt, for what might happen to you. Your care for him does you credit. But here and now it is a dangerous indulgence. If you are to ever leave this island you must pack those feelings away now and focus.

'Take them out someday, years from now. When you are, oh, twenty-five years old and far from here, sit down some sunny afternoon and have a good cry for Gry, for yourself, for what you are both enduring, here in this place. But in this moment, you must concentrate. The Masters will be scrutinising all the Keeper novices to see if they missed any others. You cannot afford a single misstep. You have done so well to last this long undetected, but it will all be for nothing, and worse than nothing if you slip now. You do not have a powerful Family name behind you, and I cannot protect you. The Masters would very quickly write you out of existence rather than endure another embarrassment so soon after my nephew. It is what they do best, after all.'

They were still some way from the top, and Eadha could see Lady Hera was tiring badly from the effort of talking and climbing.

'My lady, please, you don't want to be exhausted when you arrive before the Masters. Let me help you.'

Her power kicking quietly to life Eadha lifted Lady Hera from the ground. The two of them floated up the remaining section, their feet only inches above the steps. Lady Hera turned to her as they rose, a look of puzzlement on her face.

'I cannot sense where you are channelling from.'

Eadha was focused on keeping their feet low as they approached the surface. Without thinking she replied, 'Myself.'

Lady Hera's expression changed to one of purest shock. She opened her mouth to speak but before she could say anything Master Joen's face appeared over the rim of the light well. Eadha dropped them both in the same instant, so they were back to climbing the steps. The moment passed. Lady Hera closed her eyes, rearranged her expression and turned to look up at Master Joen. He flew down at once, making a show of lifting Lady Hera the rest of the way, apologising for having missed her early arrival. In the ensuing hubbub, Eadha slipped away unnoticed by anyone but Lady Hera, who turned to watch her go, before turning back to Master Joen.

Eadha didn't see Lady Hera again on Second Island as she was closeted away with the Masters. But two days later, when Lady Hera was due to sail, there was a knock at the door of her room. It was one of Lady Hera's personal guard. He handed her a tightly rolled scroll.

'Lady Hera bade me give you this. She believes it might help you, to endure what must be endured. When you leave this island, you will always have a home at House Crioch. Sister save you, my lady,' and bowing his head, the guard was gone.

Eadha unrolled the scroll. It was short, the ink still fresh, written in the formal style of the Channeller histories they'd studied on First Island.

The Sister

'There was once a family of one girl and four boys. The girl Leah was the first-born. As she grew towards womanhood there awoke in her a gift newborn in this world. To take the strong young life within her and with it reach down into the ground and coax seeds into life, to call the stones to bind together and rise from the earth, to turn life into light or fire or flight.

She shared her power with her baby brothers, sang them to sleep with were-lights dancing above their heads, wove beautiful stories in the air, channelled playhouses for them from the earth. As they grew, they yearned to be like her, but they did not have her gift. They became envious of their sister, for she was beloved among the people of their land for the wonders she could create.

Then one day the oldest of the boys, Erisen, found he, too, could fly, fight, create were-lights, do all his sister could, by taking Leah's life-force and drawing it into himself. He gathered his brothers then and they, too, learned the way of it.

At first Leah was happy to let them channel from her, for she loved and trusted them, and the power they drew, she gave willingly. But they grew greedy, drained her more and more. She became gaunt and weary. Soon her power was not enough for them. They began to draw the life-force from all those around them. So channelling, as it is now known, as it is taught by the Masters and used by the Great Families, came to be.

The brothers became powerful and wealthy, using their power to drain and subjugate the people in the lands all around them. Their sister wanted no part in this and at first they let her be. But as people still came to Leah for help, her brothers began to fear that her gift, whereby she gave of herself to help others rather than take from them, made them vulnerable. There was no place for her gift in the world they were building, where channelling was a path to dominion over others, not service.

So they stole her away one night, fired up with the life-force of the very people who had come to her for help. She had no chance against their might, no heart to fight the brothers she loved and the power she had helped unleash. On Second Island they imprisoned her, in an island fortress raised just to hold her. Too far from land to use her power to escape, leaving her to live out her days broken and alone.'

CHAPTER 31
ANGER

The art of Illusion was the focus of lessons in the early days of the new term on Second Island. It required relatively little power but significantly more skill and control than the crafts studied on First Island. It was a difficult art to convey as so much of it was internal; an act of imagination and focus, to conjure the images in the mind and channel them out to take shape in the air. Some who'd been strong students on First Island like Senan and Linn, struggled now, unable to catch the trick of it, forcing it so it fled from them through their reaching fingers. Others, though, were like amphibians taking happily to their second element, moving effortlessly from water up and out into air. Ionain was one such, an artist born. In class it seemed he'd always known how to create the illusions, he just needed to be reminded of that fact. Before long he'd moved far beyond the rest of them. Ruadh, the senior Master Teller, let him work on alone, simply pointing him towards paths he might explore, from which he returned with creations of such crystalline beauty it broke the heart to watch them shimmer into unbeing at the end of each lesson.

As the theory lessons ended and the apprentices began channelling in class once more, Eadha resumed her supply of power to Ionain, making sure to gift him so much he'd hardly need to channel anything from the Fodder he touched. She couldn't stand the thought of him channelling Seoda or anyone else. She was helped by his gift at Illusion, as it was the art involving the least use of power. Thrilled to have found an apprentice so gifted in the art he loved, the Master Teller even managed to have Ionain excused from some of his other lessons so he could concentrate on it.

Outside of class, she was withdrawn, either staying in her room or roaming alone beyond the House, out around the island. But underneath the carapace of fear and silence where she hid from them all, something new was growing. Born in the crucible of Senan's eyrie on midsummer night, it was fanned to flickering life by Lady Hera's scroll. Day by day it grew, taking on a life of its own, feeding itself on the plentiful scraps of humiliation, cruelty and fear that littered her days. She hunched over it at night, held it close so it kept her warm as summer cooled to autumn, though it was a long time before she knew it for what it was and gave it its true name. And that name was anger.

There on Second Island anger was an emotion of the powerful; in her weakness, to show anger would be to invite a swift and deadly retribution. She tried to bank it with the ashes of her fear and shame, but it was too powerful, the flames of it licking through and climbing within her as she lay in her bare room each night until she felt as a dragon must feel, a fire sleeping within it, longing always to roar into fiery life.

She read and reread Leah's scroll until she had it by heart, each time stoking the rage within. The Channellers, the Families, the Masters, they all lied. They'd had a choice at the beginning of things, and they chose power over others, they chose subjugation and then they hid the fact that there was ever even a choice, hid it here on this very island. And then they built their temple of lies on the very spot where the choice had died. They had lied and lied until they'd built a whole world on a lie. For all their pious intonations and ceremonies, their invocation of the First Brothers and their hundreds of years of tradition, she was more the heir of the First Channeller Leah than they were. All the time on Lambay she'd thought herself and her gift freakish, an aberration. But her drawing of her own life-force to create and to give was descended from the first sister more than their twisted corruption of power into dominance and control could ever be.

Her anger sustained her as the evenings grew dark and chill, but at a price. It had its own being within her and she couldn't control it. And it is those who love us that we will dare to show our anger to, because we trust they won't hurt us for it, while we bite our lips and smile on at those we truly hate and fear.

There was a wall between herself and Ionain, built of all the things he didn't know. A wall whose foundations were laid when she stepped in for him at his Reckoning, or further back even, when Magret told her of her power and she didn't go to him in the Keep but ran instead into the forest to race with the deer. A wall she'd always thought she could still reach across, until the day she told him all and with each secret told it would fall away stone by stone 'til she could step clear through to him.

But now she became impatient with him, at his innocence, his ignorance of so much happening around him, like some sheltered child playing on unawares in a sunny Keep courtyard while adults fought life and death battles on the battlements above him. How could he channel, fly, and fight knowing it drew on the life-force of others and not recoil in horror? How could he draw the life-force out of the people in the holds and not hate every moment of it? And why could he not see, not feel in his heart that the power flowing through him came from her, her sacrifice to preserve his honour, his pride?

It had seemed so important once, that he be lord of Ailm's Keep, that he get his dearest wish, but now she struggled to justify it to herself. In her head she kept having the same imaginary conversation with Gry deep in the hold, where he sat on a Fodder seat, shackled to the wall, a disbelieving look in his eyes.

'Let me understand this. You give your gift to Ionain, and he uses it to channel Fodder.'

She would nod, start to try to explain that it was complicated, about Lord Huath and losing the Keep to him, and Beithe's wonder tales of old, but he would stop her short, waggling his chains at her so they clanked and shook.

'Tell me you do see it's almost as bad as channelling yourself. You do understand that's how most of the truly, banally evil things in this world are justified, that it's the oldest story of all, the crazed parent or lover, claiming they're doing it all for love? As if that somehow grants them absolution? Would you let him channel me with your power? Or Seoda?'

And she would try to tell him he hardly needed to channel Fodder at all, she gave him so much of her power and he would turn to look at her and ask, 'Is that what this was really about, Eadha, power? You couldn't face the idea of being hidden away, of a life of denial, of invisibility. But your conscience wouldn't let you announce your gift, so instead you placed yourself here, at the heart of power, all innocent, maybe secretly hoping all along that you'd be discovered, our little bluebird, raised to the skies?'

And Eadha would get up, busy herself with work or study, pound around the cliff paths once more, anything to escape the questions that would not let her be.

She thought, too, about Seoda, down in the holds full-time now there were no more Channeller balls to be sent up to. As a skilled seamstress and a presentable, Eadha knew she wasn't in the most at-risk Fodder category but she'd looked so worn out, that day in the lift. Her world, Eadha realised, had been so small once, nothing but a story about herself and Ionain, with everyone else no more than walk-on players in that one, all-consuming drama. She knew now she couldn't go back to that way of being in the world.

Time and again she thought of just stopping. Of simply withdrawing her power and letting things play out as they might. But she loved Ionain too much still to do that to him. To risk him facing the same fate as Gry and worse. Instead, she grew more and more resentful of him, that he should be so blind to power, he couldn't see what was happening all around him.

In the days that followed the Midsummer Ball he'd tried again and again to catch her alone, but that was easily avoided, as she busied herself about her Keeper duties or roamed out beyond the walls. A hurt, puzzled look came into his eyes when he looked at her, knowing her too well not to guess she was holding him away.

He finally caught her alone in Senan's sitting room some weeks after Lady Hera's departure, catching her arm as she moved to leave the room.

'Eadha, please,' he said in a low voice. 'What is it? What's happened? Why won't you talk to me?'

Eadha stayed facing away from him.

'The others are saying you were mixed up with what happened between Gry and Senan at the ball, but Senan won't give me a straight answer. Please, I thought after the ball that we understood each other. But now you won't even look at me.'

She couldn't look at him. If she did, he'd see everything in her eyes. She couldn't talk to him, because if she did, she wouldn't be able to stop. So she picked up Senan's discarded underclothes and pulled away from him.

At the entrance to the corridor, without looking back she said, 'My apologies, Lord Ailm, I have my Keeper duties for Lord De Lane.

You should return to your own Keeper.'

After that she shut down completely, unable to handle the contradictions that were fissuring within her 'til she felt she must break apart. When they encountered each other in class or in the refectory, in Senan's rooms or in the temple she stared through him, eyes blank, as if he were a passing stranger.

He didn't give up at once. Day after day, he would nod at her and smile in the face of her cold stare. He stood beside her at every opportunity, deliberately brushing his shoulder against hers until she shivered with the memory of that night above the towers. He left small gifts in her room; a shining ripe apple, red-gold leaves from the autumn birches outside the House walls, shells from the stony island shore in a little pile on her bed, the way they'd collected them as treasures once as children. But he was a proud boy, a noble son of a noble Family. In the end, as she stonewalled and blanked him without end, he finally stopped trying and slowly pulled away. The little boy who'd called her out of the summer night so long ago and held her as if his entire happiness depended upon it stepped away and back into his castle, and she was left alone in the darkness with her anger.

CHAPTER 32
CONFIGURATIONS

The days became weeks, the weeks became months, and Eadha endured. As autumn faded, she woke each morning believing she couldn't get up, couldn't go through the old exhausting routine of sending Ionain her strength, holding down her anger through the haze of molash at Matins, and enduring another day of Senan's demands. But there was no choice, and so she pulled herself one foot at a time from her bed, leaned her head against the wall for support as she sent her power to Ionain in the rooms above and shambled down to the temple hardly able to hold her head up.

The morning came for the students to begin dragon combat training. The class were in the refectory, filling up on warming food before heading out into the chill of a late autumn morning. Ailbhe entered on her own, looking drawn and pale, hastening over to where her closest allies sat. They huddled together and murmurs began to spread from the little group outwards. Moments later silence fell. Ionain and Linn had come in holding hands, hair tousled and bleary eyed, heading straight for food, piling each other's plates high with fruit and sweetbread, giggling and murmuring back and forth before heading over to a corner table where they sat, backs pointedly to the watching room. Ionain reached over and took Linn's hand again, working his fingers in between hers, and she leaned into him, tucking her head under his chin.

Shock waves reverberated through the class all that day. Ionain and Ailbhe had been paired by the Masters, and most had assumed that Senan's long siege of Linn would eventually succeed. But that evening Senan dressed in his finest clothes and disappeared without a word. The next morning when he and Ailbhe swept through the doors of the classroom holding hands the Channeller world, which had momentarily wobbled on its axis, righted itself once more.

Determined to convince the world that their pairing was not a consolation prize, the two proud, ambitious creatures quickly installed themselves as undisputed king and queen of the class. Senan redoubled his efforts to take first place among the Rising Channellers, while Ailbhe had a ship sent from Erisen with the most exquisite wardrobe, offhandedly sharing it with friends and allies. They threw parties for the select few in Senan's rooms, ingratiating themselves with the Masters for Fodder and molash supply so that their evenings became the talk of the island.

The Keeper girls chattered endlessly about the new pairings, how the Masters and Families had blessed the unions, how powerful Ailbhe and Senan were together, how happy Linn and Ionain looked. Eadha sat on the fringes of the gossiping groups, hungrily listening for every detail, like someone pressing on a scab. How Ionain and Linn were inseparable, how Ionain had been spotted more than once leaving Linn's rooms in the east tower early in the morning to go change in his own apartment. They held hands during class, sitting at the back and giggling together. The Masters were so evidently relieved to see Linn paired at all they said nothing even when the two began to straggle in late for class, dishevelled and sleepy.

In the end it seemed the only person suffering from the new

configurations was Eadha. She was numb with disbelief. She'd never really believed Ionain cared for Ailbhe, even when they were paired together on Second Island. But Linn. She could offer him everything she had and much more. She was kind, beautiful and oh so talented. Her Family name was impeccable, an alliance between two revered Families. And if Ionain's power never flowered into life Linn could easily channel for the Keep, while her powerful gift guaranteed their children would be gifted, too. She was perfect. And it broke Eadha's heart.

The Keepers' lessons on Second Island were a mix of shared sessions with the Channellers and Keeper-only lessons with Fiarone. They'd begun training for their Westport posting, with its specific challenges. As Keepers, they'd be in charge of the wagons of Fodder brought west with them. It was their responsibility to ensure they were fed and watered, to monitor their strength levels and to bury any that died.

They'd studied the basics of thread manipulation on First Island, but Fiarone and her Keepers were more demanding again, expecting them to be able to read each thread precisely and switch at the exact right moment to maintain a perfect flow. How to judge the amount of time needed for a source to replenish so the thread could be taken up again, and all the other details that went into getting the very most from the limited Fodder resources in a wagon, while keeping them docile with exhaustion. It was exacting work, demanding intense concentration and a swift dexterity in shuttling between the threads.

Eadha threw herself into the lessons, into the relief they gave her from the endless circling questions. Her experience in the holds meant she was far beyond her classmates in her ability to read a Fodder thread. But still the lessons taxed her almost to her limit, as, underneath the watchful eye of the most senior Keeper in all Domhain, she stealthily blocked and protected the Fodder when she judged they'd had enough, stepping in invisibly with her own power to give them respite, well before the point of near-collapse Fiarone taught her students to aim for.

They still took classes with the Channeller students, keeping for them as they'd always done. They were the hardest for Eadha to bear, as she couldn't avoid seeing Ionain and Linn together, when they did turn up for class. She tried to hold on to the belief that the promise Ionain had made on midsummer night still held, that this was all some elaborate game. But it all seemed so real. After all, he and Linn had been friends since childhood, the two Families intertwined over generations in the way of Great Families on Domhain. Maybe it was, as Senan had said, his viper's tongue speaking truth to naivety. Maybe it had just been Ionain's innate decency, some inconvenient notion of loyalty to her that had tied him to her until she finally pushed him away and he had at last felt free to go to Linn and tell her how he felt.

As she stood watching them circling and laughing in the sky above her, all Eadha's anger came roaring back. Ionain shouldn't have given up so lightly on their whole life together. Her pain had pushed him away but she hadn't meant to drive him into Linn's arms. Seeing him so relaxed and happy with Linn, the full realisation hit her.

She couldn't go home.

She might never go home, to the Keep, to her uncle's cottage, to the woods below the Blackstairs and the lake at the heart of it all. It was all too intertwined with Ionain. How could she live there, serve as a Keeper in his household and watch him with Linn, restoring the Keep and the lands around with their power? Marrying her, having children who would run and play in the Keep gardens as she and Ionain once did.

Linn had taken her life and would live it better than she ever could have.

The anger that had sustained her splintered then into shards of pain. Her knees buckled and she sat down heavily on the ground, drawing an angry shout from Senan as he wobbled in the sky, her thread momentarily snapping. She was lost, unmoored, drifting rudderless with nowhere to make landfall before night fell.

CHAPTER 33
THE KILLING FIELD

While Eadha struggled on, the Masters had moved on to the last of the Channeller arts, dragon combat. It was also the most difficult, for the apprentices and their Masters both. The Masters sought as far as was possible by their craft and power to recreate a true dragon battle. The Master Teller would create the illusion of a life-size dragon, complete in every detail, though privately Eadha thought he deliberately made his vision more nightmarish, with none of the beauty of the real thing. Master Joen, who was the head Master Combat on Second Island, would then channel enormous bolts of real flame that roared from the mouth of the illusion-dragon as it wheeled in the sky. The Rising Channellers had to face this fiery nightmare with a Fodder wagon as their sole power source shared between them, just as they would on their dragon patrols in a few short months.

Defeating a dragon was more a matter of skill and tactics than brute force; a full-grown dragon could easily outfly or overcome a single Channeller unless they had massive Fodder resources at their disposal. During the simulations, the apprentices were expected to study the dragon, identify its characteristics and whether there were any patterns to its flight that might make it possible to predict where

301

it would go in response to the first blow. The favoured tactic was a series of quick successive blows from multiple Channellers positioned along its likely flight path that tore its wings and sent it to the ground. The danger the apprentices faced as they fought the fiery illusion was real. They were dependent on their Keepers for a steady resupply of power from the wagon as they poured it out of themselves, into their yew staffs and out as firebolts that flew at the target.

Linn, Senan and Ionain, as the strongest apprentices, were expected to take the lead in these combats, which demanded a carefully choreographed response. But beneath their superficial cooperation there was a real, enduring niggle between them, with Senan still smarting from the humiliation of Linn choosing Ionain rather than him, and a determination on all sides not to be bested by the other.

The combat ground was well outside the main House on a large rocky outcrop that jutted out to sea. There was too much risk of the dragon's flame or the apprentices' fire bolts hitting the House walls to fight within the grounds but out here they could fly on harmlessly over the water.

As they prepared for a full combat session one afternoon, Senan strolled over to Eadha, standing with the other Keepers.

'Well, Keeper, it seems this is to be our last outing together. My dear Lady De Paor has asked to be formally paired with me as my Keeper for the remainder of our time on Lambay.' Eadha kept her head down so Senan would not see the relief in her eyes.

'Yes, my lord,' she replied. Senan turned towards the combat ground and looked back briefly.

'You know, I feel I really do owe you something, some little recognition of all the trouble you caused me, between your sabotage at the spring trials and then your melodrama over nothing at the Midsummer Ball. So let's make this a session to remember, just to reinforce all the lessons we've learned during our time together, shall we?'

He lifted into the air, arrowing his thread through her and on towards the Fodder wagon parked at the edge of the combat ground. Eadha picked up the threads, counting and assessing the strengths available, dropping some as they were not yet needed; the illusion was not finished. Ionain stood by the Master Teller, helping him create and hold the dragon illusion.

There was always a polite scramble at the start of the session as each of the Keepers tried to get the best, strongest threads for their Channeller from the limited supply in the Fodder wagon. The rule was that a Keeper had to release a thread to another if their Channeller was in active combat, but some Keepers were inclined to hoard threads at the outset to reduce the risk of running low. Eadha was unconcerned by this jostling, confident in her ability to supplement the threads with her own steady power if needed, even though she was more than usually tired that afternoon as Senan had drained her late that night when his Fodder supply ran low at a party. She was not unduly worried, though; the Rising Channellers were still tentative in these sessions, wary of being burnt by Master Joen's flame.

Finally, the dragon illusion was ready. Supported by the Master and Ionain it rose into the air, flapping its enormous wings, the length of a battleship. It seemed to be truly flying rather than being lifted by the power flowing from the two yew staffs pointing towards it in unison. Throwing back its head it roared, then shot up into the sky. Senan, Linn and Coll rose after it. Watching the direction of the dragon's flight Linn shouted instructions to those behind her, established Channeller combat codes. The Channellers lifting up behind her flew into position, forming the points of a net. At Linn's word they each shot power towards each other's staffs, between them weaving a golden net of power across the dragon's path. It would not hold it but would slow it down, allowing Senan, who'd taken up position behind the dragon, to fly in and hit it from behind. He would aim for the weakest point on its back, the join where the wing sprouted from the back and there was a sliver of unmailed skin.

Something had been nagging at Eadha since picking up the threads from the Fodder wagon, some familiar sensation. As Senan flew into position above her she bent again towards the threads, held loosely in her mind until they were needed. She fingered through them like beads on a string, holding and testing them, seeing if she could catch at that sensation again. At the last thread, the weakest of those she'd chosen, she felt it again. Bending all her concentration towards that weak signal, it came to her. It was Seoda, there in the Fodder wagon. Her thread was almost unrecognisable from the summer, so weak and faded was it, but unmistakeably hers. Eadha's heart caught. As a presentable she hadn't thought Seoda would be sent out in the Fodder wagon, believed she was safe from that at least. She immediately blocked her thread so Senan could not draw hard on it, substituting as much of her own power as she could instead.

Above them Master Joen sent a gout of flame roaring from the dragon illusion. It plummeted towards the waiting Channellers. On Linn's signal the net of power sprang into life, shining dimly in the autumn sunlight. The dragon flew into the net, its wings becoming briefly entangled, its progress slowed. It roared and flamed all around it, so the Channellers had to break away or be burnt. Several strings snapped as they flew, enough so the dragon could gather speed once more. Senan came flying in from behind, staff raised, pulling a huge surge of power from the threads held by Eadha for a concentrated bolt of deadly power, but the dragon was pulling away too quickly and his bolt shot harmlessly through where the illusion had been seconds before, to land with a splash in the waters beyond the combat ground. Master Joen was normally kinder than that, letting the apprentices score hits on his illusion if the shot was good, but clearly Ionain was not inclined to let his classmates, and especially Senan, win any easy victories over his dragon.

The hunt was on then, the apprentices quickly realising Ionain was taking them on and galvanised by the challenge. Senan hurled himself into the fray, drawing gulps of power through Eadha. He was drawing so ferociously she was hard-pressed to manage the flows between the remaining threads, all of which quickly came under strain. All the while she was watching Seoda's thread, seeing it weaken further. Her block on Senan's channel was sparing her the worst of it, but she was still fading further and further, her line hardly visible in the sunlight glittering on the waves in front of them.

She squinted up at where Senan was holding position, waiting for the dragon to come back around. The Fodder wagon as a whole was dangerously low in strength. Ordinarily he would be the first to call for a pause so fresh Fodder could be called up, always greedy for as much power as possible. As she shaded her eyes, she saw him look down at her, a focused expression in his eyes. The next moment her knees buckled as he pulled power savagely out of her and the Fodder. And she knew that this vicious draining of the Fodder was all entirely deliberate on his part; his parting gift to her.

She panicked then, reaching down within her to try to find more reserves of power. But her own strength was running down too fast now, trying to cover Seoda and the other threads from Senan's clawing, relentless demands. Her legs began to tremble and dark smudges appeared in front of her eyes. Shaking her head, she tried to force herself to concentrate harder, to keep shielding Seoda, but she was weakening dangerously with each vicious draw from Senan.

Head Keeper Fiarone saw nothing, preoccupied by her own work keeping Master Joen supplied with power for his illusion, caught up in the excitement and beauty of the pretend combat that was playing out in a fiery dance above them as the apprentices traded bolt for flame and the illusion-dragon wove in and out between the massed Channellers, its wings torn but still aloft and coming back to fight on.

Meanwhile the real, invisible battle between Eadha and Senan for the life of a Fodder girl stretched and stretched like a rope pulled ever more taut. Eadha grew dizzy, struggling to focus on the lines she was defending with her very life. No longer able to stay on her feet, she fell to her knees on the ground, her hands thudding down, her head hanging, the world darkening around her. Every scrap, every hidden pulse in every nerve she sent up that silver line. Still Senan hauled, savagely, mercilessly until at last Eadha had nothing left. She toppled over, darkness rising to greet her. As she faded out, she felt something snap, a tight-drawn hawser cut loose and whipping, for a moment flying free as if filled with life, before falling limp to the ground. And she knew that Seoda was dead.

Eadha lay almost unconscious on the ground, like a swimmer under water, able to dimly hear the sounds in the air above her. She wanted to stay like this and float a while, but she felt her silver fish nudging, pushing her back to the surface. Stiffly, reluctantly, she swam back up to unwelcome consciousness. At Eadha's fall Senan's thread had broken, too. Seeing what had happened Head Keeper Fiarone had stepped in to keep for Senan, allowing him to land safely. Above them the dragon winked out of existence, the only trace it had ever existed the fireballs that raced on through the empty air, the hissing as they splashed into the waves suddenly loud in the silence that had fallen.

All of them had sensed the little life snapping out of existence. It was the first Fodder killing during training for their class. The Channellers flew back to the ground, the Keepers barely remembering to hold the threads that let them descend. Ionain and Linn came over to the group gathered around Eadha. Her heart had resumed its normal work, pumping life around her body but she could not move yet.

Senan came down last, talking loudly as he landed.

'I don't know what's wrong with her, I didn't touch her, just the Fodder. Really bad quality stuff we had today, too—that last one had hardly anything in it.'

'Thank you, Lord De Lane, that is enough,' said Master Joen, guiding the group away from the wagon and back towards the House.

'All of you, in light of this interruption, we will continue the rest of this class back in the combat room. Be prepared to answer questions on the flight path and dragon characteristics when we resume.'

Turning to Eadha, Master Joen continued, 'Keeper Eadha, you know that in the event of a Fodder wagon expiration, it is the responsible Keeper's duty to dispose of the remains and look to the remaining Fodder. You will observe this duty. It will be good preparation for your Westport posting. The soil here is too shallow for a grave. However, there is a coracle below the field, which you can use to row out an appropriate distance, together with stones to weigh down the body.'

As the rest of her class moved away, Eadha levered herself up to a sitting position.

'Why did you do it?' she whispered, her voice hoarse.

'What?' asked Master Joen.

'Why did you do it?' she asked again, louder. Senan was walking straight ahead, not looking back, already some way away from the killing field. She pulled herself to her feet and screamed after his retreating back.

'Why did you do it?' Senan looked back then, but only to roll his eyes at Head Keeper Fiarone.

'Control your charge before she gets into serious trouble.' Fiarone took her arm then.

'Keeper Eadha, that is enough. You do not speak to a Channeller in this way. Proceed immediately to the wagon and see to the disposal. That is all.'

CHAPTER 34
ASK AGAIN

After everyone but those locked in the Fodder wagon had left, Eadha sat for what felt like a long while on the short grass of the combat ground. A huddle of daisies by her feet nodded their white heads in the sea-breeze. She stared at them sightlessly. She knew Seoda was dead, knew it from the hollow place in her chest where the thread binding them together had snapped. But to do as Fiarone had ordered, to open the wagon and see Seoda's lifeless body, touch it, lift it, bury her in the restless sea. How was she to do that?

So, she sat there unmoving on the grass until at last, unbidden, there rose inside her an image of the other people still chained in the wagon, trapped in there beside the body, and the horror of that finally drove her to her feet.

Moving stiffly, every muscle protesting, she opened the wagon doors. She was met by the smell of sweat, urine and fear so familiar from the holds, its wrongness stark as it seeped out into the sea air. As she did, every face in the wagon turned to look at her; all except one. Seoda's small white face was leaning against the door jamb as if she were only sleeping a while.

She'd probably only been a few years older than Eadha but she looked far older, her emaciated body aged by the months of relentless channelling. In death none of her beauty remained except for her hair, still the same beautiful chocolate brown. Her hands lay limp, and trailing out from under her sleeve was a small strip of white silk, the same silk she'd used to make Eadha's skirt. It was tied around her wrist, with one end still coiled in the palm of her hand as if she'd been gripping onto it like a talisman, while Senan had been draining every scrap of life out of her, over and over again until he'd taken everything and she'd died.

A sob rose inside Eadha then, her face crumpling as she said, 'I'm so sorry.'

With hands that shook she unlocked the chains that bound the Fodder. But when she moved to lift Seoda out, a grey-haired woman sitting beside her said quietly, 'Grianan. This one time, while we can, let us say goodbye.'

Eadha stepped back wordlessly. As she did, one by one they began to reach across the narrow space to brush Seoda's cheek or squeeze her hand, whispering their goodbyes to her, because in the holds you could never speak out loud. Eadha turned away. She had no right to be part of this grief. They had a right, these people who'd suffered alongside Seoda. But she had no right, not when she'd failed her and in failing her, let her die.

Behind her, the men and women began climbing out of the wagon. They were clearly exhausted, but there was, too, an unyielding determination to honour their friend, as four of them carefully lifted out the little body, wrapped her in a white sheet taken from beneath the wagon and carried her down to the shore. There they placed her in the coracle, then helped Eadha push it out into the waves.

When she reached deep water, Eadha shipped her oars, but she couldn't just tip Seoda over into the sea as Master Joen had ordered. Instead, holding the body in her arms she dove down with her. As she swam, she could feel her strength beginning to return, her silver fish flickering into life, and it felt like treachery. On the seabed, she arranged a grave of stones to hold down the white sheet, uncovering Seoda's head so that her hair floated free, waving in the current, and she could see the sunlight dancing on the water above her.

As she worked, she thought of what Seoda had said, that day in summer when she'd stopped the lift to give her the dress, and Eadha asked how she could bear being drained by the Masters, and she'd replied, 'You have to break. Once you're broken you can learn how to just exist, that the only way is to go through it. And if you do come out the other side, you will never be the person you were. You had to give that person up to survive. But you might make a new person who is just as worthy.'

It had been such a small hope. To lose everything, just not to die. But Senan couldn't even leave her that.

An unspeakable rage rose inside Eadha then, looking at her hands, cut from prying up stones to weigh down the body. What was the point of this power she had, if it would never be enough to stop someone like Senan?

She understood now, why she dreamt of dragons. It was a dream of finally being able to stand against them, these evil men. Tilting her head back to stare up at the water's surface and the empty sky beyond, from the deepest part of her she sent out a great wordless cry of loss and fury and need, 'Mahera!' and just for one instant she thought she felt a response, an answering tremor along some impossibly long, invisible thread, but then it faded to nothing. Afterwards she still held herself down there beside Seoda, unwilling to let the water carry her back up to the surface because then it would truly be over, and she would have to face what came next. With her power returning, she could hold her breath a long time. Almost idly she wondered how long it would be, before her power ran out once more. Would she just fade out there on the seabed beside her friend? But in the same moment an obdurate refusal rose inside her. The Masters had brought too much death to this island already. Leah had died here. Seoda had died here. She would not give them another death.

So, eventually, she swam back to the surface and rowed ashore as the sun began to set. The people from the Fodder wagon were standing and sitting on the stony shore, watching her as she beached the coracle.

Still dripping wet, Eadha told them, 'I won't bring the wagon back until Fiarone sends someone out to look for us. When they come I'll say the burial went awry and I was waiting until daybreak rather than waking everyone bringing back a wagon in the middle of the night. So do what you wish, just try to stay out of sight of the House. But for now, I am spent and must rest. Wake me whenever they send out the guards.'

So saying, she sagged down to the ground and was asleep almost before her eyes had closed. She slept on as the sun set and the moon rose over the eastern shore, as the stars appeared, first one, then many and spun across the sky. She did not see the people wolfing down the bread stored below the wagon. She did not see as they built a fire beside her from driftwood thrown on the shore and dried all summer long, though the sweet smell of apple wood as it burned might have eased her dreams. She did not see two of them row out in the coracle and with old skill catch fish unused to being hunted in this Channeller domain of force-grown food. She did surface briefly as an old woman held her and gently tipped a warm fish broth into her mouth before drifting off once more, warm now at last, within and without. The people sat long around the fire that night, murmuring quietly back and forth, before climbing back into the Fodder wagon at the first sign of the sky lightening over the sea. The first Eadha knew was a gentle but insistent shaking. She opened her eyes to an unfamiliar face staring intently into her own in the early light of a hazy morning.

'Grianan, beware, you must wake. The fair one, he comes and you must be ready.'

She wiped away the drool from her mouth and stared at the man before her, still befuddled by the heaviness of her sleep. He turned and climbed into the Fodder wagon, closing the door after him. It stood there, inert wood and steel, no sign of the life within, nor of the death.

Eadha climbed to her feet and saw a figure on horseback approaching; someone from the holds no doubt come to check where their Fodder wagon was. She breathed in deeply, at once grateful and surprised that she felt almost fully restored to her power, her silver fish giving a welcoming flick as she bent her mind a moment to it before looking towards the rider once more. There was a light sea mist that stretched its tendrils across the combat ground, and it was hard to make out features. But something in the turn of the head, the impatient kick they gave their mount as it scrambled up onto the level ground and she knew it for Senan.

Automatically she began to construct her thought-wall as she'd done every day of the last almost two years. But as she did Seoda's pale face flashed into her mind and she stopped, unable to set the wall. The façade of mundane thoughts fell apart. Unguarded and empty-handed she raised her head to face him as he cantered up out of the mist.

'I thought I might find you here, when you didn't return to your room last night,' he said, reining in his horse and looking down at her.

'What is it you want, Lord De Lane?' she asked, staring levelly at him.

'You asked me a question yesterday. Ask me again.'

Between jaws clenched so hard they hurt Eadha said, 'I asked why you killed that girl.'

'Because I can. Because you needed to know that. Because I can see it in your eyes, even though you try to hide it. You haven't learned yet.'

Voice still steady, Eadha asked, 'What, precisely, is it that I haven't learned yet, Lord De Lane?'

'Watch your tone. It's simple. If you don't want to spend the rest of your life shackled to a Fodder seat in the holds you need to get it into your head that I control you. I own you. And I can end you anytime I want, just as I did that girl yesterday.'

'So why didn't you? If you had a problem with me, why not take it out on me? Why kill her, when she was nothing to you?'

'I did take it out on you. I didn't care whether that girl lived or died, but you obviously did and yet you helped me kill her. You kept for me and held the thread open until it snapped and she died. So, if you want to blame anyone for her death, blame yourself.'

He smirked down at her.

'Now run along back to the holds with the wagon before you get into more trouble, there's a good girl. And every time you feel guilty about your dead Fodder friend, do remember me.'

Senan had wheeled his horse about when Eadha spoke once more, loud enough for her voice to carry clearly on the rising wind.

'Her name was Seoda, and she was beautiful and strong, so much stronger than you or I will ever be.' He stared back at her as she continued, standing erect as her hair was whipped about her by a sea breeze come to blow the fog off the headland.

'She survived down in the holds, where they peel away every shred of human dignity and joy and she endured. Here on this island of Lords and Masters, she was the only person I met with strength enough to show kindness. This girl, who was starved and drained, denied her humanity in every way possible, was kind to me, gave me hope. So yes, I did care that she died. You broke my heart yesterday when I couldn't save her.'

Senan climbed down from his horse, the familiar flush of irritation suffusing his face. He stopped directly in front of her and jabbed his finger in her face.

'How dare you speak to me like that? Don't you get it? You are our resource, you hold your position here by our favour alone. Perhaps yesterday wasn't enough of a lesson for you. Maybe you need a lesson a little closer to home right now. Have you ever been really drained by a Channeller? Would you like to know what it's like, to be our Fodder, drained of every shred of your strength, over and over again? Would you like to find out, you stupid, worthless thing?'

And he seized her hair and pulled it towards him, in the same moment reaching out along the thread between them, the now-familiar pull, but more savage now, filled with rage, ready to scour her insides out with his clawing power. Eadha stood unmoving and stared straight back at him. Inside with a flick she threw up a translucent, shimmering wall so that his power rebounded straight back up the channel and into him, hitting him squarely in the midriff. She followed it with a single blast of her own that sent him flying backwards onto the perfectly smooth grass of the killing field.

All the rage, all the grief, all the pain and all the guilt over Seoda, Gry, her aunt and uncle, Ionain and the nameless numberless others she'd failed roared up within her 'til she must disintegrate if she couldn't get it out of her. With barely a flicker of power she rose in the air and flew to where he lay on the ground in the centre of the field, shaking his head to try to clear it from the blow. Looking down at his sprawled body she said, 'You ask me how I dare? This is how I dare.'

She hit him, again and again as he tried to rise, so that he sprawled on his back, arms and legs outstretched. He tried to reach out to the Fodder sat in the wagon, to draw power from them to retaliate, but she blocked his threads with ease.

'Ah, ah, fair's fair. I'm not drawing power so neither can you. Let's see how that goes, shall we?'

He had cut his lip as he fell, arms flailing. As he wiped away the blood she came and stood over him.

'Look at you. You fool yourself that you are powerful. You are an empty shell. A husk of vanity and ego needing to be filled with other people's lives, their energy, their passion to have any substance at all. See how I block you? See how easy it is, to make you powerless? See how empty you feel, all of a sudden, without all your little people to drain and make you feel the big man. Here, now, you are alone. For the first time in your misbegotten, warped life, Senan, Lord De Lane, you stand alone and you are empty. You have spent your whole life filling yourself, puffing yourself up with other people's life-force, living off other people's lives and foolish boy, you never once looked inside yourself to see that there is nothing there. You and your precious Masters. They take you and spoilt children like you and hollow you out so there is no heart, no soul, nothing left but an empty vessel good only for filling with power, endlessly using other people's lives to feel even half-alive yourself. And look where it's got you, here on this beach, with me, empty and useless.'

'You're insane! What do you think you are doing?' he half-screamed, struggling still as she flattened him once more with ease, still trying vainly to draw power from somewhere, anywhere, but there was no one that he could reach, only seagulls that circled above them and the Fodder sat silent in the wagon.

'It's as you said, my lord. As this is our last session together, we should reinforce what we have learned from each other. The lesson you can take from me is that everything you think you know is a lie. You thought you had power over me only because I let you. Because not in this world or any other world would l ever care what scum like you thought of me.

I walked straight into your citadel, into the heart of your power and none of you even knew me for what I am. With your stupid incantations and ceremonies, your pathetic need to feel important and in control and all the time we exist separate from you, uncontrolled by you, laughing at you.'

With one final blast of power, she knocked him unconscious. Taking some chains from the Fodder wagon, she secured him and rolled him over to lie hidden behind some rocks, and then drove the Fodder wagon back up towards Second House, hands trembling as she urged the horses along.

CHAPTER 35
ILLUSIONS

Back in the House she hurried through the still silent cloisters, her small bag slung across her chest carrying Magret's burnt book and her torn dress. Ahead of her the Hall of Illusions was lit from within by a rainbow of circling lights. Ionain was inside, practising in the early hours before classes began. As she came through the doors the lights started to fade. Ionain shook his wrists in frustration, not understanding why his power was faltering. Eadha hadn't gifted him anything since the morning before and he was almost out. He looked up and saw her in the doorway, took in her set expression. The remaining lights above his head snapped out and the room slowly filled with sunlight.

'Eadha, what is it?'

Taking a deep breath Eadha stepped into the room, into a sunny square of light, looking up towards the stage where Ionain stood.

'Ionain, we need to talk.'

Ionain climbed down from the stage.

'I can guess what this is. I know I owe you an explanation for the last few weeks, Linn and I.'

Eadha stopped, her mouth still open to speak, shut it again.

'I'm sorry, what?'

'Linn and I, I know it must've seemed strange, when we appeared in the ref and everything since.'

Ionain came and stood beside her, taking her hand from where it clutched the bag strap. He took a deep breath, too.

'Linn was the one who told me on First Island that the Keeper girls were bullying you because Ailbhe wanted you out of the way. I couldn't stand the idea of you being hurt because of me, especially after you collapsed just before the spring trials. I thought they might ease up on you if I pretended to choose Ailbhe and turn my back on you.'

'But what did you mean about you and Linn, these last few weeks?'

Ionain wrapped his arms around Eadha as he'd done once before, that night above the towers. Speaking into her neck, his voice half-muffled he said, 'Linn is a good friend, but that's it.'

'But you seem so happy together.'

He pulled back to look at her.

'How could I even see someone else that way? It makes no sense.' He took another breath and said simply, 'I'm part of you. You're part of me. We're one single thing. We always have been, we always will be. Other people, they don't exist, not that way.'

He looked up at her again.

'You know this. You have to know this.'

And she did. She knew this, had always known this.

They were silent together then, eyes closed, heads together, just breathing each other in. After a little, Ionain stepped back, clearing his throat.

'Ailbhe was driving me to distraction, pressing for a marriage commitment because she's desperate to avoid dragon patrol. Linn was being worn down by Senan. She's like us; there's a girl at home she's loved forever, so she was determined not to be forced into a pairing with Senan. We realised we could solve each other's problems by pretending to fall in love. The Masters would be so relieved to see Linn paired with a strong Channeller they'd sanction any couple split to make it happen. Senan and Ailbhe are too proud to want to look like losers. So, we appeared together looking suitably loved up and let the other two's egos do the rest. The plan is to stay together until we leave Second Island, then split once we're both safely home. My parents would never force a marriage I didn't want, you know that.'

Just for a moment relief, even joy flowered out from Eadha's heart, pulsed all through her so she felt alive to her fingertips. Ionain had walked them over to a window seat and sat down, putting his arm around her and kissing her gently on the top of the head.

'We've come so far, you and I. We've held on and held on, not let them warp us or change us. We just have to hold on a few more weeks now, through winter and into spring. I know it's been so much harder for you, being a Keeper and not being protected by a Family name. But if we can just hold on, don't do anything stupid, not give them any cause, then it really won't be long until we can go home to the Keep and we can go back to how things used to be, only better, because we'll be able to do so much more.'

He turned to look at her, his face serious.

'I just hope you won't mind that I won't be much of a Channeller.'

She froze. He continued, 'I don't think I could live with myself, to be a Channeller like Senan or Uncle Huath, now I've seen what it does to the Fodder.' Seeing her shocked face, mistaking it for dismay he hurried to reassure.

'Oh, don't worry, I'll still be lord. But I've become quite good at avoiding drawing on Fodder. Like getting roaring drunk at all those summer parties so Senan and the others would give up on trying to get me to play those mindless games. I spent weeks in here before lessons started learning illusions, so they'd think I was some prodigy and let me steer away from combat and the other arts that are more Fodder heavy. I know I have a gift and that to be lord, I have to channel a bit, but there are ways...'

'But you haven't,' whispered Eadha, as the fragile tower of hope that Ionain's words had built for a few shining moments came crashing down like one of his illusions, swept away like a grain of sand on the shore where Senan lay, bruised and bound by her rage.

'What do you mean?' asked Ionain. 'Of course I have to channel, so we can hold on to the Keep.'

'I mean, you haven't a gift. Or not one that's flowered yet.' Ionain stared at her. Eadha stared down at her hands, unable to look at him as she continued in a low monotone, 'That's what I came here to tell you. It was me. At your Reckoning. You were about to fail. Master Dathin was about to drop his hands. I thought it would break your heart, to fail so publicly like that, so I sent my power into you. That's what Master Dathin saw, when he raised your hand and acclaimed you gifted. My power, my gift. Not yours.'

Ionain had dropped his arm and was staring at Eadha in shock. 'What?'

'I thought it was what you wanted.' Eadha started to cry, hard choking sobs. 'It'd been your dream ever since you were little, to be a Channeller and save the Keep. After I'd done it once, I had to keep on doing it if you weren't to be found out. I couldn't be a Channeller, not when I saw what it did to the Fodder, but I pretended to be a Keeper so I'd be sent away with you and I could keep sending my power into you.'

Ionain had stood up while she was speaking and walked away to the other end of the enormous Illusion Hall, as far away as he could get from Eadha. She called after him as unspeakable fear began to squeeze at her heart, trying to pull him back to her with her words.

'Ionain, I couldn't face it, being left behind. To lose you, and to spend my life clamping down on my power. I thought I was helping you, helping your Family to stay in the Keep.'

Staring at her down the length of the Hall, Ionain said, 'What have you done?'

'I thought it was what you wanted,' she stammered again.

Ionain stared at the ground and spoke in a low voice, 'You had no right. None. I am not your puppet, your avatar for you to manipulate, to do the things you secretly want to but know you shouldn't.'

Eadha was shaking her head, tears streaming down her face.

'No, Ionain, no. It wasn't like that. I was trying to balance helping you with not harming anyone and yes, not being left behind. I thought I'd found a way. I know it's hard to hear you've no gift but I thought...'

'You thought. Always what you thought. Just once would you actually listen to me. Let me actually tell you what I'm thinking. It seems you've been projecting all these thoughts onto me for years, assuming you know my every thought, but you really, really don't. All they are, are echoes, projections of your own hopes, your own fears. If you wanted to know what I thought back then before my Reckoning about failure, why didn't you ask me? I would've told you. I would've always told you anything you asked.'

He looked up at her, tears in his eyes, too.

'Don't you see, what you've done to me, it's no better than channelling Fodder. In fact, it's worse. At least with Fodder we're honest, they know we're using them. But you, you've made a lie of my entire existence. I'm here in this hell-hole draining innocent people day after day because of you and I didn't even know it. Because you didn't think to tell me, because it didn't occur to you that I deserved to make my own decisions over my own life.'

He turned away again.

'How could you do this? I thought you loved me, I thought you were a part of me.'

Eadha cried wildly, 'I do love you, I do.'

He sat on the edge of the stage, his head in his hands, rubbing his temples as if he could rub away the hurt if he just rubbed hard enough. Still not looking at her he said, slowly, tiredly, 'No, you don't. You don't love me. You think you own me. That you can make decisions for me, that you know my every thought better than I do, that you can fool me into believing I'm something I'm not. Did you enjoy it? Did you laugh as your proxy Channeller struggled to hold on to some shred of humanity in this place? Oh, get out. Just get out. I don't want to even look at you.'

Eadha started to walk over to where Ionain stood, thinking if she could just touch him, hold him, she could make him understand. And all the time her head hammered with the urgency to be gone as she thought of Senan, lying unconscious on the stony shore. He would come to soon enough. There was no time for this and yet it was the crisis of her life and nothing would ever be more important than getting this boy in this room to look at her again the way he had just a few minutes before.

'Ionain, you don't understand, we can't do this, here, now, it's what I came here to tell you. Please, we need to talk about this properly but not now. Something has happened and you have to...'

He turned to look at her then, his eyes stone cold as he spoke carefully, levelly.

'Stop. Do not come one step closer. Hear this. I do not *have to* do anything you tell me. You will never make a decision for me again. You will respect the decisions I make for my life. And right now, I want you gone. So, if you love me, get out now.'

Eadha stopped then, as if he'd raised a wall of power in front of her, unable to take another step. She felt sick to the heart. It had all gone so wrong, the thread between them always so straight and true grown so badly knotted and tangled she could no longer find the way along it to reach him. But before she could say another word she was lifted from behind and thrown against the wall, so hard that her head rebounded off the stone and she crumpled in a heap to the ground.

CHAPTER 36
BLIND ALLEY

It was hard to think with the pain; or rather, she could think but all she could think about was the pain and how to make it stop. There were other things on her mind, she knew, but she could not hear them over the ringing of the pain. Slowly, very slowly, she picked herself up from the floor of the Illusion Hall. She had time to see the streaks of blood on the polished wooden floor and think how strangely sticky blood was, before Master Dathin struck once more. This time his power just flattened her against the wall, halfway up towards the dome. A fall from this height would break most of the bones in her body. She was pinned and helpless, unable to move a finger. The pain from the first slamming hit of body against stone began to subside a little, enough that she was not fighting to stay conscious and could focus on the familiar figure in front of her. He'd always been bear-like. Now, power coursing through him, he seemed grown to twice the size of a normal man, his black cloak and shining yew staff barely containing the might within.

He spoke calmly, the deep voice carrying easily in the silvery acoustics of the Illusion Hall.

'I am intrigued. Just what were you planning to do? There is no way for you off this island. Even if you did steal a boat there is no way you could outrun us or reach the mainland with your pathetic little candle of power, held oh so piously to your chest. Virtue may keep you warm at night, but it won't protect you against a real Channeller. You might have ambushed Lord Senan alone on a bare rock but here, stood above the greatest Fodder pool in all of Domhain, do you really think you have any chance?'

Eadha hung there, legs dangling, arms stretched out cruciform. Her tongue was thick, and she tasted blood as she forced out the words.

'Ionain, he knew nothing.'

'I don't doubt it. I sent him away. I came in at the end of your little heart to heart. You seem to have quite let him down. He was your only friend since Lord Flemin was sent to the holds, so you are rather alone now, aren't you?'

'What will happen to me?'

'Same as happens to all your kind. You'll be locked away, tested and when we're done, channelled as Fodder.' Eadha looked at him then.

'You didn't think you were the first now, did you?'

'I know Leah was the first true Channeller, before your kind warped her gift into your perversion.'

'Oh ho, strong words for someone who can't move a muscle. Yes, a few of your kind are born every generation. Most never know the power they have. Either they are sent to be Fodder, or their Inquisitor tells them at their Reckoning they're nothing but Keepers. Those few like you who stumble on your true gift we can easily deal with. That's the useful thing about being in power for several hundred years. Very little happens that hasn't happened before. You and your kind are an evolutionary dead end, entirely pointless and easily defeated. Not that I need to tell you, given your current situation.'

'If I'm such a dead end, why don't you just let me go? You're right, I can't defeat you, I'm not a threat,' she panted, breath constricting as he steadily tightened the power that enveloped her and pressed her into the wall.

'Really, that's all you've got, *please let me go and I'll be good*? I'm disappointed. You don't rule an entire culture for generations by taking anything for granted. The First Brothers were right when they brought Leah here to end her days. She might have been powerless against their might, but they understood her very existence could cause unnecessary disquiet.

The people of Domhain accept the Channeller system because they believe this is how it has to be. That only we, the elite, have the gifts needed for Domhain to survive. They accept lives of quiet hell being drained as Fodder because they believe that this is the only way.

But your gift, where you draw on yourself to give to others—that is the very essence of weakness. It would turn us into their servants, not Masters.'

He tightened his grip even further, watching with detached interest as she began to gasp, unable to speak, barely able to breathe.

'Power, as you can see in your own case, is control. So no, we won't be letting you go. You will quietly, invisibly disappear and when you die your secret will die as it has been born and died unspoken and unknown again and again every century since the First Sister came out here to end her days. But I didn't come here to chat to a Fodder loving ingrate. No doubt you have been quietly gathering your strength, hoping to make a break for freedom. So this ends now.'

He raised his yew staff to send a bolt of power towards her, enough to knock her senseless.

He was right; she had been reaching down into herself, her silver fish powering up from the depths. As she felt his bolt leave the staff she lifted her shield, shimmering and silver, so the shot reflected back towards him. His grip that had her pinioned shifted as he instinctively moved his staff to block the power rocketing back at him. In that instant she was free. She shot up into the air directly above him. Master Dathin fell into a fighting stance and began firing rapid bolts of power at her. It was a classic move for a ground-based Channeller and she'd spent many months watching the Channeller apprentices learn the sequence. She avoided the shots with ease, diving and rising like a swimmer through the patterns. She was not a large target like the dragons these tactics had been devised for and she could avoid him all day, though he had sense enough to stay near the door so she couldn't escape. After some minutes he realised he wasn't going to catch her and began weaving a net of power. Without other Channellers it took time to set the points, but he was in no hurry. She could see what he was doing; once the net was in place, he could pull it tight around her and then she really would be trapped until other Masters arrived and took her down.

She began to shoot her own bolts down at him; not as powerful as his, but precise, burning hot. He was less mobile than she, his large frame slow to move out of the way, and she hit him square in the chest so he staggered back. On one swoop she came in too close and with ferocious speed he whipped his staff around and hit her with a fiery bolt right on the shoulder. It sent her crashing to the ground, and he was almost upon her before she recovered enough to fly up again. He resumed his weaving as she leaned her injured shoulder against the wall. It was bleeding badly, and she was dazed from the impact.

Across the room then she saw a slight movement. It was Ionain, standing quietly by the entrance, behind Master Dathin. He gestured to her to fly down behind the viewing gallery at the centre of the hall, along the west wall. It would give her some shelter from Master

Dathin, though he could quickly blast it aside. She dived down, avoiding two bolts as she flew and landed with a rolling tumble behind the wooden seats. Coming up nursing her shoulder, she saw herself staring back at her. For an instant she thought there was a mirror behind the stands. But then she realised it was an illusion. From the last dregs of the power still in him Ionain had created a replica of her. More beautiful than she'd ever be in real life, a dream image of her he carried in his head, but recognisably her. As Eadha stared the illusion sprinted out from behind the stands and flew up into the air. Master Dathin immediately sent bolts after it. This was her chance. Staying low behind the stands and then racing across the open space she made it to the door where Ionain grabbed her hand and pulled her out.

The cloisters outside were as quiet and as sunny as they'd been when she'd come to find Ionain. The fountain played in the centre, and it was so quiet she could hear birdsong as she panted, trying to catch her breath and examining her shoulder to see how badly burnt it was. She looked up at Ionain standing watch by the doorway.

'You saved me,' she said between breaths. He turned to face her.

'There's no time, you have to go, he will destroy the illusion any moment now.'

'Come with me, we can go together.'

He took her face is his hands, looked straight at her with those blue eyes that could see all the way to the very heart of her, and she'd never seen such sadness, such a sense of ending.

'Eadha, I just found out that everything I thought about myself, who I am, who you are, is a lie. You have to see I can't go with you.'

Sorrow roared up inside her then until she thought she must choke with it. This couldn't be happening. She couldn't be losing him. But he was leaving her even as he stood there, holding her, he was leaving and she was alone. For the first time in her life, she was

331

truly alone.

'Ionain, no...'

His head lifted as they both heard the roar from the Illusion Hall. The windows were lit by flashes of power from within.

'Run,' Ionain said, taking her by the shoulders and turning her towards the colonnades.

'Ionain, I...'

'Eadha, RUN!'

CHAPTER 37
BURIAL AT SEA

She ran then, legs fleet and effortless. Her breath still came in gasps like one who'd run for miles, the air fighting to get through the choking lump in her throat. It was hard, rigid with tears still to be cried. The temple bell began to toll, calling all to Matins. Soon these empty halls would be thronged with apprentices and Masters, their cloaks drawn against the early morning chill. A plan half-forming in her head, she stopped at the doors opening into the Banqueting Hall. There was no one there to bar her entrance this time, no velvet rope, the room quiet and dark. In the Fodder alcove, she wrenched open the service hatch. The lift rested at the bottom of the long shaft, but she did not need it, pulling the doors after her and flying down in near-perfect darkness, enveloped by the immense weight of the granite cliffs, the only light a faint rectangular glimmer around the edges of the lift far below.

Burning through the lift she stepped out into the holds. That early in the morning the night Keepers would just be finishing their shift, a skeleton staff compared to the summer nights of parties and round the clock channelling. Her face would be known down here. If she had a convincing enough air of a girl with an errand and her luck held, she might just win through to the iron door leading out to the sea cave entrance. Ailbhe's sailboat had not yet returned to Erisen and was moored unguarded in the dock. But as she hurried through the hold, nodding to the occasional Keeper passing with a lantern, she noticed a door not far from the sea cave that had never previously stood open. Inside it was brightly lit, with carpets and furniture visible through the doorway. It had to be Gry's quarters. She veered swiftly and peered in. Gry's familiar mop of curls could be seen on a single bed set into an alcove in the wall. The quarters were confined but comfortable. Lady Hera's intervention had clearly saved her nephew from the worst of the holds. She'd thought him asleep, but as soon as her head came around the door his face lit up.

'Eadha, how are you here?' he hissed.

'Shhh. I can't stay. Are you alright?'

'I'm fine.' Eadha saw then that his ankles were chained; a long chain that allowed him to shuffle around his quarters but no more. He saw her look, shrugged his shoulders.

'Are they channelling you?' she asked, looking over her shoulder into the main hold as she spoke. No one was paying them any attention.

'No. Judicious exposure to the suffering out there, implicit warning this is what happens to bad boys, no channelling. They're not looking to start a second Channeller war.' His look changed quickly to one of concern. 'But what happened, who's after you?'

'Dathin, everyone else, too, I suppose.'

'I'm so sorry; Hera told me. If I'd realised what you really were that day on First Island I would have rowed you all the way back to Ailm's Keep myself instead of telling you to just hide your power. If you make it out of here, go to Hera; our Family will help you as much as they can.'

They both heard it then; the sound of the main hold lift clanking

334

down its shaft.

'Unlikely to be the morning delivery of pastries,' said Gry. 'If you had a plan, I'd put it into action now.'

She was halfway to the sea cave entrance when the lift doors opened. Out came Master Dathin, Master Joen and a host of other Masters and Keepers. Quickly they fanned out and began searching for her. Eadha dived into the nearest empty bunk and with all her shielding skill shut herself down into a lifeless bundle of drained Fodder slumped unconscious after a night's channelling. Every scrap of power, of energy, she hid behind a thought-wall made of her exhaustion and pain. She heard the Masters approach, talking quietly to each other as they surveyed the enormous space, trying to work out where she might have gone to ground. She waited until the line of searchers had passed her bunk and then quietly began the short walk to the cave entrance. She would have made it, too, if a summer colleague from Records had not seen her and called, 'Eadha, what brings you back down here?'

The Masters turned at once, yew staffs raised. Eadha immediately raised her shield and in the same instant they shot, one, two, ten at once, pulsing into her shimmering wall and rebounding to the shooters. After several were injured by this they changed up, aligning their shots so they all shot at the same point, one after the other, creating a continuous stream of power that overwhelmed the shield, burning through to hit her on the legs, the arms, the side of her head before she could fly up into the air. Several Masters followed at once, others remaining on the ground and she was quickly surrounded.

It was her first combat and it was the fight of her life. Without a staff like the Masters she sent her power flowing through her hands, using them alternately to shield and to shoot. The shots came from everywhere at once, from men schooled in warfare all their lives but she was a warrior born, fighting for her life. With a sure grace she danced through the hail of bolts, sending some back with interest, deflecting others, avoiding still more; leaping up into the air so the Masters were shooting at each other, using one as a shield from the others' shots. She did not have their vast reserves of Fodder power to draw on but she was drawing only from her heart, not dragging strength from the reluctant prisoners of the hold and so her shots came faster, more easily. Some of the Masters struggled to adjust to the speed of her, slow to move out of the way as she answered their long lines of power with short bursts of white fire. Where she could she blocked the threads so that the Masters' power fell away, diving through the gaps created by their faltering.

But in the end it was all a beautiful dance of death to which there could only be one end. Trapped in a narrow space with only her own heart, her own strength to draw on, surrounded by Masters fuelled and furious, there was to be no mercy shown her, no chance taken. All they needed was time; time to wear her out, to exhaust her power and close in for the kill. She dropped to the ground, too tired now to remain in the air. The circle of Masters began to tighten around her, several in a pattern above her head, more on the ground cutting off any escape route. Her shots became more sporadic, weaker; all her strength now was focused on her shielding, preventing them from landing the knockout blow that would finally deliver her to them. Panting and helpless, she backed against the wall of the Holds, feeling the familiar cold slickness behind her.

Master Dathin, who had held back during the main engagement, stepped into the group that stood around her, edging closer, yard by yard, hunters with a wild beast at bay. As she backed, she had ended up close to the cave door, close also to Gry's quarters. From the corner of her eye she saw him wave her over to him. Summoning the last of her strength, she caught the nearest Master by surprise, leaping over his head and landing with a diving roll in Gry's door.

As she landed, he said, softly enough not to be overheard, 'The metal flap beyond my door, the chute for dead Fodder, it leads straight to the sea. Channel power from me and it should be enough to get you a good distance from here.'

'I can't,' she panted, on her hands and knees, watching as the Masters parted to let Master Dathin through. 'Then I'll be as bad as them.'

'Stop it, think just once. This is a gift from me to you, not something taken, and it is about more than you and me, it is about hope for all of us. You have to get yourself off this island and this is the only way.'

Eadha pulled herself into a crouch as Master Dathin approached. She closed her eyes and for the first time since the day she almost attacked Ailbhe, she felt her way down a thread and sought out the life-force in Gry. He was strong and her silver fish leapt as the power flowed into her, steadying her, pouring down into her heart, her legs, every part of her. She heard him gasp as the life drained out of him but when she faltered he urged her on.

'Don't stop, you need every drop, I'll be fine.'

He crumpled onto the floor but Eadha did not see it, as she lifted her head to face Master Dathin. As he pointed his staff at her she felt him pause as his Keeper drained the Fodder all around him for a killing blow. She stood, flexing her fingers, standing up on the balls of her feet. With a grin she sent a blast rocketing straight into his unguarded chest. As he fell back she ran, and her run became a dive so that she was already flying by the time she hit the Fodder hatch and burst through it. She flew down the long, pitch black slide, hearing the slap of water at the end and the next moment she was engulfed by freezing, inky black sea.

CHAPTER 38
STONE AND BONE

She hung a moment in the water, trying to get her bearings, trying not to think of the bodies of the Fodder that must be lying below her. Still, when her arm brushed something she could not prevent her shuddering recoil, thrashing away desperately from the imagined clutch of some half-rotted corpse there in the darkness. Slowly she calmed herself, treading water. She could hold her breath a long time with the power within her but not indefinitely; she needed to come to the surface. Cautiously she sent out small bursts of power, creating a faint light that struggled to pierce the murky water, travelling up until they hit rock. She was beneath the island, millions of tonnes of sea and rock above her. She tried not to panic.

Her silver fish was churning inside her and she forced herself to relax and heed it. As she did it grew within her, filling her until she was all sleek power, suddenly sure and in her element. Without needing to think she stretched out then, hands forming a delicate inverted v-shape, her body undulating in a sinuous wave of power that left a trail behind her as she moved smoothly away, headed unerringly towards the surface and the light.

She swam a long time before Gry's gift gave out. There was a joy in it, in the midst of her fear and her heartbreak, to be weightless, the water's caress like a mother's hand smoothing away her pain, absolving her of all she had done, of all she had not done, not said. But the power ran out in the end and she was forced to rise, aware of being cold and wet only now as her head came up out of the water into the air. She was not far from the wooded shore of First Island. Without power she struggled in the waves that surged and crashed around the island, having to stop often when she became breathless, hands and legs working beneath the water to stop her being swept around the western side of the island to where the stony dock stood. Finally she made it onto the narrow shelf of shingle that bordered most of the island, half-swept up on an inrushing wave. The trees grew right to the water's edge, their roots visible where the sea had washed away the thin soil. She pulled herself up the shallow bank by holding onto roots and collapsed onto the ground just inside the tree line. There was not much time. It had taken her most of the afternoon to cross from Second Island. The Masters would surely send tracking parties out around First Island on the off chance she'd survived the dive from the holds.

She headed for some old ruins not far from the jetty. She could hide there overnight, gather her strength and see how she might make her way off the island and onto the mainland. Gry and Hera had both said she should make for their home, House Crioch, the last way-post on the ride west to the dragon-islands. The rightness of that thought steadied her. Ever since she'd kept her vigil beside Seoda's body and cried out to the dragons, she'd understood this was the only choice she had left.

What had once been a folly raised by some long-ago Channeller apprentice was now a ruin, stone and tree bone merged into one. Enormous roots snaked out through doorways, branches curved through windows crumbling more each year as the trees grew wide and strong. The roof had long since collapsed but the canopy provided cover. She crept in. There was a nook she'd spotted once, months ago, on the night she first made a mirror-sheath for her power, formed by two walls and some enormous roots. The roots lifted off the ground slightly, leaving a gap not visible from above. She climbed down and slipped into the root space, lying on the stone floor. She was wary of using her power but lit a tiny were-light in her hand for comfort. Shivering and sodden still from her swim she fell into a dreamless sleep.

They found her in the end far faster than she had thought. She woke to see a guard's face peering in at her. He immediately withdrew, crying as he did, 'Bring Lord Huath, I've found her.'

There were answering shouts to him to come away at once before the traitor drained him, but Eadha had no thought in her head but that she wished now she'd drowned. Huath was the one she'd always feared and hated the most, ever since that night in Ailm's Keep when he'd terrified her as a child, swooping down as if to toss her over the cross-walk. She heard the familiar sound of a Fodder wagon labouring up the hill from the school. He would not find her huddled and terrified like helpless Fodder. Slinging her bag across her chest once more, she climbed out to stand on the tangled tree roots, hard like bone, stretching up over the shattered walls. She would fight her way back to the sea and let the waters take her and Magret's book and Seoda's dress, before she let Huath touch her. Do anything to shake his impregnable certainty that the world and all that was in it was his to control.

Lord Huath's fair hair appeared through the trees, looking down at where she stood, nursing her scant store of power.

'Well,' he said, 'haven't you given us the run around?' He took up position in front of the Fodder wagon as it creaked to a halt in a clearing a little way behind.

'To think you were there all that time, creeping around Ailm's Keep, poisoning my nephew and none of us knew. I should have ended you years ago when you first defied me. This is the gratitude I get. Half the Masters on Second Island wounded, two sons of noble families needing to be reconditioned and I'm going to be late for a party I had almost been looking forward to, because it seems if I want you ended I'm going to have to do it myself. The Masters want me to keep you alive, let them study you. But they're not here and I'm not really in a studying mood.'

And he swivelled his yew staff around almost casually before sending a shot of such blinding ferocity that it burnt away her clothes where it hit her in the stomach, opening a wide gash across her belly. The choking smell of burnt skin filled the air of the clearing as Eadha toppled backwards off the tree root and onto the shattered stone. She stared stupidly down at her stomach, half-expecting to see her silver fish evaporate into the air through the gash as blood began to pump out.

But it wasn't gone. With shaking hands, she pushed the edges of the gash together; it was clean where Huath's fire had seared through flesh and skin. Bending over she wove a filigree of silver threads across the opening, a mat of power that would stanch the bleeding and hold the wound together for now. As she did, she used her feet to push herself on her back underneath the tree roots, out of sight. She pushed herself deeper and deeper as she heard the sound of feet approaching.

'I'm still sensing power, she is not dead yet,' came Huath's voice. 'I don't want my head taken off by a bolt coming over the top, so let's move this.'

As he spoke one of the walls began to shake, the stones that had been sealed together for centuries protesting as they were pulled apart, until with a slide and a shudder the wall collapsed. She was well out of sight beneath the roots, the gap where she'd slid in barely visible now in the pile of rubble. She'd stopped the bleeding, but the wound had badly weakened her. There was no way out; she was trapped. Huath could kill her any number of ways. Bring down the other wall on top of her, shatter the tree roots above, or drag her out and finish her off himself, there on the shattered remnants of the ancient building. Rage filled her then. She would not die cowering in a hole. She would make him look her in the eye as he killed her.

She put a hand on the tree root above her, to lever herself up. But something was different. Beneath her hand was not the smooth warmth of the roots, or the cold hardness of stone. It was something altogether greater, altogether more powerful than wood or stone. The next moment a jolt flowed up her arm and in her head a star exploded as a voice spoke, smooth and hissing like metal sliding on stone.

'Mahera,' it said, and the world went white.

Her head snapped back on her neck as the young dragon's power flooded every cell of her being. It was like and unlike anything she had ever felt before. Unquestionably hers, but grown so strong, so mighty, so beyond anything she could have imagined. Dimly she could hear the sounds of Huath and his men shifting the fallen stone, searching for a body. With a flick she healed the wounds on her belly and her shoulder. The power within her overflowed and when she looked behind her she saw it had taken the shape of great golden wings, hazy and transparent. Climbing up between the roots with easy steps she stood above Huath then. And she was rage, she was fury, she was vengeance. Her voice when she spoke echoed with the voices of the silenced.

'We endure and we will outlast you.' She shot up into the air, up and up, spreading her wings so they blazed in the morning light. Huath came after her, roaring to the men below as he powered up their arrows. She stopped them easily with a thought and they fell lifeless to the ground. Huath flew on, levelling his yew staff at her once more.

'Bitch, you are one, I am many. You might have pretty wings, but I have killed many with wings as pretty and you don't frighten me.'

Holding herself steady in the air she stared at him.

'I should. I am the end of your world and all of your kind. You should be frightened to death.'

With a gesture she blocked the threads from the Fodder wagon, so that he only had the power already drained to draw on. Still he flew on, too overcome with rage for caution, higher and higher so they could see the outline of First Island below them, Second Island in the distance and the sun on the white towers of Erisen. She flew easily, feeling the air rush past, the surge as her wings lifted her high on the morning wind.

He whirled his staff and with all his years of dragon combat lay down fire in her path, to catch and tear at her wings, but they were illusions, impervious to fire and she flew through them unharmed, wheeling about as she felt his power begin to fade, spent in fire bolts that fizzled into nothing. He hung there in the air, only realising then that he had no power to draw on. He reached out, as he had reached out all his life, to those around him, those he had taken and taken from in a never-ending stream of lives defiled. But she blocked them all, all the spidery, grasping threads, and watched as the realisation hit him then that a man, alone, cannot fly. Still she watched as he began to fall, unmoved and unmoving as he tumbled down the morning sky, over and over the flash of his white-blond hair, falling faster and faster towards the trees below until at last he disappeared without a sound beneath the canopy.

'Mahera,' she said then softly.

The young dragon uncurled itself from where it had lain hidden, curled around the ruins and the tree roots, returned in response to

Eadha's cry of despair.

Eadha bowed her head, returning the gift of power it had given her along the golden thread stretched between them. The dragon spread its wings above the trees and sprang like a cat into the air of morning. It flew up to greet her, girl and dragon, heads bowed towards each other, almost touching as the sun cleared the sea. A watcher would have seen their wings blaze gold in the sunlight until the girl extinguished hers with a thought, and the dragon rushed up beneath her. She caught one of the huge thorny spikes with one hand and sat astride the enormous mailed back between the wings. The dragon swung its head back towards her and seemed to smile.

Together they flew, the girl's power flowing into the dragon as it wheeled once above First House. The dragon threw back its head and sent a bolt of flame shooting towards the wall with the small oak door facing east, the new grown trees reduced to ash in an instant. Below, she could make out Masters and Fodder wagons, fiery arrows being readied, yew staffs cocked. And the dragon flew away north and west on the world's winds, its impossible flight powered by one girl's heart, beating steadily in time with the dragon's wings as they left the Channellers far behind them.

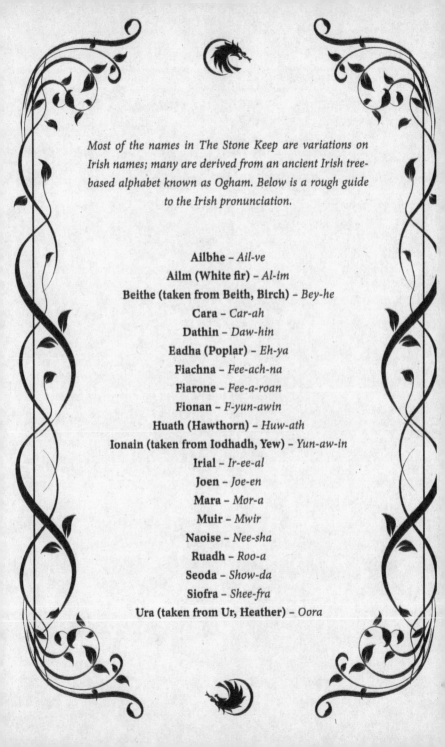

Most of the names in *The Stone Keep* are variations on Irish names; many are derived from an ancient Irish tree-based alphabet known as Ogham. Below is a rough guide to the Irish pronunciation.

Ailbhe – *Ail-ve*

Ailm (White fir) – *Al-im*

Beithe (taken from Beith, Birch) – *Bey-he*

Cara – *Car-ah*

Dathin – *Daw-hin*

Eadha (Poplar) – *Eh-ya*

Fiachna – *Fee-ach-na*

Fiarone – *Fee-a-roan*

Fionan – *F-yun-awin*

Huath (Hawthorn) – *Huw-ath*

Ionain (taken from Iodhadh, Yew) – *Yun-aw-in*

Irial – *Ir-ee-al*

Joen – *Joe-en*

Mara – *Mor-a*

Muir – *Mwir*

Naoise – *Nee-sha*

Ruadh – *Roo-a*

Seoda – *Show-da*

Siofra – *Shee-fra*

Ura (taken from Ur, Heather) – *Oora*

ACKNOWLEDGEMENTS

My daughter often jokes that the message of nearly every animated show she watches is that it's not about the quest/pony/apocalypse but rather the friends you made along the way.

I set out to write The Stone Keep in a search for joy after a run of personal heartbreak. If I'd thought about it, I'd have assumed it would be a solitary experience; me and my doughty self-sufficiency in the face of a harsh world. So, the most unexpected thing about writing this book, is how it's brought me such kindness and generosity from so many people.

For their kindness and support I want to thank Fergal & Jai Mohan, Orla O'Connor, Dermot McCullen, Jean Young, Amy Ball, Mick Brennan, Grace Smith and especially Tony Hanway. This book also wouldn't exist without coffee shops to hide away in, so thank you to the good folk in Strandfield who let me sit writing in their car-park all lockdown, in Panem where they always ask how the writing's going, and in Monart and Ardgillan.

The writer and truly good human being Philip Womack was the first person to encourage me to believe I'd written a real book, and did so much to help get it out in the world; I am eternally grateful. John Whelan and Alison Quinn provided ever-wise counsel. And the brilliant Niamh Mulvey restored my faith when it started to wobble and showed me how to make a story shine.

To everyone at Heroic, it's been a joy from the very first call with the wonderful Chris Arnold & Helen Blakeman. Thank you to my tireless editor Harriet Hirshman for your insight and determination, to Trev Fleming, Ben Ashurst and Isabel Hassan for being insanely dedicated & excellent craic, and to Aisling Leyne for doing such a great job on the audiobook.

Thank you to Maya-Rose, Éanna and Aodhán for existing, for being beautiful humans and for never once complaining that your mother is always running away to write. And last and most of all, thank you Conor for your unwavering belief in the importance of trying to create some beauty in this world, for inspiring me to write and for carrying me every step of the way.

ABOUT THE AUTHOR

S.K. Marlay is an Irish fantasy author. She's been a fruit picker, a maths teacher, a factory worker, a touring singer and a boat hand, not to mention a bunch of other jobs not worth mentioning. Before writing her first novel she was a songwriter. She thinks the discipline of having to distil a song's story down to sixty words or less really stands to you when writing a book, though she does miss being able to just repeat the chorus when stuck. She still doesn't quite believe writers are real people; this is likely to trigger something of an existential crisis now that her first book has been published.